Ghosts

Of

The

Dardanelles

**A novel of the Great War
by
Alan James Barker.**

Published by
Cauliay Publishing & Distribution
PO Box 12076
Aberdeen
AB16 9AL
www.cauliaybooks.com
First Edition
ISBN 978-0-9571330-7-5
Copyright © Alan J Barker
Cover design © Cauliay Publishing

The Turkish Memorial at Anzac Cove.

'Those heroes that shed their blood and lost their lives, you are now lying in the soil of a friendly country, therefore rest in peace. There is no difference between the Johnnies and the Mehmets to us, where they lie, side by side, here in this country of ours...You, the mothers who sent their sons from faraway countries, wipe away your tears; your sons are now lying in our bosom and are in peace. After having lost their lives on this land they have become our sons as well.'

Kemal Attaturk 1934.
Turkish President and poet.
(aka Mustafa Kemal.)

Dedications.

To my beloved sister, Elaine Evans, without whose help in scouring Australian bookshops for research material this book would never have been possible and to Michelle Coulson for her help and storyline suggestions. To Private 433 George Clark, 9th Battn AIF, a native of Ellon, Aberdeenshire, who emigrated to Australia in 1911 and was killed in action at Gabe Tebe, Gallipoli, on 2nd May 1915. And in remembrance of our great-uncle PJ/21190 CPO Nicholas Dobeson, tragically lost in the Denmark Straits onboard HMS Hood on 24th May 1941, who served in the Dardanelles aboard HMS Queen Elizabeth from March until May of 1915.

Finally, a heartfelt 'Thank You' to Euan Kelly without whose recovery this book would never have been written and to Michael. Thanks for the privilege.

A Glossary of ANZAC slang used in this book.

Babbler. Cook. Rhyming slang. 'Babbling brook'-cook.

Banjo. A shovel.

Beaut. Something or someone beautiful. Said tongue-in-cheek.

Bludger. Derogatory term for a scrounger or someone who shirks his share of work. A person to dislike. Can be a friendly insult also.

Chooks. Chickens, hens.

Cobber. Friend, pal, mate.

Cocky. A farmer.

'Crack hardy.' To 'stick it out.'

Crook. Ill, sick.

'Did my block.' To lose one's temper.

Dinky-di. A true, native-born Australian.

Dobbed in. To inform on one.

Drongo. Unintelligent, a moron. Also used as a friendly insult.

Dunny. A toilet.

'Fair Cow.' Something, a place, a situation that is unpleasant or difficult.

'Fair Dinkum.' To express surprise, disbelief. Also used to proclaim a truth.

'Fair goes.' To give someone a chance or to suggest one is lying or exaggerating.

Galah. A fool, an idiot.

Grog. Alcohol.

Knocked. To be killed. From the term 'knocked off.'

Larrikin. Someone who clowns about or is unruly, noisy.

'No worries.' Expression meaning, 'don't worry' or 'it's alright.'

Poms or Pommy. A derogatory term for anyone British.

'She be right.' Term meaning everything will become alright.

Sport. Another word for a pal. Sometimes used belligerently.

The Black Stump. An imaginary point beyond which a country is considered to be remote or uncivilised.

Tucker. Food.

Two's up. A popular gambling game, involving two coins and a stick and observing which way up the coins land when tossed up.

Waler. Australian breed of horse, origin New South Wales, hence the word 'Waler.'

Yabbies. A small Australian crayfish, considered a great delicacy.

Author's note.

It is impossible to stand at Ari Burnu or Anzac Cove, scene of the Australian and New Zealander's landings, or any of the southernmost beaches associated with the British landings at Cape Helles, as my son Darren and I did in September 2011 and not feel a sense of reverence. 'W' Beach, 'Lancashire Landing,' 'V' Beach where the SS River Clyde grounded; all of these saw heavy fighting and horrific casualties during the frantic morning's assault on Sunday, 25th April 1915. To look on these sites is to glimpse history in the raw, our Commonwealth's history born out of the blood that was spilled as thousands of young men clambered from their boats into intense machine-gun and shell fire.

To many of these men, Gallipoli was a name uttered for the first time in the final briefing before they left the battleships and transports that had carried them over the Mediterranean to this beautiful but desolate spot in the Aegean. When the last Allied troops re-embarked in January 1916 they left behind the graves of many of those who had alighted that early April morning with high hopes and a joyful enthusiasm. On recovering their land the Turks left those graves untouched, a noble gesture of reconciliation that did much to vanquish the hatred that had built up between the opponents during the campaign.

Nature has since reclaimed those valleys and gullies, with thick scrub covering the scene of so much heartbreak and bloodshed. To gaze upon them today is to ponder the madness of war and the incompetence of the politicians and generals who sent so many young men here to die. The new road through the Gallipoli peninsula has changed the face of Anzac Cove forever but will bring with it increasing numbers of tourists eager to see the battlefields where their forefathers fought nearly a hundred years previously. Their observations and deliberations will only add to the untold story of the Gallipoli campaign and the war with Turkey, a subject this book attempts to redress.

In order to maintain an air of authenticity the Turkish phrases used in this book are taken from the older form of the language in use during the Great War period.

Alan James Barker. June 2012.

Prologue.

The wind blew down the platform, cutting icily through the thin overcoats of the two waiting figures, one standing with a battered brown suitcase at his feet.

'I still wish you didn't have to go, Tom,' the younger of the two spoke, 'Queensland? It seems—so far away. The other side of the world.'

The older figure looked across to where his 15-year old brother stood, moving unconsciously from one foot to the other.

'Don't fuss so, Walt,' he said, smiling. 'I'll write you and it'll be as if I'm at the other end of the country, you'll see. Now don't go all miserable on me and spoil my leaving. Promise?'

Walter Harding forced a smile and leant his face against his older brother's coat sleeve.

'Mebbe you're right but whenever you mentioned leaving for Australia I had in mind that it was all a story, something you were just thinking about. Now look at you, all packed and ready to go. I can't believe that I won't see you, maybe never again and... '

'Walt!' his brother admonished him. 'Don't be daft, lad, how many times have I told you? When I get out there and see how the land lies I'll be sending for you as soon as I'm established. For the moment, you go and stay with Aunt Elsie until the time comes, alright?'

A loud, forlorn whistle interrupted their conversation and they turned to see the gleaming black shape of a large locomotive slowly approaching the station and the waiting passengers, wreathed in grey smoke as it hove into view round the bend.

'Here she is, bang on time.' Tom bent down to pick up his suitcase. He straightened up and looked keenly at his sibling. 'Right, come here and give us a hug and no bawling, mind. I don't want my last memory to be of you snivelling with tears on your face.'

Walt wiped his eyes and punched his brother lightly on the shoulder. 'Aye, Tom, that'll be right. You get yourself on, then, and when you're a millionaire, send us a ticket and I'll come out First Class like a swank to join you.'

They embraced fiercely as the train came to a wheezing, clanking, shuddering stop. As the steam cleared away, doors swung open and a throng alighted followed by those clambering on, all eagerly seeking a seat. Stepping back, Tom Harding gripped his suitcase firmly and swung himself easily up into a carriage. Throwing the case into the overhead rack he turned and leant out of the open window to speak. As his lips framed the words the train's whistle shrieked piercingly once more and it slowly began to move away.

'Godspeed, Tom!' Walt shouted, waving his arms furiously but his brother's reply was lost on the wind as the train picked up speed. He ran along the platform to its sloping end and stopped abruptly, watching intently until the last carriage was lost to view and the thrumming sound finally ceased from the rails below his feet. Sighing, he jammed his cap firmly on his head and moved towards the platform exit, head bent low.

Author's note. It had all began so innocuously. On June 28th 1914, a nondescript, disaffected student named Gavrilo Princip jumped onto the running board of the royal automobile on a State Visit to Sarajevo and emptied a pistol into the heir to the Austrian throne, Archduke Ferdinand, and his wife, Sophie. Their deaths caused the countries of Europe to square up to each other as old jealousies were aroused and treaties that bound several of them together were taken from the dusty vaults where they lay and examined closely.

The following political war of words spilled into military action, lining France and Russia up against Germany and the Austro-Hungarian Empire. Despite trying to remain aloof from the gathering storm, Germany's invasion of Belgium brought Great Britain and the Commonwealth into the fray on 4th August 1914 and the world found itself plunged into a bitter war such as had never before been witnessed.

--§--

The Dardanelles, 18th March 1915.

'Heave!'

In the overheated confines of the steel-walled handling room men responded and a massive, gleaming shell slid into the gaping maw of 'A' turret's hoist. The hoist door closed and the shell sped upwards, pausing momentarily opposite the charge-handling room while a bag of cordite constituting a quarter charge was carefully placed in the crib above the shell. The door slammed shut once more and shell and charge carried on their upward journey to the 15-inch naval gun breech waiting to swallow them both.

The same was happening on the opposite side of the turret as both barrels were speedily reloaded and readied for the firing sequence. From firing to reloading had taken the sweating gun crew under a minute to complete. Moments later the firing gong sounded tinnily within the battleship and she heeled over sharply as the guns thundered out their next broadside to the distant shore.

The concussion inside the turret was enormous but was soon dismissed as the gun crew prepared themselves for the next shells to arrive from the shell-room. Outside in the March coolness of the Mediterranean sun a cold breeze blew but inside the steel walls the heat of action had caused a noticeable rise in the turret's temperature and the men could feel the increased humidity amid the acrid tang of cordite.

Able Seaman Nicholas Dobeson took a moments respite to wipe his profusely sweating brow and arms with a rag he'd stuffed earlier into his white duck trousers. As he finished, the shell-hoist doors opened to admit the next massive shell into the turret and any thoughts of rest disappeared as he bent with his comrades to the task of the smooth reloading of the gun. The automatic ram pushed the shell into the gun's breech before the waiting gun crew inserted the cordite charge behind it and the breech hissed shut. Months of training and drills kicked in and each man carried out his allotted task like an automaton, servicing the guns with a practiced ease.

On *HMS Queen Elizabeth's* bridge Captain GPW Hope smiled as he watched the shells impact on the far shore of Cape Helles. His ship, the newest and largest in the Royal Navy and the first to be fuelled entirely with oil instead of coal, carried the very latest 15-inch guns and these guns were being put to very good effect.

He'd pleaded with the Admiralty for his ship to be included in the attempt to force the Dardanelles and on gaining that permission, albeit reluctantly, had raced to be with the Eastern Mediterranean Squadron. The ship had arrived off the Dardanelle Straits separating the Black Sea from the Aegean on the 19th February 1915 just in time to join the party.

'Two points to starboard, Number One. Open up the arcs and give the guns longer on their targets.'

'Aye, aye, sir. Helmsman, two points to starboard.' The metal deck shuddered again as all four turret's guns boomed and a spreading cloud of thick, black acrid smoke enveloped the ship's bows. On the outline of the fort opposite the ship, a twinkling pattern of multi-coloured flames appeared and Captain Hope smiled again. They were certainly giving the Turkish gunners over there a hard time and he took a deep pleasure in the accurate fire from his ship's guns.

Author's note.

The Turkish government closed the Dardanelles to Allied shipping in October 1914 in a prelude to declaring war. Britain's response in November was to send the ageing battlecruisers of Vice-Admiral Carden's Eastern Mediterranean Squadron, accompanied by two French battleships, to fire on the forts along the straits. Encouraged by the results, the British government envisaged an easy passage if they attacked early in the New Year but the Turks gratefully used the time interval between the two assaults to strengthen their defences and lay even larger minefields in the straits.

First Sea Lord, Admiral Sir "Jackie" Fisher, had pushed for an attack on the Dardanelles in an effort to divert attention from the Western Front, ease pressure on the Russians in their Balkans struggle and force Turkey out of the war. His suggestion would see several Greek divisions land on the Peninsula and make their way to Istanbul but Russia was vehemently against this plan, declaring that she would not contemplate Greek troops in the Turkish capital.

Winston Churchill, First Sea Lord of the Admiralty and a former protégé of Fisher's also opposed the plan and together with Lord Kitchener, the Secretary of State for War, pressed for a purely naval solution. A force of allied battleships and cruisers would take on the task and destroy the Turkish forts along the Straits leaving the way free to sail into the Sea of Marmora, capture Istanbul and force Turkey's capitulation.

By a mixture of eloquent speaking and by simply ignoring any opposition to their plan these two men set the scene for the failure that was to be the Gallipoli campaign. All intelligence that did not meet their approval was pushed to one side and forgotten with many Intelligence experts deliberately left out of the undertaking, especially if their views clashed with those of Churchill and Kitchener's. Any dissent was ruthlessly quelled, any voices of doubt stilled and preparations went ahead unchecked.

The assault would be a purely naval undertaking and the first day's action on the 19th February had been promising. A gale whipping up had sent the fleet running for the shelter of the nearby island of Tenedos and it wasn't until the 25th that the weather abated enough for the fleet to return and begin their work of demolishing the outer ring of Turkish forts and their guns in earnest.

Queen Elizabeth had put two of the guns from No.4 Fort out of action early on and fired up with their success, her crew were eager to take on and destroy many more of the enemy's emplacement.

The imaginative plan stuttered to a brief halt when Vice-Admiral Sackville Carden suffered a nervous breakdown and was replaced by Vice-Admiral John de Robeck in time for the attack on the Turkish forts on the 18th March.

Clang!

'Christ! What the bloody 'ell was that?'

'Shut up, Turner, you bloody woman.' the sweating seaman laughed. 'Sounds like a Turkish shell just ricocheted off the turret. Keep those shells coming and we'll put the cheeky beggar out of action before he can hit us again. 'An while you're at it, pass me another mug of lime juice will you, this sport's got me mighty thirsty!'

Captain Hope's ship led *Line A* of four lines of Allied battleships into the straits to finally pound the Turkish forts into submission. It was approaching two o'clock in the afternoon, a full month after their first engagement, and the ships began carrying out their allotted tasks targeting the Turkish forts and known gun emplacements. A deep rumbling noise was heard to their right and Captain Hope looked round inquisitively.

'Good lord sir! It's one of our own ships, looks like—no, it's the *Bouvet*! She's turning over, her magazine's gone, I think!'

Captain Hope followed the pointing finger of his Number One and watched as the twin funnels of the French battleship *Bouvet* slowly disappeared from view as she rolled over and sank in Eren Keui Bay. Several accompanying destroyers raced to her aid but from the speed at which she had foundered it was obvious there would not be many survivors.

'Alright! Everyone, back to your stations. Helmsman, hold your present course!' he commanded. 'We've a job to do so concentrate on carrying out your orders! Did anyone see a torpedo boat in the area? Has she struck a mine?'

No-one replied and he repeated his order to the helmsman.

'Aye, aye, sir.' The helmsman responded mechanically through the voice- pipe from his steering position in the bowels of the ship and the ship shuddered again as the next broadside screamed out of the gun's barrels. At four o'clock another explosion rumbled over the sea and they strained their eyes to see the cause. 'Sir, it's *Inflexible*, she's been hit near the same spot *Bouvet* disappeared. She's signalling. Hang on...it reads... *"Have struck mine...Taking in water...many casualties...intend to beach ship on Tenedos Island."* Message ends.'

'Roger, Number One, keep an eye on her. *Guns?* Keep our guns busy, fire on any shore battery you see targeting *Inflexible* and we'll cover her withdrawal.'

'Aye, aye, sir.' The ship's Gunnery Officer bent to speak urgently into one of the voice tubes.

'Oh my God, there's another one hit! Look at her...'

Captain Hope's normally urbane manner snapped. 'Lt Naseby, if you see something, report it properly, man! What can you see?'

'Sorry, sir, another of our ships has been hit.' More calmly. 'It's the *Irresistible*, sir. She's stopped dead in the water and listing badly. Possibly another mine, I didn't see any shell strikes on her before she was hit. Hang on, she's signalling, sir, a green flag. Odd. She's indicating she's been hit by a torpedo yet there are no u-boats known to be in the area.'

'Thank you, Naseby, does she need assistance can you see?'

'Our destroyers are on their way, sir.'

'Fine. Keep an eye on the situation. Meanwhile, gentlemen, we have a job to do so let's continue.'

The firing continued with clouds of dust and smoke billowing up as the heavy shells struck home ashore. The Turks were not intimidated by the shelling and as their own shells began falling around the Allied ships, near misses saw plumes of water and clouds of shrapnel clanging hollowly along the upper decks. Just after 6.05 in the evening, at the very moment he sensed that the Turk's return fire was slackening, Captain Hope's attention was drawn urgently to the pitiful sight of yet another British battleship heeling over in clouds of steam and ugly black smoke. HMS *Ocean* had pulled out of her column to aid *Irresistible* and after attracting severe Turkish artillery fire had herself struck a mine and come to a gradual stop, listing badly. Captain Hope thought quickly. What had started out as a perfect day was rapidly turning into a disaster.

The losses were a blow but an even bigger blow would be that of his own ship, the navy's newest, being crippled or sunk. Already, from the reports being urgently passed to the bridge, he knew that *Queen Elizabeth* had sustained nearly a hundred casualties from the accurate fire of the Turkish shore-based howitzers and to delay would mean more damage and almost certainly result in further casualties. His decision took mere seconds.

'Helmsman, reverse your course,' he ordered brusquely. 'and *Flags*? Signal Admiral de Robeck that we're moving back to the mouth of the Straits, let him and their Lordships at the Admiralty decide what to do next. Judging by the close proximity in which our ships have been lost I'm beginning to think our Turkish friends have laid a new, uncharted minefield in our operating area. Someone back home is not going to be very happy but I for one don't intend to risk my ship for so little gain. Let's go, gentlemen, I'm afraid we're finished here, for the time being at least.'

'Aye, aye, sir, reverse the wheel.'

Ponderously the metal leviathans heeled round and began the short journey back to the mouth of the Straits, chased by shells from unseen Turkish howitzers. They retreated in good order, firing as they departed but no-one onboard could foresee the tragic consequences that their attempts to force the Dardanelles would bring to the men tasked with attaining what they had failed to bring about. *Irresistible* sank at 7.30 that evening and *Ocean* vanished in the night, both ships sinking after listlessly floating in full view of Turkish batteries that wasted no time in reducing them to mere hulks before they slipped below the surface.

--§--

Author's note.

In the coming months, the deaths of thousands of allied soldiers would be laid at the feet of this day's failure. What the Royal Navy had failed to carry out with relatively few losses, the army would pay for with the blood of tens of thousands of its men. The navy's unseemly retirement lifted the morale of the Turkish defenders thus making any subsequent attempts liable to stiffened opposition.

And so it turned out to be. The naval plan having failed, it was decided to assault the Dardanelles from the land using fresh troops as yet uncommitted to the slaughter in Europe. In a hurried exchange with very little thought or strategy, General Sir Ian Hamilton was dispatched to Egypt to command the forces gathering there. The newly-formed 29th Division arrived in Britain from overseas and abruptly about-turned, following their commander and his staff to join the burgeoning forces of Australia and New Zealand who'd been diverted to Egypt to complete their training before embarking for the Western Front.

Together with French forces, these men would form the vanguard of the forces hurled against the Turks on Sunday 25th April 1915. An innovation of the ANZAC's under Lt General William Birdwood was a landing at dawn, in darkness and silence. The British plan, led by a stolid, unimaginative Major General Sir Aylmer Hunter-Weston was for a full frontal attack in daylight, preceded by a largely ineffectual naval bombardment which did nothing but arouse an already alert enemy. The heavy casualties suffered by the British that day would bear out the wisdom of the ANZAC tactics.

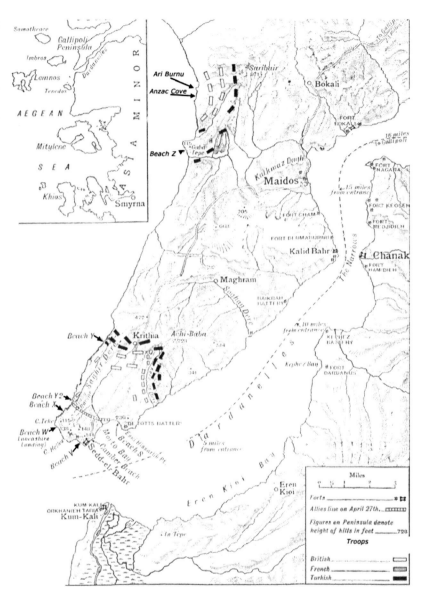

Map showing the disposition of the Allied and Turkish
forces on the Gallipoli peninsula, May 1915.

Chapter One.

Mudros Harbour, April 1915.

'Cor, would you look at all those bloody ships!'

'Christ, Peters, why didn't you let me know you were there before sneaking up and scaring me like that! I nearly had an accident, you clot!'

'Sorry, corp, I just thought I'd come up and 'ave me a look, like.'

Mollified, Corporal Walter Harding of the 7th Middlesex Regiment moved his feet to allow the other man to join him at the ship's rail and together they gazed at the scene before them. In the great, green-fringed, natural harbour of Mudros on the island of Lemnos, hundreds of ships were gathered. From majestic, grey battleships swinging slowly on their anchor chains to the smallest of steam pinnaces dashing around the larger ships, the assorted fleet filled the harbour as far as the eye could see. Motor launches, troop transports, cruisers, tugs, minesweepers, all vied for space in the immensity of the harbour

Lean-looking destroyers slid easily round the fringes of the assembled ships, aggressive sheepdogs carefully watching their flock. In amongst all these purposeful fighting ships were transports, scores of them bearing the 29th Division of the Mediterranean Expeditionary Force and the ships of the Australian and New Zealand Army Corps, known as ANZAC. All were gathered together for the day, not far off, when they would hurl themselves on the beaches of the Gallipoli Peninsula sixty miles to the north-east of where they now lay serenely at anchor.

'They say those Aussie's are good fighters, corp, I bet they're spoiling for a real fight just like us. The word going round is we're gonna fight the Turks soon, do you believe that?'

'I think we'll find out pretty shortly. It'll make a change from fighting the Aussies.' Walt replied dryly and both laughed at the memories from the meeting of both armies whilst on leave in Cairo.

Watching the spectacle, Walt's thoughts wandered back to the days preceding their arrival and how he'd grown up since his brother Tom had left him standing on the train platform five years earlier.

After Tom left for Australia, Walt went back to live with their Aunt Elsie who'd brought them up since the death of their parents. For a while the excitement of Tom's leaving and his promise to send for him had filled Walt's every waking moment but as weeks stretched into months it became apparent that Tom's situation wasn't as good as he'd hoped for. His letters home told of hardships and the failure in finding decent work which had dogged him since he'd left Britain and Walt came to realise sadly that his dreams of joining Tom were just that. Pipedreams.

When he reached the age of eighteen, Walter Harding travelled down to London and presented himself at an Army Recruiting Office, a remarkably swift and painless experience which soon led to his being sent on his way to barracks for basic training with the 7th Middlesex Regt of the Regular Army. On finishing training he'd accompanied them to Poona, India, where he spent the next two years filling out in both body and mind. Tall, with his brother Tom's black hair and open features together with dark, piercing brown eyes, intelligent and popular with both men and officers alike, promotion to lance-corporal had quickly followed. When the regiment's sick and unwanted had been weeded out prior to their embarkation for Egypt he'd been awarded his second stripe.

'I 'ad a look at some of the women on the island when we went ashore the other day, in that shop near the landing stage. Cor, there was some right dragons there, I can tell you, frightened the hell outta me! Don't ya miss those bints in the bazaar back in Poona, corp? Some right fine lookers amongst them too. Gawd, I remember them all, they could do things I'd never want my mum to find out about!'

'No I bloody well don't, Peters, you dirty Arab. I never got mixed up with the bazaar girls, you never knew what they carried. And I don't just mean in their purses.'

Jim Peters laughed aloud. 'Ah, yes, corp, I forgot, you're keeping yourself clean until *Miss Right* comes along. Ain't that so?'

Walt joined in the laughter. 'Well, at least I don't have to worry every time I go to the latrines whether anything's gonna drop off.'

Letters between Walt and his brother became sparse and eventually stopped altogether. With Tom moving around in search of work and Walt overseas in India communication became difficult until it was easier to stop writing than to chase letters halfway round the world. Tom entered his head now and again but as the years passed he'd found himself sometimes struggling to recall him.

Walt Harding's life changed at a stroke with the coming of war. Recalled from India the 7th Middlesex boarded a requisitioned liner in Bombay for the long, tiring journey home and although a submarine watch was kept they saw nothing, arriving back in Southampton on a dank, grey January morning in December 1914. Borne swiftly by train to the outskirts of Rugby, they joined other Regular Army battalions recalled from the far-flung corners of the Empire to form the 29th Division. On being allotted to the 87th Brigade, the 7th Middlesex immediately began the task of training for its anticipated move to the battlefields of France.

'Hey, Peters, do you remember when the King saluted us as we set off?'

'Aye, I'll bet he's sat in *Buck Palace* right now, kicking hisself that he didn't follow us to Avonmouth and come wi' us.'

Walt smiled wryly in recalling the day in late March when the division had been inspected by the King himself, regiments lining the road for miles before His Majesty rode past. At a command from their Commanding Officers they'd formed fours and marched in columns past the lonely mounted figure of their king as he sat at a crossroads outside Stretton-on-Dunsmore. With a grave expression on his face, George V watched his troops passing him by on their way into history. The regimental spies had been confounded when shortly afterwards, instead of heading south for the Western Front, they'd entrained for Avonmouth in the Bristol Channel.

Arriving there after a four-hour journey they were hurriedly loaded onto a series of transports before being towed out through the lock gates by tugs and released at the top of the tide to make their way down the Bristol Channel to the open sea. That night, orders for their area of campaigning were read out to the waiting men. In view of the Navy's failure to force the Dardanelles, Lord Kitchener had decided the job would be done by the Army under Sir Ian Hamilton. The 29th Division with Major-General Aylmer Hunter-Weston as its commanding officer was bound for Egypt for training before making their way to invade somewhere in Asia, the objective being kept from them for the time being.

Peters waved an arm, pointing out the hills behind the harbour. 'My old mum would've given her right arm to see this lot, you know, and here we are, having a real holiday courtesy of dear ole Blighty.'

'A holiday? D'ye really think so? We'll see. Word is we'll be up anchoring and away and then what? If you're right about what they're saying and if we're going to fight the Turks, believe you me, they're not gonna let us just land on their beaches and build sandcastles.'

'Hah! You watch, they'll run a mile at the sight of us, one look at our manly physiques and their 'ands'll go straight up. Mind you, it

3

would be better if we could ditch those helmets, we look a right set of ponces in them. The Turks? They'll be laughing too much to shoot straight when they see us bearing down on them with these stupid helmets on our heads. What do you think, corp, are we going to knock the shit outta them wearing these or will we get to go in wiv our normal caps on?'

'*My knees are brown, I have seen Calcutta and my will is with my solicitors, Short and Curly!*' Walt intoned hollowly and both men smiled at the old sweat's joke. 'How the hell do I know? I'll find out, Peters me old mucker but before we hold a confab about the comfort or discomfort of your official issue Wolsely Foreign Service Helmet, best you go and get changed. Serjeant Major Havelock'll go mad if he sees you like that. It's our turn for boat practice this afternoon, a few hours of dipping oars with our navy pals, so bugger off and exchange those ripped trousers for a good pair, quick as you like!' When he looked round again he was alone and he returned to his reverie.

The cramped voyage to Malta had taken a week, with bad food and limited exercise. Pleased to be finally entering Valletta Harbour, the euphoria had changed to anger at the knowledge that no-one but officers would be allowed to go ashore. A mutiny in the making had been averted by sailing the morning after but the injustice still rankled.

They landed at Alexandria, Egypt, three days after being escorted from Malta by French destroyers. Disembarking quickly, they then sat around watching the hustle and bustle of an army getting to grips with its logistical problems. Alexandria's huge harbour, stinking of coal dust and raw sewage struggled to cope with the enormous amount of allied shipping loading and unloading within its confines. Men of all nationalities wandered around, some bustling self-importantly on military business while others strolled around haphazardly, taking in the sights.

The regiment was eventually roused from its inertia and marched five miles down the coast to Mex where a huge tented camp awaited them on a strip of ground between the sea and a large salt lake. For the next eleven days they acclimatised to the sun, filled sandbags, practiced beach landings by boat and got drunk at every opportunity that presented itself.

During their stay, time was found to overhaul their weapons and equipment. Their SMLE's, the .303 calibre Short Magazined Lee Enfield rifle, had all been cleaned and lovingly oiled and cartridge pouches jammed with five-round charger clips for easy reloading. A quick visit to a make-shift range enabled them to sight the weapons and they then felt they were ready for anything.

April arrived and on the 7th they were marched back to Alexandria straight onto a waiting transport and bedded down for the three day voyage to Lemnos. There the division would assemble, receive its orders and make its plans for the assault on the beaches allocated to it. At long last they felt replete, impatient to be off but also slightly fearful of the consequences of the coming battle.

--§--

As Walt continued his thoughts, below decks the regiment's officers were cramped together in the dining-room. The air was humid and a weak electric fan spun slowly overhead, managing only to spread the humidity round the room and the sweating officers it contained.

'Gentlemen, take off your hats and tunics and let some air in.' Gratefully, those present obeyed their colonel's orders and breathed a bit easier. 'Right, now that we're all ready, I have our orders here at last.' Lt. Colonel Richard Compton looked round the room at each of his officers, taking in their eager, flushed faces. He looked down at the map on the table in front of him and began.

'We'll land with the force at 'X' Beach on the Gallipoli peninsula, towed in by the navy who'll release us near to the beach. Because of the narrowness of the landing area, only half of one company will go in first, the rest of the regiment will follow when the beach is secure. Tim, I've decided you and half of 'B' Company will be that detachment. Got that? You'll move over to the *Implacable* later and be landed from her.' Captain Timothy Gould, 'B' Company's commander nodded hurriedly.

'Good. You'll have the Royal Fusiliers on your right and some chaps from the Royal Naval Division out left. Packs only, each man to carry three days rations and 150 rounds of ammunition. Make damn sure everyone has sufficient water and tell your chaps to take a good drink before we leave the ship so they don't start on their water-bottles as soon as they land. John, can you see to that, let the RSM and the CSM's know?'

His adjutant, Major John Gabriel, raised a languid hand and the colonel continued. 'We know the enemy will be waiting, aerial reconnaissance has indicated that Johnny Turk is dug in and defended by lots of barbed wire and machine-guns. Luckily for us, 'X' Beach is not that well defended. Frankly, I don't think the Turks believe we'll attempt to land there because of the high cliffs so the idea is the navy will bombard all known Turkish positions as we go in and resistance on the beach should be minimal.

When you get ashore, Tim, press on and get off the beach as quickly as possible. Link up with the Royal Fusiliers, get your chaps moving forward and leave any prisoners for those coming behind you to deal with. Push on inland with the Fusiliers, assist them in taking Hill 114 to the south and then swing left to join up with the Lancashire Fusiliers coming off 'W' Beach. All this must be completed before heading for the village of Krithia, which is here, on the map.

Sounds simple but you'll only have 100 men until the rest of the regiment can get ashore in support. We don't know the ground we're going to fight over and we don't know how many Turks will be there to oppose us.'

'I say, sir, does the map you have there show much of the topography? We could get some clues of the steepness of the hills, etc. Let the chaps know what they're facing, where the Ottomans are, if you see what I mean.'

'Thank you for your timely interruption, Lt. Keats,' the colonel answered dryly, 'I have had a good look at the map, you know. Unfortunately, it was drawn up by the French in the year dot so God knows how it equates with what we'll face when we get there. They seem to have left the restaurants unmarked on it, too, damned uncivil for a Frenchman don't you think?

In fact, Keats, you could nip over and ask them. The French're attacking on the other side of the straits, going in against Kum Kale. Maybe the snails are bigger over there, what do you think?'

Archibald Keats had the good grace to flush bright red as he sank back into his chair, surrounded by his grinning fellow officers. 'Gentlemen,' the colonel spoke again, all trace of humour gone from his voice, 'when I spoke with Sir Ian Hamilton this morning he was in a fairly upbeat mood. Some of his staff wallahs are forecasting heavy casualties when we go in but Sir Ian thinks they're talking tosh. Everything seems to be in place and if we can keep our heads and push on, we'll get the job done.

Now, time for a spot of tiffin and then we'll watch the chaps practice their rowing. That'll be all for now. We'll go back over the

6

plan again later, over and over it again until you all know by heart your place in the scheme of things.'

--§--

'Look, I don't know how to fucking swim so how the hell am I supposed to get into the boat down that poxy rope ladder with all this kit on, corporal?'

Walter Harding sighed. There was always one. 'Sling your rifle over your back, put your foot in the first rung below you and go down hand over hand, Bailey,' he explained patiently, 'don't look down or you'll fall. And stop swearing! If you fall in, that nice navy cove with the sharp looking boathook will fish you out. That's if he doesn't stick you in the backside first. Savvy?'

'Sorry, corporal, it's just that I don't fancy ending up in the belly of a *Nobby Clark*, I've always been terrified of them.'

Walt laughed. 'You dimwit, there's no sharks in here. There, that's the way, keep doing that. Right, next one, move along quickly now.'

When they were all tightly packed in the boat's confines the able seaman at the front pushed off from the side of the ship with a jaunty air as the soldiers sat within its innards attempted to sort out the oars and rowlocks. At the other end of the boat a small, diminutive midshipman who looked as if he still belonged at school puffed heavily on his cigarette, moved the tiller bar over and shouted in a squeaky voice, 'Alright chaps, all together, heave!'

The result was pandemonium. Oars twisted and men and equipment fell about the boat as they scraped down the side of the transport, rocking heavily in the swell. 'Mister Pevensey!' a thunderous roar came from the upper part of the ship, 'Put that cigarette out and get that damned boat under way. Take charge, man!'

Weakly, the midshipman waved an arm in acknowledgement and attempted to bring his craft under control. It took a few minutes but gradually they sorted themselves out and began rowing in earnest away from the mother ship. The sea was beginning to whip up and they made heavy going at first, before being joined by more and more laden boats as the rest of 'B' Company practiced their new-found rowing skills.

A steam pinnace appeared, tossing in the swell, brasswork gleaming as the sailors onboard her shouted for them to throw a line. Eventually this was done and they were taken in tow as the pinnace corkscrewed round picking up tows from all the other boats. When she had a string of five boats the pinnace took them for a gentle tour of the harbour, threading her way delicately inbetween the other transports, oblivious to the jeers and catcalls from the men lining their sides.

As they came back alongside a good hour later, Walt grabbed gratefully at the rope ladder and began to swing his way up. 'Eh, corp, what's that sticking out of the water?' an indignant voice sounded at his elbow. Walt paused and looked over his shoulder. 'Oh, that? Don't you know, Bailey,' he said, trying to keep his voice neutral, 'it's a bloody shark's fin. Apparently the harbour's full of them!'

--§--

The following day the sea was too choppy to practice their boat skills and the bad weather continued into the next, causing a postponement of the original timetable. After an interminable wait of another two days due to bad weather, the transfer of the men to go with the first wave was effected. The southern group of the division, consisting of HMS *Implacable*, HMS *Euryalus* and a fleet sweeper would leave Imbros first, bound for the island of Tenedos, south of Gallipoli, where they would stay until the early hours of Sunday the 25th. That morning the assault would commence up and down the peninsula. A sombre 'B' Company boarded the boats to take them to HMS *Implacable*, the goodbyes and best wishes of their regimental comrades following them as they made their way over to the huge bulk of the battleship.

Late in the afternoon the battleships bound for Tenedos began their slow, graceful passage from the harbour, followed by Fleet Sweeper No.1. The battleship, HMS *Queen Elizabeth*, carrying the overall commander of the task force, General Sir Ian Hamilton, and his staff would follow with the rest of the division on the morrow. It was an awe-inspiring moment. From his position on the side of *Implacable*, Walt watched as the assembled fleet and their small contingent began the journey that would take so many men to the destiny awaiting them. Cheers sounded from ship to ship, the sound swelling until it became a constant roar as the thousands of men of the 29th Division saluted each other in passing.

'Fucken' poms, ain't we glad to see the back of them!' The speaker, a bronzed individual with a weather-beaten face glared at the men lining the rails of the British ships as they passed by amidships. 'Look at them, bloody white corpses, that's what they look like with those stupid sun hats on. Wait 'til they get ashore, they'll know about it then.'

'Shut it will you, Willis, you're always bloody complaining. At least we've got another day here before we have to follow the Brits.'

'Too bloody right we should. Oh sorry, mate, forgot you was one once. Just cos you wear our uniform, it don't make you a real dinky-di! Once a pom, always a pom in my book.'

His companion sighed theatrically. 'You're right, Billy, I forgot. But at least I walked down the gangway of the ship I arrived on as a free man, unlike your convict ancestor. Remind me again, what was it he was transported for? Sexually interfering with sheep, wasn't it?'

Both men glanced at each other and burst out laughing. 'Do for me, Harding,' Corporal Billy Willis grinned, 'we're gonna get on great kicking hell out of those Jacko's ashore the day after tomorrow.'

Had he but known it, at the time of the ships leaving Mudros, Walt Harding was closer to his brother than he'd been for a long time. Corporal Tom Harding of the 9th Battalion (Queensland) Australian Imperial Force, stood by the rail of His Majesty's Australian Troop Transport *HMAT Maida* and watched with detached disinterest as the British ships slid past the watching multitude. He ignored the cheering from the other ships and thrust one hand deep into a pocket as he fumbled for a handkerchief.

Although the years spent roaming the far north of Australia had not proven to be the good life he'd anticipated, Tom Harding's approach to life was still that of the eternal optimist with no lines of bitterness etched into his calm, handsome features. Tom had come to love his adopted country with a fierce pride and had been one of the first to apply when war was declared and the call went out for volunteers.

From his job on a cattle station near Windorah in Queensland, he'd journeyed to Brisbane to pledge his allegiance to the foundling Army that the Australian Prime Minister, Joseph Cook, in August 1914 had enthusiastically proclaimed would aid the mother country in her hour of need. A cable was sent to London offering the warships of the Australian navy to the motherland and a pledge of twenty thousand men. From a small standing army the AIF expanded rapidly, taking in thousands of eager volunteers desperate to join up and experience a taste of war before it was all over.

In September 1914, barely a month after making that promise the government lost a General Election and the federal administration of Andrew Fisher was returned to the office he'd vacated only the year before. During the course of his election campaign Fisher had ardently supported the AIF's expansion, an undertaking he enthusiastically embraced on regaining office.

In its usual arrogant manner the British government insisted on the Australians being under their command although in a rare victory the Australian High Commissioner in London, Sir George Reid, did wring a concession from the British that the AIF would complete its training in Egypt and not in the wintry depths of Salisbury Plain.

It was this decision that would doom many Australian and New Zealanders when the need for troops for Gallipoli became a pressing matter. Being so close to the scene of the intended assault it seemed a perfectly natural act to use the nearest troops and so the ANZAC Corps was included in the order of battle. Even so, they would go into action under a British general's command and not their own, a situation that rankled bitterly then and for generations afterwards.

'I always meant to ask you, mate, why the Jesus did you choose the AIF, why didn't you jump ship back to England and join up there with all those other fucken' poms?'

Tom thought long and hard before giving an answer. 'I dunno, I suppose I got carried away like all you other blokes. Besides which, the tucker in the pom army's lousy, I'm told!'

He blew his nose noisily and spoke earnestly. 'Australia suits me fine, the climate and the people there who've made me feel welcome. There's so much opportunity if you look hard enough. I've come to think of it as my home now. When the call came I knew I'd have to stand up and fight for what Australia means to me. What about you, Billy?'

Billy grinned. 'Ah well, I've a similar story to yours. Almost. I was working as a stockman on the Inkerman cattle station out Burdekin way. Silly old bastard sold it in 1910 to grow sugarcane and that was me and my cobbers out of a job. Plus there was a young lady chasing me, said I was the father of her kid. Me? The little bugger had blue eyes, I swear, mate.

So I did a runner from there and drifted for the next few years. Did some work for a *cocky* on a farm out near Brisbane but he was a miserable bastard so I off and took to droving, running cattle up the Birdsville Track from South Australia. Didn't last too long, the beer down there was awful! The war came and I figured I'd join up and see a bit of the world-even bought me a French dictionary to allow me to get close to those *ooh-la-la* French sheila's when we got there. Fat bloody chance I'll get to use it now, eh mate?'

Tom had thrown himself whole-heartedly into becoming a soldier and that enthusiasm had been rewarded by his promotion to corporal when the regiment was formed. For all his outwardly hardbitten veneer, Billy Willis's inner qualities and strength of character had been noticed at an early stage leading to promotion straight to platoon serjeant. A rank he'd kept. Until now.

'I never asked, Tom, just what was it you were doing prior to enlisting?'

'I was a miner back in England but there was no way I fancied going back down the mines when I arrived in Sydney so I jumped a train going north and ended up in Queensland. I did a bit of prickly-pear clearing, some sheep droving but I couldn't keep on a Waler's back long enough. They paid me off and I drifted around before ending up on a cattle station so when we declared war it seemed a good idea to join up and now look where it's landed me.'

'Hey, you're with me and together we can beat the brains out of any Abduls. Trust me, it'll be a walkover.'

'We'll find out soon enough how Johnny Turk's gonna fight, Billy. Me, I don't think it's gonna be the pushover everyone keeps telling us it'll be.'

'No worries, mate. You'll see, we'll knock their bloody bollocks off!'

--§--

Author's note.

The 9th Battalion was one of the first units of the AIF to be raised in August after the declaration of war and was the first of many Queensland battalions that served during the Great War. After its formation the 9th embarked on the transport ship HMAT Omrah at Brisbane under their commanding officer Lt. Colonel Harry Lee as part of the 3rd Infantry Brigade and sailed south in October. A brief sojourn in Port Melbourne followed before she sailed to join other transports off the harbour of Albany in Western Australia. Here, a fleet of fifty transports and their armed escorts sailed in November 1914, heading initially

11

across the Indian Ocean to Ceylon. After embarking fresh supplies they set their bows for the tip of Africa and the Red Sea until finally making their way up through the Suez Canal to Alexandria in Egypt.

On November 14th, Omrah anchored off Colombo in Ceylon and embarked 2 officers, 2 warrant officers and 44 ratings, survivors of the sinking of the German commerce raider SMS Emden by the Australian cruiser HMAS Sydney. The Germans were to be held under armed guard on Omrah and the Australians looked at their aloof captives as they boarded with decided interest. These were the men they were travelling half-way round the world to fight, the foe who was already locked in mortal combat with Australia's allies on the Western Front.

The Germans remained onboard until Omrah reached Suez where they were embarked on the cruiser, HMS Hampshire, for onward travel to a prisoner-of-war camp. Omrah travelled through the Red Sea and up the Suez Canal, arriving in Alexandria on the morning of the 4th December 1914.The journey had not without further incident, apart from the excitement of having Germans onboard for the latter half of the voyage, the battalion's first casualty had occurred when a private, one Thomas Hodges, had been reported missing at sea. Two other men were sent over to one of the other better-equipped transports for hernia operations and on embarking at Alexandria, 39 men were hospitalised with measles. Not a good start to the battalion's campaigning.

--§--

'It won't be as hard a fight as we had with those bloody galahs in Cairo. Hard bastards those Gyppos but we gave as good as we got, eh Tom? Remember that punch-up we had with the buggers in *The Wozzer*, eh? Even the Salvarmy preacher couldn't believe the damage we did there. And the poms, God, we didn't half sort those bastards out. A pity we missed the riots earlier this month when the boys smashed the place up together with the poms. That would've been a sight to see, those miserable bastards mixing in with our boys and giving the Gyppos hell!'

'Billy!' Tom protested, 'All *those miserable bastards* as you put it are our allies in this and the poor bugger's earn less than a fifth of what we get paid.'

'A fifth? Nah, you're taking the piss! Are you telling me the poms only earn a shilling a day? Who'd come over here and earn less than a sweeper-up in a Brisbane bar and get the shit shot outta him, like what's going to happen shortly? They should've joined with us and become *six bob a day tourists*, that would've made their pay up. They didn't really call us that in the Brisbane Courier, did they Tom? Six bob a day tourists? Sounds a bit offensive to me, cheeky bastards.'

'So I was told.'

'Yeah, but going back to your poms, you're not telling me that's what they really get, are you?'

'It's true, I swear it'

'Who told you that?'

'That pommy corporal I was chatting to in Fakim's Bar before you smashed the chair over his head!'

'Oh, him? I didn't like the look of him, he had a funny cast to his eyes. I thought he was giving you a hard time, mate, that's why I did my block and hit him. You mean to tell me all he was doing was whingeing about how poor his fucken' pay was? Anyway, it serves the poor bastard right. It's their fucken' officers what caused this bloody trouble in the first place, any Aussie lot would have beaten the Bosches months before. We've been brought here to sort their bloody mess out so that drongo deserved the headache I gave him!'

--§--

On arrival in Alexandria there'd been no time to stop and gaze around them as they were swiftly entrained and sent inland to the tented village of Mena Camp, Giza, in the shadows of the pyramids near Cairo. Here the entire 15th Division of the AIF was gathering, infantrymen, artillery and the mounted regiments of the Australian Light Horse. Together with the contingent of troops from New Zealand the men from Australia would go down in history when they formed the Australian and New Zealand Army Corps, known forever after as the ANZAC's.

Training began immediately in the training camp known as *Area B*, practising assaults on a well dug-in enemy and taking long marches out into the desert to acclimatise. The days were spent in searing heat but the nights were often freezing, cold enough to require wrapping up well in a blanket. A heavy dew formed each morning which meant weapons cleaning became next to godliness, a single speck in a rifle barrel bringing heaped epithets on the unfortunate's head from an outraged NCO.

Time spent training was not without further casualties, a grim reminder that on active service death was ever present and not only from enemy action. Whilst at Mena, men died of pneumonia, septicemia, went absent without leave or were held in detention for various offences awaiting sentencing. Reinforcements joined and were swiftly absorbed into the battalion, bringing its strength up to over a thousand men and officers.

Christmas came and slid by, followed by the New Year heralding 1915 and the start of a second year of warfare. Boredom set in swiftly so the chance to let steam off in the delights of Cairo was met with alacrity. Better paid than their British counterparts, the Australian troops soon garnered a reputation for enjoying themselves although many a Cairo shopkeeper found himself on the wrong side of the counter if he tried, mistakenly, to gyp these amiable, good- natured yet hardened, tough individuals. *The Wozzer* was the nickname given to Cairo's red-light district of Haret el Wassa by the ANZAC's, an area Billy had taken to his heart.

'Billy, what am I going to do with you? My head's still ringing from rescuing you from the fights we had and luckily, Mr Hatton, the Salvation Army Captain, managed to square things with those Arabs you busted up otherwise you'd still be in the pokey, my little street fighter! Anyway, I'm taking plenty of ammo with me and if I run out I can chuck a tin or two of bully beef at the Ottomans, those things are hard enough to stun an ox!'

'Good on yer, Hardie. It was a shame Simmo and Johnno were sent home, though, there's two good blokes we could've done with keeping. What was it all about? Who'd they upset, the bloody padre?'

'Billy, they were sent home cos they'd caught gonorrhea, like a whole heap of other blokes who were gallivanting round those Egyptian whorehouses.'

'Christ, try telling that to the missus! *"Sorry, love, I'm home cos I caught the clap, don't mind what the neighbours say."* Poor bastards.'

'Aye, we were sent here to fight the Turks, not fuck our way round Cairo.'

'Too right, mate! Hey, you're a bit of a know-all, Tom, what's the Turkish for, *"Hands up, you fucken' bludger?"* That oughter do it when we make it ashore.'

'Billy, I give up!' Tom shook his head in exasperation as he glanced sideways at his friend's deadpan expression.

The ethos of Australia's free spirit was engendered in these tall, wiry men in their loose, comfortable tunics and brown leather boots who played and fought hard. An all-volunteer army, the only one of its kind in existence throughout the First World War, they brought a grudging admiration from all who encountered them although their attitude to discipline appalled the rigid officer class of the British Army who shuddered to hear an Aussie private call his officer, *"Mate"*. Their own brand of self-discipline and that peculiar brand of Australian kinship, known as *Mateship* would be sorely tested in the dark days ahead.

At long last, on the 28th February 1915, the order was given for units to move out, among them the 3rd Brigade who had been honoured by being chosen to make the first assault in the coming landings. Many of the men embarking on the transports to Lemnos were in ignorance of their destination, being certain that they would soon be sent to France but grateful to be leaving the tented metropolis behind. Short of 34 men who still lingered in hospital, the battalion retraced its journey to Alexandria in high spirits where a fleet of transports awaited them and their fellow battalions.

The horse-drawn transport wagons were withdrawn as, on reaching the shore at Gallipoli, it was intended to use mules to supply the troops with and the men quickly embarked onto the transport which would be their home for the next few weeks. Once aboard they learned of their destination.

In January all the battalion's' order of battle had been changed with the six-company formation being altered to form four company's, 'A' to 'D'. A hard-bitten professional soldier, knowing they would be going into action soon, Harry Lee had quietly kept a fifth, 'E' Coy, in existence by absorbing several drafts of newly-arrived reinforcements. ANZAC HQ had turned a blind eye to his subterfuge and during their stay at Mena 'E' Company's ranks had swelled with the likes of NCO's such as Tom Harding and Billy Willis, drafted into it to provide experience and backbone. This gave the battalion an extra couple of hundred men which Harry Lee surmised would be sorely needed once they were ashore.

A curious incident had occurred on reaching Alexandria. Transferring onto the transport, *Ionian*, early the following morning of the 2nd March one of their number, a Private Davenport, had been found with his throat cut. Taken shore to hospital he was quickly reported as deceased, leaving the ship ablaze with rumours. These rumours had still not died down when the *Ionian* sailed that evening for Lemnos, arriving in Mudros harbour three days later.

They were kept cooped up on the transport for two days before disembarking into the chaos of Lemnos as a great army of men

15

gathered on the tiny island's shores. By a quirk of fate, there were enough tents pitched for only one Australian battalion and the 9th had won the honour on the toss of a coin, condemning the rest of the ANZAC Corps to eke out a miserable existence cooped up in their transport ships.

It proved a poor prize, the tents leaked and caused men to fall sick with colds with one unlucky soldier dying of pneumonia in the cold and rainy weather that had greeted them. Exercises were carried out on a regular basis to toughen them up and prepare them for action, rowing to a beach in Mudros harbour that partly resembled those they would assault in the coming weeks. All the while as they practiced landing and carrying out mock assaults their thoughts strayed towards the Turkish mainland and the almost certain Ottoman army waiting to receive them. After weeks of a miserable existence the 9th marched back to Mudros harbour and embarked on the transport that would take them into battle.

--§--

'One thing's for certain, I won't miss Lemnos,' Billy Willis said as their ship continued to swing lazily on its anchor by the harbour entrance. 'We've been here, how long now? Six weeks? An' I only bunked off the camp once for a look round. I was beginning to miss egg and bacon for five piastres and a bucket of beer in the regimental wet canteen for a penny back in Egypt. Look at what we've come to now! Bugger all.'

'If you hadn't turned up smashed that time and tried to throttle the sentry we'd all have enjoyed a bit more time in the village!'

'Come on, Hardie, fair go's mate! The bastard tried to take my grog off'n me when I tried to get back into the camp! Do you know how much I paid for that bottle? No way was he goin' to do that. It's almost…it's bloody stealing, that's what I say!'

Tom laughed again. 'I didn't see anything in the regulations that said you could have your own private supply of cognac, Billy! It's an offence, you knew that.'

'Fair dinkum! But at least the *Old Man* recognised it for what it was, he could've busted me down to the ranks but he didn't, eh? The bastard must've fair pissed himself though, watching me run round with a rifle over me head. Reckon that's where I got me dose of the trots from, though!'

The sight of ex-serjeant Billy Willis running round for a week, toting a rifle high over his head in the heat of the sun had amused them all, even the ones who had anticipated wandering around the island before Billy's exploits had ended that small pleasure for them all. He was lucky the sentry didn't press charges and the colonel had only busted him down to corporal. Good men were at a premium and Colonel Lee had realised that. Billy was one of the best soldiers in the battalion, if he could stay sober.

'At least the weather's cleared up, Billy, I was beginning to feel like your gaolbird ancestors, cooped up on a ship for days, weeks, on end and only shit to look forward to once you'd landed. We're off soon, I'm told, and good riddance to this fleapit.'

'Oi, don't you knock my antecedents, mate! Did you remember to change into clean underwear like the colonel told us to?'

'Are you taking the mickey? I laughed more at that pathetic letter General Hamilton sent to be read out than the colonel worrying about how clean our private bits are.'

'Oh yeah, I saw it too. *"The landing will be made good, by the help of God and the navy ...."* What was he before his mummy bought him a commission, a music-hall comedian? If God's tucker bag is full of .303 ammo then he can come ashore with us, if not, him and the bloody navy had best stay out of our way!'

'Don't give me that hard-bitten sense of piety, Billy Willis, I saw you at the Church Parade yesterday, you were singing as loudly as the next man.'

'Oh that, it don't count. You should know that, Tom, I was singing, not fucken' praying! Anyhow, no worries, I've seen enough, let's go and scrounge a cup of char and see how the other larrikins are doing. Shitting themselves if they've any sense. I've got a few things left to stick in me pack and that'll be me ready for the little buggers. Think we'll find a few Turkish bints waiting for us over there? You never know, if they don't know we're comin' we could catch them having a shindig, like those ones we saw in bloody Cairo, *Hookey pipes* and all. I could fair go some of that now, mate.'

'God help us Billy, what're you hoping for, a few belly dancers to put on a show? This isn't a picnic we're going on, and it's a Hookah, not a *Hookey pipe* you idiot! What am I going to do with you?' Tom turned to follow and as he did so his gaze fell upon a large ship whose anchor chain strained at keeping her on station in the centre of the harbour. She was painted white, with large red crosses on her sides and a green stripe down her length, a hospital ship, readying herself for the broken bodies and minds that would soon be filling her cool interiors. Tom shivered as a cold sensation made his spine tingle and he hurried after a still-loudly complaining Billy.

Chapter Two.

Ari Burnu, Sunday, April 25th 1915.

The sunset was spectacular, the sea a bright hue of azure as they swung round to the east. Away to their left the sun, a ball of intermingled orange and reds, slowly sank beneath the horizon, spreading its dying rays across the surface of the Aegean and wrapping the clouds lingering above in pink-tinged cotton wool. In bright moonlight the ships fell into line, each silhouetted column heading for its own particular part of the peninsula.

Prior to leaving Mudros, 'A' and 'B' Company had boarded the battleship, *HMS Queen*, along with 200 Brigade staff and so became part of the first wave of 1500 men. Safely aboard *HMS Queen*, (General Birdwood's HQ.) they were joined by *HMS Prince of Wales* and *HMS London*. The rest of the 9th were placed on the transport *HMAT Maida* and settled down fatalistically for the 60-mile journey. The battleships would head for the shore and let loose their boats within a few hundred yards of the shore then stay to back the landings with their main armaments if needed.

The next two waves would transfer from their transport to seven of the accompanying destroyers at the rendezvous point, five miles off the beach at Gabe Tebe, 3rd Brigade's initial objective. There, half of 'E' Company of the 9th Battalion including Tom Harding and Billy Willis would transfer to *HMS Ribble* along with a company of the 12th Battalion. The other half would board another destroyer, *HMS Beagle*, along with 'C' and 'D' Company and it was reckoned that 'A' and 'B', should be ashore half an hour before them on landing from *HMS Queen*. All the destroyers would head to within 50 yards of the shore, towing the boats behind them before letting go and allowing the boats to row the remaining distance. It was not a satisfactory solution to getting the men ashore but the plans were to regroup and reform the battalion once all were safely ashore

Whilst their officers pored over maps and read and re-read their orders, the men lay on their bunks, some writing letters home, others engaging in light banter with their mates. A few were silent, staring into space as they mentally worked out the chances of staying alive in the morning. These were the men who realised it was not going to be the pushover they'd been promised. Sleep would not come easily this night with everyone keyed up for the events that would unfold in a few short hours time.

Dear Ma,
        Hope this finds you in the pink. I am well and looking forward
to...

'*Gaaa!*' Tod Hammond threw down his pencil and screwed the sheet
of paper into a ball. 'How long before we go over to that pom ship?
Hey, Petersen, still got those bloody cards on you, mate?'
'What's up Hammond, got some money you want rid of before we
go ashore tomorrow?'
'Too right I have. Get them out and let's see who's gonna fleece
who!'
Ralph Petersen grinned, fished a greasy pack of cards from his
trouser pocket and beckoned the blond-haired youngster over. 'Come
on then, the wife's needing new chooks to lay more eggs so you can
supply the funds she keeps asking for every time she bloody well
writes. Put your stash down, cobber and let's get started.'
As Petersen dealt the cards, Tod jumped down off his bunk to join
him, looking round the messdeck. Men and equipment lay
everywhere, sprawled in heaps, filling every nook and cranny of the
available space. He sat alongside his friend and jerked a thumb at one
of the recumbent forms.
'Bert Ring told me we're goin' in tomorrow with only fixed
bayonets, sez the colonel don't even want anyone to have one up the
spout, never mind loaded magazines.'
'That fucken' moron, what's he wanting us to do that for? Is he
cummin' with us? Not on your bloody nelly! You can't stick a bloody
Abdul from a hundred yards away, the berk, did no-one tell him that
our bloody bayonets are only eighteen inches long? Nah, Bert's got
his facts mixed up. Oi, Bert? Where'd you get that load of nonsense
from about the bayonets, mate?'
'Straight up, Petersen, old *Laggie* says so. Here...' He fumbled in his
pocket and brought out a folded piece of paper. 'I got this off Lt
Treharne.' He scanned its contents. 'This is from Colonel Sinclair-
MagLagan, commander of 3rd Brigade. It'll be read out later but I got
a sneak copy. It sez here summat like...'*about to carry out a most difficult
operation...a high honour which we must do our best to justify...*And...'
'Yes, yes, just get to the bit about the bayonets!'
'Alright, Petersen, keep your bloody hair on, mate. Right, where is
it? Oh, yeah...'*Until broad daylight the bayonet is your weapon.*' I reckon *old
Birdy* himself asked for it. Probably 'eard about your bloody useless

results on the firing range, Petersen, and doesn't want you shooting our own blokes in the arse as we land.'

At the mention of the ANZAC force commander, Lt General Sir William Birdwood, Petersen threw his cards down in disgust and stood up. 'Jesus! If he's asking for us to use only our bayonets I'd better get writing to the old lady and tell her she'll have to wait some time for the new chooks. She can buy them with the money the army sends its widders!' He walked over to his bunk and threw himself down morosely on it.

'Hey, mates, anyone for cards? Alright, hows about a quick game of *Two's up*, then?' Tod looked round but the heart had gone out of the crowd that had gathered. Sighing, he left the cards where they lay, walked over to his bunk and retrieved the crumpled sheet of notepaper. Straightening it out, he scrabbled round for the pencil and recommenced writing.

Tension grew while they waited and with a sense of relief they were called just after midnight to transfer over to the waiting destroyers. The lifeboats used to row over in would stay with the destroyer and be employed for the coming assault. Friends embraced, old debts were settled and they silently took their places in the queue to board the lifeboats. Each man carried his rifle and 200 rounds of ammunition, three sandbags, three days rations and a full water-bottle. The packs on their backs held more ammunition, more rations and a greatcoat but the packs would be dropped on landing, to be retrieved later.

'Cheerio mates, see you on the beach. Don't eat all the fucken' ice-cream before we get there, you hear?'

'Tough on you boys coming later, we're gonna bag the best *pozzys*, you'll see!'

'Yeah, right! Will late entries into the sand-castle *compo* be taken?'

'Oi, you lot, shut it and get in the bloody boat, will you!'

The lifeboats also carried more boxes of ammunition, picks, shovels, sandbags and extra supplies of water and rations, the picks and shovels being taken with them to dig in when ordered to. Fully laden, wearing their packs and leaving their webbing unbuckled, they shuffled forward to the ladders. Some wore slouch hats but the majority of the men wore their stiff uniform caps, leather straps pulled tight to stop them falling into the sea.

Sharp-edged entrenching tools hanging from their webbing frogs caught against many a man's legs as they assembled by the side of the

21

ship but hard experience in digging trenches back at Mena had taught them the necessity in carrying this vital tool so they bore its chafing stoically whilst clambering over the side.

'I'm telling you, if one of those pom tars tries to take the mick, I'm gonna bloody crown him!' grumbled Petersen as he lowered himself down the rope ladder to the lifeboat. Sleepy-eyed, they rowed over to the sleek destroyer as she pitched and heaved in the gentle Aegean swell. Ribald shouts as they approached came from the company of their sister regiment, the 12th, which was already onboard. Making their way up the ladders they sought out old mates and began animated chin-wags amongst the crowded chaos of *Ribble's* upper decks.

A rumbling below their feet and the churning of the wake behind them was their first inkling that they were finally on their way to action. This was to be no practice landing in Egypt and Mudros but the real thing. In a few hours the ANZAC's would join the war and receive their baptism of fire. The ship's cooks sorted a meal out and gratefully they ate an early breakfast of bully beef stew and army biscuits with a mug of sweet tea. For the rest of the voyage they lay against their packs and tried to rest. Tom stood at the rail thinking deeply and looking down into the sea, entranced by the gleaming phosphorescence of waves foaming backwards from the destroyer's bows under the bright gleam of the moon. It was a cold night and the stars twinkled icily overhead, looking down with interest at so many men retracing the steps of the ancients who had come to take Troy not too far away from where they lay.

2/Lt Mark Treharne, the platoon leader, had spoken to them before they'd left the security of the transport, spreading a poorly-drawn map of the area at his feet as they sat around him inquisitively.

'Here you go, blokes, this is what we're going to be facing so pay attention. This headland here is Gabe Tebe and the one at the other end is Ari Burnu. We're going to land at Gabe Tebe, on 'Z' Beach', head inland as quick as Christ and cut Mr Johnny Turk off from retreating or reinforcing his forces on the Peninsula. We'll then stay put and let the following waves hurry through us and advance over the plain towards a place called Maidos.

When you get ashore, drop your packs off on the beach and get inland as quickly as you can, don't wait for anyone. The good thing is that we'll be accompanied by a company of the 3rd Field Ambulance so anyone catching a packet will be well looked after.'

'Excuse me, sir, is it true that we're to go in with only our bayonets?'

'Yup, that's the line, Petersen, no ammo up the spout 'til it gets light enough to see what we're shooting at. If you spot an Abdul in the bushes, give him a jab with your bayonet unless it's daylight by which time you have my permission to shoot the bugger!'

'Sir, Petersen can't bloody shoot straight, can't you order him to use his bayonet for the rest of the day as well? I don't want my arse shot off just cos of his duff shooting!'

'Fuck you, Rushton! You ain't so hot with a rifle yerself, mate.'

'Alright boys, calm down. Take a good dekko at the map, memorise what boat you'll be in and go and get some rest. Good luck and I'll see you all on the beach.'

'How's the missus bearing up, sir, still missing you, eh?'

Mark Treharne had flushed to the roots of his auburn hair. He'd married shortly before enlisting and his wife back home in Australia was pregnant. Excited as he was of his impending fatherhood, he'd kept a quiet council about his family life, one doomed to failure once his men had found out.

'She's fine, Fairlie, as long as the little bugger doesn't look like you!' he'd retorted, bringing smiles and cheers all round.

As they'd moved to disperse he'd called out. 'One last thing, gentlemen, verbal orders from the *Old Man*. It concerns women and religion.'

'Don't tell me the padre's bringing some women with him, sir?'

'Shut up, Fairlie. Right, sit back down and I'll go through it. Stop chuntering you blokes, the quicker I explain the quicker you'll get your tucker.'

At his serious tone they'd stopped fidgeting and sat quietly, looking at him expectantly.

'Right, here goes. Women. Any female encountered ashore will be treated with all courtesy, do I make myself clear?'

'Is this before we stick her with the bayonet, sir?'

Treharne had laughed aloud with the rest. 'You bloody fool, Fairlie, you and Rushton should go into the Music Hall business when this show's over, your bloody talents're wasted in the army! No, you berk, you leave her be. Now let me continue.

Where we're going there will be no women but in the event…shut it, Fairlie…that we do encounter any, you're to treat them as you'd treat your mother.'

A strangled gasp from Fairlie had brought the house down. When the laughter cleared, Treharne's amused face had changed to one more serious.

'Religion. I know most of you blokes think that God's an ugly word, given the circumstances we find ourselves in but Johnny Turk happens to believe in his God fairly seriously so listen up. Their God is known as *Allah* and this bloke is revered in the Moslem world, their main man like our own God. His followers are known as *Mohammedans* or *Ottomans* and while I can tell you when you go ashore that you can kill as many of these Mohammedans or Ottomans as you can, I must also warn you about messing with their religion.

Strict orders from Colonel Lee, treat all prisoners with respect and do not, DO NOT, under any circumstances take the mickey out of his beliefs. Do we understand each other?'

'Yes, sir!' they'd bellowed as one as they were dismissed.

--§--

After their youthful officer had left, Tom sat with the men of his section as they discussed home, families and the coming conflict. Looking round, he felt a burst of pride as each man showed he could be depended on to look after the welfare of his fellow platoon members. They'd be ashore soon and he could see some men hiding their own feelings in order to assist mates whose built-up tension and fear of impending death was making coherent thought almost impossible. The apprehension was there but they'd pull through it together.

A knot of mates lay carelessly entwined, packs and weapons in a jumble as they chivvied each other, drawing strength for the hours ahead from the close proximity of the closely-knitted group. Declan O'Neill, a bank clerk from Townsville opened the conversation,

'It's all a load of bollocks if you ask me, we're only here to bail the Brits out. Australia should be in charge here, not following orders given by some high-ranking aristocratic duffers that were found in the local geriatrics ward.' An enigmatic, fiercely loyal member of the company, O'Neill was destined for higher rank if he could only keep his sharp tongue under control.

24

'Oh, yeah, and why did you join up, then, O'Neill if you feel like that?'

Running his fingers round the rough collar of his tunic O'Neill answered with a faint smile. 'It wasn't because of the uniform, Corporal Harding, I can assure you! I was out of work for ten months before this lot started so the pay they were offering to enlist came in right handy. Loyalty to the British Empire? Don't make me laugh, mate! Here, have you seen my two boys, take a dekko at this.' He proffered a crumpled photograph showing a slim, pretty woman holding two tousle-headed boys.

'Our twins, Aidan and Kiernan, that's who I'm fighting for. General Sir fucken' Hamilton can kiss my arse.'

Another member of the group, Victor Abbott was a quiet, taciturn person, not prone to high jinks like most of the others but Australian to the core, strong and utterly dependable. Tod Hammond and Ralph Petersen were mates from a while back, having enlisted together and they were never far from each other's side. Edmund Rushton was the platoon's wit but was also a formidable fighter as many a Cairo policeman had found out to his cost.

'I just hope the fun isn't over by the time we get ashore, it'll be a pity to come all this way and not see any action. I've bin away from the missus so long these Turks are gonna pay for it.'

'Don't worry, Petersen, I wrote ahead to the Caliph and he's keeping some of his big boys back just for you to have a fight with.'

'Fuck you again, Rushton, another smart comment from you and I'll bust your nose, mate!'

'Alright, alright, knock it off you two. Rushton, stop being such a berk and antagonising Petersen, will you?'

'Aw, corp, you're not his mummy are you? I can...*Aaaahhhh*!' A lumpy ship's lifebelt hit Ed Rushton full in the face, adroitly ending the conversation.

Treharne's words had brought no comfort to Tom's mind and he continued to look down at the surface of the water. In spite of the cold not a breath of wind stirred and the sea was as calm as a millpond. After an hour of this a dark shape rose from the sea ahead of them. A figure joined him on the rail, pointing. 'That's the island of Imbros, mate, according to the tars. We're not that far from the beaches now so we're gonna wait here until the battleships arrive and the first wave goes in. We'll be next. Are you ready for this?'

'Hi Billy,' Tom greeted his pal, 'yeah, I reckon so. I'm a bit on edge, like everyone else, it's the waiting I guess. We'll find out soon enough. My head hurts with all that guff Lt Treharne gave us though, timings, objectives, who's to go where and at what time. Jesus, they talk as if it's going to be a bloody pushover but I still have my doubts!'

Through the gloom he could sense Billy Willis's anxiety, the man's natural sense of humour seemed subdued as he stood with Tom and contemplated the coming hours. After a long pause he broke his silence.

'I never thought we'd end up here, you know. When I joined up back in Oz me'n the blokes who volunteered with me thought we'd be off to France to save the Empire. Now look at us, instead of facing the frightful Hun we're all kitted up to land on some God-forsaken beach and slaughter a few Gyppos.' He broke off to take a deep drag from the cigarette he held cupped in the palm of his hand.

'They're not Gyppos and you'll get slaughtered if one of the tars catches you smoking up on deck, Billy, don't you know it's...'

'It's what? Do you think they'll put me in the pokey and make me miss the party for breakin' their stupid rules?'

'Don't get clever, I was just saying...'

'There's worse things waiting than having a crafty drag Tom but you're right. Remember Mena camp, that was a fair cow, mate, with all those bloody dust storms and locusts but not as bad as the situation we're gonna be facing shortly.' He sighed deeply and flicked the glowing end into the sea below. Straightening, he gestured out into the darkness.

'Look at it. Can you get a whiff of the smell coming off the land over there? Hard to think that in a few hours time we'll be ashore and doing our best to kill each other. Hey, Tom, do you really think the Abduls know we're coming?'

'C'mon, Billy, this ain't the Nullarbor Plain, mate, you can't pack all these men and ships in here, fifty-sixty miles from the enemy's coast and hope they don't get to hear about it. Course they know we're coming, they just don't know what a good rollicking we're going to give them when we do get ashore.'

'Yeah, I know. It's just that I don't feel too good about this. There's a letter in my pack, Tom, addressed to my old ma so if I catch a packet today will you make sure she gets it? Promise?'

'Alright, I promise but....'

'What?'

'I just don't think it right to ....'

'What? Say it. I shouldn't worry about copping a bullet?'

'You're scaring me, stop being a berk, we'll be fine.'

'I'm just saying that...if...well, you know...'

Tom glanced sideways. In the pale light, Billy Willis's face was strained, apprehensive.

'Don't talk that way, Billy. You and me'll be enjoying a cold Castlemaine back in Mount Perry this time next year, you'll see. We're natural born survivors, me and you so don't go all sad on me now, mate.'

'Tom, please. I said I've got a real bad feeling about this one.' He shook himself. 'A bit of the wind up, I reckon, seeing as how it ain't windmills we'll be tilting at shortly.'

Tom looked up, startled. 'Wow! I didn't take you for a classical scholar, Billy Willis, you do surprise me sometimes, mate.'

'Oi, Harding, I've 'ad me moments. What was that spics name again, Donkey summat?'

'Don Quixote, you berk!'

'Oh right. Well, tell that to His Highness, General Hamilton. He wasn't too pleased with us last time we messed with windmills I heard.'

They both laughed, their thoughts returning to their time at Lemnos when the 9th Battalion had been chosen to carry out a mock attack in front of no less a person than the expedition commander, General Sir Ian Hamilton, and their own General Birdwood. The 9th had attacked a row of windmills, whooping and hollering as they left the roughly-cut trenches. It had been a shambles and a depressed Hamilton had departed the scene totally unimpressed.

'Aye, I've a horrid feeling any windmills we might meet ashore are going to be filled with lots of little Abduls, all wanting to kill us. What time we going in?'

'Treharne said the first wave'll go in from the battleships about three fifteen and then we'll be taken as far inshore as possible by the destroyers and cut loose about four. What time's it now?'

'Two thirty.'

As they spoke the ship moved away from the lee of the island and began to slide slowly through the water. Shortly after that the moon dipped into the sea, heralding the approaching dawn but leaving them in an inky blackness. Time passed slowly and as they strained to pierce the night, an immense shadow quietly and purposely slid by their starboard bow. By its sheer bulk they recognised it as one of the three battleships although it was impossible to be certain which one. Low down on the surface of the water, following her like ducklings, was a string of boats being towed by a number of pinnaces. At the same time their destroyer hove to and the battleship and her accompanying boats disappeared soundlessly into the gloom.

--§--

'Four o'clock, mates, time to go.'

'Fall in, fall in! Come on men, get ready to board!' An hour had passed since their conversation, taken up by each man lost to his own thoughts.

'That's it, Tom, see you on the beach. Take care.'

'2 Section to me!' Tom roared as the troops ran round in a frantic struggle to find their boarding places. At the sound of his voice his men ran to where he stood and gathered round. Their platoon serjeant, Wilf Rickard, appeared out of the dark and flashed Tom a grateful glance when he saw most of his men were already present. Lifting their packs onto their shoulders, helping each other adjust the straps, they hefted SMLE's and made their way to the side of the ship where the rope ladders beckoned.

'How long before we go, mate?' whispered one man anxiously to his friend.

'How the hell do I know, cobber, and why are you bloody whispering? The Turks are fucken' miles away yet.'

Awkwardly, each man climbed down the ladder into the waiting boats. The outline of the shore ahead was invisible but to each waiting man's nostrils the offshore breeze wafted a sweet scent of lavender and myrtle over them from the invisible beachhead. Sailors in each boat helped the apprehensive soldiers onboard and a youthful midshipman manning the tiller pointed to where he wanted the men to sit. It soon filled up, each man packed tightly against his neighbour with no room to move. Moving aft, Tom flung himself down next to the youngster. 'How long 'til we get there?'

The youngster laughed. 'Don't be in such a hurry, we'll get you there. The first waves haven't even landed yet.'

'How old are you, son?' Tom asked curiously.

'Fifteen, and don't call me son, I'm a naval officer!' the youngster squeaked.

'Sorry, sir.' The apology, inadequate as it was, mollified the youngster and he busied himself with his maps and a compass, waiting for the off.

HMS *Ribble* started to edge slowly forward, dragging her charges with her, the tow tightening then slackening as each boat in turn appeared alongside and took on its passengers. This was repeated until all the boats were filled and they began the slow, careful approach to the, as yet, unseen beach. For all the world it appeared as if they were out for another hours energetic rowing around Mudros harbour but the grim, taut faces of the men in the boats belied the gravity of the occasion.

Under the protective umbrella of the darkness the destroyer knifed slowly forward and the shoreline became more distinct, a thin smudge that assumed a dark definition as they drew closer. The thin noise of a man whistling nervously through his teeth grated on Tom's nerves but the sound was swiftly silenced by an angry retort. He looked slowly at faces surrounding him, pale, wan discs in the moonlight, and deliberated hard. Up until now the thought of his dying or being wounded was a subject he'd deliberately ignored but as they moved silently through the water he began to consider the real prospects of either occurring in the very near future.

The fate of many would be decided in the following hours and for those who did survive, the world would be a different place from then on. He closed his eyes and counted to ten. When he opened them again, he would be back in Queensland with the sweet smell of the Jacarandas in his nostrils and the gentle murmuring of their branches in the breeze in his ears.

He blinked hard and opened his eyes abruptly. The only smell was one of naked fear and instead of the movement of tree branches all he could hear was the lapping of waves against the boat's hull.

Swallowing his fear he concentrated on watching the shore for any movement. So far no return fire had been encountered and he began to hope they'd land unopposed. That hope was dashed when a white light burst frighteningly overhead, illuminating the boats in the distance carrying the first wave and the sound of heavy firing broke out almost immediately.

'What the hell...?' The midshipman looked to his left and right, 'What're they doing, this isn't it...'

As he spoke, a loud voice from the destroyer reached them and the signal was given for the boats to disengage from the tow and make their way to the beach, now only a hundred or so yards away. 'Out oars! Get ready to start rowing, chaps!' the midshipman shouted in a weak voice before turning to Tom.

'This isn't right, we're not in the right area!' he cried in frustration, almost in tears. 'We shouldn't be here, we're all over the place.'

'What do you mean?' Tom asked, 'surely that's the beach ahead? What's wrong?'

For an answer the midshipman held up his prismatic compass.

'Look here, navigation's my best subject. I've been checking our heading and it's not right. Some idiot didn't take the current into account and we're heading too far to the north. That headland's Ari Burnu, not Gabe Tebe. It means we'll land too far to the north of where we're supposed to be.' He stood up. 'Sit down! You there! No, not there, *there*!'

Horrified, Tom rocked back on his haunches and tried to collect his thoughts as the boat lurched shoreward. Dim figures in the lightening gloom laughed nervously at their clumsiness as they frantically plied the oars. Around them a veritable armada of boats made for the land ahead and his uneasiness grew.

From his sitting position he made out the shape of stark, high cliffs appearing, cliffs, not the smooth open beaches they'd been promised and he wondered just how far from their original objective they would be landing.

Nearing the shore the sound of firing increased. The Turkish defenders were fully alert now and pouring fire onto the boats approaching their positions. It was obvious that the first wave had met with opposition and his anxiety increased. A dark, strung-out, unmoving body of men lay on the beach ahead and he wondered why they were making no attempt to rise and move off.

'What are those fools doin', corp?' the man to his left shouted, 'Why don't they get off the bloody beach?'

'Shut up, Clifford!' Tom snapped, 'Never mind them. Just watch what you're doing and get ready to hop over as soon as we ground.'

A starshell sailed high above them, giving Tom a view of momentary splashes in the water ahead as a torrent of firing erupted, all the while growing in intensity. An artillery shell exploded suddenly among the boats and they all ducked involuntarily to escape the spray and shrapnel. His stomach ached with tension and he sensed the fear in the boat as the occupants stared aghast at the mayhem and carnage whilst their boat ploughed steadfastly on into a growing maelstrom of shells and bullets.

He turned to speak to the midshipman in time to see the youngster's head snap back violently and explode in a red haze as a bullet passed through his right temple. Tom caught him as he collapsed but the boy was already dead. What was left of his face quickly turned a pallid white as the blood poured out of him, drenching Tom's tunic and hands in a warm torrent of brightly-coloured liquid. He recoiled in shock at the sight of his reddening hands whilst numbly lowering the dead boy into the bottom of the boat

In collapsing, the midshipman's hand had swung the tiller hard right and the boat now drifted helplessly sideways, parallel to the beach. Tom reached out desperately to grasp the tiller and as he did so saw a line of waterspouts race across the water with frightening speed. He let go instinctively and ducked as the machine-gun burst tore into the boat, throwing up deadly clouds of splinters as rounds punched into the woodwork and men's bodies tightly packed into its interior.

To his left, Francis Clifford groaned softly and fell backwards, a shredded line of scarlet where his chest had been and from the bows a high screaming noise sounded. A glance confirmed Tom's fears. The bullets had found targets in the packed ranks and the boat's interior was now a writhing heap of wounded and dying men intermixed with the terrified survivors. Blood intermingled with seawater added to the gory scene as a crimson wave washed freely up and down the scuppers, painting the men's boots and the dead lying in the scuppers in an obscene coating of scarlet.

Some men had violently brought up their breakfasts on seeing the carnage, making the air around them foul with the reek of death and vomit. 'Get those bloody oars moving!' Tom roared desperately at the shocked occupants, 'If we don't get ashore soon, we'll be hit again. Move, for God's sakes!'

Frantically the survivors attempted to sort the oars out from the shambles and start rowing again. A few succeeded and although not under total control they managed a semblance of timing and struck out for the shore. Tom took control of the tiller and attempted to steer a straight course for the sand.

A machine-gun opened up from their left, staccato bursts interspersed with an increase in the rifle fire pouring down on them and screams and groans from adjacent boats accompanied the sound of bullets thudding into woodwork and bodies. The gunfire was one long continuous sound now, a drumfire coming from the cliffs as the troops already ashore fought an unseen enemy and Turkish machine guns enfiladed those still on the beach.

Splashes appeared all round the boat and Tom heard the spiteful *Zzziiip!* of bullets as they whined overhead. As they approached the beach he realised with mounting horror that the large number of men they'd spotted unmoving on the sand were dead and wounded soldiers, casualties of the first wave who'd been caught in the open when the Turks had opened fire.

The boat was swept further along and grounded only yards to the north of the headland of Ari Burnu. The beach here provided very little cover and it was obvious to the terrified men that the first wave had been decimated. Huddled figures were strewn thickly along the high-water mark and he stared closely at the bodies as they neared. Some lay as if asleep, others bore the marks of horrific injuries, heads shattered by bullets, limbs torn from their owner's bodies by the explosive force of modern bullets hitting them at close range.

One of the dead lay limply on his back with his lower jaw shot away, the swollen tongue protruding in a grotesque, bloodied parody of a child pulling a face, aluminium identity disc gleaming palely against his torn throat. As Tom turned away from the gruesome sight a young officer waded quickly through the shingle and gunfire to the side of the boat, gesturing madly. 'Come on...Jesus! What happened to you blokes, looks like you copped a right packet! Corporal? Get your men out of here as quick as Christ and get up to the top of the cliffs over there on your right. Your mates need your help. Leave the wounded where they are, they'll be taken care of shortly.

Quickly now, come on, the bloody Abduls are slaughtering us here!'

Tom ducked involuntarily as a bullet *pinged!* into the water at his feet. Bullets hummed overhead like angry bees and he began to realise by standing there in the open just how exposed they were. Looking up at the cliff tops to their front he could see a winking, twinkling display of lights and realised with shock that these were muzzle flashes from the Turks firing down on them.

'Where the hell are we, sir?'

'On the wrong side of Ari Burnu, nowhere near where we should be. Some bloody idiot got his sums wrong and now everyone's mixed up all over the place.'

Tom looked down with an almost curious detachment as bullets struck sparks from the shingle by his feet and the 2/Lt's tone changed as he, too, ducked. 'Look, corporal, do me a favour, I'd love to chat but those gunners on top of the bloody cliffs are too damn good. We're also being enfiladed by that machine-gun over by Fisherman's Hut so get yourself and your men off the beach. Now!'

'Come on you blokes, you heard the officer, get moving! Follow me and grab a pick and shovel as you go!'

He looked back to watch the other boats making for the shore. The nearest weaved madly as burst after burst of machine-gun fire splintered its woodwork and he could see men flinging themselves desperately over the side to escape the deadly fire. The water's edge was tinged a bright red as limp bodies washed in and out with the surf and from the beach the screams and incessant cries of the wounded filled his ears along with the increased sound of firing.

Looking out to sea he watched a destroyer turn rapidly, her decks swept with rifle and machine-gun fire as the Turkish troops fired frenziedly at her retreating shape. With her out of range they turned their attention back to the beach and Tom was galvanised into action. Jumping over the side he waded ashore. There was no sign of Serjeant Rickard so grabbing a discarded shovel from the sand he held it high and dashed forward. 'Come on, 3 Platoon!'

Men followed swiftly, bent forward under the weight of fire now pouring down on them. One or two threw arms up and slumped to the ground but the majority reached the shelter of the low arbutus scrub, looking anxiously over at Tom as they cowered in the lee of the bank

'Drop your packs and fix bayonets!'

A clattering of metal sounded as eighteen inches of steel were snapped into place at the end of their rifles. Soundlessly he dropped his sodden pack, slung his rifle over his back and waved his hand aloft, scrambling towards a track he could see in the thick scrub. More men followed him as he plunged to his right into the cover afforded by the dense thickets of myrtle and holly bushes. The track wound its way to the base of the cliffs he'd seen from the beach and he pushed quickly through to where it began to rise steeply in an upwards direction.

A bullet snapped viciously past his ear and he recoiled in shock, crouching low against the soil lest another came his way. After cautiously estimating the risk he redoubled his efforts, grunting with exertion whilst pulling himself up the steep, sandy path by the expedient method of grabbing hold of the bottom of bushes lining the track. The prickly thorns scratched his hands with their spikes and he winced with each contact, his resultant slowness in ascending causing him to be swiftly passed by the fitter members of the company bounding alongside. Hooting and hollering excitedly they made their way upwards with renewed energy after ditching the weight of their packs.

'Stay together, don't spread out!' he called but they gave no sign of acknowledgement before passing out of sight in a highly excited state.

'*Cooee! Cooee!*' Their cries echoed faintly over the crest of the hill as he climbed. Puffing heavily, using his shovel to assist him, he followed as fast as his exhausted body could manage. A sudden burst of firing ahead caused him to look up sharply and the sound of someone screaming in agony only added to his anxiety.

He made it to the top after what seemed an eternity and looked round, heart thudding wildly in his chest. The panorama stretching before him was extraordinarily captivating and his eyes opened wide as he took in the view. In front of him, as far as he could see, was a large plateau filled with scrub, thorny ilex bushes and an occasional stunted tree. Flowers filled his view, red, purple, white and yellow petals covering the ground, adding their sweet scent to the already perfumed fragrance of thyme and rosemary wafting over them.

The expanse of open ground upon which he was standing would be named *Plugge's Plateau* but for now he was glad of the rest as he took in the view. To his left the large whitened promontory that would later pass into ANZAC folklore as *The Sphinx* thrust aggressively outwards from the line of hills, inaccessible from where he stood and he looked in vain over to its right for a better approach to the summit. The landscape there led upwards to the hills, guarded by numerous gullies and ravines that plunged away rapidly, threatening any speedy progress an invader would want to make.

He stared hard but could see no sign of the elusive Turks although the crackle of gunfire surrounding him told of contact at close proximity. As he stood there a figure burst out from the scrub and would have run past but he grabbed at the man's elbow and held it fast.

'Where do you think you're going, mate?'

'Aw, fair go's corp, my mate's over there and I was just going to join him.'

Tod Hammond pulled angrily at the pressure on his tunic but Tom held onto him.

'Just hang on 'til I get my breath back and we'll both go. You stay close, you hear?'

Sullenly Hammond nodded his agreement and both men moved off together. The air was sweet now with the smell of myrtle, an overpowering pungent perfume that stuck in the back of their throats but they moved cautiously through the scrub and small stunted trees, looking out for others from the platoon. A sound behind made them both whirl round but as Hammond raised his rifle high Tom knocked it aside.

'Strewth, where've you two been, you lazy drongoes? Christ, Tom, are you alright, mate, you're covered in blood?'

Tom gestured impatiently.

'Don't mind me, I'm fine, the blood's not mine. Billy, you bloody idiot, what are you doing up here by yourself, winning the war on your own?'

'I was with Petersen first off, Tom, but he disappeared on me.' Billy Willis replied in an aggrieved voice. 'The bastard went off in that direction.' He pointed to their left and they stared but saw nothing. As Tom turned, a fleeting motion caught his eye and he looked back quickly. 'What was that?'

'What?'

'I saw something. Someone. There, again!' A dark figure flitted between two bushes as he spoke and he pointed in the direction Billy had indicated earlier, 'It looks like someone's over there.'

'*Coo-eee*! Petersen? *Coo-eee*!' Before they could stop him, Tod Hammond sprinted towards the trees Tom had pointed out. More firing erupted all around them suddenly and both men ducked, sinking onto one knee, rifles ready, as they watched Hammond charge through the scrub.

'Hammond, get back here!' Tom shouted desperately but Tod Hammond ran on, bursting through the scrub until he disappeared from sight. Tom glanced at Billy but before he could speak a high, thin scream came from the bushes ahead.

'Oh God!'

Both men ran towards the sound. As he ran Tom fumbled hurriedly in his webbing pocket, questing fingers closing round two five-round clips of ammunition. Jerking the bolt of his SMLE back swiftly he pushed the chargers into the magazine and rammed the bolt home.

35

His last action as he and Billy burst into a small clearing was to release the rifle's safety catch.

On the far side a still figure lay huddled on its side, both arms drawn protectively round in a futile gesture to cover the hideous, gaping wound in its back. Breathing hard, Billy knelt, pulled the body onto its back and they both looked down into the pale, contorted face of Ralph Petersen.

'Christ, he's dead! Some bastard's bayoneted him.'

Tod Hammond appeared from the scrub, chest heaving with exertion as he looked down on the body of his dead friend.

'Well, at least his wife'll get her bloody new chooks now!' he exclaimed savagely, dropping to his knees in despair and reaching out gently to touch Petersen's corpse.

'Hammond, on your feet, we've got to get out of here and rejoin the others.'

Wondering what chicken's and Petersen's wife had to do with the situation, Tom pulled at the young man's sleeve for the second time that morning and Tod Hammond reluctantly allowed himself to be pulled upright.

'Which way we gonna...!' His words were cut short. *Crack!* A bright, red hole blossomed in his left eye socket and as the sound of the shot died away, Hammond's legs buckled and he collapsed limply at Tom's feet.

'Jesus! Get down!'

Billy dropped to the ground and pulled Tom with him into the shelter that Hammond's body offered. Breathing hard they looked all around but saw no-one. 'Tom, the buggers must be all around us.' Billy Willis whispered fiercely. His hands closed on a small rock. 'I'll throw it to my right and we'll go off to the left. Got it?'

Tom squeezed his mate's hand in acknowledgement and Billy tossed the rock as hard as he could. As it struck the ground away to their right a shot sounded frighteningly close.

'Now, before the bastard can reload!' They both rose to their feet and ran diagonally to their left, hurtling through the scrub, rifles held protectively in front of them. A figure suddenly rose up in their path and collided with Billy, startling Tom as both men fell down, limbs entangled.

'*Uurggh!*' Billy grunted, a long drawn-out sound of agony and remained lying on the ground as the other soldier struggled to his feet, a dripping bayonet on the end of his rifle. Shocked, Tom saw a small, wizened face poking from beneath a cloth helmet. The man's features twisted in a feral snarl as he attempted to swing his rifle upwards but pointing his SMLE automatically at the Turk, Tom pulled the trigger in a reflex motion.

The rifle recoiled savagely in his hands and the Turk dropped without a sound, a dark stain spreading on his chest. Dropping his weapon, Tom knelt desperately at Billy's side and cradled his pal's head in his arms. Billy Willis stirred and opened his eyes weakly, squinting up at Tom as their eyes met.

'The little bugger's done for me, mate.' he whispered in surprise, closing his eyes again, his breath leaking out in weak flutters. 'Stuck me good in the fucken' side.'

'Don't say that, Billy, lay here and I'll go and get a medic. You'll be alright. Just let me get some pressure on the wound.' Tom turned Billy on to his side and ripped the field dressing from the wounded man's upper pocket. The jagged tear in the side of Billy's tunic spurted brightly coloured blood in a steady stream and Tom sensed his pal slipping away. Fruitlessly he clapped the dressing over the wound but it was immediately drenched in blood. Passing the tapes under Billy's side he brought them round to the front and tied them off whilst pulling at the dressing in his own tunic.

A hand caught his and he glanced down into Billy Willis's haunted eyes. His wan face was a white smudge against the dark soil and his hands fluttered weakly as he tried to speak.

'Mate, leave it, I'm done for. Do me a favour, please. My ma. Get that letter from my pack and send it off to her. Promise?' The words were spoken with an effort and his voice trailed into a tortured silence. His breathing became shallower and his eyes rolled upwards.

'Billy, don't, you'll be fine, you see.' There was no answer and when Tom looked at his pal again, Billy's eyes were wide open and his body had relaxed in the finality of death.

'Billy! Oh God…Billy…' Tom gently cradled the dead man's head and shoulders as the full horror of his friend's death overwhelmed him. The shock of the events of the last half-hour and the violent deaths he'd witnessed rose in his gorge and he slipped loose his hold on Billy's tunic. Bending over, he emptied the contents of his stomach into the scrub. He remained in that position for several seconds before stirring and wiping his face and lips. Conscious that he needed to leave his friend where he lay and get back to the others, he straightened up and looked round. Nothing stirred although in the distance he could hear the sound of heavy firing

In rising, he lost his footing and almost fell across the body of the Turk he'd killed. The man lay curled in a ball, his *kabalak* headgear alongside him. He looked old, with shrivelled, sunburned features resembling a man in his fifties not the young man Tom had expected. The Turk was dressed in a ragged brown uniform with puttees carelessly wound round baggy, threadbare trousers from the knee down and a tunic with a large collar buttoned up to the neck. He was small in stature and Tom marvelled that he'd stayed to fight it out with them instead of retreating. If he was typical of the Turkish army they were in for a long, hard fight.

He picked up the Turk's headgear and examined it closely. The *kabalak* consisted of a cane helmet covered with a thickly-wound cloth turban, in no way able to withstand the shock of a bullet penetrating it but lightweight and cool in the present heat. Throwing it to one side he bent over Billy's body and recoiled as he looked straight into the dead man's glazed eyes.

Billy Willis's expression was one of raw accusation, a reproof to Tom for the savage way his life had ended. Swallowing hard, Tom Harding reached down and pushed Billy's face to one side, hiding the anguished look from that of his own. He stretched out and grabbed the man's limbs, arranging them as if in a funeral parlour before sticking his friend's rifle in the ground, bayonet first, to mark the spot should he be able to return later.

Taking a last look he left hurriedly, crouching low in trying to find his bearings and return to the cliffs. A half-dug trench loomed up but it looked abandoned with no sign of recent occupancy, and he increased his pace and passed it by. Sounds of firing and shouting filled his ears and he glanced desperately from side to side, trying to find any familiar landmarks. By now the defenders were fully aroused and shrapnel shells were exploding heavily all around, adding their sounds to the confusion and noises of battle.

Ahead of him a large patch of scrub had caught fire and in skirting around it he pulled up short. Among the flames he could hear a man screaming in terror. '*Aaagghh*! God! Mother...help me...*aiieeee*!' Tom peered into the thick smoke and flames but saw nothing. 'Where are you?' he shouted desperately, 'I can't see you.'

'Oh, God, help me, I'm trapped, I'm burning...*ahhhh*...it hurts .... God, cobber, get me out of here! Please!'

Tom ran frantically round to the other side of the scrub, careful to remain upwind of the flames and in the centre of the patch of burning, crackling scrub made out a figure writhing in agony. He looked on helplessly as the figure's hair burst into bright flames and an acrid smell of roasting flesh and hair drifted through the smoke to his nostrils.

'I can't reach you. I'll go and get help.'

'Shoot me...For God's sake, shoot me!' the man screamed, voice cracking, a high-pitched animal noise torn from flayed lips by unbelievable pain as the fire remorselessly ate its way through his uniform and body.

'Please...*aarrghh*! Do it...now!'

Tom's knees turned to jelly. He stood paralysed, staring into the flames, a sick feeling of helplessness overwhelming him. 'I can't, mate. Oh, sweet Jesus, I can't!'

'*Pleeeaase*!'

'God!' He turned to flee from the horror but his rubbery legs stubbornly refused to obey. Slowly, with a metallic click the rifle bolt locked as he fed a cartridge into the breech, pointed the barrel into the flames and feeling the heat blanket his arms, squeezed the trigger.

Crack! The rifle jerked violently and the figure relaxed limply before sinking back into the rising smoke

He turned and fled in turmoil, running blindly from the scene behind and the man's agonised screams echoed and re-echoed round his head whilst the nauseating odour of roasting flesh followed him all the way back across the hillside to the overhanging cliffs.

'Halt, who goes there?'

The challenge pulled him up sharply.

'Corporal Harding, 'E' Company, 9th Battalion AIF.' he shouted desperately, looking round to see where the voice had come from.

'Advance and be recognised. I'm warning you, mate, if you're a bloody Jacko you're dead meat!'

Slowly, keeping his rifle pointing upwards, Tom walked towards the sound of the voice. As he neared a small bush a private stood up, lowering his rifle and stared at Tom with concern.

'Jeez, mate, you alright? You're covered in blood. What the hell happened to your rifle, it looks sorta burnt? And look at your bayonet, it's singed—'

Tom waved the man away. 'I'm fine,' he said wearily, 'what bunch are you with?'

'12th Battalion. From Hobart, Tasmania, mate and ain't this a fucken' shambles?'

'You could say that.'

'Too right I could. Someone dobbed us in, the bloody Jacko's were waiting for us.'

'Do you know where any of the 9th are?'

The soldier pointed over his shoulder. 'You might find some of them down there, at the top of the track but everyone's mixed up. I've been put here as a sentry but some bastard's made a right beaut of this one, mate. We're getting beat all over the shop, those little bastard's are hiding in the bush and knocking blokes as they go past. I heard they got our CO, Colonel Clarke, and a heap of the officers have been knocked, too! Did you come across any Jacko's while you were out there?'

Tom looked down at his bloodied hands and tunic and the soldier's face fell.

'Sorry, mate, no offence...' Before he could speak further a loud whistling noise sounded over their heads and a second or so later the ground behind Tom heaved violently as shells exploded, throwing earth skywards in huge quantities. Both men dropped to the ground as salvo after salvo followed, the explosions working their way up and down the plateau Tom had just vacated. '*Wheeee*! Come on you poms!' the sentry shouted gleefully 'About time their guns started whackin' the bastards, that'll teach them to mess with Australia!'

As the man continued to shout, Tom rose and stumbled through the scrub towards the point the soldier had indicated. A minute later and he was on top of the cliff, looking down on the scene below. The sea was filled with boats in the midst of making for the shore. Out to sea he could see the flash of a battleship's guns as she fired another salvo to keep the Turk's heads down. The Turk's were replying defiantly and the sky around the boats was covered in puffs of white cotton wool as exploding shrapnel shells lashed the air.

Away to his left a narrow strip of shingle was rapidly filling with troops and supplies. The sound of firing still carried on the air from all sides but he was amazed to see how unconcerned the troops on the beach seemed as they moved boxes and crates from the boats and dropped them further up the beach. A pile of limp bodies stacked to one side testified that the landing had not been without cost and Tom's thoughts returned to the deaths of his friends as he gazed down on the bodies.

'Harding! Where the hell have you been?'

He turned to see 2/Lt Mark Treharne waving furiously from a shallow trench to his right and ran across to join his platoon commander.

'Christ, I thought you were dead, corporal, no-one could tell me where you'd disappeared to.'

'Sorry, sir, I followed some of the blokes to bring them back here, they'd all run off chasing the Turks.' Tom explained sheepishly.

'And did you?'

'What, sir?'

'Did you bring the blokes back with you?'

'No, they're dead. Petersen, Hammond and...and Corporal Willis.'

'Damn! Sorry, Harding, I know Willis was a good mate of yours.'

Tom nodded dumbly. A vision of another dead man entered his mind but he suppressed it quickly, guiltily. The scrub held too many memories, all of them unpleasant.

'We've been told to dig in here for now. The Turks are still active over to our left and Christ knows they could attack at any moment. We've taken a heap of casualties, the bastards that planned this debacle need shooting themselves, we've lost far too many good blokes today.' Treharne snapped angrily, ducking as a woolly puff of shrapnel exploded overhead. 'And where's *our* bloody artillery? I haven't heard a single gun of ours open up on those Jacko bastards, don't tell me the guns're still on the bloody transports?

Look, forget that, some of the lads are round the other side of the bloody headland so Christ knows when we'll see them again. I've also noticed a lot of blokes sneaking away down to the beach so keep your eyes open and stop anyone you see buggering off in that direction, we can't afford any stragglers at this time

Meanwhile, go over to the other side of this gully and grab some blokes, can you, send some back for more ammo and tell the rest to dig in alongside me and my blokes. I saw Private Ring and Rushton in a hole over to your left so get them back with us. And be careful, there's snipers everywhere.

Oh, last thing Harding, Sgt Rickard is missing so take on his duties 'til we can replace him. One of the blokes reckons he saw him get hit and fall overboard on the approach to the beach. Either way, he's not been seen since we landed so do as you're told and get me those blokes, eh?'

41

He thought of telling Treharne about the burning man, a way of unburdening himself but now was not the time. Later, perhaps, when the madness of the day had passed and they could sit and collect their thoughts. For now there were other things to worry about.

He walked dutifully over to where his men cowered, selected a few and brought them back to where they dug shallow holes and waited for orders. The sun had risen fully by now, a burning, beautiful red dawning and was beginning to warm them with its rays. Tom noticed several men's hands fumbling for their water bottles and he called out angrily.

'Leave it! If you're thirsty, stick in and bear it for now. What's in your bottle's got to last you until we get replenished and God knows when that'll happen. Take small sips if you must but don't ask me in an hour for a swig of mine cos you ain't gonna get one!'

Rolling over he pushed his rifle into the lip of the hole and eased his cap forward onto his brow. With eyes shadowed he tried to relax and relived all that had happened in the hours since they'd left the destroyer. Petersen and Hammond, Billy's death, the poor unfortunate screaming out his agony as he burned to death. Nothing had prepared any of them for the savagery they'd witnessed on this first day and he wondered if their leaders had any idea of the ferocity of the struggle that must lay ahead.

He looked down at his hands, scratched and bloodied and thought about using his own water bottle's contents to wash away the memories of Billy and Tod Hamilton's deaths. The thought left his mind as quickly as it had appeared and feeling totally exhausted, thirsty and drained of all emotion he pushed the cap further over his head and closed his eyes. He'd fetch Billy's pack later and retrieve the letter but for now he could do no more.

Lifting his face, he let the sun's rays warm his features and revelling in the warmth snuggled down into the comparative security of the scrape, pushing his hips into the earthen sides in an effort to obtain a more comfortable position. All around him the firing increased in intensity and next to his right ear a strange insect *chirruped* loudly but his tired brain stubbornly shut out the sounds of conflict and he slipped into a deep sleep.

Author's note.

In the late afternoon of the 25th April, the fresh Turkish troops of Mustapha Kemal's 19th Division flung themselves on the battered survivors of the, by now,

42

thoroughly mixed-up Australian and New Zealand brigades. Throwing men forward with no thought as to casualties they were savagely beaten back. The guns of the battleships with their flat trajectories were unable to seek out the enemy troops sheltering on the reverse slopes and the decision to retain their own artillery onboard the transports until the landings were well underway cost the ANZAC's dear. By sheer will and grim determination they clung onto their narrow beachhead, killing great numbers of the attackers until nightfall brought them a welcome respite.

A panicked call to re-embark was turned down by Sir Ian Hamilton and the men began to entrench themselves in their positions, positions they would hold for the next eight bloody months. The assiduous way in which they burrowed into the hillsides and slopes around ANZAC Cove to shelter from the Turkish guns earned them the nickname that would be forever synonymous with the ANZAC soldier. That of 'Digger.'

Chapter Three.

'X' Beach, Sunday April 25th 1915.

'Walt? Wake up! Wake up!'

Walt Harding groaned softly at the words in his ear, tired brain registering the fact that his shoulders were being shaken urgently.

'Wassa marra ....?' he grunted, attempting to turn over and drift off back to sleep but the touch on his shoulder became more insistent. 'Walt, for God's sake, wake up man. It's three thirty, time to get ready.'

Alert now, he sat up and rubbed his eyes. 'Why didn't you say so?' He swung his legs over the side of the bunk, yawned deeply and stretched his aching limbs, painfully aware of the fetid smell of the messdeck they'd inhabited on the overnight journey from Mudros. He'd stayed up until late sorting out stores, spare ammunition and a thousand other things before tiredly making his way to the messdeck. A kindly tar seeing his fatigue had given up his bunk for Walt and his eyes had shut the minute his head hit the mattress.

Puffing and panting he pulled on boots and webbing, grabbed his rifle and pack and made his way up the companionway to the open air, feeling the welcome freshness of the morning as he appeared through the hatch. All around him in the gloom men were talking in low voices and he was grateful to see that they'd obeyed his orders and that no-one had lit a cigarette. *HMS Implacable* was wending her way towards the distant land mass slowly but surely, the throbbing below his feet coming from her engine-room several decks below.

Gallipoli was a faint smudge in the dark and looking round at the crowded deck Walt wondered how many of them would be standing when darkness fell again at the end of the day. He shivered involuntarily at the thought but a loud thudding noise made him peer over the rail and he caught sight of a string of empty boats swinging against the ship's side as they were dragged along. These were the boats they'd be clambering down into shortly and his shivering had nothing to do with the cold of the morning.

While joining his men for a welcome breakfast, the Lancashire Fusiliers destined for 'W' Beach silently passed by and boarded their boats, followed minutes later by a company of 2/Royal Fusiliers. The replete 100 Middlesex men were last to board. When everyone was seated they settled down under the watchful eyes of the sailors accompanying them for the long tow towards the beaches. The vast majority wore their Wolsely helmets but he noticed some were sporting their army issue caps.

During the approach a low muttering, grumbling sound from the north caught their attention and many men craned their necks in that direction as they futilely sought to catch sight of the origin of the noise.

'Alright, alright, settle down. Cut the chattering.' Walt realised this was a signal that the attack had already started with the landing of the ANZAC's and his fear increased as he thought of the Turks lying in wait for them, fully aroused now.

The sound carried with them all the way to the shore, increasing in intensity as they neared their first objective. After nearly two hours the Lancashire men's tows were slipped and they began their approach to 'W' Beach, joining up with the rest of their battalion under tow from HMS *Euryalus*. Watching the boats disappear, Walt felt the tension building inside, a foreboding and with it a desire to get ashore and face the worst. Waiting drew deeply into men's souls. Robbing the faint-hearted of what little courage they possessed, the long, drawn-out emptiness before battle allowed all one's deeply-concealed fears to rush to the surface in their ugliness and destroy a man's self-composure.

For most, it would be their first time in action proper, a big difference to their days in India and shooting at a few Pathans who would obligingly fade into the distance as the British advanced. He looked round at the strained, tense faces wondering who, if any, would let them down; yet at the same time feeling reassured by the look of determination on many of the faces. When it was all over, would they meet as friends and mull over the events of this day? He shivered anew.

'Don't load your rifles until we get onto the beach. I'll sort out anyone I spot shoving one up the spout before we land!' The warning was unnecessary, they were jammed in too tight for anyone to have access to his ammunition pouches but his words helped relieve the fear etched on the sea of white, frightened faces gazing up at him.

By now dawn had come and gone, any slight mist disappearing as daylight heralded a fine day to come. The tows were slipped and they began to row for the thin grey smudge of land rising up from the sea. A massive sound of thunder made them start and Walt turned to see huge flashes of flame-flecked black smoke erupt from *Implacable's* 12-inch gun turrets as she fired on the rising cliffs in front of them. The battleship had slipped so close inshore that it seemed to many of the onlookers she must ground at any moment but she swung away sharply and continued her broadsides unhindered.

He fixed his attention to their front and observed the narrow strip of beach they'd been allocated approaching fast, secure under its mantle of high, forbidding cliffs. It was these cliffs that *Implacable* turned her guns upon and they were all heartened to see columns of dust and smoke erupt as the heavy shells slammed into the crests.

The roar of her guns was continuous as Walt's boat grounded in the shallows and he had to raise his voice to shout hard at his men to galvanise them into action. 'Out, out! Come on, get out and get moving!' For the time being there'd been no return fire from the Turks and it looked as if they might land without a fight. The beach looked impossibly small, only a few hundred yards long and not wide enough by far to accommodate the numbers of troops attempting to land.

His men obeyed willingly, leaping awkwardly over the side and splashing ashore through the shallows. As they waded onto dry land, *Implacable's* fire lifted and her shells began landing inland, seeking out the Turks to prevent them opposing the troops below. Walt saw their company commander, Captain Gould falter and fall heavily and he ran anxiously over only to see him regain his feet. 'Damn fool, I tripped over a bloody branch. What a way to start my war, eh, Harding? Injured by a sneaky Turkish tree!

Right, now that I'm back on my feet let's get moving and join up with the Fusiliers. Grab your men and go find Serjeant Johnstone, corporal. Tell them to fix their bayonets and let's find our way to the top of these cliffs to see what's going on.'

Walt whirled round and waved his men on, repeating Gould's orders in a harsh shout. They crossed the narrow strip of ground at a run, fixing bayonets as Capt Gould pointed to a body of men moving off the beach up the cliffs by way of a track and gesturing for them to follow. The rest of the company joined them and as they began the long, hard climb up the track a crackle of rifle fire alerted them to the fact that the enemy had been sighted and they redoubled their efforts.

The top was reached in double-quick time and, puffing hard, Walt waved at his men on hearing the sound of increased firing to their front. Some took the time to view the scene below them before being angrily urged on. Against the setting of a sparkling, blue sea two battleships moved menacingly along the shore, joined by other ships pouring out their cargoes of troops. Boats approaching from all directions heading for the strip of beach to disgorge their cargoes before hurrying back for the next group.

The ground consisted of dense, sweet-smelling undergrowth with small inter-weaving goat tracks leading off into the distance. There was no barbed-wire at the top of the cliffs and at a signal from Gould they moved hurriedly inland along one of the tracks and into open farmland. In the far distance rose a low menacing mass of hills and below them to their right a gleam of white houses told where the village of Krithia lay. The crackle of rifle-fire grew louder and they gripped their weapons tightly in nervous apprehension.

'Here! Over here!' A loud voice stopped them in their tracks and the figure of a young 2/Lt burst out of the undergrowth, his face a mask of fresh blood. Gould ran over but he brushed him away. 'I'm alright, sir, it's only a flesh wound. Thank God you're here. Quickly, follow me. The Turks have twigged we're ashore and are massing for an attack. We need as many men as possible to hold them otherwise we're all in grave danger.'

He wheeled round and they followed him with alacrity towards the sound of the gunfire and shouts in a strange tongue. '*Allah! Allah!*' The shouts sounded close and they perspired freely whilst running alongside the subaltern urging them on.

'Come on, come on, they're attacking!'

The sound of firing was frighteningly close and they burst from the scrub onto a small plain filled with shallow holes occupied by scared-looking soldiers. Throwing themselves to the ground, rifles were hurriedly loaded as a large body of men approached through the morning haze. Flags waving and bugles blaring the Turks bore down on them, shouting hoarsely as they ran. A British officer stood upright in full view, impervious to the rounds zipping past him.

'Wait for it! Wait for it! Ten rounds...rapid fire!' Rifles cracked sharply and the front row of Turks crumpled and fell as if struck down by a giant hand. Undeterred the remainder leapt over the bodies of their fallen comrades and carried on their advance, many firing wildly from the hip.

'Keep firing. Don't stop!' the officer shouted, trying to make himself heard above the noise but a bullet smacked into his chest and he slid to the ground in a nerveless heap. For a second or two the fire slackened as they watched him fall but Capt Gould dashed forward and took charge of the situation.

'Aim low and take your time, men, make sure you hit your targets!'
Hearing his voice the firing picked up once again and more Turks tumbled to the ground as the men heeded Gould's words. Walt fired and reloaded frenziedly alongside his neighbour, the heavy rifle pounding his shoulder with each loud report. Fresh sweat pouring down his face hid the results of his shooting but he continued firing into the mass of men bearing down on them. A *click*! informed that him that his magazine was empty and he fumbled hurriedly in his pouch for fresh clips.

They were not having it all their own way, several incoming bullets had found targets and imperceptibly the British fire began to die down as more men were hit. By now the screaming mass of Turks had advanced to within forty yards of the makeshift defensive line but just when it seemed they would be overrun, the Turks swerved to their left and began to retreat, leaving their dead and wounded in untidy, scattered heaps.

'Would you look at that, we beat them corp! Gave them a right bloody nose, eh?'

Walt turned to the man on his right. 'Look to your front, Woods!' he exclaimed, 'This is just the start of it. They'll be back, mark my words, and with more men.' He raised his voice. 'Check your ammo lads and dig in deeper, this ain't over by a long chalk!'

The exultant look on Wood's face faded as he looked fearfully round. 'Christ, I thought that was it. We must have killed heaps of them. Don't tell me they ain't got the message...?'

'Start digging in now, lad, they'll be back. Keep an eye on my stuff while l go and see how the wounded are.'

Walt rose and walked over to where the medics had set up a small area for treating the wounded. Jim Peters wanly held up a smashed hand with three fingers missing and tried to smile as a medic began pouring iodine over his field dressing before attaching it to his mangled hand.

'Wotcha, corp, that's me wiv a right Blighty one. Aaargghh...Go easy you bloody scabpicker, that stuff bloody well stings!'

'Oi you, sit still, I'm only trying to help!' the medic huffed peevishly.

'Aye, Jim, the things people do to get out of peeling spuds.'

Both laughed but Walt recognised the pastiness creeping onto Peters' face and delved deeply into the top pocket of the man's tunic pocket. 'Here, have one of your fags. A few puffs and you'll feel a lot better.'

He left the grateful invalid to the care of the medic and walked on. The bodies of the dead were being carried away, down the track to the beach and he walked over to the cliff-top to view the scene below. He'd scarcely snatched a hurried look before a warning shout from behind made him start.

'Watch out, 'ere they come again, 'undreds of the bastards!'

Running back swiftly, he picked up his rifle and threw himself down into the scrape he'd recently vacated. Ramming a fresh cartridge home, he locked the bolt and eased the safety catch off whilst peering to his front. In a pattern repeated up and down the peninsula on the first day of the landings, using a tactic that would become wearingly familiar over the following months, the Turks attacked again

A huge, greyish-brown mass swiftly coalesced into hundreds of running, shouting men heading in their direction, flags waving. Behind the mass of troops he heard the guttural shouts of their officers urging them on. Walt caught his breath sharply but a calm voice sounded from his left, that of Capt Timothy Gould.

'Alright chaps. Now, give them hell!'

Rifles barked as one and a volley tore into the screaming mass of men. A shell landed short of their protective holes, its hot breath knocking Walt over but he regained his composure quickly and continued firing. More and more shells burst among them, shrapnel tearing into men and flesh as they struggled to contain the attack. In the midst of the fighting, Walt spotted a small figure crouching low, a Turkish officer urging his men on with a vigorous waving of his hands. He took a snapshot and watched with grim satisfaction as the officer crumpled and collapsed. Rather than dismay the enemy it seemed only to spur them on and they made a concerted rush at the line held by the men of the Middlesex Regiment.

On the point of collapse, Walt and his pals were saved by the intervention of newly-landed reinforcements from the Border Regiment who flung themselves at the Turks in a frenzied bayonet charge. Assisted by two Maxim guns landed with them the Borders pushed the Turks back nearly six hundred yards, taking a grim toll of the attackers, breaking up the cohesion of their assault and forcing them back to their start point. In fleeing, their enemy left behind fresh mounds of their dead and dying and a battleground filled with the cries and groans of the wounded.

Breathing hard, Walt rose and wandered amongst his men, sickened at the sight of so many still bodies. The medics arrived and began working frantically on the badly-injured, performing a crude triage as they decided who would best survive the arduous journey back to the beach and the medical staff waiting there. Platoon serjeant Clarence Johnstone walked over and stood next to him as they surveyed the scene.

'Christ, Walt, what a do. We've lost some good lads today. Lt Keats is dead, took a round to the guts. The Turks fought well, better than we'd been led to believe.'

'You can say that again, sarje, we're lucky to still be here.'

'I reckon the rest of the regiment should be landing soon so when they arrive I'll pinch some men and we'll get a burial party underway then. Can you take a dekko and maybe make up a list of who's dead and who's injured? The colonel will be sure to ask and he'll feel better if we've sorted it out before he arrives with the rest of the lads.'

Crack! A spilt second later a faint report sounded and Walt gazed round in surprise

'Ow! Shit!'

Serjeant Johnstone had dropped abruptly onto one knee, furiously rubbing his head as he scrabbled in the soil to retrieve his fallen cap.

Anxiously Walt dropped down next to him, peering curiously at Johnstone's face. 'Are you alright, sarje, what happened?'

'Give me a second. Something hit me on the side of my head, fair took the wind out of me, it did.'

'Christ, I see what you mean. That's some bruise you're gonna have.'

Wonderingly, Johnstone straightened up holding a small misshapen lump of metal in his hand.

'No wonder it hurt. Would you take a look at that! It's a bullet, Turkish by the shape of it, if it'd been a .303 round it would've taken my head clean off!'

Walt laughed, relieved at Johnstone's lucky escape. 'I don't think it would be one of our lads who fired at you, sarje, God knows you've upset a few of them on the way over but they know which side their breads buttered on. Who'd tuck 'em up at night if you were gone?' He peered closely at the serjeant's scalp. 'It's not broken the skin, just made a massive bruise. Must've hit you side-on.'

'Aye, lucky I have such a thick skull. Oi, Harding, mind you don't repeat that now!'

Johnstone joined Walt in laughing then looked around. 'It'll 'ave come from that place over there, I'll wager,' he said grimly, pointing in the direction of Krithia. 'Some Johnny Turk's had a go before he legged it. Thank God the round was a spent one or I'd have more than a headache to worry about.'

He picked up his cap and inspected it. 'Look, there's a tear on that side where it struck.' He smoothed the tear with a wet finger and gingerly fitted the cap back on his head. Pocketing the piece of lead he turned to Walt. 'I'll send that to the missus when we get a chance to write next. I won't tell her how it was that the blasted thing nearly did for me, don't want her and the kids worrying. Walt, could you get the blokes together and get on with those errands?'

'Rightho. I'll make sure the ammo supplies are topped up, too, and see if I can get some sort of a meal going. Corporal Whetten has put his lads to digging deeper trenches so if the Turks attack again at least we'll be under better cover.'

From the south and up north also, the sound of heavy firing continued unabated. The men on the other beaches, 'W' and 'V' seemed to be copping a right packet and for a fleeting moment Walt was glad he wasn't with them. For all its close vicinity, three miles to the north, he could hear no sounds of fighting from 'Y' Beach for the moment but a distant rumbling from further north was a portent of the hard fighting going on between the enemy and the ANZACS. The sight of the casualties amongst their own troops brought him back to reality and he strode grimly on.

Chapter Four.

Author's note.

The first day's landings cost the ANZACS an estimated 5000 casualties, including 2000 killed, among the 12,000 men who were landed. British losses in the first five days amounted to 187 officers and 4,266 other ranks. No great gains were made by either army, the Australian and New Zealand troops clinging onto a small toehold on the peninsula which would prove to be the only ground they would hold over the coming months. The British and French fared no better, their advances at Cape Helles amounting only to just under a mile. There, all of them would stay for the next eight bloody months.

Above Anzac Cove, May.

The flowers had long disappeared under the torn earth, the petals' sweet scent replaced by a new kind of smell, one of dead men and putrefaction. Unrecovered corpses from both sides of the fighting lay out beyond the parapets of the Australian trenches. Badly-swollen torsos lay strewn in macabre abandon, straining to burst through the stitches of clothing holding their burnt and blackened remains together. The living cowered in their newly-dug trenches, and gagged on the stench of death, a dry, malodorous smell of rotting flesh that filled their noses and mouths with every breath.

Ping!

'Yup, the little bugger's still out there.' The soldier moved his head and spoke sideways as the bullet passed overhead and struck a coil of barbed wire. 'Pass me one of those jam-tin bombs, mate, and I'll see if I can give him a scare.'

'Hey, O'Neill, keep your head down and leave it be. How'm I gonna write to your wife back in Townsville and tell her you were shot by a Jacko sniper cos you couldn't keep your bloody head down?'

O'Neill peered owlishly down the trench. 'See now,' he exclaimed reproachfully, 'I could report you for that, Corporal Harding. I have rights and refusing to let me throw a bomb at a dirty Turkish sniper who wants to kill me is denying me those rights. It's all a matter of oppression, you know, keeping me from killing that boyo out there just because you're a Brit immigrant and I'm an Irish immigrant.'

'Is that right, O'Neill? I thought it was because I'm a corporal and you're a private and I tell you what to do and you do it. And where did these bloody rights you talk about come from?'

'I'm talking about the rights that were denied us in our own land, when yous lot threw us out. It was the potato famine you see, drove us all to Australia or to America. Caused by the Brits and...'

'That's enough, O'Neill, put a sock in it. Famine? Get your facts right before making accusations like that. You certainly don't look as if you've ever gone hungry!'

'There's no need to get personal, Corporal. Harding.'

Ping...spang!

'Alright, you win.' Tom said wearily. 'That Turk's not going away. Give O'Neill a bomb someone!'

In the week since the landing, the attack had stalled. The rest of the ANZAC Corps had disembarked and reached the beach, literally digging in where they'd landed and in those first strung-out days General Birdwood had sent a message to Sir Ian Hamilton suggesting an evacuation, a suggestion frostily turned down. Colonel Sinclair-MagLagan's exemplary command of the 3rd Brigade in those early days had so exhausted him that he was relieved for a brief rest, being replaced by Colonel HN MacLaurin. The new Commanding Officer's orders were to hold the ground at all costs, even if it meant dying there. From an initial sporadic response to the assault, a freshly-reinforced Turkish army had spent the time since Sunday in building up its strength and attacking along the lines in waves. So far all attacks had been driven off with great courage shown by both sides.

The trench in which Tom and his men were crouching in was taller than an average man, the parapet lined with sandbags and a firing step high enough to enable them to see over the top. The soil had proved to lend itself to easy digging and the ANZAC's had burrowed assiduously into the landscape. Long lines of trenches wound their way through the countryside, backed up by saps, communication trenches, barbed-wire entanglements and netting designed to catch any Turkish grenades

Dug into the arid soil every few yards was a small hole, big enough to admit a man and his pack. Here the men slept, when they could, and tried to find shelter from the shrapnel balls that rained down on them. At least it was dry, it had rained on the first evening but so far no more had fallen and although the nights were cold, now that their packs and raincoats had finally reached them a man could make a fist of being comfortable. A few blankets had arrived but most suffered the night's intense cold in stoical silence

Today was peaceful except for the persistent Turkish sniper somewhere in no-mans-land intent on adding a few more *Kufirs* to his tally. Tom and his platoon were entrenched on the eastern end of Maclaurin's Hill, part of the newly-named high ground above Anzac Cove. The rest of the battalion were nearby, filling other deep trenches that had sprung up since it was obvious there would be no early advances. The ground around had been swiftly named so all would know what part of the line was being threatened and respond quickly. Shrapnel Valley, The Sphinx, Walker's Ridge, The Nek, all these and more would eventually pass into folklore but for now the men manning these parts of the line looked more to their own welfare than the emptiness of history.

'Ouch, careful, you bludger! Sorry, sir, didn't see it was you.'

Mark Treharne grinned as he slid in next to Tom. 'We could do with this being another foot or two wider, Harding, save your blokes from getting crushed to death when someone passes.' Tom grunted sourly, waiting for the 2/Lt's next words. 'I've just come up from the beach and heard a few things we'd better watch out for. The 4th Brigade has already gone out to our left, in an attempt to drive the Turks off the heights over there, Baby 700, and we're to stay here for now but might be called up as a reserve to support them. Can you make sure your blokes have all their gear and ammo ready if we're needed?'

'Christ, sir, that's a fair bit from here. We'd be in full view of Jacko and his mates if we were to leave this trench and it'd take an hour or two to reach them, if we could. Who thought this one up?'

'Calm down, Tom. I said we might be called up, not we will be. Reason being that aerial recco's seen a fair body of the enemy heading our way so we might end up ourselves needing support soon. Keep a close eye out and *coo-ee* if your sentry's see anything. I'll be in the communication trench along the ways so just holler.'

'Excuse me, sir, try sticking your head up above the top here and you'll cop one smartish. How're our sentries supposed to see anything?'

'I'll leave that up to you Tom, but I think you'll hear the Turks long before you see them. Cheerio for now, shout if you see anything, mind!'

He left as quickly as he'd arrived, leaving Tom grumbling as he gazed after Treharne's departing figure. The 2/Lt wasn't a bad bloke, quite the contrary but his orders were a sure sign of the shambles the landing and its aftermath had become. He and Mark Treharne had spent an evening or two on the ship during their sojourn in Mudros talking about politics, cattle, the world and the madness into which it had plunged. For a rich, well-educated man the officer had shown no airs or graces and argued his corner fiercely with Tom. Both had come to respect each other, comfortable in one another's company and glad of the chance to speak about matters other than just the war.

Turning to his pack Tom fumbled with the straps impatiently and thrust his hand inside, feeling a hard metallic object which he withdrew carefully. It was a small set of binoculars with the words *Binocular Prismatic No.3 Mk I. Ross London 1914* engraved on one of the lens-holders. A fierce haggling session in a Cairo bazaar had seen him return to Mena Camp with the binoculars hidden from prying eyes. The glasses were a military set, an officer's property and stolen without a doubt but he'd coveted them as soon as the shopkeeper had slyly brought them up from under his counter.

He rolled onto his side and wriggled to where the trench angled to the left, hiding him from the Turkish lines and pulled the binoculars to his eyes. Whilst trying to make sense of the ground before him by squinting hard he could see away in the distance to the right of The Sphinx the prominence known as Baby 700. As he stared, the sound of gunfire reached him and he swung the binoculars round. Spindly figures came into view scurrying along the ridgeline and he recognised them as their own. 'You beauts!' he breathed and looked back down the trench.

'Hey, you blokes, listen to this. Looks like we've taken Baby 700. I can see our own blokes on the top but no sign of any Jacko's.'

A burst of cheering rang out as the men sat along the side of the trench celebrated. 'Good on ya, sports, give them one up the arse for me!' Suppressing a shout himself, Tom turned back to watch as a shrieking noise rent the air and the ridgeline filling his glasses exploded under the impact of several shells, throwing limp bodies into the air before his horrified gaze. A strangled gasp escaped his lips as more shells impacted, adding their explosions to the earlier salvo.

'They're our own bloody shells...Stop it you bloody morons...You're killing our own blokes!' he shouted impotently as more and more salvoes screamed overhead, smothering the ridgeline in the distance until it was wreathed in smoke and flames. Stunned, he slumped against the trench, placing his head in his hands as the glasses dropped unnoticed at his feet.

'Tom? Tom, are you alright, mate?'

'You wouldn't believe it, we've just blown the hell out of our own blokes!'

'Fair dinkum?'

He waved a hand in a weary gesture of hopelessness, the other covering his eyes as he took in the full magnitude of the horror. A sudden shout brought him back to the present.

'Look out, mates, here come the Turks!'

'Stand-to! Stand-to!'

Rifle bolts rattled, rounds were fed into breeches and men sprang up onto the firing step, weapons at the ready. A loud hullabaloo warned of a line of Turkish soldiers bearing down on them, shrieking and dancing as they rushed forward to the incessant sound of bugles blaring. An enemy Maxim added its spite to the conflict and bullets hummed angrily as Turkish gunners sprayed the parapet. Shellbursts sent shrapnel whirred wickedly through the air, slicing easily through flesh and bone where it struck home and to Tom's right a man sighed and slumped awkwardly, sliding from the firestep to the floor of the trench in a tangle of limbs. Tom forced his eyes to remain on the screaming wave of men to his front and his sweating finger on the SMLE's trigger.

Rifle barrels wavered under their nervous owner's grasp but lack of experience counted for nothing now. The men racing towards them were bent on destruction. Waves of small men in dirty brown uniforms sweeping across the scrub with rifles held high. The killing time had arrived.

'Hold your fire! Let them get closer...Now! Let them have it, mates!'

The volley from their trenches sounded shockingly loud, a massive crackle and the Turks melted away in front of them. A second wave appeared and rushed forward, meeting the same fate. Again and again, more Turks rushed down the slight incline with no thought for their lives and screams and shouts of *Allah!* rose up above the barking of the guns.

At last, one of the allied machine-guns joined in the fray, scything Turks down in even greater numbers but still they came on.

'Ammo...bring more bloody ammo, I'm out!' An anguished cry rose up but no-one answered the man's call. Tom fired again and again, frenziedly working his rifle's bolt and ramming fresh clips into the magazine when needed. Several of the Turks wore white summer tunics, making them easier to pick out and these men were swiftly shot down.

Very few Turks reached the enemy trenches but when they did they were ruthlessly dispatched. One solitary Turk tripped and fell, rolled over and landed in the Australian trench, being savagely bayoneted before he could pick himself up. The world around each man dissolved into one of grey smoke, the tang of cordite, a rifle butt thumping into a shoulder, screams of the enemy and the incessant sounds of rifles firing at close range as men fought on. Loading and reloading like automatons, they fired into the mass of men before them, one or two jumping up onto the parapet in order to direct their fire from a sitting position.

An eerie silence descended abruptly as the Turk's charge petered out, leaving only the still bodies of their dead and squirming bodies of their wounded lying in great heaps before the Australian lines. Men whose minds seconds before had been joyfully filled with the visceral feeling of killing slowly lost their glazed look as normality returned. Shocked, they contemplated the results of their shooting and the ghastly wounds the .303 bullets had inflicted on their targets.

Turkish bodies lay in tangled heaps as far as the eye could see, hundreds who would rise no more, their deaths a simple confirmation of a willingness to die for *Allah* and Turkey. Peasant conscripts untainted by the riches of the West who knew only of their devotion to their leader *Enver Paşa* lay sprawled in the obscene, ungainly postures of the dead. Here and there an arm moved feebly as a badly-wounded man moaned softly and sought attention for aid that would never arrive.

'Great show, Tom, that showed the buggers. We knocked a few of them, eh? Not bad for our first proper taste of action.'

'You could be right sir but we've not come out of it scot-free.' Tom greeted 2/Lt Treharne and pointed to the stretcher-bearers hard at work removing the wounded for attention further down the line. The lucky few who'd come through it unscathed sat in a daze cleaning their weapons automatically, picking up the heaps of brass cartridge cases and speaking in low voices.

'Yes, Yes, I know, young George Clark got knocked, I'm told, poor bugger.' Tom tried hard to put a face to the name. He hardly knew the man Treharne had mentioned but the loss would be felt keenly by his mates. Treharne plunged on. 'Didn't we bloody Johnny Turk's nose for him! I couldn't believe it, they just kept on coming, straight into our fire as if they had no fear of dying! Great bravery but so bloody futile against our fire, poor bastards.' Treharne sounded exultant but Tom stayed silent for a while before answering.

'What would you do if, instead of Turkey, this was Australia? Wouldn't we feel the same if they'd invaded our country, sir?'

The tangled heaps of the dead and wounded laying only yards away from where they spoke filled him with a sick feeling inside. 'There'll be a few mothers and wives grieving after today, on both sides,' he added simply, pointing to the mass of bodies, 'whoever and whatever they thought they were fighting for. Did they really deserve this?'

Chastened, Treharne's face fell. 'I see what you mean, when you put it like that. They're just men like us, after all, defending what they saw was their country's honour. I never thought war could be like this, all this killing. And for what?' His face changed as he looked over the parapet, pointing eagerly.

'Forget the morbid philosophy, Harding. Look over there. That bloody flag. It's huge. We could do with a trophy like that, gee the blokes up for what they did here today.' He jumped up and strode into the shattered ground before Tom could react.

'Get back here, sir!' he shouted desperately.

A large coloured flag with a crescent moon and bright star emblazoned on it lay yards away and Treharne bent to pick it up. Waving it triumphantly over his head he began to walk back. *Crack!* Treharne slumped limply to the ground.

'Shit! Cover me!' Tom shouted and sprang over the parapet towards the young officer. *Crack!* He felt a bullet pass through his left sleeve and fell to the ground on his face. Staying motionless for what seemed a lifetime, heart hammering in his chest, he slowly moved his head. Treharne lay three yards away, head and face drenched in blood. As Tom watched, his arm moved slightly. *Crack!* Treharne's body jerked under the impact of a second bullet.

He swore softly and began to crawl towards the inert form, inching his way along, attempting to keep a stiffening Turkish corpse between him and Treharne. *Crack!* A thousand needles pierced his flesh as a bullet skimmed along his forearm, causing him to gasp in pain. He writhed soundlessly, rubbing the affected area to try and deaden the pain. *Crack!* This time the sound was different, deeper, and he tensed for the impact of a bullet. Nothing happened and as he resumed crawling a voice shouted urgently.

'Quick, corp, grab the bugger and get yourself back here!'

Needing no urging, Tom ran to Treharne's body, taking in his condition at a glance. Mark Treharne lay on his back, face covered in blood and a large pool of blood issuing from a wound in his lower side. Grabbing the man's arms Tom began to pull him back to the safety of their trenches. Two men appeared and between them they swiftly bundled Treharne into the trench, leaving Tom to follow. No shots followed and he collapsed gratefully over the parapet, crouching low on the trench floor while he struggled to regain his breath.

'How is he?' he gasped.

'No worries, Tom, the galah's gonna make it. A few holes in him, but at least he's still breathing. Medical orderly's on his way so we'll get him patched up in no time, mate. How 'bout you?'

'I'm fine.' Feeling drained, Tom sank onto his haunches and stayed that way until Treharne's unconscious body was removed. The medic wiped Tom's arm clean with antiseptic and applied a wound dressing before disappearing with his charge. He sat for a while controlling his breathing and thinking deeply before a figure joined him and he squinted up at the sight of Declan O'Neill calmly watching him.

'What is it, O'Neill?' he asked hoarsely.

For an answer, O'Neill stuck out his hand with a wide smile. 'Just to let you know, corporal. I'll be withdrawing my complaint, you deserve a friggin' medal for going out there. Jesus, you could almost be Irish! Oh, and thanks.'

'Thanks? For what?' asked Tom bemusedly as he automatically shook the man's outstretched hand.

'I used your binoculars to see where that Jacko sniper was hiding. Had to wait until he'd had another go at you first, though.'

'You did what!'

'Fair go's! I knocked the bugger once I found him. He was hiding behind one of our blokes' body. Poor bastard must've been killed in that stupid assault we tried a few days ago cos he sure was bloated. The Jacko hid behind him to have a pop at us, didn't do him any good, I just shot the bugger through the corpse. He was already dead so he wouldn't have minded but you never know, the dead man might have been a pom too. Sort of counts as two in one, don't you think. See you shortly, corp, gonna go and have me a smoko now!'

Before Tom could answer, Declan O'Neill dropped a pair of binoculars into his lap and made his way back down the trench leaving Tom staring after him, thunderstruck.

--§--

That evening they gathered in a small group away from the trenches to bury their dead. The conversations were muted as the stiffened corpses were reverently laid to rest in a shallow hole, each man wrapped in a blanket tied with rope or string. A chaplain arrived, uneasy at the sounds of gunfire nearby and aware of the men's contempt as they watched his hurried administrations.

'...*dust to dust, ashes to ashes*...' As quickly as he'd arrived, he disappeared, duty done, leaving them to fill the holes up with shovelfuls of red, dusty soil.

'George Clark? Never knew him meself, did you, corp?'

'No.'

'And this bloke here, Private William Eldridge?'

'I think he was the bloke killed alongside Rushton in the last attack. Rushton says he took a bullet in his head.'

'Was he with us when we landed?'

'No, O'Neill, I think he was one of the new blokes who arrived day before yesterday. Poor bugger, he didn't last long.'

O'Neill straightened from throwing soil onto the wrapped corpses and lifted an arm in the direction of the sandy-coloured hills in the distance.

'Look at it this way, he's out of it now and we're still here. Why?'

'You heard Mr Treharne, we're striking at the underbelly of the beast here. If we can win it'll open the way up through Europe and make the Kaiser beg for peace before we arrive to tear his guts out. So stop bloody grouching and get on with it.'

Tom fixed Declan O'Neill with a hard stare but O'Neill returned the stare unblinking.

An uncomfortable night followed as they waited for an attack which never materialised. In the light of day Tom snatched a wary look over the parapet, withdrawing his head quickly before a sharp-eyed Turkish sniper could draw a bead on him. The dead lay in contorted, frozen heaps and during the night the temperature had dropped, leaving the corpses decorated with a faint beading of dew, giving them the surreal look of marble statues.

60

After a hurried breakfast he squirmed down the trench and sought out their company commander, Captain Vivian Finch. Finch readily agreed with Tom's request to go down to the beach and find out how Mark Treharne had fared.

'Good show, Corporal Harding, the boys told me how you pluckily went over and pulled 2/Lt Treharne in. I'll make sure you go into my report, you deserve a mention for the bravery you displayed. No worries. Bugger off for now and see how Treharne's doing, the Turks won't be attacking again for a long time after the bloody nose we gave them here. Before you come back see if you can get more water up here, the men's canteens are running dry. Oh, and more ammo, lots if you can. Sort out those supply bastards on the beach will you, let them know just how dire thing's are up here. We need those blankets we were promised too, don't they know how damn cold up here it is of a night?'

--§--

It took some time walking in a half-crouched position to reach the beach. He found a shallow entry from Walker's Road into Shrapnel Valley, one of the major thoroughfares leading down to Anzac Cove, and joined the soldiers moving along its steep sides. A mass of people moving in both directions ducked under the lash of the shrapnel shells bursting frequently overhead and halfway down the track Tom had to step back to allow a strange combination to pass. A tall, smiling, muscular Medical Orderly led a soulful-looking donkey up the gully, a Red Cross Armlet tied above its muzzle and a rope tied to its face harness. As he stared, the soldier smiled and spoke.

'Arlreet?'

'Fine, thanks.'

Another smile and the man and his donkey passed by and disappeared up the track. Shaking his head in wonder, Tom carried on down the valley, eventually arriving at the beach and looking around curiously. A passing soldier glanced at him and Tom grabbed his sleeve. 'Where would I find the casualties who came down yesterday?' he enquired. The soldier thought for a moment then pointed.

'The 2nd and 3rd Field Ambulance have their Dressing Station over there but I did hear that they were getting ready to evacuate a lot of the blokes who came down here to Egypt.'

'Thanks mate. By the way, who's that bloke with the donkey I just passed?'

The man's face brightened. 'Him? That's John Simpson the mad Geordie medical orderly, *Jack* we call him. He and the donkey became cobbers after the first day and he's been taking wounded on it up and down Monash Gully and into Shrapnel Valley for the last week or so. I've heard he calls the bloody animal *Duffy* or even *Murphy* sometimes. Don't ask me why, I haven't a clue. Mad bastard, he'll catch it one of these days but he's there, going up and down all day. Round here he's known as *The Man with the Donk*. Should get a bloody medal for what he's doin', mate.'

Tom looked round at Anzac Cove, eyes widening with astonishment as he took in the small township that had sprung up since the ANZAC's had stormed ashore a week ago. The small cove, barely half a mile long, had been transformed with dugouts proliferating the steep hillsides and wooden entrances poking out from every opening. Men scurrying into and out of the openings like gave the scene the appearance of an agitated ants. Blankets had been pressed into use as awnings and already the cove had an air of permanence with smoke issuing from myriad campfires.

Criss-crossed tracks leading up and down the hill and the narrow strip of beach, less than the length of a cricket pitch wide, wound their way in and out of boxes of stores and great dumps of equipment and food. Cases of bully beef, boxes of biscuits, fodder and ammunition cases in large numbers sprawled over every available space and at the water's edge, a pier for landing stores had swiftly been constructed after the landings and was already in use.

The Aegean was a beautiful colour of deep, sparkling blue with an orange sun overhead dancing on the wavelets as they placidly came to rest on the shore. The quiet scene looking out to sea belied the urgency of the operations being carried out behind him as he swung his gaze round and looked inland once more. Men were everywhere. Australians, bronzed New Zealanders and swarthy Indians scurried purposely to and fro, engaged in unloading wooden lighters tied alongside the pier and stacking supplies further up the beach. Others simply waded, trousers rolled up, in the coolness of the sea. He stared, overcome at the scene, wondering how and where he'd find Lt Treharne. Another passing soldier directed him to a large opening in the hillside and he waited patiently by the dugout's entrance, basking in the warmth of the sun.

'Get on to Bridges and tell him we need more supplies for Christ's sake! We're nearly out of morphia and I haven't seen clean swabs for a day or so!' A haggard-looking individual wearing a blood-stained rubber apron shouted over his shoulder as he stood in the doorway and contemplated Tom with a look of impatience on his haggard features.

'Yes?'

'I'm sorry, sir, my lieutenant was wounded yesterday and I've come to see I how he is–2/Lt Treharne, 9th Battalion.' he finished lamely.

'Come to see how big the butcher's bill is, son, eh? Lemme see. Treharne, Treharne? Ah, I remember, nasty case.' He pointed with a bloodied hand at a lighter pulled up on the shingle in the middle of the beach.

'Your Mr Treharne should be being loaded on there right now, if I'm right. A hospital ship will be taking him and the others to Alexandria for more specialised treatment shortly. Typical of this foul-up, the bastards made no provision for the wounded. I'm short of bandages, drugs, in fact everything you could mention except patients. I've hundreds of those, all of who are frightened, in pain and needing urgent medical care.'

'Specialised treatment? Is he alright then?' Tom asked hesitantly.

'Alright? What passes for alright in this bloody madness? Your officer's alive if that's what you're asking me but alright? You'd have to ask him that?'

'I'm sorry for asking but the wound's didn't look that severe, sir, we just took it to be a slight wound to the head. He'd also been shot through the side but we managed to stop the bleeding around that wound fairly quickly.'

'Humph! The first aid he got probably saved his life but he may not want to thank you for it. The head wound looked innocuous but proved to be particularly nasty, by hitting him in the temple it's almost certainly wrecked the optic nerve. I'm afraid he'll be blind for the rest of his life, *if* he survives the journey to Alexandria. The other wound needs another operation, and quickly. We did what we could here but couldn't dig the rest of the bullet out.'

He pointed again and spoke wearily before disappearing back into the depths of the dugout. 'Go on, see if you can find him, you never know, but if I were you I'd leave talking to him for now. Let him get used to the bad news first, if he survives. You could write. Be careful

63

if you do go over there, the Turks are still firing down on us.' He disappeared back into the depths of the dugout.

Tom followed the doctor's finger. Lines of men lay on the open beach, a momentary tell-tell whisk of sand erupting from the sand showing where a Turkish bullet landed among the stretchers. Medical orderlies wandered among the wounded, seemingly indifferent to the bullets and he shuddered, fearful of what he might find if he walked over there. Amongst the shattered husks of men waiting to be loaded, men who'd laughed and joked only hours ago, was the blinded body of a man he'd admired and looked to for guidance and comradeship.

He stared past the recumbent forms, glance resting on the far horizon. Was it really only a few short days since they'd left the safe embrace of Mudros to journey here? Faces flooded his memory, the young faces of the men who'd sailed with him from Australia on the greatest adventure of their lives only to end up here, lying on a coarse stretcher covered in blood and in pain. Wounded, blinded and maimed, the lucky ones would leave this place to return home, leaving behind the crosses marking those who'd remain here for eternity.

The sun overhead was the same sun that would be watched in this moment while it set thousands of miles away in Australia as people glanced up and thought of their husbands, fathers and brothers. Who could tell them of the horror of this place and the hell that was surely to come? Would anyone believe their story or appreciate the sacrifice these young men, his comrades, had made? He resisted a bitter inclination to laugh. How would Mark Treharne, newly married prior to enlisting, read any correspondence now that he was blind?

A shrapnel shell burst overhead with a white-tinged *whoof!* and he ducked automatically as the shrapnel balls hissed into the sea nearby. A passing medical orderly glanced at him and spoke.

'Those Abdul bastards keep the shells coming most of the day. Some of the blokes lying out there on the beach waiting to be evacuated get hit again and again and there ain't a damn thing we can do about it. We're a legitimate target but they're still bastards!'

--§--

Slowly, numbly, he made his way off the beach. On the way back up Shrapnel Gully he met again with the orderly and his donkey, this time coming the other way. There was no smile on his face now, no humorous greeting. Under the shadow of his slouch hat, John Simpson's eyes were full of concern as he hurried down the track, a free hand supporting the limp, bloodied form hanging askew the donkey's back.

--§--

Back at the front line, one of the first people he met was Captain Finch.

'How's 2/Lt Treharne, Harding?'

'He's fine, sir–well, sort of. You see…'

'And your arm, how's that?'

'It's fine too, sir, I've had worse.'

'Good. Did you get those supplies I asked for?'

'No, sir, there doesn't seem…'

'Bugger. Well, not to worry, we've had new orders, we'll be moving out soon. We're to join the 2nd Brigade as a spare company, along with the New Zealanders. The *Old Man's* furious at our being used like that but I think he accepts it as part of the price of our having the extra company. Whatever, the reason, we'll be buggering off shortly. The poms need our help in an attack on the Turks in a day or two at Cape Helles so we'll be embarking tomorrow and going down there by way of a transport ship. I'll see if we can scrounge some extra supplies when we get back to the beach.

For now, go and catch up with your blokes, let them know what's going on and be ready to move at any moment. Get yourself a cup of char and something to eat then come back and find me, you and the other NCO's have got lots to get through before we bugger off to the beach.'

Author's note.

The landings were over and the troops clinging tenaciously to their toehold on the peninsula long before a single official word of the campaign was transmitted to the Australian and New Zealand governments by the British. The providers of so many of their finest men were shamefully kept in ignorance of the outcome of the landings until well after the men were ashore. Official requests for information were blithely ignored and neither government was given a say in the consultations that took place prior to the landings.

The national newspapers were quick to print the news as it arrived back home through reporters such as Charles Bean, the long lists of the dead and wounded bringing heartache and dismay to the general population. The growing casualty lists were a shocking indication as to the profligacy and incompetence of the British commanders, whose ill-thought out ideas and wretched indifference to their troops would ensure the deaths of many more over the coming months.

--§--

Inland of 'X' Beach, May.

Author's note. Owing to the narrowness of the beaches, it took nearly ten days to land General Aylmer Hunter-Weston and the rest of the 29th Division. The sands of 'X' and 'W' Beaches ran red with the blood of the British casualties on the first day and 'Y' Beach had had to be evacuated owing to the inability of the British to fend off increasingly ferocious Turkish attacks and a hurried, unordered retreat to the beach took place. The French fared much better in their objectives on the opposite side of the straits at Kum Kale but a panicked Sir Ian Hamilton caved in to the French commander's requests to withdraw, a decision that would haunt him in later months to come.

Now that all his troops were safely ashore and had established themselves inland, not withstanding the debacle at 'Y' Beach, General Hamilton decided they would assault the village of Krithia which lay in their path. Barring their way to the heights of Achi Baba, the village would need to be taken before the advance could continue towards Istanbul. On the first day of the landing, the commanding officer of the Royal Marine Light Infantry and his adjutant had strolled unopposed from 'Y' beach toward the undefended village before returning and passing on their findings. In the chaos of the landings the information had gone unprocessed and unheeded and the Turks had quickly turned the village into a fortress.

The first attack on Krithia on 28th April failed with 3,000 casualties, a well-entrenched Turkish army simply wiping out the Allied troops sent against them. Poor medical facilities only added to the bill with many of the wounded dying for lack of proper treatment. Being short of resources after the debacle of First Krithia, Hamilton decided to use the men of the ANZAC corps to assist and so the 2nd Australian Brigade and the New Zealanders were shipped down from Anzac Cove to join up and take part in the second attack on the village.

Second Krithia opened on the 6th May with a frontal attack by the British being fiercely repulsed. It was decided to throw the ANZAC's into the attack in the hope that their presence would make the difference.

66

'It's a warbler, I tell you.'

'Nah, you're wrong, Bell, that's a corn bunting. Definitely.'

The other man sighed, more in exasperation than anger. 'For Chrissakes, 'ow can you say that, listen...hear that? It's a bloody warbler.'

'Oi, you two, what the bleeding hell are you arguing over now?'

'Sarje, Bell here says that bird over there is a warbler but he doesn't have a clue. It's a fucking bunting, I keep telling him but he won't believe me.'

'Listen, if you two tits don't stop faffing about I'm gonna get pretty hacked off with the pair of you. Birds? There's a bloody war going on around us, if you clots hadn't noticed and all you can do is sit here and argue about who saw what bloody bird and when. Jesus, Mary and Joseph!'

'I saw a kestrel the other day, sarje...'

'Hopkins, do not tempt me, laddie.'

'G'day, mate, how's it goin'?'

Lewis Bell stopped and gawped in astonishment at the ruddy-faced individual smiling at him as he passed by. The strange soldier with badges resembling flaming suns on the collar of his loose khaki tunic raised a hand in greeting and ambled lithely past, followed closely by a long column of similarly-clad men. Some wore rumpled shorts but the majority wore trousers and puttees, their uniforms dirt-stained and heavily creased. Slouch hats with one corner turned up completed their casual appearance but there was no rust on the barrels of their SMLE's and the rifles' wooden furniture gleamed brightly.

A thin grumbling, muttering sound of artillery faintly echoed off the distant hills as the Australians moved past and moved into an adjoining communication trench. 'Hey, corp, 'oo the 'ell is this lot?' Walt Harding straightened up and turned to regard the strangers as they disappeared. 'Bell, you clot, they're Australians, what the hell did you think they were? The Bosches?'

'Yeah but wot are they doin' here, then?'

'I haven't a clue, Sir Ian forgot to write to me and let me know how the campaign's going, the mail's been late in arriving this last week or hadn't you noticed? How the bloody hell am I supposed to know!'

'Alright, alright, keep your 'air on. I was only asking...' Lewis Bell followed the soldiers as they moved steadily past the Middlesex trenches. 'Bollocks, I forgot to ask that bloke 'oo spoke, 'e might've 'ad some grub on him! We could 'ave done a trade.'

'What, his bully beef for some of your bully beef? Aye, a right good trade that would've been, or did you think theirs is made from kangaroo meat?'

'Now you are takin' the piss!' Lewis grumbled as he bent to empty some more dirt into the open sandbag at his feet. Walt grinned briefly and joined Bell and the others in digging deeper and using the spoil for the bags. Their trench was coming along nicely, with a good depth to it and the wall of sandbags lining the parapet would provide them with better protection from the ever-increasing shelling.

It was the third day since the opening of the assault on Krithia and so far the Middlesex had been held in reserve. The attack was going badly and they sensed that before long they would be called into the fray.

--§--

'Oi, Bert, who was that you were speaking with?'

Bert Ring spoke over his shoulder without breaking stride. 'Just some pom filling sandbags, corp, seemed a nice enough bloke. I was goin' to ask him what the hell the poms was doin' there resting while we were off to do their fucken' fighting for them but it seemed like I'd've started an argument. He didn't look like he was enjoying his work but he's got a hole to shelter in and what've we got, mate?'

'Keep walking, Ring, we've a fair ways yet to where we're going.'

'You're the corporal.'

Tom Harding looked back as they marched on past the trenchwork being built along the Krithia road. The company had disembarked on Gully Beach in the British area north of Cape Helles, the HQ of the 29th Division, and been shepherded immediately into the welcoming mouth of Gully Ravine. The entrance looked similar to ANZAC Cove, with its dugouts and a host of bell tents covering its southern approaches but there all similarities ended. The ravine widened enormously as they'd trudged partway up its two and a half mile length and they were surprised to glimpse traces of stores, workshops and even a full-size Dressing Station in its depths. After covering a mile or so under its protective cover they swung sharply to their right and emerged amidst open countryside once more.

The British soldiers occupying the trench were bent over, busy filling sandbags and all he could see were their backs so he swung his gaze back in the direction they were heading. His arm stung sharply under the sleeve of his tunic but he welcomed the pain, the sharpness reassuring him and providing him with the feeling of being alive. An orderly at the Regimental Aid Post had dressed it securely after liberally disinfecting the raw, red weal that had scored his arm but it still itched although each day it hurt a little less.

It was mid-morning and the sun shone warmly on their backs. Overhead, a large bird of prey was slowly wheeling in the clear, cloudless, blue sky, its primary flight feathers spread wide as it sought to catch every bit of the thermals in order to soar over the marching column below. Tom looked up, idly wondering if the bird could see both sides of the conflict and the long snake-like lines of rough trenches that separated the protagonists and the pockmarked ground inbetween. On the horizon the brooding pimple known as Achi Baba glowered down on them in the midday sun and he mused whether the bird nested in its heights.

From the height it soared majestically over the battlefield the ugliness of war would be hidden from its questing eyes and he envied the bird its innocence. As he watched, a heavy outburst of shelling began, causing them all to duck involuntarily even though they were now in the protection of the trench's depths and the bird's wings dipped sharply as it fled the battleground. When he looked up again, the sky was empty.

'Keep your heads down, lads.' The voice of their new platoon commander, Second-Lieutenant Godfrey Truscott rang forcefully in their ears. Mark Treharne's replacement was trying his best to fill his predecessor's shoes and the men had responded gratefully to his easy manner. He'd appeared from the beach and slipped into his new duties without a fuss, easing his way into their presence with determination and an air of confidence.

The shelling arcing over from the Turkish defences was falling a long way short of their position but they were wary nevertheless. 'Over here!' a voice commanded and they swerved to where a hand waved vigorously from a breastwork. Serjeant Matt Carr greeted them as they slid into the shelter of the fire bay.

'Nice to see you bastards made it at last, I was starting to get worried. G'day, sir, we're to sit here until the poms ask us to come up and clear the way for them.'

69

'Thanks, serjeant. Where are the poms and how far is it to the Turkish lines?'

Carr waved a diffident hand over to his left. 'The poms are a few hundred yards down this track, sir, but as for the Abduls, I couldn't tell you, they're out beyond the *Black Stump* for all I know! No-one seems to know what the fuck's goin' on and no-one gives a stuff about us from what I can see. All I know is we're to sit on our arses here until we're needed, if that happens.'

'Alright, serjeant, you and Corporal Harding attend to the men and I'll see if I can find out what the hell's going on, there must be someone round here who has a clue. I'll be back as quickly as I can so see if you can scrounge a meal and some water from the poms, eh? See if they can spare a billy of tea, too.'

'That'll be the day!' Carr shouted but Truscott had already left and disappeared further up the trench.

'Sarje, there's some poms digging a communication trench down the road. Leave it to me, I'll take some men and go and have a word with them, see what we can cadge from them.'

'Rightho, Tom, take Ring and Rushton but don't be too long about it.'

'No worries, sarje. Bert, Rushton? This way, you two.'

The three men started back down towards the British trench they'd passed earlier but after only a few paces there came a hurried shout and Tom turned to see Carr waving him back.

'Stay here you two.' he ordered and ran back. 'What is it, sarje?'

'On second thoughts, Tom, let those two drongoes go by themselves, best if you stay here with me in case Truscott comes back and we have to get a move on.'

--§--

The bird gazed at by his brother was also seen by Walt Harding only yards away as he groaned and straightened up, easing his aching muscles whilst slamming another sandbag onto the parapet. After watching it soar above them, a movement down the track caught his eye and he took his eyes off the bird as it wheeled away, watching closely as two strangers appeared, walking towards them.

Walt turned. 'Eh, Bell, what is it you're wearing? Some fancy kind of toilet water? Looks like you've got some admirers, there's a couple of those Aussies walking this way. Probably goin' to ask you to walk out

70

with them so get back before it gets dark, alright, and for God's sake put on clean underwear! Tell them to get under cover quickly, the Turk's will soon spot them and we'll all cop some shells.' He laughed at his own facile joke and returned to the matter of the sandbags.

--§--

Whilst waiting for 2/Lt Truscott to return, the Australians took in their surroundings. It was a far different landscape to the scrub and dirt that they'd met around Anzac Cove. Here near Cape Helles were tilled fields, shattered olive groves and boundary hedges with an occasional stone dwelling dotting the landscape. The countryside had an air of permanence laid down by the efforts of the local farmers spread over generations. War had come suddenly to this quiet part of the world and the effects of its passage would leave scars on the land and in the minds of the locals for years to come.

The noise of the shelling increased, a loud rumbling to their right and as they stared anxiously in that direction, Godfrey Truscott appeared from his briefing in a highly excited state. 'Serjeant Carr, get the blokes moving as quickly as possible, we're to move up to the other company's area and await orders. Looks like we'll be going into action soon. The poms and the French have already tried to make an entry into Krithia but got their arses kicked. Come on, let's go!'

'You heard the officer, mates, grab your gear and let's get goin'.

'What about the two blokes I sent off, sarje?'

'Christ, Tom, Bert Ring's like a fucken' homing pigeon, we're not going that far, mate, just up the trench! He'll find us, don't you worry.'

Time passed slowly. The frenzied burst of activity in moving further along petered out once they reached their goal and they were forced to sit round waiting for further orders that never arrived. Heavy shelling continued unabated ahead of them but in the absence of any positive information the men grew restless, the hungry and thirsty scouting round for something, anything, to slake their thirsts and appease their hunger. Bert Ring and Ed Rushton had finally appeared with some supplies the sympathetic Middlesex men had given them and Bert Ring set-to to provide a sparse meal.

'Did you manage to get some spare water off'n the poms, eh, Bert?'

'Not exactly, Morrison but I managed to fill my water bottle and a nice guy gave me a spare of his own. Sez it came from an old well

71

nearby but he'd put purifying tablets in it. Here, have a swig if you want, let me know how it tastes.'

'*Gaahhh*! Bert, you bastard, are you trying to kill me? It tastes like there was a dead donk down there before he filled the fucken' bottle!'

'Some people are never satisfied. Right you bunch of no-hopers, any more complaints while we're at it?'

'Yeah, now that you mention it. I...'

'I knew there'd be one! What are you fucken' moaning about now, Fairlie? Jesus, you're never satisfied are you, mate? You and that mate of yours over there, you and Morrison, always bloody complaining. Ungrateful bastards!'

'Naw, I'm not, just saying this tastes good, like a bloody stew should do. You're a damn good babbler, Bert, what did you do, put some dead Jacko in it?'

Bert Ring grinned. 'No worries, it's bloody Marmite, I got a jar off one of the poms. Glad you like it, nice to have my culinary efforts appreciated once in a while.'

'It doesn't taste that good, Ring.'

'Oi, Rushton, shove your stew where the sun don't shine, mate. You can do the fucken' cooking from now on!'

In the distance, the heights of Achi Baba were a menacing reminder why they were there but no orders came and they silently began to believe the day's fighting was ended. Tom began the task of bivouacking, trying to make a semblance of order out of the jumble of men spread around but a commotion from the mud ramparts they were sheltering behind caused him to look up sharply. 2/Lt Truscott stood staring down at him in a state of agitation.

'You're not going to believe this, Corporal, get the men together. We're going in. Where's Sjt Carr?'

'Here, sir, what's up?'

'Quick. Serjeant, get your men ready. Orders have just come in, we're to advance up to the front line and take Achi Baba. We'll be supporting the 5th and 8th battalions. Come on, come on, there's no time to lose, this is it!'

'There's got to be some sort of mistake, sir, look at the bloody time. It's coming up five o'clock, it'll be madness to try to attack just now.'

'Just do as you're bloody well told, Carr! Get the men moving. Now!'

'Alright you blokes, sling your gear on and let's get going.'

'Where we headed for, Sarge?'

'Mr Truscott has all the details, Abbott, so don't let him out of your sight. We don't want to get lost before we get to grips with the Jacko's, do we?'

They passed through a crowded trench full of dark-skinned, smiling men who waved and greeted them. 'Hi Johnny, *aap kaise hain*? How are you?' The Australians waved back, bemused to see foreign skins clad in British Army uniforms.

'It's alright, they're Indian, Hindustani.' Tom shouted, trying to make himself heard against the increased noise of shelling and frightened babble of voices. 'Don't look so scared Bert, they're not cannibals.'

'Thank Christ for that, corp, one of them was giving me a right looking over! An' he was sharpening a fucken' big knife.' Bert Ring replied.

The laughter lasted all the way up to the forward area where more troops were assembled, fussed over by officers and NCO's alike. A runner arrived and handed a New Zealand captain a letter which he read quickly before stuffing it into his trouser pocket and shouting loudly.

'Alright, men, listen carefully to what I've got to say and pass it down the line. In about ten minutes we'll jump off from here and make our way forward to the British front line, about two hundred yards away. We'll be supported by our own New Zealanders and these Aussies who've just appeared in time to join our jolly party. The nobs in the British HQ have decided to make one last push today and we're included in it.

Our objective is Achi Baba, that big hill you can see in the distance so the poms are going to start shelling the Turks hard in about five minutes to keep their heads down. Make your way forward quickly, don't get left behind. The ANZAC's will advance together so keep close, Krithia's directly ahead, about a thousand yards so the shelling should keep the Turks busy until we're in amongst them.

The poms and the French have retired with a bloody nose so it's up to us to show them how ANZAC's fight. Do not let me or our country's down. Use your bayonets if you have to. Don't stop if your mate goes down, leave him for the medics. All got that? Load your rifles now and fix bayonets.'

A rattle of metal from scabbards and the long bayonets were hurried fixed in place. Tom looked round at the tense, frightened faces, men clasping and unclasping their rifles as they waited for the off. A

73

sudden outbreak of noise made them duck as the air was rent by the sound of shells screaming overhead. Far away in the distance a line of dirt and smoke erupted upwards as the shells struck home. More and more shells passed over them and Tom began to believe that perhaps this time it was going to work, they'd rush the Turkish trenches and be on top of Achi Baba before darkness fell.

Their breathing became ragged as they waited, the only way to keep one's hand from shaking was to breathe deeply and easily, no mean feat when shells were screaming overhead. Tom looked down, held his breath and exhaled slowly, marvelling at how steady his hands were.

Pheep! Pheeeeeeep! Whistles shrilled loudly, awakening everyone from their thoughts. 'Right, follow me!' 2/Lt Truscott raised his right hand and waved it vigorously and without hesitation they followed, accompanied by a long strung-out line of similar troops moving forward along the line. He could hear cheering and shouting from all directions but Tom kept his mouth firmly closed, concentrating on breathing and kept his eyes fixed on the horizon.

Waves of men advanced fluidly, flowing rapidly over the wide-open farmland opening up ahead of them, bounding onwards with great energy. *Wheeeee-Crump!* A shell landed shockingly close, bowling over several men near Tom and he flinched, cursing the British gunners for firing so short. *Wheeeee-Crump! Crump!* More shells impacted amongst the running men and he realised with mounting horror that these were Turkish shells.

For the first hundred yards a grove of olive trees had sheltered them from the Turk's view but now they were fully exposed in the open the Turk's reaction was swift and deadly. 'Keep going, keep going!' a voice roared nearby and Tom recognised the sound of their platoon officer's voice. He turned to acknowledge the order in time to see a shell burst alongside the running figure of the officer.

Stunned and deafened by the explosion, 2/Lt Godfrey Truscott staggered drunkenly from the centre of the smoke. The young officer's shoulder still moved but his right arm was a bloody stump spraying bright, red blood in a wide arc as he urged his men on. While Tom watched helplessly Truscott staggered sideways before pirouetting slowly, revealing a wide, bloody rent in his right side. He stumbled forward a few faltering steps more before collapsing onto his face.

'Don't stop, keep going!' A new voice entered the fray and Tom abandoned all efforts to breathe normally, lungs drawing in huge gasps of air as he pounded across the open ground, crouching low to escape the fire-storm. A swishing noise passed from his left and he heard the staccato bark of a machine-gun. The dry, greyish earth kicked up in straight lines as bullets tore amongst them and from behind he could hear the sound of screaming. Now within range of the Turks rifles, a thunderclap filled the air with the sound of humming as bullets whined over before dropping in amongst the running men.

Bodies were dropping in ever-increasing numbers and Tom tensed, waiting for the shock of a bullet tearing into him. More Turkish machine-guns were sending burst after burst into the densely packed men, bowling them over like skittles and he ran desperately in an effort to keep ahead of their fire. To his left he saw an arm waving furiously and angled his way towards the figure hidden in a fold in the ground. As another burst of fire narrowly missed him he threw himself into a shallow trench, colliding with the soldier who'd waved from the edge of the reddened earth parapet.

'*Ooof!*'

'Sorry, mate, are you alright?'

'I'm fine, just winded. Christ, you Aussies weigh a fucking ton! Pleased to meet you, Charlie Deveraux, Middlesex Regiment.'

'Tom Harding, 9th Battalion AIF.'

He looked round. 'What is this, I thought we were the only fools in the area?'

'Don't you ruddy well believe it! This is the front line, or what passes for it. Our company's been here for some time in a holding action. Krithia's too well held, the Turks are too well dug in and those stupid fuckers at HQ still persist in sending lads forward to their deaths. They should be made to take part in the next attack, the useless bastards, it'd soon be stopped!'

Tom looked back. 'You could be right, Charlie.' he said sadly, looking at the scattered heaps of inert bodies which filled the open ground as far as the eye could see. Here and there a man lurched drunkenly to his feet before collapsing again. The Turkish fire was increasing, the shellfire an incessant drumming noise as shells burst violently and their shrapnel threw bodies and limbs in all directions.

It could only have been minutes since they'd charged but already Tom could see that they'd suffered grievously. In amongst the sounds of war, the gunfire, shells exploding, shouts, screams, the piteous cries and groans of the wounded he was also aware of the overwhelming silence of the dead. Another soldier dropped in beside them and he was relieved to see the face of Declan O'Neill smiling at him. 'Christ, Corporal Harding, this is hotter than a dockside bar in the dry season!' He held out his hand and Tom shook it, grateful for the contact of another fellow human.

The British shelling had slackened and as he listened it died altogether. He cursed the gunners volubly, picturing them sitting on their gun trails whilst he and his fellows died through lack of fire support. It was true, the Brits weren't to be trusted and his anger grew as he continued to look at the mounds of piled and twisted bodies.

A sound of shouting to his left jerked him round and he made out the figure of an Australian officer atop the broken parapet, gesticulating with his hand towards the Turkish lines. Most of what he was saying was too indistinct to be heard but one sentence stood out. He recognised: '...*Which of you men are Australians?*' The answer was a deep-throated roar as the 2nd Brigade survivors rose up and charged into the teeth of the Turkish fire.

'God, this is senseless!' Tom cried but found himself staggering to his feet to join his comrades, followed without hesitation by Declan O'Neill. Charlie Deveraux caught at his sleeve but he shook him off. 'Let go, they're my mates!' He ran forward as Charlie's words were whipped away by the storm of firing ripping into the Australian's ranks.

His rifle bucked savagely in his hands and looking down he saw a deep groove where a shrapnel ball had smashed into the butt, splintering the woodwork. Muttering a short prayer for this salvation he ran on, crouching to try and make himself a smaller target, feeling the fear and the exhilaration rise up within his soul as he ran.

Men fell, rose and fell again. In short rushes they worked their way forward but raw courage and frail flesh could do little to deflect copper-tipped Mauser bullets and jagged-edged shrapnel tearing into them. It had to come to a halt and it did. Another miraculous five hundred yards further on from the ragged trenches they had just left. On this spot it was evident that to advance any further would spell certain death so the shocked, wounded and utterly spent survivors fell to the earth one last time and began to dig in.

Behind them, stretching back for five hundred yards were the dead bodies of their friends and the slowly writhing figures of the wounded. Mates they'd sailed with from Albany seven months before with high hopes and spirits were now ripped, shredded corpses stiffening in the cool of the evening.

Lying in the small hole he'd hacked out when going to ground, Tom looked round wildly. Declan O'Neill had vanished from his side in the mad rush, one minute he'd been running alongside and then there was only an empty space. He glanced along the row of holes but failed to see in any of them a sight of the curls O'Neill had been so proud of and his heart sank. In the deepening gloom he continued to dig as the crackle of gunfire slowly died until it stopped altogether.

To his right he could hear the sound of sobbing and rolled out of his hole onto his back, wriggling over to investigate. A young soldier, hatless, sat with his back to the Turks, hands beating the ground in a futile gesture of hopelessness.

'Are you hurt?' Tom enquired, 'Get under cover before you're seen.'

The boy's tear-stained face looked up at him. 'Hurt? Me? No, it's me mates, they're gone. All of them. Gone! We never even fired our rifles, never saw a fucken' Turk but they killed all my mates, there's just me left out of the platoon. This isn't war, it's bloody murder.' He began sobbing again. Tom looked back at the hunched, scattered bodies. A flock of dark birds had landed nearby, cawing loudly as they flapped their way over the broken ground to investigate the dead.

Crows, he thought, an apt appearance, the harbingers of death. A word the youngster had used struck him as he stared at the birds. Murder. Wasn't that the name for a collection of crows? A murder of crows? Never before had it seemed so fitting, here of all days on this field of death. He turned back to the youngster.

'I know how you're feeling mate,' he said gently, 'but get your rifle and come in here and join me. There's blokes out there, the wounded, who'll need our help and I've a feeling it's going to take most of the night and as many men as we can round up to assist the medics. Come on, up you get.'

--§--

The wounded lay where they fell, hoping for rescue as night drew in and the temperature dropped. Some lucky ones were able to drag themselves to safety but for the majority it meant a long, painful night as wounded limbs stiffened but continued to bleed nevertheless. A few, the unlucky few, slipped into unconsciousness and death but hundreds more clung tenaciously to life, straining their ears for the welcome sound of stretcher bearers combing and re-combing the ground.

Piteous cries and groans from out of the darkness spurred many of the survivors into action and they joined the stretcher bearers in searching for the wounded and for lost friends. All night the searching went on but by daybreak it was apparent that many more still lay out in the open, grievously wounded and in need of aid. To move during daylight meant a death sentence for any searcher from a sharp-eyed Turkish sniper so the wounded were left in the hope that some would survive until nightfall fell again and another search would find them.

An overwhelming factor which decided who lived and who died was the fact that the nearest Aid Stations lay some distance away and each casualty had to be laboriously carried there manually. In a further twist to the story of the wounded it became blindingly obvious that the provision of medical services prior to the assault on Krithia had been shamefully neglected to the point of being almost non-existent. This caused more deaths amongst those lucky enough to reach the Aid Stations but who would die in a vain wait for attention. Many wounded who might have survived undoubtedly succumbed to their injuries through spending the night out in the open alone and untreated, the major factor in hastening their premature and unnecessary deaths.

The men of 'E' Company spent the day stabilising the line and reorganising themselves, their weapons and kit. The Turks kept up a steady fire all day but the Australians managed to keep their losses to a minimum whilst sheltering in the scrapes they'd dug the day before. A roll call showed thirty men missing. Nine had been seen to fall, including 2/Lt Truscott but the other twenty-one lay out on the battlefield, had been evacuated to Cape Helles for medical attention or were simply "*missing*". The cries of the wounded lay heavy on the minds of those sheltering in the trenches and many a man was pulled back by his NCO when he looked as if he was prepared to go out.

'Oi, where do you think you two are going?'

'Fair go's, corp, me and Rolly were going to sneak out and see if we could find any of the missing blokes. They can't all be dead, we reckon a couple of them are laid up waiting to be found so we were gonna bunk off and find them. Declan O'Neill's out there somewhere, a good cobber and I ain't gonna let him just lie there.'

Tom sighed. 'Look, Fairlie,' he said, 'I know you and O'Neill were looking out for each other but if you go over now searching for him, two things are going to happen. One, Captain Finch is going to roast my arse for letting you go and two, Johnny Turk is going to see you in this light and blow several large holes in both of you.'

'I know, I know, but we just can't sit here and ... '

'Who said we're just going to sit here? It'll be dark in an hour or so. If he's survived so far another hour won't hurt, pardon the pun. You two park your bums on that stretcher while I have a seat and then we'll see about finding O'Neill.'

'Do you mean you're coming with us, corp?'

'Hallelujah! The penny's dropped. You two, sit. There!'

Rolly Morrison and Pete Fairlie grinned and dropped alongside Tom.

'Bonzer! You always were a good sport, Corporal Harding. Haven't I always said that, Rolly, I said—'

'Fairlie! Shut up and let me have my breather in peace.'

'Rightho, corp.'

A quick meal of bully and biscuits washed down with a tepid mug of tea and they were ready. Easing themselves carefully over the parapet, the three men crawled gingerly into the scrub. 'Quiet and follow me.' Tom Harding whispered, trying to acclimatise. 'Morrison you berk, go back and get the bloody stretcher, what do you think we're gonna do, drag the blokes in by hand?'

'Sorry, corp.' Rolly whispered, abashed, and promptly disappeared, reappearing seconds later with the rolled-up shape of the stretcher he and Fairlie had stolen earlier in the day. Satisfied they were now fully equipped for the search, Tom pulled quickly at each man's boot and they began slowly crawling into the stygian blackness in response to his touch. Nothing stirred but every now and then a faint cry would reach their ears, bringing them to a halt as they tried to ascertain the direction the cries had come from.

Adrenaline made Tom's heart thud madly in his chest and his pulse race. He jumped as a whisper came out of the gloom. 'Over here.' He crawled towards the sound. 'Sorry, false alarm, this cove's dead, poor bugger.' Fairlie's quiet voice reached him and he backed away.

They crawled on. A flare rose and they lay still, bathed in its white brilliance but nothing happened, no shouts of discovery or shots so after waiting for it to sink to earth they crawled on. 'We'll have to go back soon, corp, otherwise we'll all find ourselves in fucken' Constantinople.' Rolly's voice sounded close to his left and in spite of himself Tom smiled. Trust Morrison to find some humour in the situation.

'Over here, quickly!' He sped up and crawled quickly towards the sound of Pete Fairlie's voice. Fairlie grabbed at his sleeve and gestured with his other hand. A still figure lay huddled up before them, the face unrecognisable in the dark. As Morrison joined them, the figure rolled over and began to snore.

'Jesus, it's O'Neill. Fancy that, the lazy bastard's just having a bloody kip. Oi, O'Neill, wake up you bludger!'

O'Neill's weak voice answered his friend's insults. 'Hi, Pete, what took you so fucken' long? I've been lying here all day waiting for you drongoes to come and find me. Where've you been?'

Fairlie leaned forward and shook his friend's shoulder, a gesture that made Declan O'Neill draw his breath in sharply. '*Aaah*, mate, careful there.'

'What! Are you crook? Did they get you?'

'Naaah, I just thought I'd lie here to get out of fatigues, Pete.'

'Enough!' Tom ordered, 'Let's get him on the stretcher and get the hell out of here.' As they dragged O'Neill's limp form onto the stretcher Tom detected a pungent smell and leaned over, gagging on the odour coming from O'Neill's right arm.

'Jesus, Declan, your arm bloody stinks.'

'I know, mate, 'O'Neill spoke wearily, 'a Jacko bullet went straight through it, took me bloody ages to stop the bleeding. I can't feel it now. Reckon its gone numb on me so I suppose those butchers of medics will want to take it off. God, that'll be right, me a one-armed cripple selling matches outside the bloody station.'

'Hey, look at it this way, Declan, at least you'll get to see your twins now.' There was no answer. He looked down. Declan O'Neill lay unconscious against the stretcher rail.

'Alright, you two, lift him up and let's get the poor bugger back.'

Straining, they lifted O'Neill's dead weight onto the stretcher and began the long slow journey back. Tripping over stiffened bodies, catching their faltering steps in unseen shellholes, the nightmare task of bringing Declan O'Neill back to the safety of their lines seemed to take forever. Eventually, they stumbled in amongst the waiting sentries and handed O'Neill over to fresh arms and legs. As his inert form was hurried away his three rescuers dropped to the ground exhausted and cuddling together for warmth, they slept.

He woke an hour or so later, the smell of burning flesh in his nostrils and a haunted sense of failure uppermost in his mind. Cautiously he looked round but no-one stirred, all around him men slept, deep within their own memories and nightmares. His failure to banish the images coursing through his mind of the poor wretch burning to death in the scrub unsettled him and in an effort to dispel his depression he leant over and nudged Fairlie's inert form.

'*Worra...?*'

'Sorry, mate, I can't sleep, I just wanted to talk.'

'Gawd, corp, d'you know what fucken' time it is?' Fairlie answered sleepily, 'It's still dark for crissakes and I was just having a beaut dream about a quiet spot with the missus. Now you've bloody well spoilt it! I'm frozen too, when're we goin to get those blankets you promised us?'

'God knows. Go back to sleep then. Sorry.'

Fairlie hunched down and was snoring again within seconds, leaving Tom lying next to him, eyes wide open as he looked into the dark. He wrapped his arms around his upper torso in an attempt to keep the bitter cold eating its way into his bones and mentally totted up their recent losses. Faces swam into and out of his conscious thoughts; a bloodied, ravaged face writhing in the heat of a fire, Tod Hammond's skull shattered by the force of a Mauser bullet and the agonised stare on Billy Willis's features as he lay dying in a pool of his own blood.

His breath a white hoar frost against the blackness of the night, Corporal Thomas Harding lay shivering and remembered. The 9th Battalion's casualties at this point were in the region of 45 killed, 28 wounded and 199 men missing. The butcher's bill was mounting steadily.

Chapter Five.

Anatolia, Turkey. May 1915.

The sky was a vivid blue and though it was the last week in May the heat from the sun brought a warming sensation to her back as she tidied up her garden implements and lifted the grain-carrier from its place behind the back door. A cooling Anatolian breeze swept across the backyard but her reverie was disturbed by the sound of jingling harnesses and the faint voices of men heading towards the Armenian village of Merghem in the south-eastern part of Turkey known for centuries as *Cilician Armenia*.

The chickens clucked impatiently at her feet, demanding to be fed but she ignored them. Instead, Hegine Seferian shielded her eyes from the low noonday sun and gazed upwards, trying to make out the approaching figures as her young son ran down the hillside towards her, shrieking excitedly in a high, piping voice. Far away in the distance the blue outlines of the Taurus mountains shimmered starkly in the haze but it was in the opposite direction to their heights that her attention was drawn.

'Mama, mama! Soldiers are coming, will papa be with them?'

His words caused a faint flutter of unease in her stomach but she said nothing. Impatiently brushing a stray lock of her dark, lustrous hair from her eyes she replaced the grain-carrier on the floor and motioned him to her side and together mother and son watched the strangers approach. The soldiers marched imperiously out of sight and Hegine and the boy walked round to the front of the small mud-bricked house to await their coming.

Other inhabitants of the village came out of their houses and joined her, all craning their heads to see who the approaching strangers could be. She moved to the cool shade of the hazel tree standing next to the well in the square and hushed her son. 'Quiet, Khat, be still and let's wait and see who comes.' He tried to squirm away as young children are apt to but she grasped his hand firmly and held it tight.

The first sound to reach their ears was a loud braying noise. Walking sedately, a whitened donkey rounded the corner of the church heading towards the square. Seated on its back, swaying languorously with the donkey's movements sat a fat man in the uniform of a Turkish army captain with a lamb's fur *kalpak* perched perilously on his bald, glistening forehead. He held a flywhisk diffidently in his left hand and was smoking a long cigarette with the other as the donkey's reins hung loosely around its neck. A parasol fixed to the rear of the saddle waved incongruously with the donkey's movements, giving it the impression of a ship lost at sea.

Behind the donkey puffed a squad of armed soldiers, uniform jackets stained with sweat as they tried to keep up with their leader. At the rear of the column another donkey loaded down with sacks of supplies and water skins staggered drunkenly in the men's footsteps. All came to a stop in the dust and the officer astride the white donkey coughed up a large piece of phlegm which he carefully spat onto the ground before straightening to look around him.

He glanced over to the knot of villagers who waited anxiously for developments as if seeing them for the first time and clearing his throat, he spat again.

'Listen to me! I am *Yuzbashi* Halit, a captain of the Turkish army and I come with a message from your government the *Ittihad ve Terakki Jemiyeti,* the Committee of Union and Progress. Where is your *Naib?*'

An old man detached himself from the throng and approached the waiting officer, blinking nervously and bowing deeply. '*Hosh geldün efendim,* you are welcome, sir. If it pleases Your Excellency, my name is Nahabed Yaralian and I am he. What brings you and your men here, Captain?'

The fat officer looked down at the headman, lips curled in contempt.

'You *dhimmî,* you have no sense of honour! For years you've enjoyed special privileges granted you by the people of this country, people you turn your back on and despise.' His scowl deepened. 'Well, no longer! Know this, *people of the book* that I've been sent here on a special mission to dispense important information. It has come to the attention of the authorities that criminals in this village have been harbouring and giving aid and assistance to bandits operating in the *vilayet* under the guise of *ermeni* resistance fighters. This will not be tolerated and an example will therefore be made.

As a result of His Excellency, *Talât Paşa,* Minister of the Interior's decision, you're all to leave this province immediately for relocation elsewhere in order to deny these bandits the succour they seek. We are at war with the *infidels* from the west who have invaded and anyone not showing their support for the country at this time will meet with the severest penalties.

83

The government has further decreed that all belongings left behind shall be forfeited and will become the property of the state. You now have thirty minutes to gather what you can carry and we will then escort you to where you'll make your new lives, *Inşallah*, God willing.'

'Thirty minutes? What is this? Surely, Excellency, there must be some mistake. No-one in this village supports bandits, as you infer. We are all loyal Turks, captain, *ermeni* by birth, yes, but true Turks nevertheless. Look around you, all our able-bodies men have gone, taken to serve in the army. Can you not see how patriotic we are? How can you say such things? We were not informed of this...this decision. Leave? Where are we to go?'

For an answer the officer pointed his flywhisk carelessly in the direction of the interior. 'You must all go to the east, the government has prepared a camp at a place called Deir ez Zor, in Syria. You'll start your march today and be joined by other *ermeni* also sent there for their own protection.'

'Syria? But there's nothing out there, just scrub and desert! How shall we go there? An hour to leave our homes, our livelihoods? Impossible, this is impossible what you ask! I beg you, Excellency, give us time to learn more. I must speak with your superiors for more information before we can accede to your demands.'

Ignoring the man's pleas the officer leant on the donkey's back and twisted his head round, addressing the nearest soldier waiting in the sun.

'Hang this pig!' he ordered softly. The soldier looked up, perplexed, and the captain repeated the order, this time more forcefully. 'Hang him. Now!'

Obediently the soldier took off at a run to the supply animal and returned carrying a length of rope. Before the shocked crowd's incredulous gaze he and another soldier pulled the headman roughly around and bound his hands behind his back with twine. Kicking and shoving him they manoeuvred him under the tree by the well, pushing those gathered there out of the way.

Hegine and her son sank to the ground and looked up in horror, her arms wrapped protectively around her son as the soldiers fashioned a noose out of the rope. They tightened it over the headman's head and flung the free end over a low-lying branch of the hazel.

'Excellency!' the terrified headman entreated, 'Please, mercy, I've done nothing wrong. I've...*eeuuuchh!*' His words were cut off in mid-sentence as the rope tightened and he was lifted bodily off his feet by three soldiers hauling on the free end. Kicking and struggling, face turning puce, he was lifted still squirming, several feet off the ground in front of the horrified villagers.

Soldiers barred the way from anyone trying to escape watching the spectacle, loaded weapons pointing loosely at the crowd.

'Don't move!' roared the fat officer, his face streaming. 'This is what happens to anyone who defies my authority. Watch and take heed!' He took a large, red handkerchief from a pocket and dabbed at his face. As he choked and gurgled above them, the dying man's bladder relaxed and a stream of urine pattered to the ground beneath his feet, catching those unlucky to lie in its path. Hegine felt the warm flood hit her leg and the soldiers roared with laughter as she moved swiftly away from the tree, dragging Khat with her.

At last, all movement ceased from the man swinging above them and at a signal from their officer the soldiers released their hold on the rope. The corpse fell nervelessly to the ground, raising a plume of dust as it collapsed into the dirt, a swollen tongue protruding from its mouth.

'Now, listen to me once more, you *ermeni* whore's children! You now have only...' He took a timepiece from the same pocket which had held the handkerchief, opened it and inspected it minutely. '...thanks to this dog's disobedience you now have only fourteen minutes to gather up all you can carry and come with me. Anyone not wishing to accompany us will share the same fate as this cur. Go now and make ready.' He snapped the timepiece shut with an air of finality.

'Mama?' Khat cried, 'What's happening, where's papa?'

'*Shh*' Hegine chided him, terrified he would bring attention to them with his cries. She pulled him away, ignoring his snivelling as she made for the front door of their house. Once inside she looked round, her head whirling. How had this nightmare come upon them...? Think, think! Oh, Artoun, strong, capable Artoun, if only you were here you'd know what to do. What to do....what to do...What to take and for how long? The thought of leaving her home, their home and their meagre belongings filled her with a mounting dread but she tried to calm herself, think logically and pick out some belongings for her and the boy.

'Khat, watch the door while mama sorts our clothes.' she ordered, 'Quickly now or the bad men will get angry and shout at us.'

'But mama...?'

'Now, Khat!' His face crumpled and she ran over to soothe him. 'Please, little one, help your mother. Do this for me. Alright?' Obediently the boy did as he was told and she moved into the bedroom to pick out some clothes for them. Artoun's tools and implements lay where he'd stored them weeks ago but she passed them by without a second glance. The clothing draped by her sewing-machine was ignored as she thought frantically. A seamstress's skills were not needed at this present time, what was required were the things that would guarantee their survival until it became clear what was to happen to them. Outside, a sudden scream cut-off in mid-cry spurred her on and she shuddered in fear at the noise's import.

What belongings she selected she wrapped and tied in a coarse blanket from the bed, making a bundle that would fit over her shoulder. She moved quickly, still unable to believe what was happening, panicking as she darted here and there trying to decide what to include. From outside, loud shouts and screams spurred her on into making her choices quickly.

The other room held some bread and goat's cheese on the window so she pushed a loaf and hunk of the cheese into the depths of the blanket. On the table, a half-eaten chicken caught her eye and she stuffed that also into the blanket. It was a bird that had died of old age but nothing was wasted and it would help stave off any hunger pains until they got to ...where? A large water skin, half-full, dangled from a peg and she made sure the stopper was firmly fixed before lifting it from its peg. As she hefted the blanket awkwardly over her shoulder the doorway was filled by a soldier, eyes flashing angrily as he cuffed Khat over the head. Ignoring the boy's cries of pain he gestured at Hegine.

'You heard my Captain, out now you bitch or you and the boy die here!'

'I don't understand,' she cried, 'what have we done, why is this happening to us?'

He moved forward swiftly and struck her hard across the face, a cruel stinging blow, knocking her to the floor. 'Get up now and take your bastard with you. Move!'

She scrabbled across the floor, keeping away from his path, the blanket rolling round to her front. Pushing it back into place, face smarting, she grabbed Khat's outstretched hand and staggered upright. Mustering her courage she looked squarely into the soldier's angry, twisted face.

'My husband is a soldier serving in the same army as you. Is this how you treat women and children? I need more time to gather things for the boy, for myself. Women's things.'

He had the grace to look discomfited. His hand, ready to hit her again, dropped to his side at her quiet words and he gestured roughly.

'I'll wait outside. You have two minutes only and then you must come with me.'

As he left she sprang back into the small room where their bed stood, the marriage bed Artoun had lovingly crafted for her and where he had held her tenderly in his strong arms through the dark nights. There, too, the round fireplace where they'd sat and discussed their dreams of a better life before Artoun's enforced departure. Unable to raise the required *bedel*, a tax that would have exempted him from conscription, he'd left with a promise to return as soon as he was freed from his military obligation.

Squatting on the floor she reached underneath the bed and her questing hand found the small leather bag she sought. The bag contained all the money she and Artoun had gathered since their marriage, money to pay for Khat's education when he grew older and for any large bills that might come their way unseen. It jingled as she brought it out from its hiding place and she held her breath in case the soldier standing just feet away heard the noise and realised its portent. Straightening, she moved over to the chest of drawers and silently opened the top draw.

Hidden under some handkerchiefs was a small box containing her jewellery, the chains and bangles she had brought with her on her wedding day along with some silver coins and she carefully slid the box's contents into the depths of the leather bag. Putting a finger to her lips she motioned for Khat to stand still as she slid out of the back door and crept stealthily to where the chicken coop lay on the dirt floor of the garden.

The chickens had long since fled at the sound of the commotion so she was able to place it to one side and dig a shallow hole using a small piece of wood as a trowel. Satisfied it was deep enough she laid the bag into the scrape, filled the hole up with the earth she'd disturbed and replaced the coop.

Moving back into the house she took a final look round before heading to where the soldier waited. Although it was small the house represented all she and Artoun had striven for, her job as a seamstress and his as the village carpenter; the signature of their lives were written here in these small few rooms and her eyes filled with tears as she contemplated the bleakness of the future waiting on the other side of the door.

Her terror-stricken neighbours had already assembled, herded into a rough semblance of shocked order and surrounded by soldiers they were marched to the edge of the square where the rest of the village waited in blank silence. Two bodies lay sprawled in the square, their belongings already having been ransacked and Hegine's horrified gaze took in a fresh corpse swinging slowly above that of Nahabed Yaralian's. Stepping back with a start she recognised the long-bearded figure of the village clergyman. Pastor Krikor Kazazian gazed down with lifeless eyes as his flock was brutally gathered together in the shadow of his martyrdom.

At this point the teenaged boys and a few older men were separated from their families and herded out of sight from the remainder by a squad of soldiers. 'Where are you taking my husband?' a woman cried in an anguished voice but her answer was a rifle butt in the stomach. Crying with pain, she gained her feet and sought shelter in the arms of an old woman, looking fearfully in the direction the men had been marched away.

'Move.' said the captain and as one the column of eighty villagers moved off silently down the street into the open country. No-one looked round as they marched off, the menacing looks from the accompanying soldiers was enough to keep each villager's eyes locked firmly to their front. As they left the last house behind a volley of shots crashed out, followed by another. Numbed, the people glanced at each other with wide eyes but a shouted order quelled any words that might have formed. Children cried as the adults tried vainly to silence them and their noise only increased the soldier's anger.

Khat held tightly to his mother's skirts as the soldiers vented their rage on the helpless villagers, running up and down the column and swinging fists into the marching throng, ignoring the gasps and squeals of pain. The first death came an hour into the march. An old woman, her energy gone, sank to the ground, resisting the entreaties of her husband to rise. A soldier strode over quickly, took in the situation with a glance and struck the woman a fearsome blow to her head with his rifle butt. Her skull shattered like an eggshell, spraying blood and matter over the soldier's sandals and he kicked the dead woman's body angrily before pushing her distraught husband back into the column and walking off without a word.

A collective gasp issued from those who witnessed the brutal murder but they inhaled deeply and lapsed into a terrified silence as angry faces were turned in their direction. Leaving the body behind the march resumed in shocked obedience, the hot sun beating down on their faces and shoulders causing a mounting desire for water. Two hours later, at a signal from the officer, they halted and sank down gratefully. A young woman squirmed over to Hegine and Khat, all the while keeping a watchful eye on the guards.

'What's happening to us?' she hissed, pulling her shawl low over her eyes. 'Your Artoun's in the army, surely you must know why we've been forced from our homes?'

Hegine turned her head, shaking it sorrowfully. 'Like you, I know nothing. Artoun's been gone for some months now and none of this....*shhhh*...careful!'

A soldier turned his baleful glance in their direction and the woman crawled back to where her family waited. As they sat huddled in fear they were joined by the soldiers who'd marched the men and boys away.

'Back on your feet, move. That's long enough!'

With a groan the villagers stood up with an effort, and began to slowly shuffle forward. The soldiers crowded round, forcing the reluctant ones onwards with the butts of their rifles, pushing and pulling them into a column. At a sharp command they moved off as one group, stepping along the track that stretched in front of them.

During the remainder of the day more villagers faltered and were dealt with in the same manner as the old woman. A swift blow to the head and the column moved on. In this way they travelled for several miles before the setting sun heralded the approach of nightfall. Opposite a small stand of trees the officer raised his hand and the column halted. He shouted a brief command and the nearest soldier turned to them.

'Down here, we stay the night, now. Do not move from this spot, you'll be watched through the night. Any movement from where you lie will mean death.'

Shivering, the villagers obeyed. They sank to the ground thankfully and began to huddle together in groups for warmth. It soon became obvious they were not going to be fed by their guards so their packs and bundles were opened surreptitiously and small morsels and water sacks brought out. Those unlucky not to have anything with them went hungry and thirsty. Hegine and Khat ate and drank quickly before she hid their supplies back in the depths of her bundle.

Swiftly, the soldiers erected a small tent they'd unpacked from the back of the protesting pack animal and the officer crawled inside. As night fell the noise of screaming arose from the group nearest the tent and Hegine's neighbour turned to her, distraught.

'Oh God, they've taken two of the young girls into the tent. God help them!'

Hegine clutched Khat tightly to her and listened with mounting horror to the screams and wails coming from out of the inky blackness. She tried to drown out the sounds by holding her hands to her ears but the screams penetrated her skull nevertheless and she lay pressed to the ground in this manner as she tried to rest. In the early hours of the morning the sounds stopped abruptly.

Dawn arrived slowly, a thin streak of red on the horizon that stretched into bands of yellows and blues as the sun rose. Stiffly, the soldiers stood and moved amongst the groups of huddled frozen villagers, kicking them awake. Hegine rose slowly, her limbs stiff from the cold and where she'd grimly clung to Khat during the long, cold night. Her gaze fell on the tent where a yawning Captain Halit made his appearance before striding off to the shelter of a stand of trees. He was back in minutes, fastening his trousers as he shouted angrily at his men.

They rushed to strike down the tent, packing it away on the supply donkey's back before kicking and pushing the villagers into a semblance of order, ready to march off. There was no sign of the two young girls and they were quickly forgotten as the column stepped off slowly once more. A loud sobbing from the head of the column stopped in mid-cry as a soldier wielded his rifle butt and they marched on with eyes averted, passing the corpse of another female victim, that of the missing girls' mother.

Shortly, the trees and green fields gave way to sand and they began to slow down as they floundered their way onwards through the drifts, shouted and bawled at all the way by their guards. Two hours later, as they entered a small valley the officer held up his hand and they stopped, exhausted by their efforts to keep up. 'Now we wait.' he said and they subsided gratefully to the ground amongst the sparse scrub. The soldiers circled them once and satisfied that no-one looked to have the energy to resist, sank onto their haunches and waited, staring towards the west.

The waiting was not long. A cloud of dust told of the arrival of more strangers, a large band of evil-looking Turks on horseback who circled the column whooping and hollering, terrifying the villagers as they huddled tightly together. The captain rose from dozing under his parasol and waved a hand in greeting. He dismounted stiffly with the help of a soldier and walked over to a swarthy, one-eyed individual mounted on a dark horse.

'My brothers of the *Teshkilâti Mahsusa*, men of the Special Organisation, we greet you. May *Allah* be merciful unto you!'

Ignoring his greetings the leader twisted and from a saddle-bag lifted a large, heavy bag which he thrust into the captain's eager hands. Carefully counting the coins it contained, Captain Halit nodded curtly. Turning to his waiting men he made a chopping motion and was helped back into his place on the donkey's back. Striking her flanks with his flywhisk he moved away in the direction from which they'd approached, his men following. Neither he nor the soldiers looked back.

Hardly were they out of sight than the thugs leapt from their horses and ran into the frightened, tensely waiting villagers, knocking men, women and children out of their way in their eagerness to examine their newly-acquired prisoner's belongings. Some stood menacingly quiet on the periphery, hands on hilts of swords that protruded from their waists. Hegine watched carefully, if anything was to happen here it was these men who would begin the action. She pulled Khat close, feeling his heart thudding like a bird against her breast and her anxiety grew.

'No! Don't! Leave us!'

One of the older men stood to remonstrate with one who pulled at his pack but his attempts to ward the Turk off were ended by a sharp, curved dagger slicing into his stomach. Coughing blood, the man collapsed limply to the ground as his wife screamed in horror and dropped to the side of her stricken husband.

Her shrill cries were the trigger for an orgy of death as the Turks turned on their helpless captives, drawing large swords, axes and sharp daggers from under their clothes. Throwing themselves at the villagers they showed no mercy, hacking and stabbing in a mad frenzy of killing, the piteous creams and harrowing cries of their victims passing unheeded as a merciless sun shone down.

'No...please...mercy...ahhh!' An old woman knelt, hands entwined in a desperate plea but her killer soundlessly buried his sword up to

91

the hilt in her chest before kicking her limp corpse backwards and striding on in search of another victim.

The younger females were herded together in a crying, wailing group whilst the boys suffered the same fate as the adults. Unable to speak, Hegine watched with mounting terror as the full horror took place in front of her unbelieving eyes. 'Oh God, we must go!' She took Khat's hand and scrabbled away, desperately trying to find somewhere to hide but was pulled up short by strong hands grabbing hold of her long, dark hair.

'Where are you going, my pretty, thinking of leaving us?' She was painfully jerked off her feet as the speaker, an unshaven unkempt member of the band stood leering at her, bloodstained knife in hand. She moved to run past but he punched her hard in the stomach, forcing the air from her lungs in a loud *whoosh!* and she fell in agony to the hot sand. At this assault on his mother Khat burst into frightened tears and his cries spurred her on.

Weakly she regained her feet and tried to catch her breath but her assailant struck her again and she felt a black veil of unconsciousness loom as her legs wilted. He pushed her unresisting towards the shivering, sobbing blank-eyed group of women and young girls the band had gathered away from their other victims.

'Abdullah, here's another pigeon for the flock!'

'My son! My son! Khat! Khat!' She tried to push past him, wild-eyed, frantic as her eyes looked unseeingly round the nightmarish scene. 'I must have my son!'

He hit her hard across the face this time and she fell back. 'You stay here, woman, leave this group and you'll be meat for the jackals!' he growled.

Distraught, she ran again at him but he laughed and knocked her down again. This time she stayed sprawled on the ground, her strength gone as waves of pain threatened to overwhelm her. Hours, or was it minutes, passed and in her agony she hardly felt hands turn her over and bind her wrists together. Dimly she became aware of being picked up and draped roughly face-down over the pommel of a horse, the sweaty, leathery smell of its mane filling her nostrils.

Her world dissolved into a painful bumping sensation as the horse cantered away from the killing ground, her captor holding onto the waist of her skirt with his free hand. Her mind slid unfettered towards madness and she screamed soundlessly...Khat—Khat—

Khat! the image of her young son's scared face still imprinted within her tortured mind.

Behind her, the vultures wheeled, high, in a clear blue sky before landing clumsily and hopping forward awkwardly, eagerly, over to the piles of stripped and scattered corpses.

--§--

A few hours to the south, Artoun Seferian rolled over and yawned as his sleep was disturbed by his head slipping from the comfort of his pack. He rubbed his eyes and looked around the freight car he and his fellow conscripts were housed in. Six hundred of them had been travelling for some hours now, bumping and clattering along the narrow-gauge track from Syria, bodies and legs intertwined as each man tried to find a suitable place to rest. Now and then the foul, black smoke from the locomotive blew in through the gaps in the sides causing a paroxysm of coughing and covering them in tiny soot particles but for the moment the air was clean enough.

His infantry unit, a battalion of the Anatolian 66th Regiment attached to the 6th Ottoman Army Corps was composed wholly of Armenians in the service of their country of birth. They had been posted to Aleppo in Syria as a garrison unit at the outbreak of the war last December and now after five months they'd suddenly been recalled, the explanation being to allow more seasoned troops to be released from lesser duties and fed into the major battle that had erupted on the Gallipoli peninsula. The Western Powers, jealous of Turkey's growing might had forced this war on them but these unwashed unbelievers would soon learn what it was to face the Turk in battle at Çannakale.

The *infidels*, the British, French and the ANZAC Corps containing men from Australia and New Zealand had gained a toehold on Mother Turkey and they were to be thrown back into the sea. As a result the 66th had been recalled from the backwaters of Syria allegedly for guard duties elsewhere in Turkey whilst more seasoned troops hurried to the front.

He lay back on his pack again, dreaming of home and his wife and son. Hegine and Khat would be feeding the chickens about now, he reasoned, by the height of the sun and at the thought of his four-year old son a broad smile lit up his sunburned face. Khat had his mother's eyes, you had to say that but his heart was that of his

93

father's. What did women know about bringing up young men? When his army service was finished he would return to his village and he and his son would live as brothers. Perhaps he could enjoy some leave with them after the battalion arrived at its destination. The thought of seeing his family again brought another smile to his face but those thoughts were rudely interrupted by a sound of shunting and the noise of the brakes being applied. A loud squealing filled the air as the train slowed to a stop.

'What's happening, Artoun, can you see, have we reached Islahiye already?'

His friend, Nareg, rolled over languidly and glanced up at him. The tunnels of Ayran in Mount Amanos were still under construction so the railroad ended in the foothills of the Amanos Mountains. Having left Aleppo earlier, the troop train was headed for the eastern terminal at Islahiye where they would disembark and march the twenty or so miles through the hills to the western terminal at Osmaniye. There a fresh train would be waiting to take them further into the hinterland to Adana and onwards to their new duties.

'Not yet ...That's strange, I can't see...'

'Not yet?' his friend interjected, 'What do you mean, not yet? Why not, what's going on? You're supposed to be our *onbasi*. I thought you NCO's knew everything!'

'I'll give you *NCO's* Artoun growled, 'being a corporal does not give me the ability to see through walls or foretell the future so shut up whilst I try and see what's going on! We've stopped but I can't see why. There's nothing out here, just wilderness. I wonder what ... ?'

'Out! Everyone out!' A loud, stentorian voice filled the air as the train came to a shuddering, squealing, clanking halt in a cloud of steam. The voice spoke in Turkish but everyone onboard had spoken Turkish since their early youth and all obeyed the command. Scratching tired faces, rubbing tired eyes they poured from their wagons and looked inquisitively at the large knot of soldiers gathered in front of a barrier opposite the locomotive.

'Men over here, NCO's and officers this way, quickly now.' The loud voice boomed again and all looked round to see if they could spot where its owner stood. Artoun's face broke into a smile as he recognised their commander, Colonel Misakian striding along the track towards the locomotive, a severe look of displeasure on his otherwise genial features. This should prove interesting.

'Hold on there. You! Come here! What do you mean by stopping us here in the middle of nowhere and forcing us to detrain?'

The leader of the detachment of around fifty men, a sullen-faced lieutenant, walked slowly to meet the irate colonel. 'My orders from the Army Council of Enver Pasha are quite clear, colonel, sir,' he answered, almost insolently, 'your men are to surrender their arms and you must all wait here until arrangements can be made for you to travel on to a different destination. This train is returning to Haleb as it's needed elsewhere.'

'What orders are you talking about, man?' the colonel snapped. 'And since when did the orders of a *mulazim-i-evel*, a lieutenant, take precedence over those of a *mirilai*, a colonel? Or did you not see the difference in our ranks, lieutenant? Well? Surrender our arms, what is this nonsense? I was never informed of this before we left Haleb. Who's in charge here, I would like...?'

There was steel in the lieutenant's answer, although he tried to speak in a deferential manner. 'My apologies, sir, no disrespect was meant but I must insist, I have my orders. You and your men are to form a labour battalion, an *amele taburlari*, for service but where I've not been informed.' His lips curled. 'It would seem all you *ermeni* are to be treated this way, the order went out months ago but for some reason your regiment was overlooked or forgotten. Until now. All I know is that men are required to build the new roads we need and decisions have been made by the Army Council to use troops. You have been chosen and must surrender your weapons and accompany me and my men over there.' He pointed vaguely to his left.

'There's a quarry two hundred yards up the road and it will be better for all to rest there in the shade while we wait for another train to take you on to Islahiye. There's a war going on and matters change from minute to minute as you know, sir. I do not give orders, only obey them.'

'I still don't understand ... Another train? ... what train? ... when?'

'Soon, I'm told, sir.' The lieutenant's voice changed to a soothing tone. 'We've stockpiled bread and water for the men so you can take refreshments while you wait. There are also olives and cheese to be shared out. Come, come, eat.'

'A labour battalion? What's the world coming too? Who the hell thought this one up...?' The colonel followed, grumbling, behind the suddenly affable lieutenant but the thought of some decent food

95

raised his spirits and he spoke quickly to his more senior officers before allowing himself to be led away.

Artoun frowned as their company commander detached himself and came over to repeat the Turkish lieutenant's request. All their arms were to be piled together and they would march up the road to be fed and watered whilst waiting for another means of transport to take them to—God knew where. For all he was a simple man, something didn't sound right and he watched the accompanying Turkish troops carefully as they fell in alongside his own men. These men's rifles were held loosely enough but they'd quietly assumed a threatening stance

'Leave your packs here, too, brothers!' a Turkish *chaoush*, a serjeant, shouted, 'It'll save you carrying them back again when your new transport arrives. Would all officers and NCO's follow me please, my men will show the rest where to go.'

'Huh! That's something new,' Nareg spoke at Artoun's elbow, 'since when did a Turk care for the lot of we *ermeni*?' Nevertheless he shifted his pack from his shoulder and dropped it gratefully on the ground. 'Come on Artoun, you heard him, there's food and water up ahead and if we're too slow those pigs from the other companies will eat it all. Come on or I'm off.'

Artoun raised a casual arm in answer. 'Go, you heard the man, we NCO's have better fare to look forward to!'

'You look just like a Turk, never mind an NCO.' Nareg jeered, 'Speak to them nicely and you'll get better food than we *ermeni*!'

Instead of taking offence, Artoun merely grinned. With his dark, swarthy looks and full moustache he could easily pass for a Turk, something his comrades had teased him with since his joining the battalion. 'On your way, *nefer*,' he grunted, 'before my boot comes into contact with your backside.'

Nareg spat disgustedly before hurrying away to the head of the column. As his friend raced off, Artoun's suspicions hardened. Just why had they stopped here of all places? Why didn't the train simply take them onto Islahiye where they'd receive the orders to march to their new destination and who had ordered this sudden change of plan? Most importantly, why separate the officers and NCO's from the others?

All these questions crowded together and he slid carefully out of sight round the back of the wagon. No-one saw him go and he carefully eased his head round the corner to watch events as they unfolded. If caught it would be easy to make an excuse of needing to relieve himself but for now he remained unseen and narrowed his eyes as he watched his friends and comrades march up the dusty track towards the quarry opening on the hillside.

While he watched, the Turkish lieutenant moved across the track, heading for a small building at the quarry's entrance. There followed a brief argument before the officers and NCO's, apart from the colonel, were taken inside and the door firmly closed with sentries left guarding the entrance.

Ahead, the long snake of soldiers wound its way slowly up the track until it disappeared out of sight over the crest of the rise and into the quarry's welcoming mouth. Artoun's breathing quickened as twenty or so of the escort hung back to bar the quarry entrance. His disquiet grew and his heart thudded wildly in his chest. What was going on, why...?

He ducked back quickly out of sight as a soldier appeared from the quarry mouth and waved his arms frantically at the locomotive. In response the locomotive's steam whistle began to shrill wildly, long loud piercing blasts that filled the desert air with sound.

Artoun reeled back at this sudden assault and, frighteningly, above the sound of the whistle a new sound reverberated, this time from the quarry, the fierce staccato stutter he recognised as that of a Maxim machine gun. It was swiftly joined by another and the air was rent with the sounds of firing interspersed with blasts from the whistle.

His legs lost their strength and he would have fallen had he not clung onto the edge of the wagon. Above the sound .of the firing he could hear the screaming and shouting of men being cut down and his stomach jumped. A loud yelling came from within the quarry building and his attention switched to that as the Turkish sentries pounded on the door with their rifles, shouting angrily at the yelling coming from inside.

The firing carried on incessantly in long bursts, *Brrrrr! Brrrrrrr! Brrrrrrrrr!* before stopping as abruptly as it had started. The steam whistle, too, stopped its demonic wailing and silence returned to the desert sands but only for a short space of time. After a pause, single shots sounded out and Artoun's horror mounted as he realised that those fortunate to have survived the slaughter were now being finished off. The sharp *cracks!* carried on for a minute before they, too, mercifully ceased.

He pulled a rag from his pocket and wiped his sweating features, as if by doing so he could wipe away the memory of the last ten minutes. He was given no time to gather himself as the body of Turks appeared from the quarry and headed purposely towards the building the officers and NCO's had been imprisoned within. Reaching it, the Turkish lieutenant harangued those inside angrily, although Artoun was too far away to hear his words.

Slowly the door opened and a face appeared. A short conversation took place before the lieutenant lunged forward and dragged the man out from the entrance, brandishing a pistol in his face. After more shouts from the armed Turkish soldiers the rest of the men inside the building appeared, exiting hesitantly in ones and twos. When the building was empty the lieutenant languidly strolled over and struck one man, an officer, in the face, screaming loud imprecations at him. Two of the guards sprang forward and pulled the man to a spot at the side of the building as, almost casually, the lieutenant raised his pistol and shot the officer through the forehead as his horrified comrades and Artoun watched.

He bit hard down on his clenched fist so as not to cry out as the corpse crumpled to the desert floor, a man Artoun recognised as Major Cazian, the regiment's Adjutant. Cazian's death was the signal for the others to die, a few at a time they were dragged forward from the main group and shot at close range. Some died praying, some pleading for their lives, all met the same end. A rifle bullet at close range before a bayonet was plunged into the corpse, the butchery continuing with no let up until all were summarily dispatched Most died silently, implacably, staring disdainfully at their executioners until the bullet tore the life from them, while others screamed hysterically until their cries were silenced forever.

As the last shot died away, Artoun saw a figure being escorted to where the corpses lay. It was Colonel Misakian and from where he was crouched Artoun could see the agony the colonel felt as he was marched over to where his men had died. A short conversation followed with much shaking of heads by both the colonel and the lieutenant before the Turkish officer strode away without a backward glance.

The colonel was pushed roughly away from the building and his uniform jacket torn brutally from him by the *chaoush*. A group of men with rifles erect stood forward and took aim at Misakian. Standing there, head held high, his braces dangling down his sides, the colonel stared at them before slowly, deliberately, turning his back on the firing party. A brief interval followed before the *chaoush* rapped out a curt order and the rifles barked as one.

Fighting the urge to release his stomach's content over the sand, Artoun knelt by the wheel of the wagon, white-faced at the barbarity he had witnessed. A shout brought him to his senses and he jerked upright, fearful at having been seen. The shout came from the lieutenant who now shepherded his men back down to the trackside.

'Leave those dogs where they lay, others will come and clean up the mess!' he shouted, 'Throw the *khanzir's*, the swine's, packs and *tufeks* into the wagons and let's get on our way. Well done, men, there'll be extra rations all round tonight.'

Surreptitiously removing his jacket with its regimental facings and dropping it behind the wheel, Artoun slid round the corner of the wagon, his pleated *kabalak* protective headgear pulled low over his face. He made a show of throwing the packs and Mauser rifles nearest to him into the depths of the empty wagon and was rewarded by a hearty wave from one of the soldiers thirty yards away who had been advancing towards him. Seeing the job ahead being carried out already, the other man turned and walked back to another wagon and began clearing the trackside there.

His work finished, Artoun eased himself over the lip and down onto the wagon's floor, hoping that no-one would see or join him. His luck held again and after more shouting and banging a silence came over the train before the jerking noise below him told of the train's onward progress. As the train picked up speed he held his head in his hands and sobbed at the violent deaths of his friends and comrades, body convulsed with tears as the train picked up speed. Nareg, oh Nareg, my dear, dead friend, what is this, what's happening, has the world gone mad? Lapsing vocally into his native Armenian tongue, one word escaped his lips. '*Inchoo?*' Why?

He waited for a portent, a sign but none came save the gentle swaying of the wagon and the humming of the rails below. Defeated, he slid back to a sitting position on the floor. Evil had come to these simple men, soldiers in their country's service who had been butchered by the very men they had served so faithfully alongside. What had led to this day of atrocity, what was behind the slaughter of so many innocents and where would it lead? What crime had they committed simply by being Armenian? True, since the Young Turks coup in taking over the government years ago things had become difficult for non-Moslems but this...?

His racing thoughts jumped quickly to his family and he shuddered. Hegine—Khat. They would need him now, his family came before all else and instantly made up his mind to quit the train when it passed near to his village and walk the remaining miles through the hills to ensure their safety.

Formulating a plan, he pressed his face into the nearest pack and tried to sleep, drained by all he'd witnessed in such a short space of time. It was a forlorn undertaking. He tossed and turned restlessly as the faces of his murdered friends and comrades made for uneasy dreams whilst the train clattered its way northwards, those disturbed thoughts drawing him ever onwards towards his home.

Stiffly, painfully Hegine regained consciousness from where she lay on a hard-packed dirt floor. A faint cry of pain escaped her lips as she tried to stand, only to find herself bound, her arms tied in front of her round the rough leg of a table. She looked around and by the moonlight spilling in through a splintered crack in the shuttered window by the door spied a crumpled heap lying under a tattered blanket on a filthy straw mattress on the floor not five feet from her.

As she watched, a loud snore rent the quiet of the room and the blanket heaved with the exertions of the invisible figure beneath. A second later silence reigned again and it was then that the full import of her ordeal struck her. Stifling a moan she took in all before her as her memory returned from the dark spaces into which she'd retreated.

Dimly she remembered the journey face down astride the horse's neck, her captor striking her roughly each time she'd cried out at the horror of it all. On reaching a village she'd been thrown to the ground like a rag doll whilst he'd emptied his side panniers of the booty he'd looted from the massacred people of her village. Satisfied everything had been unloaded he'd come back for her, picking her limp figure up and dumping it on the floor inside the hovel.

Her memory failed her in parts after that moment. She knew he had become angry at her unresponsiveness to his crude fumblings at her skirts and his sharp slaps whilst parrying her feeble attempts to stop him had developed into a full-blown beating. He'd stopped from

100

time to time to drink deeply from a wineskin before renewing his attack on her, the beating becoming more ferocious until she'd slid away into unconsciousness.

Mercifully, he'd sunk into a drunken stupor himself shortly afterwards, the drink rendering him unable to violate her but not before he had given her a few more angry blows and tied her hands round the leg of the table. Now, fully and painfully awake, she pulled experimentally at the table leg but it was too solid and the table too heavy to budge. The rope looked her better option and she began picking at the knots with increased urgency.

Her head and sides ached but she worked on, terrified he would waken and begin a fresh assault on her, one she knew she'd be unable to resist this time. The snoring from beneath the blanket carried on at regular intervals, causing her heart to lurch but she bent and twisted the knots frantically as she tried to loosen them.

Eventually, hardly daring to believe it, she felt the rope sag slightly and her hands and fingers picked up speed as she pushed and pulled at it. The knots loosened by the second until it released its grip on her hands to fall limply at her side. Blood pounded through her head and she eased herself slowly from the table and made her way softly to the door. The blackness of the night offered her no assistance as she groped her way forward but she reached the door eventually and her hands twisted the handle this way and that before stopping, dropping in anguish to her sides. The door was locked.

She turned back into the room; defeat a sour taste in her mouth. The beast would wake soon and the terror begin anew. Stifling a sob she backed up against the door, watching the blanket and the still figure with terrified eyes. Khat sprang unbidden into her mind and she summoned every mental facet of her being in reaching out across the miles to touch her son but felt no answering contact, no spark, only the coldness of a wind blowing across the icy mountains. Khat was lost to her, she knew it. Her beautiful son, the very essence of her love for Artoun Seferian lay somewhere lifeless in the scrub, his remains an invitation to the scavengers of the night. The awfulness of that revelation almost unhinged her and she looked desperately round.

A low moan escaped her lips and she clapped her hand tightly across her mouth lest she wake the man under the blanket. Making her way softly to the table, she strained to see what it held. Something gleamed in the dim light and she felt the cold embrace of a long, sharp knife which she drew towards her. The handle fitted her hand perfectly, a comfortable feel in her grip and she dropped to the floor and began to crawl towards the blanket.

He slept on in his drunken dreams, unconscious of her presence, a stale stench of wine surrounding him like a halo as she softly peeled back the blanket. His eyes were firmly closed, a faint hiss of foul breath escaping his lips as he arched his unshaven face and neck to find a more comfortable sleeping position. She reached out hesitantly, cupped her free hand near his mouth and strengthened her grip on the knife. '

'*Whaaaa-aarrcccch*...!' The blade slid easily, deeply, across his windpipe and she pushed his head hastily away from her as hot blood spurted out under great pressure, spattering the wall and her hands. His one good eye opened wildly and both hands beat feebly against her body while the blood continued to spurt in great gouts, a fountain pulsing with the failing beats of his heart and the falling note of his gargled, choked breath.

She almost threw up from the copper stench of fresh blood but controlled her breathing and sat panting on the floor a few feet from the twitching corpse, wiping her blood-stained hands on the folds of her skirt. Clutching the knife to her body she padded over to the window. No cries of alarm from outside reached her ears and she turned back to drag the table over to the window.

The weight of it nearly defeated her but eventually she pushed it to a position where she could look out through the crack in the shutters and up to where the stars twinkled high above her in the firmament. Forgive me, Artoun, darling, light of my life. Pray for me, for Khat your son. She took a firm hold and placed the knife handle down on the top of the table. Arching her head and fixing her eyes steadily on the nearest star she bent over the table, felt with her other hand for the left side of her chest and positioned it over the knife's sharp point.

Mentally she sought the comfort of her son's arms around her once more and as she did so, relaxed to let her body slide down onto the knife. A sharp, fleeting moment of agony and she would once again feel Khat's embrace, a pain she would willingly endure to salve that of losing him. The blade wavered and she paused.

'Oh my son, forgive me, I cannot.' she whispered, tears filling her eyes. The knife dropped to the hard-packed floor as her body was racked with sobs. Artoun. What would become of him, how would he live with the loss of his loved ones? How could she be so selfish as to leave him alone in the world without her love to protect and keep *him* safe? He would need her, more than ever now if their beloved child was indeed lost to them and these thoughts strengthened her resolve. Deep within her breast a faint hope grew that somehow, miraculously perhaps, Khat had survived and even now was lying in hiding, waiting for her to return and sweep him into her arms.

Wiping her eyes she rose and made a search of the hovel. In one corner of the darkened room a crumpled heap of discarded clothing lay on the floor and she looked at it speculatively before unpinning her skirts and slip. Letting them fall to the floor she extricated a pair of rough trousers from the heap and wriggled into them whilst trying not to gag at the smell. They were too loose but she tore a strip from her slip and fixed them tightly to her satisfaction. A filthy cotton coat, hooded and deeply-stained, hung on a peg on the door and she shrugged into it and drew it close.

The smell of sweat almost overwhelmed her but she moved more comfortably within its depths and made a careful survey of the room for foodstuffs. There was very little, the spoils of the massacre he'd brought with him held no food and all she found in a box were some rancid vegetables but she stuffed them into a pocket and continued to search. She found nothing more of value to her and looked back to where the dead man lay.

The corpse lay unmoving in the moonlight and she walked slowly over to his stiffening body. His boots looked worn but she sat down, cross-legged, and tugged them off, averting her eyes from his face as she did so. Breathing hard she completed the task and drew them on. They were far too loose so more of her slip was ripped into bindings wrapped round her feet before she tentatively tried them on again. This time they were a tighter fit and she grunted in satisfaction.

That left only the door. A few seconds in pulling and tugging was sufficient to enlighten her, there would be no escape from this avenue and she looked across to the window in desperation. Moving the table that was now blocking any attempt to open the warped wooden shutters she lifted the latch and pushed hard. They failed to open under her administrations and she ran back to where the knife lay and retraced her steps. Wedging the blade into the gap between the latch and the locking frame she dug deeply into the wood.

Something gave and she staggered back suddenly as the blade broke. Heartened, she moved back to the window and pushed once more. This time it moved slightly and that spurred her on. Holding her breath and leaning against the frame she pushed mightily and was rewarded by a low squeaking noise as the shutters, freed from years of grime, slowly gave way and opened a fraction. After several more minutes of effort it widened still further and taking a last look round she moved the table back against the opening and climbed up. Turning round, Hegine pushed her legs out of the window and dropped lightly onto the dirt outside.

She stood for a moment, listening intently for noises coming from the houses around her. Nothing but the faint sighing of the night breeze reached her ears and she eased away from the cover of the house and began to walk quietly into the darkness's cloak. Before pulling the coat's hood up over her hair to disguise her outline she took a long look at the sky, seeking a direction from the stars.

Over her head the stars twinkled coldly and she squinted hard and tried to mentally picture how they had appeared from the sanctuary of her own back door. She moved the image around in her head, making an overlay and nodded as the two intertwined. South, she should head south for a while, that should take her back to where the bandits had robbed and killed her fellow villagers and where she had last seen her son.

As his face flashed before her she shuddered, suddenly feeling very cold. Khat may lie out there, somewhere, discarded like unwanted rubbish and she resolved to find him. No matter what, she would not leave her son alone for the wild animals to find. If the worst *had* happened she, Hegine Seferian, would discover his last resting place and give him a mother's love and a proper burial. The thought comforted her and she moved off with a fresh purpose.

Somewhere in the darkness dogs barked but the noise was soon left behind and she heard no sounds of pursuit. She needed to move quickly, the discovery of the body in the morning would bring avengers out looking for her and any distance between her and the village would greatly increase her chances of survival. Her feet slipped within the confines of the ill-fitting boots but she put her head down and grimly walked on through the night.

Within minutes she'd crossed a track leading in the right direction and she paralleled it from the cover of bordering trees. A mile or so down the track she came to a stream and stopped abruptly. Dimly, she remembered being splashed by water as the horse upon whose back she was being carried had cantered through water and she nodded. This confirmed her earlier decision to head south and it gave her heart to know she was heading in the right direction. Ignoring the cold shock of the water she ploughed across the stream and emptied her boots on the other side before steadfastly continuing.

An hour later she heard a faint drumming sound and spun round. Silhouetted against the night sky and drawing closer with every second was a dark mass heading her way at speed. Fear lent her wings; without a moment's hesitation she threw herself into the safety of a large bush and drew the coat's hood over her face. The shapeless mass of the coat together with its multi-coloured stains made a perfect camouflage, cloaking her in darkness and the stern-looking body of horsemen clattered past without giving her hiding-place a second glance. When she was certain they'd gone she stood up and commenced her march.

Hegine walked through the night without faltering, weary but filled with a grim determination to reach the site of the massacre and find Khat. A light overhead flashed across the sky and she watched the progress of the falling star with renewed hope and vigour. It was a portent telling her of Khat's survival, she decided, and carried on walking with a grim determination.

Several times she heard rustling in the undergrowth around her but kept to her pace without faltering and was relieved when the noises faded behind her. At one point she tripped over a large branch and after gaining her feet used it as a walking stick, planting it firmly ahead of her and pulling herself towards it.

Dawn rose slowly, the shadows of the night surrendering reluctantly to the rising sun and she exulted to feel its warming rays on her tired features. The track petered out in a large, wide expanse of featureless sand, the same volcanic sand they'd struggled through on leaving the safety of their own village and she looked round helplessly for clues. To her left a welter of hoof prints showed up starkly against the soil and she ran gratefully over to it before following them into the sand. The breeze blew stray tendrils of sand over the boots as she walked but she made her way determinedly along the scrapes and signs of the horse's passage.

Not knowing why, her eyes were drawn upwards and forwards to the horizon where a number of vultures wheeled slowly, black silhouettes against the blue of the sky and her heart leapt.

Floundering through the sand she struggled in the direction of the birds, her breath escaping in large gasps as she tried to make some headway through the cloying embrace of the desert soil. A raging thirst grew but she pushed her desire to drink and the resultant pangs of hunger that accompanied those thoughts to the back of her mind. Let her find what had become of Khat and then she could attend to her body's demands but not now, not when she was so close to him.

After an hour of hard, physical effort she came to a rise in the ground and it took several long minutes before, finally, standing atop the dune she looked keenly around. A mile or so away in the distance flashes of colour danced, alien sights in the drab olive and brown of the desert and she dropped down the other side of the dune and headed in that direction. The overhead sun burnt her hair and she placed the hood back over her head, accepting the increase in expended energy and her thirst in return for relief from the sun's rays.

After an age she reached what looked like thin scraps of torn clothing caught in the thorn of the scrub clinging to the valley floor. None of it was recognisable and she continued to walk on. A marbled object draped over one hump caught her eye and she moved towards it, recoiling violently as she realised it was a severed arm with bloodied strips of withered flesh and tendons hanging from the bone.

Her hand moved automatically to her mouth and she swallowed hard. Moving gingerly to one side, avoiding the sight of slash marks on the limb, she continued to glance around her. A frenzied throng of vultures rose flapping upwards, screeching their annoyance, and she hurried past the shredded corpse they'd been busily consuming before resuming searching.

A dry, musty smell overpowered her olfactory senses and she knew that she'd reached the epicentre of this place of death as more and more ripped and torn remains of bloated torsos came into view. All had been stripped of their clothing by the bandits before the birds had ravaged them but the odour and sight of the white, bloodless limbs and numerous bones filled her with an overpowering sense of nausea and this time her stomach failed her and she fell to her knees and retched helplessly into the sand.

When she'd recovered she rose, using the branch and once on her feet leant heavily on it as she looked around and tried to make sense of the ground and where she thought her and Khat had been parted. Tears of frustration filled Hegine's eyes as nothing looked familiar, those frantic, fearful minutes of the massacre had robbed her of any sense of direction and her heart sank. Far away, faintly on the wind she heard the word *mayrig* (mother) and spun round with renewed hope.

'Khat,' she murmured brokenly, stopping to listen intently but nothing reached her ears save the sighing of the breeze and squawking of the fractious birds. A white rag fluttered some distance away and she ran over to it eagerly but it held no trace of him and her spirits dropped. Turning away, she would have walked from the scene but something held her there, a faint foreboding, and she walked past the rag to a large hummock and climbed it before looking down.

There, huddled against the soil at its base was a small shape and though she could not tell for certain by looking down from her lofty position, in her heart she knew she was staring at the remains of her son. She slid down the hummock and landed next to the pitiful remains, those of a small child.

He lay fully-clothed with knees drawn up in a protective position, hands crossed against his face as if asleep and she carefully prised his small arms apart and looked deeply into the empty eyes of her dead son. The back of his skull had been crushed like an eggshell and though the birds had miraculously left him alone, no doubt for bigger, juicier prey, nevertheless she caught a sharp, acrid tang of deteriorating flesh and knew instinctively that the onset of putrefaction had already begun.

Gently she cradled her son's remains in her arms, laid down with him and wept for the loss of his innocence. She broke down, keening as she recalled his birth, the years of his infancy and the promise of better things to come that her and Artoun had wished for. Crooning softly, she continued to hold him and as the reservoir of her tears emptied, told him of her love and how she would forever grieve for the life together that now could never be. His dead eyes held a vacant, fixed stare and she wished she could join with him on the journey he had now embarked on. Looking at him, Hegine realised with a terrible finality that almost unhinged her that Khat must face that journey without her.

Somewhere, she knew not where, Artoun her husband still held them in his heart and when he discovered the awful truth of his beloved son's death he would need her more than ever. A fierce determination welled within, she had to be strong for Artoun's sake and that meant living, not dying, welcoming though the latter might seem at this moment.

She lay there and slept with Khat in her arms for a while but at last rose and cast round for a small implement to aid in digging. The edge of a wooden box peeped up amidst scattered rags and she pulled it free before returning to where Khat lay. Digging methodically, tiring quickly but resuming her task after resting for several moments, a large, shallow hole was soon fashioned from her efforts and she bound strips of rags around her son's face and hands. Her last act was to remove and pocket the thin silver chain from around his neck that Artoun had purchased for him from a travelling merchant before reverently lowering Khat into his make-shift grave.

It took even longer to pack the earth around him but at last it was finished and she stood above the disturbed earth and wept again. There were no stones at hand to place over the ground and keep the jackals away but she hoped there would be enough in the immediate area for them to leave Khat's resting place alone. Hegine placed a small green piece of scrub tenderly in the centre of his grave before taking one last look and reluctantly walking away; there would be time to grieve properly when she and Artoun were together again but for now this would have to do.

As she walked away she recognised the torn remains of the blanket she'd worn over her shoulder when they'd left the village under the soldier's guard and bent to pick it up. The food was gone but from within the tattered strips the water skin flopped down onto the ground and she picked it up eagerly, aware for the first time in hours how thirsty she was. Shaking it vigorously she was heartened to hear the contents sloshing around inside and pulled the stopper from the top before drinking greedily.

The water was tepid but in her dehydrated state it tasted like nectar and she had to stop herself consuming the entire contents there and then. It was at least two days walk back to the village and she would need all her luck and what water she could find or carry to make it without being discovered. Slinging the skin over her shoulder she walked away, turning every now and then to look back at the spot where she'd buried her son.

It was growing dark again and the stars beckoned eagerly so she responded to their invitation and began walking with a purpose in the direction she knew her home village and house lay. When night overtook her she walked on for some distance in the gloom but soon succumbed to an overwhelming tiredness. Lying down on the hard ground, she wrapped herself in the depths of the stolen coat and slept, an image of her son's face uppermost in her mind.

--§--

Nothing disturbed her and she slept fitfully, the hard ground and her troubled thoughts of Khat and Artoun making sleep an uneasy experience. In the coldness of dawn she woke early and stretched stiffly before rising and making a small meal of the vegetables she'd looted from the bandit's house. After packing the remains in a pocket and taking a small sip of water to slake her thirst she began to walk again. She walked all day with few halts, conscious of a burning desire to find the sanctuary she was seeking. The land seemed devoid of human existence and she saw or heard no-one as she marched along, stopping every now and then to look behind her to look and listen for any sight or sounds of pursuit.

To the north a tendril of smoke rose lazily into the sky and she stared hard in that direction. Nothing stirred through the shimmering heat haze and after a while she resumed her solitary journey, satisfied that any pursuit was nowhere near her. A mental image of the bandits discovering their comrade's ripped throat afforded her a feeling of grim satisfaction but she swiftly quelled the thought and plodded on.

Eventually, at the end of the second day, as a roseate glow of evening shone on the landscape she wearily crested a hill and looked down on her village. A thin finger of smoke rose up from one of the chimneys and she dropped swiftly to the ground before cautiously looking over the brow. A small child ran from one of the houses calling excitedly and she frowned. What was this? The village had been emptied by the soldiers and had consisted solely of Armenian families so where had this child come from? Did its presence mean that Moslems had found the deserted houses already and come to take their fill of the plunder?

Under her questioning glance, another child ran out and the two children began to scurry around at play until a woman wearing a white shawl over her dark dress appeared at the doorway of the house and called sharply to them. They ran immediately to her and disappeared inside, leaving Hegine perplexed. She watched for a while longer but no-one else appeared and scanning the other houses saw no signs of habitation. Satisfied there were no soldiers in the vicinity she eased herself down the hill and walked into the village.

No dogs barked to warn of her presence, an eerie silence was all that preceded her slow progress down the street to her house and when at last she reached it and stood outside the doorway all she could hear was her own heartbeat. She placed a faltering step forward, prior to entering.

'Mama!'

A small voice split the silence and her tautened nerves snapped. She leant against the doorway for support, blood pounding in her ears as a young girl in a tattered, filthy dress of indiscernible colour appeared suddenly, staring at her wide-eyed.

'Elise, where are you?' A woman's voice sounded frantically and from the house opposite a young woman rushed into the street. 'What have I told you, don't stray without your brother. I'll…Oh!' She stopped and her face took on a fearful look as she spied Hegine. Rushing over she swept the child into her arms and continued to stare. Both women's eyes locked as they regarded each other and it was the stranger who turned to back away.

Hegine put a restraining hand out. 'Please, don't. Who are you? You're *ermeni*, aren't you? What are you doing here?'

The young woman turned back to Hegine. 'I thought…I thought you were the soldiers. My children. We…it…'

Soothingly, Hegine spoke. 'Look at me, do I look like a soldier? I have an idea I'm like you, hiding from the military but I belong here, this village is my home. And you, where have you come from?'

The woman relaxed and placed the child on the ground. 'I'm …*Shhh*, Elise, let mama speak. Go and bring Jan here, go, go and get your brother.' The child stopped trying to speak and ran into the house opposite, returning seconds later with a younger child in tow, a boy this time. Together the children walked warily over to where the women stood. Jan, the boy, ran round the back of his mother and peeped shyly at Hegine from the folds of his mother's skirt as she addressed Hegine.

'My name is Marem, Marem Abalian and I live, or at least I did live in a village to the east of here. Three days ago the village was invaded by soldiers and we were told to march away with them. We were neither told why nor allowed to take anything with us and they killed several of the villagers as we walked, for the most trivial of excuses.' She broke off and tears welled in her eyes before she could continue.

'I got scared that something bad was going to happen and two nights ago, when we camped and everyone was asleep, I told the children we were going to play a game. We were to sneak past the guards without a sound and—'

'We did too! And mama gave me a big hug for it and told me I was—'

'Yes, yes, Jan, let mama finish, there's a good boy.' She carried on speaking rapidly, the words tumbling from her mouth. 'We got away and made our way over the hills behind you and found this place. It was deserted and we were hungry and thirsty so I thought we could rest here a while before we…I, decided what to do next. I did wonder where everyone had gone but saw no harm in resting here a while with the children. And you? What of you?'

Hegine gathered her thoughts before she answered. 'We befell the same fate as you; the soldiers arrived and marched us away into the desert. You were right, it *was* bad what they had in store for you. Bandits arrived and slaughtered all but the young girls and women, carrying them off and robbing the dead of their possessions. I, too, was captured but managed to kill my captor and make my way back here.' A picture of Khat filled her mind and her voice faltered.

Marem Abalian leant forward, a look of concern on her face. 'It's alright, you don't have to tell me everything now.' she said, softly.

'No, thank you, Marem, I will tell you, if you can bear to listen.' In a low voice Hegine completed her tale, recounting Khat's death and her discovery of his body after she'd escaped. Both women's eyes filled with tears as she recounted her story whilst the children looked on with wondering eyes at their mother's distress.

When she'd finished speaking, Marem reached over impulsively and hugged Hegine as she cried softly into the folds of the young woman's blouse. 'There, there, it's alright. You poor thing, come with us into this house and let's see what we can find to soothe you with. God has kept you safe for a purpose. He—'

Hegine straightened, pulling away from the young woman's embrace. 'Thank you, Marem, for those kind words but…God? Where is the God I prayed to save us when my son was murdered? Where was that God when my village was torn from its roots and forced into the desert to be butchered like a tethered goat? The past few days have seemed like a nightmare but I know it's real, I need no prayers to tell me that God saved me for a purpose. God is gone, he longer lives here. Khat, my son, is gone too and all I have now to keep me going is my husband, Artoun. He's with the army at present but will return one day and I must be here to greet him.' A thought struck her and she looked askance at Marem Abalian.

'Your husband. Is he in the army also?'

It was the other woman's turn to look downcast. 'No,' she replied sorrowfully, 'my husband, Tajat, died several months ago, of the sickness. We couldn't afford to pay for a doctor so he died.' Her eyes filled now and Hegine took her arm.

'We've both known tragedy, Marem, you've lost your husband and I a son. Come, let me take you into *my* house, Hegine Seferian's house, and together we'll see what is to become of us. If those bandits haven't robbed us blind there should be some chicken feed left and I'll put it out. The chickens will come back soon, you see, and we'll all have fresh eggs for the morning.

As for today, let me rest for a while and then we'll go round all the houses before it gets dark and see if there's any dry food we can use. The children can draw water from the well while we search. Between us we should be able to build a store of foodstuffs and later tomorrow we can go into the hills and seek out any of the livestock that's up there. They won't have gone far and there's plenty of grass for them. The goats should bring fresh milk and we can always slaughter one for meat.'

Marem lowered her voice. 'I can't ask the children to fetch water. There are…bodies lying in the square. And a hanged man dangling from a tree.'

Hegine blanched. 'Of course, I'm sorry, I forgot. They hanged our *Naib* and Pastor Kazazian when they arrived as a warning to make us obey them and killed some others for not being quick enough to make ready. We'll put the children out to play at the opposite end of the village, tell them to watch for strangers while we bury those poor unfortunates.' She laughed grimly. 'You see? It takes more than a bunch of renegade Turks to see off a determined *ermeni* woman. Our men might think they rule the roost in their houses but we know the real truth, eh, Marem Abalian?'

In spite of herself, Marem allowed a smile to crease her face. 'But what about the soldiers, what if they come back? Won't they just…?'

'Shh! Don't scare the children. Come, let's make a start.'

'Hegine! Look!'

Hegine followed Marem's shaking finger and her eyes narrowed. Sitting in the dust not ten feet from her, its eyes fixed on her was a large, black dog. It must have sneaked up unseen whilst they were talking and now it watched them both. She moved slightly and the dog's eyes followed her movements, unwavering and unblinking. Marem started forward and the dog growled, a low rumbling noise rising up from its throat. Around its neck hung the chewed remains of a halter and as she watched, Hegine saw the hackles on its neck rise and knew that if the woman next to her moved again the dog would strike.

'Marem,' she said as calmly as she could, 'don't move, if you frighten the dog he'll attack you. Sit there and try not to scare it.'

'Scare it? It's me that's terrified! Look at it, look at those teeth! It could—'

'Hush! The poor thing's probably as scared as we are and I don't doubt, as hungry too. Wait! I know this dog. It belonged to the baker, Kachadorian. What was it he called it...? No, I think...'

'Hegine, for God's sake hurry up and remember, it's starting to crawl towards me!'

There was sheer terror in Marem's voice and Hegine struggled to plumb the depths of her memory.

'I know, I remember, he called it *Oğlan*. It's Turkish for *boy*. That's what he called it.'

At the mention of its name the dog's ears twitched and it stopped and looked back towards Hegine, hackles relaxed and whining softly. She laughed delightedly.

'You see, it's just a big, soft thing, it needs a friend. *Oğlan*, come here!'

Obediently, the dog rose from its haunches and trotted over to her, lowering its massive head and allowing her to bury her fingers in the thickness of its mane. A low, contented rumbling issued from its mouth and it pressed harder against her.

'Look, Marem, we've got a friend now. He'll make a good sentry for us and a protector for the children. Come, let's find that food I mentioned and give this new addition of ours a drink and his supper.'

'Huh!' Marem walked nervously over to Hegine, looking sideways at the dog. He lifted his head to inspect her and after staring closely, closed his eyes and bent back to Hegine's administrations. 'Just don't ask me to pet him, Hegine, I still value my fingers.'

Chapter Six.

Anatolia, Turkey.

He woke suddenly, bathed in sweat and looked round wildly before becoming aware of his surroundings. A cold shadow had crawled across his heart and Artoun Seferian shuddered at the dark edges it had left on his memory before scrabbling to the wagon's side and taking a careful peep. Across the blackness of nightfall a few lights flickered but gave him no clue as to his whereabouts. He crawled back to his resting place and began searching through the packs of the dead men he'd left far behind as the train thundered onwards.

Food was what he was looking for, food and water bottles but though he discovered plenty of the latter he was unable to fill his pockets with much in the way of anything edible. A few stale biscuits and some rancid cheese was the sum total of his search but he stuffed the pieces into his trouser pockets and pulled the straps of several water-bottles over his shoulder.

By his reckoning they would arrive in Islahiye soon so he eased himself carefully over the side of the wagon and held on until the train slowed momentarily to negotiate a bend before letting himself drop onto the ground. Although the speed was negligible he hit the ground hard and rolled three or four times before coming to a stop. Winded, he raised himself to a sitting position but no cry of discovery followed his exit and the train clattered serenely out of sight, leaving him alone.

He sat in this position for some time, gathering his thoughts and his strength. Eventually he dragged himself to his feet and began walking. As he walked he thought of Hegine and Khat. They would have to leave the village, word would soon reach the authorities of his arrival and questions would be asked that could lead to severe consequences. No, better they left in the night without anyone seeing him and make a fresh start elsewhere, if such a thing were possible in these troubled times.

He had his carpentry and metalworking skills to back him up and there must be someone looking for a village carpenter and blacksmith. Buoyed up by these positive thoughts he strode on, feeling more at peace as he thought of holding his son and wife in his arms once again. The horror of a few hours ago was still foremost in his mind but by concentrating on his family he was able to push the dark scenes to the back of his thoughts.

114

Dawn was breaking when he spied a wisp of smoke in the distance and worked his way carefully through the sparse trees to where he could observe without fear of being discovered. A stone farmhouse loomed out of the grey, positioned on the edge of some tilled fields and he carefully slid round to the back of the building. A line of washing hanging inert in the stillness of the dawn caught his eyes and he ran quietly over and scanned the clothing. A tattered blue shirt flapped feebly by its sleeves and he pulled it from the line before turning away. By the back door he saw a line of footwear and ventured closer, picking up a worn pair of leather sandals.

A low growling from inside the building made him start and he held his breath. The growling turned to a fierce snarling and from the depths of the farmhouse he could hear a man's sleepy voice cursing the dog before a yelp ended the animal's interest in him. Gratefully, Artoun returned the way he'd come and walked away with a quickened pace. When he judged he was far enough from the scene of his crime he unrolled his puttees, tore off his army issue shirt and wrapped the two garments together before thrusting them under some large stones.

The shirt was a tight fit but he buttoned it and left it hanging freely. In this way it covered the top of his issue trousers, a sure giveaway. The sandals pinched his feet but they were better than nothing so his army boots followed the rest of his other clothing. Satisfied by the change to his appearance he walked on with a growing confidence.

The sun rose towards its overhead position in the sky and he ate a piece of stale cheese and took a grateful swig from one of the water-bottles as he stood by a crossroads in the track. To his left were more tilled fields and in the distance he could discern some buildings whilst to his right was just sparse scrub and stunted trees leading upwards into the hills. His mind told him to turn left and as he did so a voice called out in Turkish and he froze.

'*Orade dur*! Stand still there!'

He turned slowly and his heart sank. Ambling slowly towards him from the opposite direction, rifles at the ready were three Turkish soldiers and a mounted officer with drawn pistol. His mind raced as he tried to fix a story in his head. Assuming a welcoming smile he walked back down the track to meet them. The nearest private lifted his rifle and snarled.

'*Nereden geliyürsiniz*? Where have you come from?'

Artoun gestured dumbly over his shoulder, pointing in the opposite direction the soldier's had appeared from.

'*Yalan söüliyorsiniz!* You're lying!'

Before Artoun could answer, the officer leaned over the neck of his small black pony. 'Be a good fellow and please answer the *nefer's* question truthfully,' he said almost pleasantly, 'or I shall be forced to flog you here and now. Where have you come from? Don't lie, I shall know if you do and it will cause you much pain, my brother.'

Throwing himself to the ground, Artoun pressed his face into the dirt and whined, '*Efendim*, I am just a poor farmer in search of work...'

'Oh dear,' the lieutenant sighed, 'now I know you're lying, there are no poor farmers round here, not with the prices they charge to supply the army. And those water-bottles, they look like army issue to me. No, this is a serious matter. I'm afraid. Kayaoglu, bind this man tight, we'll take him to meet the captain.'

Hearing his name the nearest *nefer* dropped his rifle and sprang forward. Taking some twine from his pocket he roughly forced Artoun's hands behind his back and bound them tight. Placing themselves around him the three privates marched off behind their officer, a slow pace that Artoun was grateful to be able to match. As they marched along he thought frantically of a story that would hold water or at least cause them to think before they condemned him out of hand.

No-one spoke, the silence broken only by the wheezing of their breath and the jingling of the pony's harness. An hours marching brought them to a small village of a dozen or so houses. In the centre of the village a figure in shirtsleeves sat in the shade beside a small table and it was to him the men marched up to. Sliding to a halt the lieutenant threw a diffident salute and cried.

'Captain sir, I have the honour to present you with this suspect we found walking in the hills.'

'Yes, yes, lieutenant,' the captain answered in a bored manner stirring the plate of stew in front of him and sipping from a glass of hot tea, 'another ferocious bandit no doubt. You! Name?'

Artoun was taken by surprise. 'What...?'

'Are you deaf? Name!'

He thought furiously. To admit to being Armenian now would be a certain death sentence. Oblivion beckoned.

'*Efendim*,' he tried to screw a pitiful look on his face as his mind raced. 'I, that is…Yilmaz. Seref Yilmaz.'

'Well, Seref Yilmaz, if that is your real name, what were you doing out there in the hills to cause my men to bring you in?'

'Please, *efendim*, I am just a poor farmer looking for work. I was walking from village to village to see if I could find work and food when your men found me and brought me here. You see, I am…'

'Silence!' the captain thundered, rising to his feet, eyes hardened in temper. 'Do you take me for a half-wit? Open your shirt!'

'My shirt, *efendim*?'

'Question my orders once more and I shall have you shot for your insolence, you dog. Open your shirt, now!!!'

Artoun unbuttoned the shirt quickly with fumbling, trembling fingers and stood stock still as the captain rounded the table and flicked the shirt open with a short horse whip he'd picked up from the table. The captain spoke over his shoulder to the lieutenant.

'Good work, Kemal.' He turned back to Artoun. 'Those are army trousers if I'm not mistaken, you're no farmer, just another filthy deserter who would let your comrades die in your unworthy place. The sort of scum we've been searching these hills for over the last week.'

'Please, *ef…Aaaah!*' Artoun reeled back in agony as the whip slashed across his cheek.

'Which battalion did you run away from? Answer me!'

Artoun said nothing, his face burning, head hung low.

'I won't ask again. Which battalion did you abscond from, you scum?'

Artoun raised his head and looked defiantly at the captain, face blank and lips thinly compressed.

The captain's face turned a mottled red, his moustache quivering violently as he confronted Artoun's dumb insolence and he raised the whip again. Gradually the fire died in his eyes and he lowered the whip before continuing calmly. 'Lieutenant Kemal, how many does that make now?'

'Fifteen, sir, with this swine.' The lieutenant answered hurriedly.

'Good. That's enough for one week. I for one am tired of the smell of shit in my nostrils. We'll march to the track just north of Osmaniye with our captives tomorrow and catch a train for Konia. His Excellency, Colonel Osman, can then decide what to do with them.

Put this one with the others, give them bread and some water, after all, we are merciful and we'll all take it easy for the rest of the day.'

Artoun was roughly marched to the dusty wooden doorway of a barn-like structure and the door unbarred. His bonds were untied and he was pushed inside, the door closing with a solid thud! His heart gave praise to the fact that his swarthy, tanned features had passed the test of being taken for a Turk, his late friends in the regiment had always ribbed him that he didn't look like a true Armenian and now he was grateful for that very fact.

In the dim light inside the building he made out several forms lying on a thin covering of straw. The atmosphere was humid and stank of musty grass, together with the rank smell of unwashed bodies and human waste. He gagged and coughed as his lungs reacted in protest at the acrid taste. A rustling sound came from his right and he jumped involuntarily as a hand grabbed at his ankle.

'Water, for the love of *Allah*, brother. Please, give me water.'

'I'm sorry. I'm a *yessir*, a prisoner like yourself.' he spoke in a hushed tone, 'I have nothing but the officer said they'd bring bread and water soon.'

A dry laugh rose from the darkness. 'And you believed those turds? You'll soon learn, my friend, not to believe a word those sons of Satan say. In their eyes we have forfeited any right to live. If it were not for their fear of *Mirilai* Osman in Konia they'd have slit our throats and returned to the comforts of their barracks days ago.'

'Is he that bad, this Osman?' Artoun asked hesitantly.

'We'll all find out soon. If he doesn't...'

The conversation was halted with the opening of the front door. A hand appeared and hastily threw in a scattering of crusts before withdrawing. A second later a large waterskin was also thrown onto the floor before the door was pulled shut again.

'My friend, my apologies, you spoke the truth. Quick, move before we lose out!' the voice from the darkness commanded and Artoun found himself scrabbling across the floor towards the door. Sounds from the darkness told of other bodies in the building and the floor was soon covered by a mass of heaving humanity as the other captives fought and cursed in their attempt to find the crusts that had been thrown in.

Artoun's hand found one piece and he pushed backwards through the throng and found an upright pole in the centre of the building where he sat and gnawed at the bread. It was stale and smelled of mould but he ate hungrily, being the first food he'd had since the morning.

'Here,' the voice spoke again from the gloom, 'quickly, take a drink.'

Gratefully Artoun took the proffered waterskin and drank deeply before handing it back. His companion did the same before throwing it towards the door. A fresh commotion took place as the others fought over this new gift of life and the voice chuckled softly as its owner watched the fray.

'Fools, they'll soon wish they were dead.'

'Why do you say that?' Artoun demanded.

'Because it's true. You'll find out when we're hauled up before the colonel.'

'But I'm just a poor farmer, caught up in some terrible mistake...'

'Yes, yes, and I'm the fucking Caliph of Medina!' the voice answered sarcastically. 'Look, friend, we're all here because we deserted, scarpered to avoid going to the front. Don't lie, you wouldn't be here if they didn't take you for a deserter. My name's Arif, Arif Bilgili, by the way, late of the 18th Battalion. And from which *farm* did you escape, my friend?'

Artoun framed an indignant reply but the dry humour in Arif Bilgili's voice made him laugh instead. When the moment had passed he spoke quietly. 'Yilmaz Izmiroglu. Let's just say I went into enforced retirement.'

'Have it your own way, Yilmaz, son of Izmir,' Arif grunted, 'and now, try and get some rest. It might be your last for some time.' He turned over and burrowed down into the musty straw and within seconds was snoring loudly. Thoughtfully, Artoun joined him, in spite of the heat he felt cold with only a shirt on and he was glad to gather a handful or two of the straw and wrap it round himself.

The rest of the day passed slowly and as he lay back and tried to doze the scene at the quarry kept repeating itself over and over in his mind, the sound of the machine-guns, the screams of his friends and the final outrage when the officers and NCO's were murdered in front of his disbelieving eyes. Sleep was a long time in coming and when it did he thrashed around restlessly. All around him in the darkness, bodies moved, men coughed, spat and whispered cautiously amongst themselves. No-one bothered him and he lay there with his vivid memories ever-present throughout the long night.

'Up! Get up you swine!' A loud voice pierced his consciousness and he struggled into wakefulness. Opening his eyes he peered blearily at the commotion by the door where two armed *nefers* stood, bayonets fixed as they shouted at the sleeping men. Looking round in the gathering light, Artoun saw other mounds of straw heave as the men beneath struggled to their feet, stretching cramped limbs and yawning copiously.

'Yilmaz?'

Artoun turned with a start to contemplate the figure at his side. He saw a wizened face, a large moustache and thinning hair. The rest of the man's body was hidden under a long, shapeless robe which reached to his ankles as he stuck his hand out and grinned wryly. 'Arif Bilgili. Ah, I see you too have met the captain's whip.'

Artoun returned the grin and rubbed the weal on his cheek before shaking Bilgili's proffered hand vigorously. Before he could speak a hidden voice roared out. 'Get those bastards over here, now!' The soldiers waved their rifles menacingly and everyone moved towards the door in obedience. As each man passed through the door his hands were bound and linked to a long piece of rope that joined them all into one long string. When all were joined in this manner they were pushed down the track to where the other soldiers and both mounted officers waited impatiently in the dawn of a watery sun.

At a signal they moved off, the other soldiers taking up a watchful position around the captives, the officers leading. In this way they passed out of the village and along the road, heading north. The sun climbed higher overhead and it was near midday when they came across the railway line. Here the captain gestured them to halt and everyone, soldiers included, subsided gratefully to the ground whilst they waited. Any attempts at conversation attracted a swift blow from a rifle butt so Artoun lay low and conserved his energy.

A thrumming of the tracks told of the train's approach long before it appeared round a bend in the distance and Lieutenant Kemal rose to walk into the centre of the track, waving his arms imperiously. The train, each freight car crammed with soldiers, puffed slowly to a stop, black smoke belching from the locomotive whilst its driver leaned from his cab and shouted angrily at the soldier barring his way. A heated conversation ensued before an old uniformed conductor angrily dismounted and led the party along the track to a freight car at the rear of the train. Conscious of the enquiring glances from those soldiers who leaned out of the windows to gape at their passing, no-one spoke.

The freight car door opened with a squeaking, grinding noise of dry rollers and planks of wood were swung down to allow the officer's ponies to be led docilely up into the interior. The captives followed, escorted by the soldiers whilst the two officers accompanied the conductor back to the body of the train. A short blast of the whistle and they were on their way.

The journey seemed endless and at one halt stale bread and water was passed in but this time the soldiers ensured everyone had their fair share. No attempt was made for the provision of toilet facilities so those unfortunate to need to relieve themselves were forced to do so where they lay, cursed by those around them.

The ripe aroma of excreta, both human and equine swiftly became unbearable and those lucky enough to be positioned near the car's sides were forced to press their faces to gaps in the wooden slats and take huge draughts of fresh air into their lungs.

It was late evening when they finally arrived in Konia, having swiftly passed through Adana and other, smaller, stations on the line. The train slid stiffly to a wheezing stop of steam as the exhausted captives lay in the freight car that imprisoned them. Eventually the door squealed open again and the lieutenant stood there contemplating them with a profound look of distaste as the smell reached his nostrils.

'Get them out!' he commanded, 'We've to turn these scum over to the authorities before we can go home tonight, so move! The captain has already left to see his lady friend so if you wish to join him we need to get these dogs offloaded. Now!'

'Up! Up! You heard the officer,' the *chaoush* in charge roared, 'up you whore's sons or I'll make you wish you'd never been born.' Stiffly they raised themselves up and stood waiting nervously, craning their necks to try and see outside. At a barked command they shuffled forward and were helped back onto terra firma. It was a long walk to the end of the platform and after a sharp turn they found themselves out into the main street.

People glanced at them curiously before hurrying on, fearful of being drawn into their plight. With soldiers either side of them and the lieutenant leading they marched along the street, young boys following them making raucous calls in their direction until curtly silenced by the grim-faced *chaoush*. The stone walls of a barracks loomed and they were quickly hustled through its portals and into a high courtyard. Here, their bonds were untied and they were led inside, rubbing their chafed, numbed hands.

A long cool corridor stretched away in front of them but the lieutenant made an angry gesture for them to halt just inside the door as he strode over to the nearest door and knocked deferentially. At a deep command from inside he opened the door and disappeared, to re-appear seconds later.

'You!' he pointed at the nearest prisoner, 'In there! The rest of you, stand against the wall until you're called forward.'

With a frightened, drawn expression the first prisoner did as he was told. Flanked by two soldiers he passed through the door which closed behind him. Almost immediately a voice began a haranguing, hectoring diatribe, becoming shrill and incoherent in its rage. The door was flung open suddenly and the prisoner appeared, sobbing, his feet dragging the floor as the two soldiers bore him away down the corridor. As he passed, Artoun could see the man's courage had failed him, a dark stain saturating the front of his trousers where his bladder had emptied. He watched with pity and fear as the man was dragged from their sight, his cries echoing and re-echoing eerily until they were cut off abruptly with the opening and closing of a door.

As a second prisoner was ordered inside a muffled volley of shots reached their frightened ears and all jumped nervously as one. The second examination was as swift as the first, a minute or two of loud shouting resulting in the prisoner being led away, protesting loudly. Another volley of shots sounded deafening close-by and the remaining men began to cringe away from the door.

In this manner they were all dealt with. Some received a different reception and emerged relieved; to be led off in a different direction but the majority suffered the same fate as the first two men. When Arif Bilgili was summoned he shook off his escort, squared his shoulders and walked into the room with a firm set to his face. This time the shouting was less intense and a few minutes later he emerged, a broad smile on his face. He was made to stand against the wall and watch the fate of the others, a task he engaged in with mounting interest before, he too, was eventually led away.

Finally, just Artoun and a thin, swarthy character in a tattered uniform tunic and baggy pants were left. The door remained firmly closed and Artoun's fear grew, giving way to an aching knot in his stomach and the feeling that his bowels would void at any moment. As he looked desperately round for a reason for their being overlooked the door opened and an officer in the facings of a colonel appeared.

Before them stood a stocky, grey-haired individual with a crisp white shirt under his uniform, wearing spectacles and a regulation moustache, tinged grey like his hair. This man looked more like a university professor than a loud-voiced, hot-headed examiner of deserters and Artoun's confusion and fear grew. Colonel Osman turned to walk away without sparing them a glance but the lieutenant barred his way. 'Forgive me, your Excellency but there is the matter of those two over there.' He pointed towards Artoun and the snivelling wretch alongside him and Artoun's bowels turned to water as a cruel pair of piercing, icy eyes swung in their direction.

'These two are the last, colonel, sir.'

'Damn! I was told there were no more and I'm late for an appointment with those damned *Ittihadists* from Constantinople, it seems they wish to speak with me about the *ermeni* problem. *Allah* preserve us from morons in the government but it bodes ill for anyone not singing to their tune. Take these two away and...no, on second thoughts bring them in here. *Chaoush?* Bring them here and give me those dice you have in your trouser pocket. Don't gape, man, do you think I haven't seen you fleecing the new conscripts in the back courtyard? Quickly, or you'll feel my anger if I'm late.'

Artoun and the other prisoner were pushed into the room and made to face the desk by the window. Impatiently the colonel snapped his fingers and the serjeant fumbled hurriedly in his pockets, finally producing two polished, ivory dice which he meekly handed over.

'Not too far away from where we stand many of your comrades are dying bravely in the service of their country. You two dogs chose to abandon Mother Turkey in the hour of her need by deserting those very comrades who are now buying the very air you breathe with their lives in the Çanakkale battles.

However, don't let it be said I'm not a merciful man, I've no time to listen to your pathetic excuses so I'm going to make a deal with you. Throw the dice, if you roll a three or less you die. If it's a four or above, you'll still die but at a later date, of your country's choosing.

'Here, throw!' He handed each of them a dice and gestured at Artoun's companion. 'You first. Throw!'

Trembling uncontrollably, hands shaking, the man cupped the dice and let it fall from his nerveless fingers. It spun briefly before landing with a number facing upwards. A two. He collapsed, grabbing the table edge for support and wailing loudly.

'Please, Excellency, mercy. I have three children. I...'

'Congratulations. There are now three more orphans in the world. *Chaoush*, take this pig away.' Osman looked over at Artoun and his voice hardened.

'Now, you. Throw!'

Palms sweating profusely, Artoun rolled the dice along the table and looked away, the fear inside leaving him incapable of watching to see where it landed.

'A four, *Allah* is smiling on you today, my friend. You'll join what few of your friends remain for a special undertaking from which, of course, none of you will return. Take him away.'

'Yes, Excellency. Right you, move it, or you'll feel the weight of my boot.'

Artoun was manhandled along the corridor and out through a door into a different courtyard. A volley of shots echoed sickeningly close and he heard the sound of a body slump to the ground. At the far end of the corridor a large barred door was inset into a small stone building with an armed guard outside. Opening the door with a brass key, the *chaoush* thrust Artoun inside and relocked the door.

As his footsteps receded a quiet voice spoke in the darkness.

'Well, well, if it isn't my old friend Yilmaz. So glad you could join us.'

'Arif?' Artoun whispered, scared to speak loudly in case the guard heard him.

'Who else, you numbskull? How did you survive your meeting with that snake, Osman?'

'A lucky throw of a dice. You?'

'I made him laugh. So much so that he forgot his anger and cursed me for a camel's offspring. He said he had one or two places left in a special unit and as a comedian did I want to volunteer for it or join my dead relatives in Paradise? It wasn't much of a choice so here I am. What did he say to you?'

'Just that by throwing a four I'd survived being shot immediately but not to make any special plans to celebrate another birthday.'

Arif chuckled. 'That's what I like, a comedian like myself. We'll do well together, you see.'

'So you say but what did the colonel mean when he said he'd saved us for a special undertaking? I don't understand.'

'Oh that! We're to form a punishment unit, you, me and all the rest of us scum. Don't you know there's a battle going on in the Straits of Çannakale? Well, my brother, we're being sent there tomorrow, initially to the town of Gelibolu, around two hundred of us in all, deserters and criminals to sort out the *kufirs*, those *infidel* unbelievers from the west who've invaded our glorious homeland.

We heroes are to join up with our comrades in the Ottoman 5th Army, to be placed in the forefront of every attack so the foreigners can use our bodies as receptacles for their bullets. Our comrades can then sweep down after us and capture the enemy position while we're busy dying.'

'Gelibolu? Where the hell is Gelibolu?'

The humour vanished from Arif's voice as he quietly answered Artoun's question. 'That we'll find out soon enough, my friend.'

As they were marched away, Artoun's thoughts returned to the colonels words. Just what had Osman alluded to when he mentioned '...*the ermeni problem?*'

Chapter Seven.

Author's note.

The campaign lurched on with no end in sight as the very thing that the assault on the Gallipoli Peninsula was supposed to avoid came to pass. Poor planning and non-existent preparations to exploit any local gains led to the rapid development of trench warfare, one that far exceeded in brutality the conditions being encountered at that time on the Western Front in France and Flanders.

The government in Britain were kept in ignorance of the real war being fought in the heat and dust of Gallipoli, optimistic dispatches fooling those back home into believing the campaign was being fought and won with little cost except to the Turkish defenders. The reality was known only to those who were paying with their blood for their commander's incompetence and indifference. One thing that could not be hidden from the fighting men in flowery language and vague references was the mounting butcher's bill.

ANZAC Cove, May.

'Come on Tom, get your kit off and join us. The water's lovely, mate so get a bloody move on!'

'Hang on a mo', these puttees are wound round my legs like a snake.' Tom exclaimed, falling over to loud hoots of laughter as he wrestled with his boots. The laces were badly knotted and took an age to undo but once free of the heavy boots he dropped his trousers, pulled off his uniform shirt and ran, naked, across the shingle to join the others splashing in the shallows.

'*Aaaaaah!*' he gasped as the water engulfed him, 'It's bloody freezing you mad dingo's, why didn't you say something to warn me?' His answer was a loud raspberry and a heap of epithets hurled in his direction. '*Chaaaaaarge!*' Ed Rushton ran full tilt at him from behind and both men collapsed into the sea, showering all nearby in a tidal wave of water.

'I'll get you for that, Rushton.' Tom spluttered on surfacing but a paroxysm of coughing robbed him of the power of speech as the sea-water he'd ingested choked him and he doubled over in an attempt to catch his breath.

'Sorry, mate,' Ed cried, pounding Tom's back vigorously, 'I didn't reckon on drowning you, corp! Take a deep breath...There, there, that should do it.' Tom responded weakly and Rushton backed away warily. Seeing his corporal on the road to recovery he immediately lost all protective feelings and any thoughts of contrition and rejoined the others splashing about in mad abandon.

Wearily, Tom staggered back to the shingle beach and lay down at the water's edge. The battalion was spending a few welcome days out of the firing line in Reserve Gully, for re-equipping. The last two weeks had kept them all under a great strain and it was good to be able to relax for a change without being covered in swarms of flies and itching continually under the scourge of lice infesting every part of their clothing. The two existed in the beach area but the coolness of the water made life in reserve that much more bearable.

Mail had been delivered along with two week-old newspapers and for a while the war had been forgotten as they'd caught up with family news and tales from back home. Disappointingly, none of the papers was recent enough to have news of the landings but it was enough to have this contact with home again and their spirits rose.

They'd all been subdued for a while after they returned from the disaster of Krithia but it wasn't long before natural high spirits had returned. New reinforcement drafts had arrived, bewildered youngsters who'd swiftly been absorbed into the various platoons and sections, filling the gaps left by the battalion's growing numbers of dead and wounded. Today they'd been given a few precious hours away from fatigues and his men had elected to go swimming. A spout rose up in the water near one of his men and he stood up, nettled.

'Oi, Rushton, stop throwing stones, you'll put someone's eye out!' Tom admonished sternly and Rushton looked up in astonishment. 'Strewth, corp, that ain't me, it's the bloody Abdul's firing at us!' Another spout of water sprung up next to him and he pointed at it. 'See, that's a sniper up on the headland over there, bugger's taking a crafty potshot and hoping he'll hit someone.'

'Right you lot, out you get, we've enough blokes pushing up the daisies without giving the Jacko's a free shot at adding to the score.'

They grumbled as they obeyed him but he was having none of it. Men became fatalistic if they weren't chivvied occasionally and he kept a close eye on them, watching for any obvious signs of them giving way to fear and abandoning any precautions for their own safety.

'Alright, boys, dry yourselves off and we'll try and scrounge some fresh water for our blokes before we bugger off back.'

A loud explosion made them turn out to sea. A Turkish shell had exploded squarely on a barge being towed towards the jetty and they watched in bemusement as she slipped swiftly beneath the waves in a cloud of white smoke.

'Christ, I hope she wasn't carrying any fancy tucker for the fucken' officers.' someone said and they all snickered.

Ed Rushton's sombre voice broke the silence. 'You can forget scrounging water before we go back, mates, if I'm not mistaken that was our bloody water supply on the frigging barge. Looks like we'll go thirsty for a while longer.'

'Corp' Harding, there's a heap of dead fish floating out there, can me and Rollie go and fetch some?'

'No!' Tom snapped, and stoically withstood their grousing all the way back round Ari Burnu and under the shadow of The Sphinx to the reserve bivouacs.

On arrival back at the dugouts they'd made their home in on the side of the gully, Tom received a message to appear at the Company HQ. He sent the others on their way and trotted along to the dugout which served as HQ. The shaded interior was like a furnace and despite the cooling swim he began to perspire freely. Captain Finch waved a wad of papers over his face as a fan while addressing Tom.

'Good to see you, Harding, had a bonzer rest?'

'Sir?'

'Never mind, let's get straight down to it. Forget the heat, it can eat a man up but I've got other bloody matters on my mind. And it ain't these bloody flies. Can't open your mouth without killing a whole generation of the little bastards!'

Tom kept his lips compressed in a tight line and waited.

'Some fool at Brigade has been looking at the map and decided we've got a bit of a wonky stretch, here.' He leaned over and picked up a damp piece of paper. 'According to this bumf the company is going back into the line tomorrow, here, The wonky bit's there, on the other side of Plugge's Plateau right opposite where you and your platoon will be situated shortly so it's up to you and your men to straighten the line out. Get what I mean?'

'How're we supposed to accompany…'

Finch sighed deeply. 'There you go again. No…' he held a restraining hand up. 'Don't. We'll go on all day like this with me getting angry. When we go back tomorrow to the shithole we call the front line, you and your men, together with some blokes who'll accompany us, will straighten the line out so that Brigade can sleep a little bit easier. Simple, don't you think?'

128

'I still don't understand, sir.'

'What do you know about mining or tunnelling?'

'Me?'

'Yes, Corporal. You!'

'Nothing, sir.'

'That's not quite the truth, is it? I've seen your records, Harding, you were a bloody miner in civilian life, don't lie to me. That's why you're going to be involved in this little lot. Brigade acknowledge the fact that the Turks are too close to shell out of that position so they've come up with something different. We're going to be visited by some engineer fellows tomorrow who're going to blow the hell out of Mr Turk and you, Corporal, and your men, are going to dig a hole under the Turkish front line so these blokes can plant their mine.'

'How big a hole sir, and how far are we expected to dig?'

'There you go once again, asking too many questions. The word's *tunnel*, Corporal Harding. You and your blokes are going to *tunnel* under the Turks and fill the hole with explosives. The engineers will then blow the hole up and we'll rush forward in the confusion, take over that part of the line and, *Hey Presto*! the line is now straight again. Simple really, or so I'm told by Brigade.'

'I'm not convinced sir.'

'You don't have to be convinced, you're a corporal and I'm a captain and either way none of our opinions bloody well count. I've chosen you because apparently in this shambles you're beginning to look like someone who knows what he's doing and can follow orders. So bugger off, grab some tucker and a cuppa and we'll talk tomorrow when we get back up to where we're going.

On the way out, send in 2/Lt Nevett could you, he's the pale-looking bloke wondering what the hell's going on here. And by the way, he's your new platoon commander.'

The following morning they were roused before dawn and set off shivering in the icy coldness of the day. The Turkish artillery was silent in the hours before daylight spread its fingers of light over the peninsula and they were grateful to reach their destination without any harassing fire. Waiting in the trenches were two grizzled, unshaven men wearing engineers uniforms and Finch made his way down the trench and pointed them out to Tom.

'These are the two blokes I told you about on the way up, Harding, Serjeants Stubbs and Holdsworth. Get your blokes settled in and then we'll all have a chinwag.'

An hour later, Captain Finch, a nervous and self-conscious 2/Lt Nevett together with Tom Harding and the two engineer serjeants stood over a wooden table outside the company dugout and looked down on the map Finch had positioned on the table-top.

'Right you blokes. As you can see here,' he pointed deftly at the map with the blunt end of a chewed pencil, 'the Turks have pushed their line well forward making a salient that they're using to fire on us from three sides. Brigade want us to eradicate that salient, smooth the line out, so to speak. What you lot are going to have to do is tunnel beneath the little bastards, pack the hole with explosives and then blow them to Kingdom Come.'

He turned to the engineers. 'How much gunpowder do you have?'

The older of the two laughed, an amused bark. 'Sorry mate but we don't use gunpowder anymore, went out with Napoleon I reckon. We fancy using some explosives we stole from the navy, they use it as a filling for their shells. Doesn't half make a big bang though, should be right up our street for this job. And if you don't want us to dig too far out under the Jacko's we can do the whole thing in pretty good time, too.'

'Keep me right then, what's it called?'

'Trinitrotoluene.'

'What the bloody hell is that when it's at home?'

'Oh, sorry, didn't mean to baffle you with bullshit, mate, we know it as TNT.'

'How much of it do you have?'

'Enough to take half the peninsula out.'

Finch grinned mirthlessly. 'That'll do for me but we just want a tiny bit of it to disappear and, hopefully, without taking any of us with it. Just ensure all those you kill are bloody Turks. Got it? Corporal Harding here will assist, he's an ex-pom miner.'

'Pleased to meet you Serjeant Stubbs.'

'Call me Amos, mate.'

They made their way to where Tom's section waited, struggling up the roughened trench and easing their way past the grumbling prone figures who barred their way. 'Oi, watch yer fucken' feet, could you!'

'Sorry, mate.'

'Ouch, my bloody head!'

'Beg yer pardon.'

At last, chests heaving in the heat of the sun they arrived and leant against the trench wall to catch their breath. Amos Stubbs gestured at Tom 'How far away are the Turks.'

'Not too far.'

'Mind if I take a peep?'

'I wouldn't recommend it if I were you but if you're still determined, use one of these.' Tom lifted up a long, slim, wooden box and Stubbs looked down at it curiously.

'What the hell is it?'

'A homemade periscope. Some of the blokes on the ships out there can't shave because we've nicked their mirrors to make these contraptions.' He offered it to Stubbs who took hold of it gingerly. 'It does work, you pop it over the top of the parapet, squint through the bottom piece of glass and you can see for miles. Go on, try it.'

Stubbs took a long, hard look at Tom's deadpan face before slowly raising the periscope skywards. 'There ain't much to see out h—.' *Crack*! Stubbs slid down the side of the trench in consternation as the instrument jumped out of his hand, watched with amusement by the men either side of his prone form.

'Jesus, that was close! Just how far away are the bastards?'

'We reckon about fifteen yards but no-one's been able to confirm it, for the same reason as you just found out. Every time we try for a looksee, some Jacko sniper shoots the damned thing out of our hands.'

'Strewth!' Stubbs leant back and mopped his sweating brow with feeling.

When the laughter had subsided, Tom drew closer to the two engineers and using the map given them by Finch they plotted where to start digging. Tom saw the wide grins on his men as they watched his conversation and he leaned up and spoke. 'Rushton, Abbottt, O'Neill, nip off and come back with those banjos and picks Mr Nevett snaffled for us, can you? We're going to dig us a hole in the side of the trench where these two blokes are going to show us. Bugger off smartly, I reckon that'll wipe the grins off your ugly mugs.'

Declan O'Neill ignored Tom and shuffled over to where Stubbs stood recovering his composure.

'G'day mate, feeling better now?'

'I should say so, Christ, I nearly got my head blown off.' He poked the soil absentmindedly with the toe of his boot while ruminating on his lucky escape.

'This stuff's fairly sandy, we should be able to dig a shaft under the Turks in a few days, you see if we don't.'

'Yeah?' O'Neill squatted down alongside him. 'Smoko?' he enquired, proffering a crumpled packet.

'Naw thanks, I packed up some years ago, breathing in explosive fumes did it for me.'

'Oh, righto.' He lit a cigarette adroitly and blew smoke into the air. 'So how'd you get into this lark, then?'

Stubbs pointed at the silent figure of Serjeant Holdsworth. 'Me'n Sydney here, we're both miners. Syd comes from New South Wales and I'm from Charters Towers, Queensland. When the war started we joined up and were posted to the engineers on account of our explosive experience, we met up in training and came out here together, sort of a matched pair. He doesn't say much, the old bastard but we get on really well.'

'Charters Towers? I used to go up that way on the train from Townsville with my boss.'

'Fair dinkum. You're from Townsville?'

'Yeah, I was a bank clerk there, in the Royal Bank of Queensland. My boss used to travel up to Charters to audit some of the accounts there, lot of big money coming out of the gold mine.'

'None of it came in my bloody direction, I can assure you!' Stubbs laughed bitterly.

'Me neither.' Declan answered blithely. 'I got to go cos I was his bloody run-round, did all the messages while he wined and dined with the bank bosses. Then they got rid of me. Still, we had a good time up there, stayed in the.... Bloody hell, what was the name of the hotel, it was just off...?'

'Wasn't the Waverley, was it?'

'That's it, the Waverley. Good tucker, too, if I mind right. Did you stay there?'

'I couldn't afford that bloody luxury, mate I was in digs off Gill Street. I...'

'O'Neill, when you're quite ready ...'

'Coming, corp, just having a chat with a fellow...'

'Now, O'Neill, not next bloody week!'

--§--

Holdsworth had been busy with a prismatic compass, taking various headings to ensure they were digging in the right direction. Under his urging the men began slowly digging into the sidewall of the trench with the picks and shovels, pushing the spoil behind them to be taken away later. A lack of wood meant shoring up the sides was difficult but Amos Stubbs assured them that for the short distance they'd be digging a lack of support wouldn't matter that much and the hole widened and deepened gradually under their combined efforts.

Captain Finch begged and pleaded with Brigade for the artillery to help out and reluctantly they added the area to their fire plan, throwing shells over at regular intervals to mask the sound of the digging underground. The plan was for teams to dig in shifts, eight hours on and sixteen off and to drive at least twelve feet forward in each of the eight hours. This would also include removal of the spoil in bags for emptying.

On the third day, Stubbs held up a warning hand as Tom approached. 'What's up?' Tom enquired.

'You'll bloody well have to come and see for yourself,' Stubbs replied grimly, 'follow me into the shaft but don't make a sound.'

Mystified, Tom followed the taciturn ex-miner into the shaft entrance, carefully wriggling through the narrow entrance until he could stand up and grope his way forward. The tunnel was claustrophobically small and the atmosphere inside was hot, fetid and with a fierce humidity that struck him like a blow.

His mind turned back to a similar scene years ago in the Lancashire coal-fields. The darkness was the same gloom he'd toiled in, longing for the sight of a blue sky, all that was missing here in this shaft was the haunting sounds of pit ponies. Immediately he began to sweat, wiping his face with his hand in a futile gesture to keep the beads of sweat from running into his eyes as he tried to see where Stubbs had disappeared.

'*Shhh!*'

The muffled command brought him up short and he stopped shuffling forward. A whisper came from the gloom. 'There! Can you here it?'

Tom strove to listen, extending his head to the side in order to catch any sound. After a while, he heard it. A faint *tap..tap..tapping* noise to his right and he reached forward and grasped Stubbs's shoulder in acknowledgement. Both men turned with difficulty in the narrow confines and stealthily crept back the way they'd come.

He dragged in huge quantities of air, collapsing onto the trench floor, aware of Stubbs's amused glance before the Queenslander flopped alongside him. 'What was that noise?' he asked, dreading the answer.

'It's the Jacko's,' Stubbs replied, 'they're digging towards us. Must be planning to do to us what we're trying to do to them.'

'Can we stop them?'

'Naw. At least, not right now. We need to be a few more feet along and then we can settle with them. We'll just have to keep going. Tell the blokes to ignore the noise, it's when it stops that we oughter worry. If we keep going the way we are I reckon a couple more days will see us right.'

'They must be able to hear us, what if they blow theirs first?' Tom asked, horrified at his men continuing to dig with this extra knowledge weighing on them.

'No worries there then, we'll never feel it!' Stubbs laughed, punching Tom lightly on his shoulder. Tom opened his mouth to protest but his companion continued. 'Don't worry, mate, I've got a little surprise for Mr Johnny Turk.'

'What?'

'A camouflet.'

'A what?'

Stubbs explained patiently. 'It's a sort of countermine. We'll place a charge alongside where the sound's coming from and when that and the main charge go up we'll kill two birds with one stone. Simple.'

Tom shuddered. 'That's awful. I wouldn't want that to happen to our lads.'

'Better them that us.' Stubbs replied, 'Now where's Syd buggered off to? I'll need him to help work out the size of the charge.'

Extra teams were brought in to help complete the work faster and at last the small gallery was finished, the spoil having been taken away every night in bags and dumped. Amos Stubbs and Syd Holdsworth wriggled their way along the tunnel to inspect it and exited minutes later, grinning.

'It ain't pretty and the sides won't hold up for long but it'll do the trick. Our blokes are bringing the final lot of explosives up tonight so we'll pack it in and tamp it down and tomorrow...*Boom*! Goodbye, Mr Turk.'

'What if they heard us digging, we could explode it and find no-one at home. Fat use that'll be if they've evacuated the area already.' Captain Finch asked Stubbs anxiously.

'They know we're doing it but not when.' Amos Stubbs replied confidently. 'Even better, mate, if the Jacko trenches are empty you won't have any casualties when you go and take over what's left.'

'Good point, serjeant. Call me when everything's ready.'

--§--

Dawn brushed away the last tendrils of night as Tom and the two officers waited outside the narrow hole that was the tunnel entrance. Like a rat from a sewer pipe, Serjeant Stubbs wriggled free and crouched down beside them followed by Holdsworth carrying a small box with wires attached.

'That's us,' he panted, 'everything's ready. The charges are right against the gallery wall, wired them up and the camouflet's wired up in parallel. All we need do is to retreat down the trench and blow this lot up. Are you and your blokes ready, sir?'

Finch smiled evilly. 'Too bloody right we are. My men are poised, waiting down the other end of this traverse with bayonets fixed. Any Turk that survives the main explosion ain't going anywhere.' His smile deepened. 'I went down to the artillery lines last night and had a chinwag with their boss. His blokes are going to fire a few rounds off, make the Turks man their fire-steps in case of an attack so we'll catch even more of them in the big bang.

Right, boys, time to go I reckon. The artillery should be on the go in, ah...five minutes. Can we set your lot off then?'

'No worries, sir,' Stubbs replied unhurriedly, 'lead the way and we'll pay the wire out. There's plenty of it so we can set it off from the beach if you fancy.'

'Wish I could, serjeant but my boss would have my guts for garters! Corporal, get back there with the others and we'll wait for the live show to begin. Five minutes after this little lot goes up the artillery are going to shell the rear lines to stop any Turkish reserves interfering. Let's get over there as quick as Christ and dig in before the little bugger's react and start to counterattack. Our lot haven't got that much ammo to play with so we need to be out of here like rats up a drainpipe as soon as the shelling stops.'

They retreated back fifty yards down the trench where a packed mass of waiting men watched them with strained faces and rifles at the ready. Some wore uniform caps while others had slouch hats jammed to one side of their heads. All were adorned with a variety of clothing, from ripped shirts to sweat-stained vests and trousers with putties, to crumpled shorts. What they all had in common was an air of utter determination as they waited for the action to begin.

Holdsworth finished paying out the cable and nodded to Stubbs who took the control box from him. Inspecting it minutely, he raised a hand to Captain Finch.

'That's it, boys, wait for the bang and then over you go!'

The next five minutes seemed like an eternity before in the distance they heard the cough of an artillery piece.

'Here they come, get your heads down.'

The shells screamed overhead and impacted with loud explosions. Hoarse shouts sounded from the Turkish lines and Finch grinned fiercely. 'Sounds like someone's copping it. Good, less for us to worry about. Stubbs, time for you to do your stuff now.'

Stubbs nodded.

'Take cover!'

Looking round, Amos Stubbs settled himself and flexed his fingers before grasping the control box firmly and pushing down on the plunger. Those near to him waited breathlessly for the sound of the explosions but nothing happened. Frowning, Stubbs pulled the plunger up and pushed down again. In spite of the shelling, the silence in the trench was deafening and he turned to Finch with a desperate, panic-stricken look on his face.

'It's not working, there's something wrong.'

'I can see that, you bloody idiot!' Finch snarled, 'What's up?'

'I don't know. Maybe the wires joining the main charge and camouflet have parted, I just don't know!'

Before Captain Finch could open his mouth in answer he was pushed roughly to one side and the lean figure of Syd Holdsworth wriggled past and soundlessly made his way to the shaft entrance.

'Syd, hang on a minute!' Stubbs shouted but with a backward wave of his hand Holdsworth disappeared into the depths of the shaft.

'I think he's gone to check the connections, make sure nothing's come undone.' Stubbs spoke in a relieved tone but Finch was in no mood for niceties. 'We'll give it another go when he comes back.' 'The artillery will be opening up again shortly, to cover our approach so he'd better get a move on!'

Vivian Finch's face was a deep puce colour but before he could vent his spleen on the unfortunate serjeant looking anxiously down the trench a double explosion reverberated from the tunnel entrance and the earth heaved soundlessly in front of them. The sound grew to a deep roaring noise which overwhelmed their senses, a pressure wave knocking Finch flat as it passed swiftly overhead. In front of their shocked eyes, earth and soil rose a hundred feet in the air in a massive dust cloud, pausing briefly before settling back to earth in a blinding, stinging blanket that enveloped them all. Another dust cloud billowed from the tunnel entrance, adding to the discomfort as they struggled to breathe through the thick, cloying waves of thin soil that assailed their throats and nostrils.

Tom opened his mouth wide to try and equalise the pressure threatening to rupture his eardrums but only succeeded in ingesting large quantities of dust and soil. Eyes streaming, he bent double in a paroxysm of rasping coughs and frantically sought fresh air to soothe his tortured lungs.

Coughing equally vigorously alongside him, Vivian Finch punched Francis Nevett's arm. 'Go on, go on! Get the men moving, quick, before the enemy gets his breath back.' 2/Lt Nevett brought his whistle to his lips but the dust had robbed him of his ability to blow so leaving it to dangle from the cord around his neck he stood tall and urged his men on.

'Come on you blokes, get over and start running!'

He joined in the melee of men who leapt the parapet and began running hard for the other side of the line, rifles held at the high port. Tom jumped over with them, sparing a backward glance at the despairing form of Amos Stubbs knelt in disbelief at the tunnel entrance. All thoughts of Holdsworth left him as he sprinted hard for the smoking earth of a fresh crater that towered around the lip of the shattered Turkish trench. Around him came the sounds of laboured breathing, shouts and wild cheering as they sprinted across the short distance separating the two combatants and he felt adrenaline coursing through his veins as he ran with the mass of men converging on the Turks.

The mine had done its job well, neatly pinching off the salient as intended and leaving only a gaping hole where a trench and living flesh had been seconds before. A high, thin scream caught his attention and he glimpsed a Turk drenched in blood, staggering in the open and shaking his head as he vainly tried to clear his shattered eardrums. A sideways movement in his peripheral vision and Tom turned in time to watch the Turk fall slowly forward as a bronzed figure in vest and shorts stepped up and savagely bayoneted the screaming figure. The sharpened steel sliced easily through unresisting flesh and the screaming stopped abruptly.

Shots barked out as the attackers poured over the freshly-riven soil in an unstoppable wave. Their impetus carried them into the remnants of the Turkish trench where only the dead and body parts waited to greet the victors. As Tom reached the edge of what remained of the parapet he drew breath sharply. The fresh stench of the dead filled his nostrils pulling him up and forcing him to inhale and exhale noisily through clenched teeth. Below his feet the crater yawned, at least ten feet deep and full of churned earth, complete with bent and twisted equipment intermingled with debris from the trench walls.

2/Lt Francis Nevett appeared alongside Tom and gaped at the destruction before them. 'Jesus, that was some bang, eh, corporal?' Without waiting for a reply he raised his voice. 'Over here, to me! Dig in, men, the barrage'll start shortly and we need some cover.' He turned to Tom. 'See that the prisoners are taken care of, will you, corporal…Why are you shaking your head?'

'Prisoners, sir? There won't be any prisoners.' Tom laughed grimly.

'What are you saying?'

'Look around you, sir, this is Gallipoli, not bloody Brisbane. Don't be naive, we don't take prisoners. Neither side does.' He strode off leaving Nevett gaping foolishly after him.

The line held and they dug the new stretch into the existing trench system. The artillery barrage held the Turks off long enough for more reinforcements to reach the raiding party but they knew it wouldn't be long before the Turks mounted a determined attack to win back the ground they'd lost. It was all a matter of time, the one resource both sides had in abundance.

Tom retraced his steps back to their original line later in the cool of the evening. Looking down the trench he spied a familiar figure and made his way to where Amos Stubbs stood forlornly at the entrance to the mine tunnel.

'I'm sorry you lost your mate, serjeant,' he said simply, 'this war will see a lot more good cobbers lost yet.'

'Thanks, mate.' Stubbs sighed, 'Poor old Syd. He always reckoned a mine would do for him but I don't think even he reckoned it would be here, today, like this.'

'Did you know him before you volunteered?'

'Naw. He was from New South Wales. Funny how life goes, ain't it? He told me once about being caught up in a mine disaster back in 1902 at Mount Kembla. There was a gas explosion which killed nearly a hundred blokes and Syd only survived because he let his mate go down the shaft before him.'

'So what happened here, then?'

'I'm not sure. The main charge didn't go up when I pressed the bloody plunger but we did put a secondary means of firing it when we set everything up. I can only assume the poor bastard tried to rig the secondary charge to set the main one and the camouflet off and the fuse fired prematurely.'

He scuffed the soil.

'Beaut, eh? You survive a bloody great mine disaster in your own country only to get blown to bits trying to kill some bloody Jacko's! Take care of yourself, corporal, you could be right, the bastard's running this stupid war are gonna do for a lot more of us yet.'

Plugge's Plateau, May.

'Gahd! Glory days, eh boys?' He waved a hand expansively. 'Oi, Fairlie, mate, don't we have anything but bloody bully to eat these days? I had a tin of apricot jam but some dingo pinched it from me swag. Bastard! What about some cheese, has anyone got a bit of cheese for me cos if I see one more tin of bully and those bloody biscuits I swear I'm gonna knock some poor bastard off! How much are the Poms charging good old Australia to serve up this kind of shite? You'd think for the money we're paying we'd get decent tucker, like a few yabbies you know, but not this.....this...!'

'Fair dinkum, Ed!' Pete Fairlie laughed, 'You can always bugger off over to the other side and see if the Jacko's restaurant has had any fresh supplies of donkey! Do them a swop, tell them our bully's really steak!'

Ed Rushton ignored him and rolled over onto his stomach on the parapet, looking pleadingly towards Tom Harding as he sat poking morosely at his mess tin. 'Come on, corp, there must be some better tucker we can snaffle instead of this crap every day. I've waited days for a decent meal and this is all we ever get, rancid bully beef that comes outta the tin like a bloody liquid stream of turds. I'm outta water too, my water-bottles emptier than a fucken' wallabies pouch an' I've eaten more than my fair share of this fucken' dust! What's the point of goin' on I ask you, when are we going to get some decent...?'

'Don't bother me when I'm trying to find something in here amongst this sand that looks edible, Rushton,' Tom intoned, pointing at his mess tin, 'I feel just the same as you about the situation but until things improve it's all we've got so shut up and leave me to my supper. Keep your head down, it's getting dark but if the Turks start shelling I don't want you out in the open exposed like that. And stop bloody scratching will you, you're making me feel itchy.'

'Sorry, but I'm alive with the fucken' things. In my head, under my arms, the little bastards have even taken a fancy to my balls, something no-one else's bothered with for a while. Will we get new clothing soon?'

'Enough back chat, will you shut up? I'm trying to eat!'

With the advent of warmer weather new phenomenon had entered their battle with the enemy and nature, an infestation of lice and the appearance of millions of flies. In the cramped confines of the trenches the lice multiplied incredibly, conquering new territories daily and adding further misery to an already depressing existence. The endless itchiness they brought made sleep almost unthinkable, making nights spent in scratching or cleaning already filthy infested clothing to try and rid oneself of the pests.

The flies had rapidly gorged themselves on the swollen bodies of the dead, multiplying and clustering so thickly it was sometimes impossible to make out the figures of the fallen. Their buzzing filled the air with a sickening hum stretching already taut nerves to breaking point. To open one's mouth to eat was an invitation to ingest a swarm of the pestilent creatures along with the morsel and the paltry latrines had become a veritable breeding ground. Typhus and dysentery were becoming a deadly problem, along with the illness known as *Enteric Fever*.

'Please yourself, I was only asking...' Rushton grumbled, returning to a scrape in the trench with his mess tin and peering closely at the contents. 'And no, before you ask, I don't feel like singing a chorus of *"Australia Will Be There."* Bloody stupid song, anyway. If the galah who wrote those words could see us now he'd throw a fit!' He put his

140

face nearer to the rim of his mess tin. 'Hey, I've got a fly in here, the silly bastard's broke his teeth on a biscuit. Anyone want some fresh meat?' No-one answered and he threw the remainder of his food high over the parapet into no-mans-land. 'Go on, you little bugger, get out and walk! That's it cobbers, I'm off to the dunny for a...'

A shot sounded out, further down the trench, followed by a great roar and Tom whirled round in alarm. 'What's going on?' he cried, 'Was anyone hit?'

'Nah,' a voice shouted out. 'Abbott and the boys were playing 'Two's up,' Corp, and he threw the bloody coins too far in the air. Bloody Jacko sniper hit one of the fucken' coins in mid-air and now Abbott's mad cos he's down a penny before the bloody game even started. Says he couldn't even see if they'd landed "Odds" up or not. Cripes! Great shot, though, that sniper's a fair shooter.'

'Abbott! I'll see you later, what did I tell you about trying to fleece the lads? Put that blasted game away before you're caught, you ass!'

'Oi, corp, watch it, here comes Mister Nevett!'

Tom looked up from his administrations to see the boyish figure of their platoon commander bobbing along the trench towards them, stopping every few yards to speak quietly to the men. Stowing the mess tin at his side, Tom waited for the young officer to reach him and as he did so, Nevett squatted low alongside and raised a hand in greeting.

'G'day, Harding, how's the boys bearing up? I've got some real aussie tobacco for you lot, some packets of Vice Regal. I got them off a fellow from Hobart.'

'Good stuff, sir, the boys'll appreciate a change from that awful pom tobacco we've been issued with. It don't make for a decent smoke. They're bearing up well, considering. When we arrived back here after that debacle down at Krithia I was a bit worried about our morale but the blokes have picked up and are ready for anything. The mining do cost us a few more of the regulars but the new draft we got are settling in fine. The tucker's pretty bad, sir, a few of the boys are threatening to go crook because of it and we're pretty short of water, too, is there anything we can do about that?'

2/Lt Laurence Nevett's face twisted in exasperation. 'Look, Harding, I know how bad it is but it's the same for all of us, officers included. Tell them they need to crack hardy!' he said. 'I'm not here to talk about tucker or water, there are more serious matters on the horizon. We've had a bit of intelligence that Abdul's going to be

141

coming over in strength at some point tonight so we're going up into the firing-line. We'll cross Monash Gully this evening at seven pip emma and get alongside our blokes near Courtney's Post. Got that?'

'Yessir. The boys won't appreciate me telling them they need to hang on, sir, they only want to know when …'

'Just do as you're bloody well told, will you, I want you to make sure all your men are on their toes. Every man's to have as much ammo as he can muster alongside him and try to acquire as many bombs as you can. Before I go, how's that arm of yours, I saw you bandaging it earlier? Are you alright, Harding?'

'It's the bloody climate, sir, the darn thing won't heal.' He pulled his shirt sleeve up and Nevett recoiled from the sight of the raw, angry weal. 'You told me earlier it wasn't that bad, you fool, look at it. When tonight's over and done with, assuming that the Turks *do* mount an assault, I want you to go down to the cove and get that arm patched up properly. You'll lose the damn thing if you don't watch it, so do as you're told and let the medics take a look. Alright?'

'Sir.'

Nevett glanced up. A low speck in the sky, growing larger by the minute, was droning towards them and Nevett frowned at the interruption to his talk. The shape was an aircraft, a biplane, heading slowly but purposefully towards them at a low altitude as the pilot clawed for height in his underpowered craft. Before Nevett could speak again a rifle sounded. The shot was followed by another and then another until a steady fusillade of shots was being aimed in the aircraft's direction. The men saw it falter and a ragged cheer broke out as its wings dipped sharply and it lost altitude, barely skimming over them at tree height before turning back towards the island of Imbros.

More shots followed as the engine note lost its cadence and began misfiring badly. Thinking furiously, Nevett leapt to his feet. 'Stop it, you bloody fools, it's one of ours! Stop firing!' His commands were lost in another fusillade and he slid back down angrily.

'Look here Harding, stop those bloody men shooting will you, it's one of our own reconnaissance aircraft. Christ, if we shoot the bugger down there'll be hell to pay.'

A ringing noise broke the air as a sentry beat furiously on a shell case and in the distance a loud coughing noise could be heard. Tom recognised the sound of a Turkish 75mm howitzer and ducked instinctively.

'Get your heads down, boys, the bastard's artillery is on its way. Take cover.'

'Alright, Harding, forget the aircraft, he'll have to take his chances, it's started. See to your men, I'm back off to HQ. Send a runner if things get too hairy. Got it? Oh, and word's just come in, you're a serjeant now so sort some stripes out after this lot's over.'

'Yes sir!' Tom exclaimed at Nevett's retreating back, nettled at the man's absurd order. Serjeant's stripes? When they couldn't even guarantee fresh food and water? He shrugged philosophically. Nevett was in a bit of a funk but he wasn't the first and wouldn't be the last.

Forgetting the encounter he cowered down into the trench, pressing his body as hard as he could into the coarse dirt. *Wheeeeeee! Crump! Wheeeeeeeeeeee! Crump! Crump-crump!* Dirt pattered down onto his shoulders and shrapnel whirred wickedly through the air. All thoughts of the aircraft above were forgotten in the hail of shells bracketing them and fresh screams above the noise of the shell's explosions were an indication of new casualties.

He thought of investigating but drew back sharply. To move now would be suicidal, far better to stick it out with the others and wait for a lull in the shelling before venturing out to see how his men were faring. It seemed to go on for ever. He kept his mouth wide open to avoid the pressure from the bursting shells from damaging his ear drums but instead of slackening the shelling increased in its intensity. The Turkish artillery had worked the range out to a yard and the ground erupted around the men of 'E' Company as the shells flayed them, killing and wounding indiscriminately as high explosive rounds and shrapnel bullets worked their way along the parapet.

Nothing could live in the barrage, Tom reasoned, any minute now and a shell would find him, slicing him open and eviscerating him along with the others. His head ached with the incessant pounding and he slumped against the wall of the trench, staring at his dirt-engrained fingers with a studied detachment. What was the use, why bother, it would all be over soon enough.

He was wrong. The bombardment continued throughout the remainder of the afternoon and into the evening, slowing for a while before picking up again. During the lull, the men from 'E' Company assembled their weapons and scrambled into Monash Gully. Moving quickly along the track they climbed the gully's side and arrived at the trenches bordering Courtney's Post, shoving their way in alongside the men already standing–to. A few minutes later the Turkish artillery started a fresh round of shelling.

He lost count of the numbers, his numbed brain hardly registering each new concussion. After a while those around him lost all fear, a weary fatalism settling over them as they endured the bombardment which violated their very souls and left them incapable of conscious or cohesive thought. Ignoring the mounting pain from his arm he even slept and on wakening, opened a bleary eye. It was nearly midnight and in his fatigued state he longed only for more sleep.

Whoosh! The shelling stopped abruptly and a new sound caught his attention as the flare ignited above them and drifted down, bathing them all in its eerie, white glare. From out of the darkness came the sounds of hoarse shouting and as his befuddled mind considered this new intrusion he realised the noise was coming from out beyond the shattered parapet. The Turks were attacking!

He leapt up onto the firing step and stared over at the mass of enemy troops pouring from the cover of the dense scrub and rushing towards them with an all too familiar cry on their lips. '*Allah! Allah!*'

'Stand to!'

In a throwback to the suicidal attacks of the early days, the Turkish soldiers rushed headlong at their entrenched enemy, whooping and ululating with no thought to their own safety. A rifle cracked out, splitting the blackness like a spark and a body fell but the Turks leapt over their fallen comrade's corpse without a glance and ran on unfalteringly. Single shots turned into a fusillade, bowling scores of Turks over in increasing numbers whilst flares bursting overhead added to the surreal scene, casting strange eerie shadows as the Turks danced and writhed along the length of the barbed-wire entanglements of their enemy.

As one man fell it seemed another emerged from the scrub to take his place, throwing themselves into the impenetrable wall of bullets with a fanatical stoicism. A machine-gun picked up the beat, stuttering fiery bursts adding to the infernal din as it scythed men down in rows, bodies dancing and jerking as metal-jacketed bullets tore into them. Many fell to rise no more but others staggered back onto their feet and staggered around drunkenly until slammed down again by a well-aimed rifle bullet.

Darts of light indicated the Turks return fire, pinpricks of flame bursting from the gloom momentarily lighting up the soldier's faces but these fireflies only served to indicate to the Australians their enemies' position and the fusillade from their own trenches increased to a roar. Blood-lust up, the Australians lost all sense of cover and rose to stand on the parapet, shouting and calling wildly as they picked off one man after another.

'Get down, you idiots!' Tom shouted but if they heard him they ignored his command and carried on firing. Incandescent with the heat of battle they stood exposed in the open and fired repeatedly without respite, loading and reloading until the ground was littered with spent cartridge cases and charger clips. A small knot of Turks broke through, rushing within yards of the trench before being met head-to-head in a savage melee of boots, rifle butts and bayonets. A fierce struggle ensued until the broken remnants retreated back into the darkness, leaving the jubilant Australians screaming their defiance.

The bark of the rifles and noise of exploding grenades was lost in a whistling noise sounding above the carnage and the first of a shower of Turkish artillery shells landed close to their positions. *Crump!* The explosion threw up huge clods of earth and Tom ducked as heavy pieces of metal whirred wickedly over his head. *Crump!* Another shell landed and this time he felt its hot breath envelop him as the force of the shell spent itself on the parapet to his left.

A man groaned next to him and reeled away before collapsing in front of the trench, his face a nightmarish, reddened horror in the dim light where a shell splinter had carved its way through soft flesh. Another, one of the new draft, he noticed, slowly collapsed onto his knees, dropping his rifle into the dirt and assuming the slumped, hunched-over stance of one at prayer. The firing continued, increasing in intensity as more and more Turks appeared, throwing themselves against their hated enemy without respite.

The noise of the shelling only added to the confusion, each man fighting alone in a microcosm and narrowing of vision, the world consisting only of the rifle in their hands and the yelling, screaming shadows rushing at them beyond the wire. Sweating hands feverishly grasped weapons tighter as the attack progressed. Nothing mattered except to work the rifle's bolt and feed cartridges into the greedy maw of the breech. *Snick!* Bolt locked, a finger slowly took up the pressure and caressed the trigger. *Crack!* The rifle bucked, a flame flared briefly and another running figure flopped to the ground.

In this manner time passed as in a vacuum, the focus of a man's existence taken up by the slow-motion act of jerking the bolt back, pushing it forward to reload and squeezing the trigger. Bombers among the troops began throwing their deadly charges, the sharp *cracks!* intermingling with the deeper bark of the rifles. A few egg-shaped Turkish grenades appeared out of the gloom but their long fuses enabled them to be picked up and hurled back and they caused more casualties among those who had first primed and threw them. The ground in front of the Australians soon filled with inert bodies and others moving aimlessly in the way of badly-wounded men. An eerie silence fell over the battlefield as the Turks suddenly melted into the darkness and the artillery fire slackened then stopped altogether. The firing died away to a sporadic crackle of desultory shots and the men stood, chests heaving as they gazed at the pile of bodies lying thickly in front of them.

No-one spoke, each of them staring fascinated at the broken humanity thickly carpeted around their trenches like autumn leaves.

Tom reacted first. 'See to our own blokes.' he shouted curtly.

'What about the Jackos?'

'Never mind them.'

'Oh God, look! Here they come again!'

'Right, get back here you lot, take cover and watch your ammo.'

The rifles cracked as a fresh wave of Turkish soldiers erupted from cover, following the same suicidal tactics as those who had gone before. A machine-gun opened up alongside the rifles, savagely tearing into running men and flinging them sideways with the impact of its bullets. Tom fired like an automaton, his shoulder aching from the repeated thumping of the SMLE. He was aware of men falling alongside him as Turkish bullets found their mark but these were only a few set against the enormous casualties the Turks were taking.

Phantoms gibbered and howled, ghostlike in the moonlight as the Turkish soldiers hurled themselves at their enemy. Faces capered and danced by the flare's ghastly light before sinking from sight into the dark, torso's shot through by a copper-jacketed .303 round. As Tom watched in terrified awe, a large, fiercely-mustachioed Turk ran through a hail of fire and picked up a multi-coloured flag which he waved vigorously over his head, urging his comrades on with a high, bellowing voice. Rifles swung in his direction and his chest erupted under a volley of gunfire as he sank slowly to the ground, still clutching the flag.

More explosions sounded, more shells and the firing of rifles that seemed to go on forever, intermingled with the hoarse yelling of men and the screams of the dead and the dying. A stabbing needle of pain tugged fiercely at Tom's shoulder and he spun violently, looking down to see blood oozing darkly from a wound high on his arm but he shrugged it off and continued firing. The pain was a stinging sensation lancing into his arm but he ignored it and shouted encouragement to the men firing on either side of him.

'Watch it!'

A shout and the man next to him spun round as a Turk leapt the wire and landed winded in the trench, followed by two more. The first gained his feet, breathing heavily, frantically looking for the rifle he'd dropped on landing but was smartly bayoneted by a cursing figure before he could straighten up. 'Shit!'

The bayonet stuck in the dead man's body and in trying to free it the Australian was himself bayoneted by one of the two surviving Turks. A shot rang out from the darkness and a Turk slumped lifelessly to the ground. The remaining enemy soldier raised his hands in mute supplication but a frenzied figure hacked him down with a sharpened entrenching tool as the attack melted away.

'Oh, sweet Jesus, look at those poor bloody galahs, would you!'

Tom twisted to see what the unseen voice meant and a quick glance showed him as he sucked in breath sharply.

Bodies and human remains lay everywhere, strewn thickly upon the blood-drenched, pock-marked ground. Scarcely a yard showed in the blackness of the night that wasn't occupied by the still form of a dead Turkish soldier. Body parts clad in ragged strips of uniform littered the ground and everywhere he looked the ground appeared to be soaked with darkened pools of blood. An arm waved weakly from a pile of bodies to his right but a rifle barked and the arm dropped abruptly from sight.

His mouth opened in protest then closed firmly. There would be no taking of prisoners, where would they put them? As to the enemy wounded, forget it, their own medical system was hard-pressed to assist its wounded let alone the hundreds of Turks that must be lying out there amongst their dead. Another rifle cracked as badly wounded men that could be seen were mercifully put out of their misery.

He jumped up onto the parapet for a closer look. A torn-off leg lay a few feet away, the bloody stump a raw, shredded mass with the white of bone showing and his stomach churned in protest. Further out the blue-white obscenity of coiled intestines lay draped in a surreal pattern alongside their fallen owner. The air was filled with the sickly, sweet aroma of freshly-spilled blood and he observed some of his men leaning over and choking, the noise splitting the eerie silence.

'God, corp, it's a bloody massacre.'

Tom turned and confronted Victor Abbott, all traces of humour gone from the young soldier's face, mirroring his own horror he as they gazed on the mounds of bodies. The ground above the parapet and the trench floor were littered with freshly-expended cartridge cases and he planted his feet solidly to avoid slipping as he took in the nightmare-ish scene.

'Why did they do it, these blokes must've been mad to keep on charging like that? Christ, some of them didn't even have rifles, did you see that, corp? You're bleeding, are you alright...? LOOK OUT!'

He spun round. Two Turks, one bare-headed, his face streaked with blood and tunic shredded from shrapnel, had tottered unsteadily to their feet a yard away and was feebly pointing a rifle in Tom's direction. The other held a broken bayonet in his hand and across the short distance the two enemy's eyes locked. Somewhere behind him, Tom heard the bark of an SMLE but the wounded Turk's rifle barrel spouted flame and he felt a mighty blow to his forehead as the world turned black.

Chapter Eight.

Krithia, May.

'Here, Yilmaz, take some of these olives, they taste delicious. Quickly, before the others see them. I'm sorry it's not a drop of *fuhl* but beggars can't be choosers as my mother would say. Ach, do you remember the taste of *fuhl?* Done in millet fat with flat *pide* bread to wash them down with, a meal for a caliph, wouldn't you say? Eat them quickly before these accursed flies take every morsel!'

Gratefully, Artoun took the olives from Arif's outstretched hand and placed one in his mouth, angrily brushing away the hordes of flies that had magically appeared. 'I can't say I was that taken with broad beans cooked in fat but you've certainly made me feel hungry with all this talk of food. Where did you get the olives?'

'Don't ask! Alright, I stole them from the captain's supply tent. *Shhh*! I said, don't. If you utter a word about this, we're dead.'

They ate together in silence, leaning against the roughness of the trench they were whilst looking over their shoulders to see if they'd been noticed. 'Aah, that's better.' Arif stretched expansively and belched, flexing his shoulders and looking up. 'Yilmaz, my friend, where did you say we were in this forsaken land?'

'I heard the captain say these trenches were near a place called Kirte. He says the *infidels* are no more than a few hundred yards away and that we should look forward to dying soon as there will be plenty of opportunities.'

'Arsehole, we'll see about that. I have no intention of dying for anyone yet and that includes our ass of a captain.' He leaned over and farted noisily.

'Better out than in, as my mother always said. What? Why do you look at me like that, Yilmaz, do you not have bodily functions like other men or does your shit smell only of flowers?'

'You should be like me and sit downwind of your friends sometimes,' Artoun said with a wry smile, 'that way the smell of camel's dung coming from your arse wouldn't offend.'

'Huh, I could...'

'Alright you two whore's sons, on your feet!'

They jumped as one at the harsh words.

'Follow me.'

The *chaoush* spun around and both men followed him hastily, trying to keep pace with his hurried steps. The morning had a bracing feel

149

to it and the sun overhead added to the feeling of peacefulness. In the distance was a noise of desultory shelling but here in this corner of the peninsula the war seemed far away. The *chaoush* stopped eventually outside a dugout entrance and gestured curtly for them to enter. Adjusting their eyes to the gloom they became aware of a calm, mustachioed figure in the uniform of a captain seated at a rough wooden bench, smoking a long cigarette. Next to him sat a middle-aged, pale-skinned soldier in a strange grey uniform and their apprehension grew. No-one spoke and after an awkward silence, Arif cleared his throat in a deferential manner.

'*Nabahiniz, hair olsún, efendim.* Good morning, sir.'

'Silence! Speak only when I allow you the privilege.' The captain calmly carried on reading through a sheaf of papers held in one hand as he tapped cigarette ash on the dugout floor, filling the small room with clouds of evil- smelling smoke whilst exhaling through his teeth. Fighting the urge to cough, Artoun looked through narrowed eyelids at the other man sat patiently next to the captain. The stranger returned his gaze unblinkingly, shifting his gaze from Arif to Artoun and back again.

The captain lowered his papers and took a delicate sip from a thin-walled china cup. As he tilted the cup, Artoun caught the fragrant smell of cardamom-flavoured coffee and he swallowed noisily in a futile gesture of yearning. The captain's hand paused in mid-air and he looked up at the two soldiers. Pointing an exquisitely manicured finger at Artoun he reflected almost languidly. 'You and your cowardly friend are part of the punishment squad sent here to this battalion to bolster the real fighting men of our country. My orders are to expend you on tasks my own men would deem suicidal so rest assured, my friends, I shall follow my orders to the letter.

I have such a task for two men and you fit the bill. We know the *infidels* are to attack soon; the numbers of men arriving opposite our lines are a certain giveaway. They think us fools but I need a good pair of eyes in the ground between us to give a warning lest they should attack during the night. We gave them a bloody nose only a few days ago but they have vast numbers of men to expend and I for one am ready to send them to hell.

That's where you come in, you and your stinking friend will lie out in no-mans-land and keep watch. If you hear preparations being made to attack one of you, I don't give a damn who, is to crawl back and inform me.'

'But if it's daylight, we'll be spotted, sir?'

The captain studied Arif's face with a calm detached air. 'If they shoot you then we'll know they're ready to attack, won't we? And if you think by being out there you can crawl away when night falls and give yourself up let me tell you, I shall personally find you, cut your balls off and feed them to the jackals. Do I make myself clear?'

They nodded dumbly, too afraid to speak. The stranger leant over and spoke in faltering Turkish. 'Captain Çelik, should we not arm these fellows, just in case they...?'

'In the name of *Allah*!' the captain cried, 'Arm them, do you know what you're saying, Brückner? These men are criminals, condemned men, giving them a weapon will allow them to murder my own men and make their getaway. No, they go out there unarmed, more for our sakes than their own.'

He glared at Arif. 'Let me introduce you to Leutnant Brückner of the Imperial German Army, not that you'll have too long left in this miserable life to make his acquaintance. The Leutnant is part of the *Aleman* team assisting us in throwing the *infidels* back into the sea and is here to glean what he can from our operations. Do me a great service and at least show him that we Turks can die bravely. Now, the *chaoush* outside will give you more detailed orders, where you're to go and observe. Goodbye, it was nice meeting you but it ends here. Get out of my sight!'

'You were right, Arif, the captain is an arsehole!' Artoun growled as they crouched together in a small scrape just five yards in front of their lines. They'd waited until nightfall before being urged into the uncertainty of no-mans-land by the impatient *chaoush* and had silently crawled out into the dry grass. Counting the distance covered by the number of leg movements they'd arrived at their present spot and dug urgently with bare hands to make a hiding place where they hoped the keen eyes of the enemy would be unable to spot them.

Arif lay on his side, facing Artoun inches away from the other man's face. His foul breath washed over Artoun like a breeze and he tried to ease his head back as far as he could to escape. If he saw the movement, Arif gave no acknowledgement.

'Don't I know it, this is just like fucking Sinai, always getting the shitty jobs! What is it with some people, they fall into shit and smell of jasmine. Me? I fall into shit and come up smelling of...guess what? Shit! You're dead right. Why me?'

'*Shh*! They'll hear you.'

'Oh, right, they'll hear me. And do what, you fool, kill us? That's what we're here for, or had that fact escaped your notice?'

'Arif, calm down, I have no wish to arrive in Heaven sooner than I need to.'

His companion looked at him suspiciously. *Heaven?* That's for Christians, what are you doing invoking their beliefs? Did you not mean *Paradise, Allah* be praised?'

'I meant anywhere but here, Arif, does it matter whose God I invoked?' For a moment, Artoun thought of confessing his origins to Arif Bilgili but caution stilled his voice and he remained silent. Although he seemed a decent man, what would Arif think of his newfound friend if that friend turned out to be an Armenian refugee from a battalion recently slaughtered by fellow Moslems? No, best hold one's tongue and change the subject. Quickly.

'You said Sinai,' he asked. 'did you serve there too?'

For an answer, Arif thought deeply before he spoke again in a low voice, devoid of all emotion. 'I was mobilised into the *Nizam*, the Regular Army in the normal manner in March of 1913. I had a good job in *Stamboul* and a family but I didn't mind, everyone has to serve so I entered the army eager to do my bit. My service with the regulars which should've lasted two years before transferring to the *Redif*, the Army Reserve, would have ended this March. The *Seferberlik*, war mobilisation, of last October ended all that and I was told I must stay with the regulars until the conflict ended.'

'But surely the government had to honour your original service?

'That's what I assumed but when I pointed that out I was transferred to a unit heading for Russia and the winter conflict there. I cursed them all, *Allah* included, may I be forever penitent, but to no avail. I froze there along with thousands of our soldiers, fighting a war we were totally unprepared for but I was lucky, I returned after the winter...'

'But Sinai, you said—'

'Let me finish! When we arrived back in Turkey we were told we had dishonoured the country by not returning victorious so as a punishment we were shoved on a train and sent in the opposite direction to the Sinai Front to try and take the Suez Canal. The *infidels* slaughtered us there just as the Russians had slaughtered us in Russia and it was at that point, my friend, I decided that I'd had enough. I deserted my battalion and wandered around for a while but there was no work to be had and I was starving so I decided to try and make it back to *Stamboul* and my family but was caught, like yourself. As a result I now find myself here, lying in a hole, waiting to be slaughtered again!'

Artoun fell silent at Arif's words, mindful of the great sorrow his friend bore so stoically. 'And you, Yilmaz, what happened to you and don't give me that story again about being a poor farmer caught up in all of this. You have the air of someone who's soldiered before so tell me, how do you come to find yourself here?'

'You're right, I was a soldier. My unit was based in Haleb and I missed my family, very much like you, so I decided one day to go home and see them. I was caught and the rest you know.'

'What battalion were you with?'

'Why?'

'You seem very touchy about your past, my friend.'

'I don't like answering such questions, why do you persist?'

'I have a lot of friends in Haleb, with different battalions. You might know some of them. Do you remember a private called...?'

'Arif, please, don't you think it's bad enough being here without having to remember the circumstances that led to my imprisonment?'

'Don't be so hasty, my friend I was only—'

'What about your family, what news of them?' Artoun interjected quickly.

'I've had one message. Since then, nothing. If I thought about them for too long, my wife and my two boys, I'd go mad. Instead, I've banished them from my mind and accepted my fate. *Allah's* will is that I never see them again but it hurts, Yilmaz, it hurts so badly... Do you not feel the same about your family, the utter hopelessness of never seeing them again?'

'We'll survive, Arif, you and me, don't talk like this. We'll survive and go back home to our families, you'll see.'

Arif Bilgili stared at Artoun with pain-filled eyes. 'Yilmaz, please, take that thought out of your head. Our bones will bleach the peninsula, we're not going home, ever.'

'But *Enver Paşa* said, I read it, he promised...'

'*Enver?* Don't make me laugh! That arrogant camel's offspring led us into battle against the Russians and watched on as we were slaughtered in our thousands at Sarikamiş! He should not have been given command of a squad of donkeys, let alone an army of men. They say our losses were 75,000, good men sorely needed today but he squandered them, just like we're being squandered here. Now, enough, leave me rest for a while. If the *infidels* should attack please don't bother to wake me, I'd rather not see the bayonet before it's stuck into my guts!'

While Arif dozed, Artoun sat thinking about the events that had brought them here. After their miraculous survival at the hands of Colonel Osman in Konia they'd been transported by rail to Istanbul and from there endured a week's march to Kirte via Gelibolu. Occasionally the naval guns of the allies had hindered their passage but they arrived with few casualties and after a vitriolic haranguing from an arrogant captain marched onwards, arriving into the trenches to await further orders.

His thirst grew so he fumbled in his tunic pocket for a small, round pebble he'd placed there earlier and began to suck on it. He had a small water-bottle attached to his left hip but he reasoned if the day grew any hotter he'd need it then. The pebble drew a small welcome amount of saliva into his mouth so he lay alongside Arif, listening to his friend's even breathing while he kept a cautious ear pricked in the direction of the enemy trenches.

The wrinkled khaki uniform they were clad in was that of the regular Turkish Army but as a sign of their fall from grace the unique coloured patches denoting their unit, normally stitched to both sides of their collars, had been ripped off. This was the ultimate sign of disgrace, a confirmation of their low status among their fellow soldiers and on the march down the peninsula more than one grizzled veteran had spat on them with contempt in his eyes.

They remained in their burrow for the rest of the day, dozing in fits and starts, each taking a turn listening. All to no avail, the British soldiers yards away carried on their own troglodytic existence unaware of the two men lying just yards away and the day passed with no movements from the trenches to their immediate front. A cold night was spent in the same manner as the day and just before dawn the friends stiffly and cautiously withdrew.

'*Dur!*'

At the shouted command to stop from a nervous sentry, Arif lost his temper. 'It's us, you fucking offspring of a she-camel, who do you think would come crawling towards you like dogs with their arses in the air? The Caliph of Damascus?'

'*Yakin gel!* Come closer.'

As directed they slowly came closer to where a rifle barrel poked waveringly over the barbed wire in their direction.

154

'Is that you, Kaplan, you cretin?'

'Oh. It's you.'

'Yes, it's us. Now poke that barrel somewhere else and keep an eye over our shoulders as we pass through the wire.' In moments they were safe within the narrow confines of their own trench and squeezed along its length in search of some food and a drink.

Captain Çelik was apoplectic at their reappearance. 'Who said you were to return?' he demanded hotly, 'You dogs, you were to stay there until orders were sent for you to return! I've a good mind to—'

'Captain,' Leutnant Brückner interjected softly, 'what were they to do without food or water; they would be too weak to fulfill their function of providing an early warning.'

'Food? Water? It was not my intention to supply them, they were sent there to die! I tell you, Brückner, an example should be made, I will not have my orders disobeyed.'

'In which case their return is immaterial, sir, you would have had no early warning of an attack at all if they'd stayed and died there.'

Çelik calmed visibly at the leutnant's attempts to soothe him. 'Alright, alright, I agree, perhaps I was too hasty in sending them without explicit orders. No matter, fresh orders have come through, the *infidels* known as *Australians* are pressing us back, away to the west, and we're to travel there as quickly as possible. We join our brothers of the 19th Division and a new assault there will see us push them back into the sea and force a ceasefire or a great victory. Get the men ready Bruckner, you and the *chaoush* ensure we've enough supplies for the march and we'll set off before nightfall.'

'Sir.'

The Leutnant disappeared, leaving a nettled captain glaring with distaste at Arif and Artoun. 'What are you staring at? You two follow him, get out of my sight for now. Go!'

--§--

'Did you manage to acquire the *tufeks* your friend promised?' Artoun whispered as Arif crawled alongside him. Arif Bilgili shuffled closer and spoke quietly. 'Rifles? I got nothing a beating for my troubles, my friend, and lucky to escape with only the beating.' Shocked, Artoun pulled at his friend's sleeve.

'*Aaaahhh*, for the love of *Allah*, please don't do that.'

'I'm sorry, does it hurt?'

155

'Like someone's plunged a hot dagger into my shoulder, Yilmaz, I should've known. That bastard of a *Buluk Emini*, he'll get his throat slit yet and from behind if I have anything to do with it.'

At Arif's mention of the Battalion Quartermaster, Artoun became anxious.

'But you said he'd help get us a weapon and some bullets, we can't go against the enemy with our bare hands, Arif. What has he done?'

'Sold us out, that's what! Some of the other prisoners made him a better offer and he sold them the two *Mauser tufeks* he'd promised us. Rusted-up, useless pieces of shit they were, too but at least we could have scrounged a bayonet for them and had a decent chance when we go into action. When I complained that he had better examples he could let us have the bastard took a metal cleaning rod and beat me, knowing that if I opened my mouth the captain would have me shot.'

'What do we do now?'

Arif pulled at his moustache, twisting his lips and showing crooked, yellowed teeth. 'Leave it to me, this is not over yet. Did you get some rations for us?' Artoun lifted the small sack from the floor. 'Here, take it, there's plenty. I got about 50 *dirhems* of *pilaf*, some small onions and a hunk of mutton. There's no bread but some should come up tomorrow, if we're still alive by then.'

'Huh!' Arif grumbled. 'At least they're feeding us well, fattening up the calf before the slaughter, eh?' He plunged his hand into the bag and withdrew a moist ball of boiled rice, stuffing it into his mouth and chewing noisily. The mutton was next; tearing a shard of meat off the bone he devoured that along with another handful of rice, following it up with a long swallow from a goatskin water-bag.

'That's better, I always feel better with some food in my belly. Now, before that pig of a *chaoush* comes along to disturb us I think I'll take a small nap to allow my wounds to heal. Keep and eye out for him, Yilmaz and give me a swift kick if you see or hear him coming our way.'

'You're always sleeping.' Artoun grumbled.

'Eh? Just watch, will you and stop complaining.'

'Me, complain? Me?'

--§--

The forced march over the hinterland had taken two days as the regiment advanced towards the enemy positions in the north-west.

Toiling in the growing heat had taken its toll of many of their number but swift kicks from the NCO's ensured no-one dropped out at the side of the track for too long. Arriving at the 19th's Division's positions they had been speedily moved into the front line to take part in the planned forthcoming assault on the *infidels*.

The evening cooled into night and Artoun shivered in his thin tunic as he and Arif manned the front-line trench with the other prisoners. Throughout the day the sound of shots and exploding artillery shells had kept their nerves on edge and they'd crouched low in order not to be seen by their hidden enemy. Snipers from both sides were active and a single shot was often followed by a sharp cry as a bullet found its mark. With his experience of earlier fighting, Arif withstood the sounds of battle stoically whereas Artoun jerked and winced spasmodically with every shot.

'Stay there, don't jump about so,' Arif jeered, 'you can't make yourself any smaller and if you can hear the shot it's missed you. The one you don't hear is the one that kills you, my friend and by then you'll be in Paradise and far too happy to be bothered about your former, miserable existence on earth.'

'Why are you such a dreamer?' Artoun snarled. 'Paradise? Every time I hear a shot I nearly shit myself. Arif, they're trying to kill us, me, and all you can fucking do is chatter about being happy about dying. I want to live, can't you get that into your thick skull?'

'Oh, so that's how it is now, is this the thanks I get for trying to help? I was only trying to make you understand how th—'

'Don't! My bowels are like water as it is! Soon, very soon, we're going to meet men over there who will try to kill us and what will we have to defend ourselves? A rock, a stick or do you have a magic trick that'll make us invisible? Pray, do tell me because from where I'm looking we're doomed.'

'Why must you go into battle unarmed?'

A quiet voice broke into their argument and they both started at the silent form of Leutnant Brückner. The Leutnant had approached unnoticed along the trench and now crouched next to them with a questioning stare. His Turkish accent was thick but there was no mistaking the meaning of his fumbled speech as he repeated his earlier question.

'I asked why must you go into battle unarmed?'

It was Arif who spoke for them both. 'Has the captain not explained who we are, sir?'

'He said you were all criminals, deserters who'd been sentenced to be at the forefront of any attack but he made no mention of denying you weapons to face the enemy with.'

'Didn't you hear him when he sent us out on sentry duty, sir, we left unarmed?'

'Ah, that. I thought that was just his way of ensuring you didn't fire at the enemy prematurely and give your position away but this, this is different.'

Artoun studied the Leutnant's face and saw only earnestness in the officer's expression. 'The colonel has his orders, sir; we're to go into battle unarmed in order to draw the *infidel's* fire to ourselves first. That way our comrades can approach without fear of losing their lives needlessly.'

'No, no, this is not right!' Bruckner insisted, 'Stay here and I'll be back directly.' He slithered away and disappeared into the gathering gloom.

'Ah well, that's that.' Arif said scornfully, 'He's gone to fetch us that stick you mentioned earlier or maybe even a sharp rock we can hurl at the *infidels* before they mow us down. And you, Yilmaz, what did you tell him that bullshit about comrades and losing lives needlessly? Losing lives? I don't give a fig for theirs, it's mine I'm more concerned about. How are we supposed to fight without arms?'

'Arif, shut up will you! I'm sick to death of your moaning, do something positive for a change and think about how we can come out of this alive, can you!'

'Me? Moaning? May *Allah* the merciful strike you dead for your unkind words, Yilmaz, it's me that's been keeping you alive, not the other way round. Don't forget, back there in Osman's office it was me that told you...'

'Just shut up, will you! How many more times must I tell you?'

A stunned Bilgili sat there in awe at his companion's angry outburst. A silence followed until he could bear it no longer.

'Look, all I was saying was...'

'*Shh*! Someone's coming.'

They fell silent as a metallic clatter reverberated along the trench. Panting with the effort, Brückner reached the two men and deposited two rifles at their wondering feet. 'Quickly, take them.' He ducked awkwardly in the confines of the trench and offloaded a full bandolier of ammunition from around his shoulders.

'Here, take this too. Hurry.'

'The Blessings of the Prophet be upon you, sir!' cried Arif reaching for the bandolier, 'How did you manage to relieve the Quartermaster of such beautiful *Mauser tufeks*? And so many *Kershuns*,too.'

Bruckner smiled, a slow thoughtful smile that failed to reach his eyes. 'Let's just say we came to an agreement, I wouldn't inform the captain of his, ah, other *activities* if he *donated* two fine rifles to me and some cartridges with no questions asked. Stout fellow that he is, he saw the wisdom in my argument and gave me the weapons and ammunition without a fuss.'

'I knew it! The rumours about that jackal selling our rations and pocketing the money just had to be true!'

Brückner looked at them with innocent eyes. 'Did I say that?' he replied in his quaintly spoken Turkish. 'No, my friends, let us say that the Quartermaster came to realise your needs and was only too happy to assist me in fulfilling them. Take good care of the weapons and if we go into action shortly at least I won't have you on my conscience.'

'Why would you do this for us, sir, if the captain were to find out that you'd helped us he would not be too pleased.'

'The captain has his own ideas on how to treat soldiers and I have mine,' Brückner replied, 'and my ideas do not include sending men into battle without the means to defend themselves. That does not mean to say that I disagree on everything the captain says, just this particular subject. There is a problem, though, what if he was to find you with these arms, how would you explain them?'

'Have no fear, sir,' Arif interjected hurriedly, 'we'd never involve you. Please, you have our grateful thanks and as the captain considers us dead men already how could he punish us further if he found us with these weapons?'

Nodding his assent, Brückner turned to leave and noticed Artoun looking at him thoughtfully. 'You!' he demanded. 'Why are you looking at me like that?'

'I'm sorry, sir, I was wondering how you, a foreigner came to be with us. As a simple soldier I do what I'm ordered but you, you've come from so far away to help us. Why?'

Brückner relaxed. 'I'm glad you said foreigner and not *infidel*. It's quite simple really, I was an Islamic scholar in Berlin well before the war. I was called up to the Reserve in late 1913 and when I heard that General Von Sanders was appointed as Inspector General and had begun to assemble a team to come to Turkey to assist your army, I volunteered to join him in early 1914. So now, here I am, sharing in

159

the shit and the heat like yourselves and wondering why I was foolish enough to volunteer.'

'You've picked up a lot of our language, sir, although your accent is atrocious, if I may be permitted to say so.'

Brückner laughed. 'You're impertinent, I'll give you that but I'll take it as a compliment. German with all its complexities has given me an ear for other languages so I hope in the eighteen months that I've been learning Turkish I've picked enough up to be understood.'

'Certainly, sir, and if you need any translation please come and speak to me or my friend here and we'll be happy to help.' Arif bowed obsequiously, butting in on the conversation.

When the Leutnant had departed, Artoun rounded on his friend. 'Oh yes, sir, three bags full, sir, anything you need, sir, *just come and see me.*' You fool, Arif, he may of helped us but he's still an officer, whatever country he comes from. I don't trust these *Alemans*, why are they here, what benefit is there in helping us? Mark my words, that man is not to be trusted.'

Arif spat on the trench floor. 'Pah! You're just jealous he favoured me with his words rather than speak to a country ruffian like yourself. Didn't he bring us these fine *tufeks*? Now we can shoot back at the infidels who want to kill us, rather than just caper about and act as a human target until we're filled full of holes.'

'What was it you did before you were called up into the army?' Artoun asked.

'I was a carpet salesman. Why?'

'It shows, you're so eager to make a sale you've overlooked the holes in the carpet. He's not to be trusted, I tell you, he is an *infidel* after all, even if he's a supposed ally.'

Arif snorted his contempt. 'Look at you, the fucking philosopher! On that note I declare this conversation ended so leave me whilst I have a cigarette and then attempt to try and snatch some sleep before the captain thinks up another shitty task for us. Check the *tufeks* out while I snooze. And in answer to your unspoken question, yes, I do sleep a lot. What else is there for us to do? Go on, go!'

He rolled himself up in his greatcoat and after belching large clouds of smoke from a crumpled cigarette was snoring within seconds. Shaking his head, Artoun laid down next to Arif. He pulled the rifles over and examined them closely. Both were the standard 1903 Pattern 7.65mm Mauser rifle, the breeches pitted in some places but otherwise in a clean and functional condition. The bandolier held two hundred rounds in clips and he carefully loaded both magazines before placing the bandolier and rifles to one side.

Sleep was hard to come and he tossed and turned, evincing grumbling and mutterings from the sleeping figure next to him. Eventually his tiredness overcame the thoughts jumbling round in his head and he slipped into a troubled slumber.

--§--

'Artoun! Artoun! Wake up!' He rolled over and stretched luxuriously, grinning at Hegine's anxious face as she leant over him. The smell of cooking wafted over his nostrils and his smile widened further

'I smell food, is that what I hope it is?'

Hegine smiled back at him. 'Aha, I thought that might wake you. You soldiers are all alike, it's only food that gets your attention. Yes, husband, I'm cooking your favourite. Manti with garlic yoghurt and Sumac. When you bother to get up, that is!'

At the mention of minced lamb and onion pasta balls, Artoun's stomach growled in anticipation.

'What is it my love, can a man newly home on leave not sleep in once in a while? Are you waking me to serve some food or just to chastise me?'

She smiled back at him, relieved at his good humour. 'Your son is waiting to play with his father, what shall I tell him, that you're too busy sleeping to bother with him?'

'Alright, alright,' he protested, 'I'm awake. Look, I'm getting up now, go tell Khat his father will be out presently to attend to him. I promise, we'll have a good time, you'll see.'

'Good. He's been running around since early this morning, eager to be with his father again. I told him you were sleeping but you know what boys are, in one ear and out the other. Go to him and the two of you can share a meal together' '

Her face darkened. 'He does miss you so, as do I. When will the war end, this madness that keeps us parted can't go on for ever, can it?' She made as if to speak further but a sound outside caught her attention and she stopped, cocking her head to one side as she tried to make out its meaning. Her face changed suddenly, becoming distant, a look of terror and fear appearing in her eyes.

'Listen, can you hear that, horses, and coming this way. Oh God, Khat's outside! There's danger coming. Artoun, Artoun, save us, for pity's sake!' She dropped the broom she was holding and ran for the doorway of the hut. 'I must go to him and make sure he's safe.'

'Hegine! Stay here, I'll go and see to the boy!' Artoun protested but his words were lost in the emptiness of the room as the figure of his wife faded into a light, ephemeral mist. Frightened at its import, he began to rise and as he did so the morning light streaming through the open doorway began to change, becoming dimmer and darker as if the sun's light had been suddenly extinguished. Anxiety gnawed at his stomach with a sharp blade. A sudden scream from outside brought him bolt upright as the drumming sound of horses hooves rose to a deafening crescendo before stopping as quickly as it had begun, leaving him standing in an eerie silence.

Thoroughly awake now, a dull ache in his gut, Artoun stepped away from the blankets on the floor. *'Hegine? Khat? Come back...Come back, don't leave me here like this. What's happening?'*

From outside came no answering call but inside the darkness grew, filling the room and enveloping him in its cloying embrace, slowing the movements of his limbs until it felt as if he were wading through quicksand and his breath escaped tortured lungs in agonised whispers. Slowly, the dark tendrils whirled round, picking up speed until they resembled a dervish spinning in the market-place and his head reeled with the giddiness of trying to keep pace. The blackness beckoned and he succumbed dizzily, falling headlong into space.

--§--

His eyes opened abruptly and he squinted into the glare of the morning sun, looking stiffly up into the curious face of Arif Bilgili. 'Yilmaz, my friend, you were having a bad dream, what was it you had to eat last night?' Offhandedly he added. 'Who's Hegine?'

Artoun thought swiftly. 'An *ermeni* woman I knew once, a long time ago.'

'Was she pretty?'

'Well...'

'Well, was she? A simple question that begs a simple answer. Was this woman pretty?'

'Very.'

'You sly dog, you. Did the *Imam* find out and flay your worthless hide'?'

'It wasn't like that, you don't understand...'

'Oh, I understand all right, my friend. Still, forbidden fruits taste all the better when consumed in private. Although I'm told the fruits are drying up, if that idiot Kaplan is to be believed.'

'How do you mean, Arif?'

'He told me of a rumour come from the east that many *ermeni* villages have been emptied and the villagers sent into the desert. No-one ever sees these people again and...'

'Who says these things?' Artoun demanded, his stomach lurching and head pounding at Arif Bilgili's words as he remembered his recent dream

'I told you, cloth ears, that fool Kaplan's been spreading this rumour around. He reckons elements of the government are paying off old scores and cleansing certain districts of all *ermeni* on suspicion of them aiding the Russians. Live and let live, I say, everyone's the same to me as long as they support Turkey but you know how some of those arseholes in *Stamboul* feel about any non-Moslems. A nod's as good as a wink for them to sneak away and carry out all sorts of wrongdoings.'

'He's wrong, he must be, how does a simple private come by this sort of information?' muttered Artoun, the half-remembered anxiety of his dream returning to cause a sharp, empty feeling in the pit of his stomach for the second time that morning.

'He says he heard the *chaoush* discussing it with the Quartermaster and the *chaoush* had heard the captain talking with the German officer about it. Yilmaz, are you alright, you've gone quite pale? This woman you knew, Hegine, did she live in the east?'

Artoun hid his face to avoid Arif seeing the conflicting emotions that he felt must scar his features and give him away. 'Possibly, I don't know, it was a long time ago, I told you.'

Arif smiled. 'Memories. Something to keep a lonely soldier company on the dark, cold and lonely nights. Let's not have any more talk of this. Come, I fancy if we sneak round to the cook's stove we might cajole him into giving us something nice to eat. I'm starving and the day's drawing on so empty your head of these dismal thoughts and drag those lazy bones of yours in this direction.

By the way, I've examined the *tufeks* and they please me greatly. I shall kill many *infidels* with mine, and from a distance too. Whilst our brothers close with the enemy and beat them to death with their bare hands we can lie on our bellies and pick the *infidels* off from afar. *Allah* is good, my friend and I shall include the Leutnant in my prayers tonight, if we still live. Now, drop what you're doing and follow me, I've heard that the cook's made a fine bean and lentil stew.'

163

With that he moved down the trench, crouching low. After a moment's hesitation, Artoun followed him, his mind a mass of confused thoughts. What did this mean, which villages? Were his wife and son safe? The dream, was that a sign? An ill-omen of bad news to come or...? His head threatened to burst under the weight of his foreboding, a vein began throbbing painfully in his forehead and he tried to still the sense of dread as he hurried after his friend.

Under a fierce sun the day passed as they sought refuge from the unforgiving heat overhead. Their *kabalaks* afforded some protection but sweat still stung their eyes as they endured the rising temperature. Any movement caused an outbreak of sweat from armpits, groins and chests, causing them to scratch fiercely, alerting their personal colonies of lice which only added to the overall discomfort. At noon, one of the company runners appeared, festooned with water skins and some stale bread and raisins which they consumed greedily.

Arif poured a torrent of tepid water down his throat before Artoun managed to snatch the goatskin from him, grimacing as the dank-smelling warm liquid disappeared down his gullet. Hunger and thirst appeased for the moment, both men squatted whilst soundlessly allowing their bodies to digest the food.

Whilst they rested, Private Kaplan squirmed towards them. 'Psst! The *chaoush* said to warn you we'll be attacking tonight so stay where you are until further orders are passed to you.'

'When?'

'He didn't say, just told me to tell you to hold yourself ready. It's a big one, the whole company's been told to be ready.'

'Arsehole!' Arif growled, 'What a way to fight a war. Luckily we'll be fighting in the dark, because if I saw that fat pig up there I'd be tempted to...' He caught himself before he could mention the rifles lying hidden under their greatcoats.

'Alright, piss off, tell him you've seen us and we're quaking in our sandals!'

Moments after Kaplan had left Arif sighed and turned to Artoun. 'It's no good, I need to go and make my prayers. Will you come with me?'

'Where?' Artoun replied, surprised.

'I scrounged a piece of cloth that will pass for a prayer mat so I thought we'd shuffle down this trench to that corner and make our prayers that way. *Allah*, praise his name, will understand, don't you think?'

164

'You go. I'll stay here and watch.' Artoun spoke tersely and Arif looked closely at his friend.

'What's up, we're going to fight shortly, don't you want to make your peace before we go?'

Thinking frantically, Artoun replied. 'Look, Arif, when I was captured and sent here I made a promise to myself that I wouldn't think of prayer or religion until I was safe in the arms of my family again. The *imam* keeps his distance from us as he thinks we're doomed so you won't mind if I keep myself to myself until this is all over and we go back to a normal life.' He looked sideways at Arif, wondering if his companion was beginning to have suspicious thoughts about his reticence to go to prayers but his fears were soon allayed.

'Please yourself.' Arif shrugged and moved away. 'I won't be long, although preparing oneself for entering Paradise is a serious business. Are you sure you don't want to...'

'Go!'

They dozed away most of the afternoon, keeping their movements to a minimum. As the sun began to set Artoun nudged Arif and they looked down the trench to watch the *chaoush* approaching. Puffing fiercely he pulled alongside and glared at the two men.

'Right you two, orders from the captain. We'll be attacking when it gets dark so when you hear the bugle sound, you and the other sacks of shit are to rise up and start running towards the *infidel's* trenches. Make lots of sounds, make sure they hear you coming. Get it?'

'Which direction would that be, sir?' asked Arif innocently.

'*Rahat dur, keep quiet!* Don't get smart with me, you jackal or...'

'I was only asking because if we run in the wrong direction I wouldn't want you or the captain to think we were deserting and start shooting at us.'

The chaoush stared, baffled, unsure if Arif was making fun of him. 'You'll soon know, you buffoon,' he snarled, 'the only shots you'll hear will be the infidels shooting at you. No need for me to bother, they'll do the job for me.'

'Aren't you coming with us, sir?'

For an answer the *chaoush* began to scramble back the way he'd come.

'See you in Paradise!' Arif shouted after his retreating figure.

'Now what?' Artoun demanded.

165

'We wait.' Arif answered simply, slumping to the bottom of the trench and closing his eyes.

The shadows lengthened and night began to fall. Their vicinity to the sound of their artillery shelling the enemy trenches made their heads hurt but for some reason where they crouched the war seemed far away. The air was sultry, warm and stifling and Artoun eased his collar in an attempt to stop the coarse cloth of his tunic making his neck itch. In the absence of any meaningful sounds a hope began to grow that maybe the attack had been abandoned but a sudden rustling to his right and the faint noise of men whispering alerted his senses. He strained to see but the stygian blackness was too deep for his eyes to penetrate.

'Arif...?'

'I'm here.'

'I think it must be time, there's...'

The loud, strident blast of a bugle pierced the night and he felt Arif Bilgili squeeze his shoulder. 'Let me get up first, Yilmaz, and I'll help you.'

'I must tell you something before we leave, Arif. This madness, so much has changed in our world and not for the better. It's Artoun, Arif, my real name's Artoun Seferian.' Arif's eyes opened wide in surprise and disbelief. He stepped back, shaking his head.

'Seferian? That's an *ermeni* name! How did you...?'

The bugle sounded again, its braying noise more strident and Arif straightened up, all thoughts of interrogation gone from his mind.

'We'll talk about this later. For now, let's get moving before the *chaoush* finds an excuse to shoot at us. Here, wait a moment.'

With a series of loud pants, wheezing heavily, Arif heaved himself up out of the trench and reached back down for Artoun's hand. Gratefully, Artoun grasped the rough fingers and was swiftly hoisted up onto the crumbling parapet. He bent down immediately and straightened up with a rifle in his hand. 'Here, Arif, take this while I get the other one.'

Both now armed, they peered round before Arif took Artoun's shoulder again. 'This way, follow me and do exactly as I do.' The sounds of running feet echoed all around them and they began to trot across the broken ground under their feet before breaking into a run.

Whoosh!

The darkness was suddenly rent asunder by the dazzling brightness of a flare exploding high above them, casting the surreal shadows of hundreds of men running alongside them into sharp relief. An orange spot flickered in front of Artoun and he heard the sharp *crack*! of a rifle as a bullet hummed spitefully over his head. He pulled up sharply but Arif urged him on. 'Don't stop, keep going!' At the sound of the shot a thousand voices gave vent to their feelings, screaming and ululating wildly as they plunged on, rapidly closing the gap between the two sets of trenches. ·

Another splash of orange appeared and another, until the air was filled with the deadly sounds of rifle bullets whirring in their direction. He felt, rather than heard, men stumble and fall, their passing marked by a surprised cough or faint yelp as the bullets struck home. The flare spluttered and died, to be replaced by another which relit the landscape, showing the fallen, humped figures of the slain. Artoun found himself yelling with the rest, the same high ululating sound escaping his lips as he ran on. A bullet plucked at his sleeve but he ignored it and ran on as all the while his tortured breath escaped from his lips in loud sobs with the effort of keeping up.

He tripped and stumbled suddenly, sprawling full length. The men alongside flowed past him in an unstoppable wave as he stared wildly round. From the darkness of the enemy trench the staccato stutter of a machine-gun added its sound to the noise of battle and he watched in horror as those who'd so recently passed him jerked and writhed under the impact of the bullets before flopping limply to the ground.

He regained his feet and pointed his rifle loosely in the enemy's direction, pressing the trigger. The sudden recoil sent him flying backwards but by gripping the rifle tighter and working madly at the bolt he reloaded and fired again in a maniacal frenzy, firing until the rifle clicked on an empty breech. A hand tugged at his arm but he shook it off wildly, swinging the rifle round in a furious defensive sweep.

'Artoun, it's me, Arif.'

The madness in his eyes died and he looked blankly into the shadowed features of Arif Bilgili. 'Quick, duck down here!' Arif shouted and pulled him down behind an outcrop of rock. Before he could speak, a loud shrieking noise filled the air overhead and the shell slammed down thirty yards away, the massive explosion sending dirt and shards of white-hot metal in every direction. They cowered behind their shelter as more shells lit up the night, the red and yellow centres of each explosion casting an eerie backdrop to the fierce fighting raging on all around. Hot pressure waves battered their eardrums, deafening them, rendering coherent speech impossible and forcing them to remain curled up into tiny balls in a desperate attempt to escape the force of the explosions.

The Turkish soldiers recoiled and broke against the defences of the Australians as waves on the shore, ebbing and flowing in repeated charges through their own shellfire and the rifles and machine-guns of the enemy. As each wave lapped at the enemy wire they left behind a series of dark shapes strewn carelessly on the ground. During a lull in the firing Arif gesticulated urgently. 'Look, over there, the *Sansác.*' Puzzled, Artoun followed his gaze and recognised what his friend meant. Lying beside a limp body was a large flag, their regimental colours. Arif made to rise from behind the rock but Artoun pulled him back.

'Don't! Arif, it's madness to go out there, you'll be shot down like a dog.' Arif jerked himself free, dropping his rifle and rising to his feet. He leant over and shouted hoarsely into Artoun's ear. 'I can't let the *infidels* mock us. We'd be dishonoured forever if they gain possession of our colours.'

'Arif, we don't owe this regiment anything, they sent us here to die, remember?'

Arif looked down at him and smiled, his face gleaming palely in the brightness of another flare. 'Remember what I said previously, Artoun Seferian. Live and let live, Artoun, live and let live. I think somewhere deep in here,' he prodded his chest, 'a soldier still lurks. Take care. I hope you live to see your family again. Goodbye, my friend.'

Before Artoun could respond Arif turned back and ran towards the flag. Bearing a charmed life in the hailstones of bullets he reached it unscathed and scooped the pole up with both hands, waving the *Sansác* in large sweeping motions as he roared fiercely at his fellow soldiers.

'This way, come on you whores, come on you *askers*, do you want to live forever? *Allah!* For our motherland, for—'

A fusillade of shots smashed into him simultaneously and his chest erupted under the impact of several bullets striking at once. The flag dropped from nerveless fingers and he slowly collapsed onto his knees before limply falling forward and rolling over onto his back.

'*Arif!*'

An anguished sound tore from Artoun's lips as his friend fell onto his face and he rose in an effort to cross over to where Arif's body lay. He'd taken only a few steps before a grenade exploding nearby blotted out the other sounds around him and he was flung violently aside in the heat of its explosion.

Slowly he came to his senses, shaking his head as if awaking from a deep slumber. His left side ached agonisingly with each sharp intake of breath and a wet sensation made its presence felt down the lower half of his body. The sounds of the battle had faded, leaving in its place the noise of sporadic gunshots and he tried to rise but his strength had deserted him. Rolling over he weakly raised his head and looked round.

Arif Bilgili lay on his back ten yards from him, arms outstretched, a quizzical expression on his face. His eyes were slightly open but the light had left them, leaving his pupils with a fixed, glazed look. Grief overcame Artoun as he stared at the dead face of his friend, becoming aware as he did so of approaching steps. By turning his head slightly, he saw the figure of a tall enemy soldier moving slowly but purposefully, bending low as he examined the bodies of the Turkish soldiers lying thickly nearby. Anger burned hotly in Artoun's mind at this defilement of the dead and his questing fingers closed around a shattered bayonet's wooden handle.

He leapt to his feet at the same time as a badly-wounded *nefer* who had been laid alongside him. The enemy soldier turned in surprise at their presence and from over the soldier's shoulder a voice cried loudly and urgently in a strange tongue. Artoun and the foreigner stared soundlessly at each other before Artoun brought the bayonet up and started forward. The sound of a shot was shockingly loud in the silence and as he watched the foreign soldier slump to the ground another shot sounded almost simultaneously and he sensed the *nefer* slump to the ground beside him.

A small object landed at his feet, hissing and sputtering and he looked downwards in puzzlement. As his tortured brain tried to make sense of his surroundings the grenade detonated with a loud *crack!* and he pitched onto the dry, arid earth and was still, with only a rapid fluttering of his eyelids showing of his struggle for life. A wetness seeping down from his shoulder, around his neck, oozed slowly over his torso, causing a sharp, stabbing sensation in his arm as he tried to rise. Giving up the struggle he subsided back to the ground and lay still once more as the foreign voices broke over his head like waves on the shore.

Chapter Nine.

Cape Helles, May.

Walt Harding grunted with the exertion of standing and pulled at his trousers, the gnawing pain in his lower belly exploding into a fireball as he straightened.

'*Aaahh...*'

The burning sensation inside grew to an urgent need and he frantically pulled his trousers down again and squatted as a stream of liquid erupted from his bowels, splashing boots and puttees with a foul-smelling rush. Relief at this evacuation was short-lived as cramps doubled him over, a sharp, visceral sensation akin to rats kneeling on his abdomen and gnawing their way into his innards. Clutching his belly with one hand he tried to stop himself from falling backwards into the depths of the crude latrine dug into the earth at the back of the trench.

'Walt, are you alright, lad?'

'No, come to think of it, I don't feel all that chipper, sarje.'

'Bloody 'ell, that stinks! When you're finished, get over here and I'll send one of the lads for a medical orderly. You look like death warmed up, lad, what's ailing you?'

Walt Harding grimaced and stood, pulling stiffened trousers up around his waist. 'If you don't mind, sarje, I'll sit on the other side of you, the downwind side. My guts are killing me. I've been like this since early this morning, shitting through the eye of a needle.'

Clarence Johnstone peered closely at Walt. 'I think we'd better get you seen to quick, it looks to me like you're running a temperature, forgive me if I don't come close enough to confirm that. You've probably caught a dose of the dysentery that's doing the rounds or it could be start of this enteric fever I'm hearing about. Stay where you are and I'll send someone. Oi, Waddell, get yourself over here pretty damn quick. Move it!'

After sitting around and waiting out the debacle of Third Krithia without becoming involved the 7th Middlesex had been sent back to holding the line near Cape Helles. An indifferent diet and the unsanitary conditions into which they were plunged began an invidious sapping of their resolve and strength. Men fell sick in numbers that threatened to overwhelm the medical staff and no amount of entreaties or official demands brought a response from HQ. The result was an epidemic of cholera and dysentry amongst the troops, all of which could have been greatly avoided if the right precautions had been taken.

After Private Waddell had been swiftly despatched for help, Clarence Johnstone commandeered some filthy blankets and wrapped him securely in them, ignoring Walt's protests. Waddell returned thirty minutes later with two indifferent medical orderlies bearing a stretcher and Walt was gingerly placed on it and borne down the trench. The jerking motion caused the pain in his stomach to erupt again but the stretcher bearers stoically carried on, oblivious to his groans.

He began to feel sick and the world slipped into a series of blurred movements and muted voices as he slipped in and out of consciousness. A sense of delirium overtook him and he began imagining he was back in England but the dream was short-lived as an aggrieved voice dragged him back to reality.

'You dirty bastard, you've shit yourself again, and all over my fucking stretcher!'

Walt opened his mouth to protest but instead found himself slipping down a warm, liquid slope. Ignoring the stretcher-bearer's bitter accusation, he relaxed and sleepily enjoyed the headlong rush into oblivion.

--§--

ANZAC Cove, May.

Tom Harding awoke to a strange swaying sensation, that of being borne aloft. His head ached and he craned his eyes and tried to see who was carrying him but all he could see was the bright, blue sky overhead and in the distance the gleam of the sea. By turning slightly he could make out a high-sided inlet, festooned with awnings and wooden entrances and his mind relaxed as he realised where he was.

The men beneath him grunted continually with the strain of carrying him and just as he was beginning to enjoy the ride he was roughly dumped on the ground, seeing only the sight of their boots as the bearers departed for another stretcher. A thick bandage swaddled his head and his left arm was immobilised in a sling but if he squinted hard enough he could just see underneath the bandage and make out images beyond the overhang of the stiffened linen.

'Hi, how you doin', sport?'

He jumped at the sound of a strange voice and moved round on the stretcher to see a friendly face beaming down at him. His tongue felt furry and he motioned to his lips but the stranger shook his head.

'Sorry, mate, you've a head wound. Nil by mouth 'til the guys onboard have had a proper look at you.'

'Onboard?' he muttered hoarsely through gummed lips.

'Yeah, you beaut, you're off to Alexandria shortly, when those pom bastards get their fingers out've their arses and get here. We're sending you off to one of their hospital ships, a real treat if you ask me. Full of pom sheila's, all sex-starved an' just waiting for heroes like you to get their teeth into.' His new-found friend giggled at the fantasy.

'How long have I been here?' Tom asked slowly.

'Day before yesterday, mate. We dressed your arm no bother but the doc was worried about that head wound of yours. We've had to wait for a hospital ship to be made available so we brought you here for evacuation to have the docs onboard take a proper look. Enjoy yourself and don't be in a hurry to get back to this.'

An artillery shell exploded nearby and Tom ducked his head. 'Don't worry, mate, that's *Beachy Bill*, the howitzer. The bastard's up in the Olive Grove sling a shell over now and again to let us know they're still in this fucken' war!'

'How's it going then, what's been happening since I copped this?' Tom asked.

'Well, the Abduls attacked the other day, the same time you caught yours and we dropped them in the thousands. And I mean thousands, mate, they say the bodies are lying out there in front of the trenches like flies round shit. We lost some blokes but not as many as the bloody Abduls. Christ, one bloke who passed through here said he got his trying to decide which bastard to shoot at, there were that many.'

His face changed, becoming grimmer. 'Poor old Simmo caught it, though, bastard was bringing some poor wounded larrikin down the track and a Jacko machine-gun got him. Killed him instantly. His donkey lived, though. Funny thing, eh?'

Before Tom could reply he was gone, talking to another stretcher case to Tom's left. Moments later a shadow fell across his face as another stretcher crew arrived and lifted him up. They bore him down to the water's edge where a large, flat-bottomed barge lay in

172

wait and he was gently lifted aboard and placed at the far end of the barge.

Aware of a low murmuring, he looked around. As far as his limited vision could tell, the barge was filling up with stretchers, most bearing blood-stained forms swathed in dirty bandages. The noise came from swarms of flies clustering round the blood-stained bandages and the lips of the wounded, some unconscious but all sharing in the pain of the bullets and shrapnel that had left their painful mark.

He lost count of time but began to feel better lying in the warmth of the sun and at one point became aware of a gentle rocking motion as he gathered that they were now at sea. The steam pinnace towing their barge sent a small plume of black smoke up into the sky and he watched with fascination as they moved along a placid surface, a sharp tang of salt in his mouth making him ever more conscious of his mounting thirst.

After several minutes the barge shuddered as they came alongside a larger vessel and a group of men appeared, moving busily, shifting stretchers and lifting them high, oblivious to the cries and curses of the occupants. Tom's turn came and he was lifted up onto the deck of what appeared to be a trawler. The stretcher was carried over to a side of the open deck and unceremoniously dumped in the lee of its bulwark. More stretchers joined him and a muted thumping noise from below signalled their departure.

A face and shoulders in army uniform appeared by his feet and he cried urgently lest the man left him. 'What's happening, where are we going?' The soldier looked at him keenly before replying.

'Don't worry me old china, we're off to Lemnos to drop you lot off. There's too many of you, the hospital ships can't come in close enough here so we're taking you lot over to the island to embark you there.'

'Look, mate, I'm dying of thirst, you couldn't get me some water could you? Please.' Tom implored him. The soldier contemplated Tom's tunic, looking for the tag tied there. 'I dunno, you lot ain't supposed to get anything 'til we gets there but leave it to me, you look done in so I'll take a chance and bring you something. Don't tell them I did though, I'll get my arse reamed if you do.' He was as good as his word and returned shortly with a water-bottle from which Tom drank deeply. He tried to retain it but the soldier snatched it from his grasp and left.

His raging thirst slaked for the time being, Tom rolled over painfully and tried to relax but the stretcher's carrying cloth had sagged and the vibrating decks beneath bit into his back, making him feel every motion of the trawler as she scudded along. Gradually, the motion lulled him into a sense of tiredness and he slept.

In this way, several hours passed as the ship carrying its precious cargo of shattered humanity made its way serenely to the island of Lemnos, scene of their departure weeks earlier. Eventually, they entered Mudros harbour and made for the bulk of a large ship rocking slowly at anchor as she patiently awaited her next batch of wounded. Tom's world turned from a harsh vibration to gentle movements as the trawler came alongside.

The trawler's motion transformed into a harsh bumping noise and he looked up as the sun was blotted out by the massive steel sides of a hospital ship. She was painted white, with a large green stripe down her side, a huge red cross in the middle and he wondered idly if this was the same ship he'd seen at anchor in Mudros harbour the day they'd departed for the peninsula. The thought rekindled memories of Billy Willis and another, darker time and he retreated quickly from the pain those memories triggered.

HMHS Fyvie Castle moved gently in the swell of the harbour. A large, four-funnelled liner of the Castle Line, she'd been requisitioned as a hospital ship early in the war. Built by John Brown & Company of Clydebank in Scotland, she was launched in 1912 and was 560 feet long with a beam of 67 feet and had a GRT(Gross Registered Tonnage.) of 17,580 tons. Steam turbines turned two huge manganese-bronze propellers, giving her a maximum speed of 16.5 knots. Her insides had been stripped of most of their finery as the larger rooms were turned into wards for the wounded. Some of the sumptuous cabins were left unaltered in order to accommodate the senior medical officers who would need pleasant surroundings to relax in after a long day's surgery but for the most part the ship had been gutted and rebuilt to the Army Council's orders.

As Tom lay beneath her towering decks, a box cradle was gingerly lowered and his stretcher placed into it. In seconds he was moving upwards, a journey that took forever as he creaked his way aloft against the brightly-painted sides. He forced himself up into a sitting position in order to observe the panorama stretching before him but the effort was too great and he fell back with a stifled groan. Before he'd time to recover he was deposited on the wooden deck of the ship and a gang of men ran over to undo the ropes and send the cradle seawards again for the next stretcher.

An icy fragrance filled his nostrils and he lifted an arm to shade his eyes from the sun whilst attempting to identify the vision in white bending over him and inspecting the tag fastened to his tunic. It was a woman, a uniformed nurse by the look of her, smelling for the entire world as if she'd just left the Garden of Eden and her perfume caught the back of his throat as he inhaled deeply.

'Let me see, just who do we have here? Welcome aboard, soldier. Oh, you're an Australian…' A pleasant, musical voice filled his ears and he heard the crackle of starched linen as she bent closer. In spite of the pain in his head he tried to rise but she forced him gently back onto the stretcher with her free hand. .

'What…are…you…doing…later?' he hissed through pain-clenched teeth and she laughed, a warm, throaty laugh that wafted a fresh wave of perfume over him.

'You Australians, you're all the same, see a woman and there's no holding you back. Now lie still while I check your tag against my clipboard. Right, what and who do we have here. *GSW hd and lft arm.* That's: Gunshot Wound to Head and Left Arm to you, my lad…Corporal Harding. Corporal Thomas Walter Harding, 9th Battalion Australian Infantry Force.' She stopped speaking, a note of puzzlement in her voice as she released his tag.

'Hmn, that's strange, you're already onboard, I'm sure I've seen your name on another list. Harding, yes, I'm sure I've seen your name already. Oh, don't tell me there's been another foul-up.' She sighed. 'It happens all the time, why can't they get it right. I'll sort it out after we've seen to you.'

'Don't tell me I've got to get off,' Tom gasped, 'just when we were getting to know each other. And it's Serjeant Harding, I've just been bloody well promoted.' The effort of speaking made his head pound and he fell back onto the stretcher.

She laughed again, a low, amused laugh that made him forget the pain. He was aware of her scrutiny but in his exhausted state was unable to respond.

'You're not going anywhere, *Corporal* Harding, we'll get you comfortable and then I'll go and solve the mystery of why we seem to have two names the same. There's no way we want stowaways on this ship, not unless they're going to work their passage to

Alexandria! And I don't care what you say, you're down on my list as a corporal.'

She turned and spoke to someone out of sight. 'Alright, chaps, make this man ready for the operating theatre could you, Colonel Horrocks is waiting to start the days work.' She bent over him, filling his nostrils with her perfume again. 'You'll be in good hands; Colonel Horrocks is one of our best surgeons. He'll treat and dress the wound to your left arm first but it's your head he'll want to have a good look at. I'll be up to see you later, when you're safely tucked up in bed. Good luck, corporal.'

Minutes later he was lifted tenderly from the stretcher, rancid clothes quickly cut from him with large scissors and he was taken down through a door into a bright corridor. The interior of the ship was cool and welcoming but from within its bowels he heard a man's voice cry out in mortal agony and he shivered. Faintly, from a distance, he heard the faint hum of a generator as he was carried gently through another door and laid on the firm padded board of an operating table that had been set up in what was once the First-class Lounge. A white-gowned face leaned over him and he narrowed his eyes to accustom them to the yellow light.

'Ah, you're still awake, Corporal Harding. I'm Colonel Horrocks and I'm going to take a look at that head and arm of yours. You're going to have a nice sleep now and when you awake everything will have been taken care of.'

Before Tom could form a reply a cotton pad was placed over his mouth and nostrils and the sweet, cloying smell of chloroform sent him sliding into a dark canyon where all the horrors he'd endured awaited him.

--§--

The thing that had once been a human being reared up and turned reddened, accusing eye sockets in his direction, a bright crown of flames surrounding its head forming a perfect halo of light as it snarled and yammered fiercely. Dawn and the sun's rays formed it into a golden silhouette and the figure's outline shimmered and sparkled as the spasmodic undulations of its limbs threatened to engulf him. He gagged at the smell, the acrid stench of burning hair and his legs turned to water under its gaze, rifle slipping limply from his grasp as he twisted and stumbled backwards in terror from the nightmare of its burnt and blackened, outstretched arms.

176

He awoke abruptly with a fierce headache and fresh bandages on his head and arm in a white-linen cot that matched the uniforms of the nurses bustling up and down the ward as they attended to men lying in similar cots. The room itself was spotless, painted a bright white with portholes along its length but the brightness of the room failed to keep out the rank, tart smell of antiseptics and sour flesh. There were other underlying states that he faintly discerned, unseen but there nevertheless, those of pain and hopelessness.

His uniform was missing and he was dressed in hospital garb. He looked round self-consciously to see if any of its occupants had witnessed his vocal awakening but the vast majority were asleep or unconscious. The cot was suspended from the ceiling at each corner and as he looked groggily around him, from across the way a friendly face beamed in his direction.

'You're awake then, matey? How do you feel?'

Tom tried to answer but his lips were stuck together. Seeing his distress the man shouted at one of the nurses. 'Oi, miss, this cove 'ere needs his mouth wetting. Fellow can't speak.'

Within seconds a uniformed girl with dark hair and pleasant features crossed over to his cot. 'Ah, good, you're awake,' she said simply, 'Matron will be pleased. We were getting a bit worried about you. You didn't want to wake up.'

He raised a limp arm and gestured weakly at the covers.

'Wait there and I'll be back shortly.' She returned as promised and slipped a long-necked glass bottle under the covers. Gratefully he fumbled with his good hand and felt the tension inside ebb as he relieved himself. Waiting patiently, she slid a deft hand under the covers once more and retrieved the bottle, placing it carefully under a cloth with a bowl of water before disappearing into a room at the end of the ward.

Moments later she was back with a bowl of clean water and a large cloth which she rinsed first before wiping it over Tom's face and lips. He tried to suck it but she snatched it away. 'Naughty! You're to have nothing for another hour until the anaesthetic wears off and then Matron says we can give you a cup of tea.'

'Please,' he pleaded hoarsely, 'I've had nothing all day, nurse, I'm just about passing out with thirst. Please, a few sips.'

She looked round. 'Oh, alright but don't tell. You'll get me into trouble and then what?'

He grimaced and pointed to his head. 'Me? Get you into trouble? Like this, how could I?' She laughed coyly at his innuendo and wrung the cloth out in the bowl. Holding it carefully over his mouth she squeezed it gently and a few drops of cool water ran down the inside of his teeth. The water tasted like nectar and he spluttered violently as the liquid tickled the back of his parched throat. 'Oh no, don't do that! I don't want you passing out on me!' the young nurse gasped in dismay and wrenched the cloth away.

'What's going on here, Nurse Weatherall?' A voice of steel broke in and Tom saw the consternation in the young girl's eyes as an older woman, a severe expression on her face, appeared next to the cot. Tom spoke hurriedly, the taste of water giving him the strength to form the words.

'I'm sorry, it's my fault entirely, I tried to take the cloth from her but the nurse wouldn't let me.'

'I see.' The elderly woman looked sharply at him and the board at the end of the cot before turning to the girl. 'In future, Nurse Weatherall, be more careful how you deal with these men's demands.' She turned about and marched off, head held high.

'Pig!' the young girl said with feeling and they both laughed. She moved closer and plumped Tom's pillows. 'There. Thanks for saving my life, Miss Green, Matron Green, she's really a nice woman but doesn't brook any nonsense on the wards. I'll be back in an hour's time and give you that nice cup of tea I promised.'

She bustled off and Tom was left to contemplate his surroundings. 'Nice to meet you.' The friendly face from over the way spoke with an effort and Tom looked up hastily.

'Oh, what. Yes, g'day to you mate. How're you doing?'

'Fine, I'm sure.' The man waggled his body under the covers. 'Lost me legs to a Turkish shell, took them both clean off. Surgeon said he couldn't have made a better job hisself and that the stumps should heal beautifully. The names Fred Wooller, from London, here with the Middlesex, what mob are you wiv then? Did she say you was an Aussie, you don't sound like one to me?'

In spite of the pain Tom grinned. He was warming to the chippy man across from him, one who'd had the misfortune to lose his legs but could still joke about it. 'Questions, questions…I'm from England myself, I come from Lancashire originally but emigrated to

Australia before the war and when it all went up in smoke it seemed the natural thing to do to join up there. Tom Harding, 9th Battalion AIF, by the way.'

'Harding. Harding?' mused Fred Wooller. 'I knew a Harding once, now where was that?'

As Tom waited for him to speak again, Fred's eyes drooped tiredly before he reopened them with an effort and glanced over as Tom's hand lifted to his mouth in a reflex gesture. Seeing his inquisitive frown, Tom smiled. 'My pipe, I used to smoke one once but gave it up before we sailed for Egypt. Now when I find myself stressed, I still reach for my pipe, like a baby and its bottle.'

'You can't smoke 'ere, mate, Matron'll have your balls if she sees you with a pipe in your 'and.' Fred's voice trailed off and when Tom looked again Fred Wooller's eyes had closed and he was asleep. Suddenly feeling very tired himself, Tom hunched down in the cot and joined his new friend in a deep sleep.

He woke to a gentle hand tugging at his foot.

'Are you ready for that cup of tea now?'

The voice was different yet familiar and he opened his eyes and stared at a young, pretty woman clad in white gazing back at him. Frantically he tried to remember where he'd heard her voice but she spoke before he could dredge the fact from his memory.

'You look puzzled, Serjeant Harding but not half as puzzled as I've been for the last three hours. Do you know what trouble you've put me to, discovering who you really are?' She laughed at the blank look on his face. 'Remember me? We met on the upper deck when you first came aboard.'

He saw a woman in her late twenties, he guessed, tall with a full figure and green eyes set in a smiling face, surrounded by a mass of auburn curls neatly tucked under a white nurse's hat. She returned his frank gaze with equal candour.

'Now that we've had a good look at each other I do rather think it's time for that cuppa, you must be thirsty after your operation. Nurse Weatherall told me about the episode with the cloth so you must still be feeling fairly dehydrated in this heat. Here, take this glass of water first. Slowly!' she admonished him as he greedily drank from the glass she offered him. 'Don't spill it all, you clot! Good. Now lie back and I'll get you that cup of tea, the sugar in it will do you the world of good.'

She moved away, taking the glass with her and Tom stiffly raised himself up.

'Thanks, nurse, that was...'

'It's Sister...Sister Mathers and lie back down now, we don't want Colonel Horrocks' good work undone just because of a cuppa, do we?'

She returned in seconds, carrying a white cup and saucer which she placed carefully alongside his cot before offering him the cup. It was full of hot, sweet tea and he took an appreciative slurp before looking up at her as he sank back onto the mattress.

'How'm I doing?'

'You're doing surprisingly well, Serjeant Harding. That head wound of yours looked pretty nasty but once we'd cleaned it up in theatre, it wasn't too bad at all. The bullet took a small piece of bone from your forehead but Colonel Horrocks removed any debris that was left in there, pulled your scalp forward, stitched that up and everything should heal in a month or two. We then cleaned and sorted your left arm. You're going to live, after a few months convalescing in Alexandria. Lucky you.'

'My eyesight's blurred, is that normal?'

'You men! You've had a nasty blow to the head so it's perfectly normal to be slightly concussed. Your eyesight will return soon, I promise.'

'And the others that came onboard with me?'

Her eyes darkened.

'Poor boys, there's some shocking wounds among them. Now that you've reached Mudros we'll be staying here overnight and tomorrow, to allow Colonel Horrocks and his staff of surgeons time to operate and for us to pick up yet more wounded for the journey over the Mediterranean. Once all the urgent cases have been taken care of as best we can, we'll be sailing for Egypt.'

She lowered her voice and he strained to catch her next words.

'Look around you, serjeant, some of these men, a lot of them, are going to die over the next few days because of the state they were in when we brought them onboard. No amount of care is going to save them now, if the authorities had provided that care on the beaches or inland our job would be so much easier. All we can do is sit with them, hold their hand and ease their passage into the next world with the least pain possible.'

180

She moved as if to leave and while he digested her sombre words he thought desperately of a reason to keep her alongside his cot for another minute or so. 'Sister, you said you'd sorted out the mystery of my name. What was there to be puzzled about?'

'Oh, yes. It was a weird co-incidence that's all. I thought I'd already booked you onboard but I couldn't have. We picked that Harding up from a delivery of British wounded from Cape Helles before you Australians arrived. Funny though, his name was nearly the same as yours only the other way round.'

She smiled and turned. 'I'll come back later, after theatre and see how you're doing. Bye for now, Serjeant Harding.'

'It's Tom,' he said cheekily, 'Thomas Walter Harding. Remember?'

She looked back and a frown creased her pretty features. 'That's what was so strange,' she murmured, 'that other chap. His name was Corporal Walter Thomas Harding. The same name and rank as yours when you boarded only his Christian names were the other way round. But he's English, in the Middlesex regiment, I think.'

'Walt Harding! I thought I'd heard his name before, it's bloody Walt Harding, Corporal Harding, and he's in 'B' Company. I know him!'

Thunderstruck, Tom looked from the nurse's face over to where Fred Wooller had wakened and was sitting upright in his cot.

'Walt? Here? Oh God, Walt...' His eyes filled suddenly and he reached up one-handed to wipe his face, ashamed of his visible emotion.

She moved closer, a look of concern on her face. 'What do you mean? Walt? Who's Walt? I say, are you alright?'

He lay supine, memories crowding in. 'I think,' he answered weakly, 'if what Fred over there is saying is the truth I think the other Harding could be my brother, Walter, Walt. It can't be, though. We've not seen each other for years...'

'Please,' she said softly, 'don't distress yourself. Look, I'll go to this other Harding's ward and have a word, see if he is who you think he is. It could be just a huge coincidence you know, these things do happen, there must be thousands of Walter Hardings in the world. Especially with the war and so many men congregated here it would be a common name, don't you agree? Names still get mixed up for no apparent reason, although I do see...'

'What's the matter with him, this man, is he badly wounded?' Tom asked in a whisper, interrupting her.

'I'm not sure, if I remember he has a very bad case of dysentry. It's starting to affect large numbers of the men so we're taking as many patients suffering from it away from the battlefield to give them a proper chance to recuperate. Please, don't upset yourself, I'm needed in theatre shortly but I'll be back and we'll get to the bottom of it.'

The next few hours were spent in an agony of suspense waiting anxiously for Sister Mathers to return. His mind tried to accept that the other man might not be his brother but his thoughts were a whirlpool of emotions, jumbled memories of Walt and their early life together flooding his mind and leaving him on a knife-edge of trepidation.

Nurse Weatherall found him moving restlessly around the narrow cot when she arrived back on duty that evening and hastened to reassure him. 'You really must try to rest, serjeant, you'll only make yourself ill if you don't.'

'Sister Mathers, is she...will she be...?'

She laughed gaily at his concern. 'Don't you worry about Bridgette, if she said she'd be back, she will be. Very particular about her duties is our Bridgette. And her men. Oh dear, forget I said that, will you? Now, you just lie back while I sort these covers out, there's some nice soup coming shortly and I do hear the cooks have steamed some fish. How does that sound?'

'Bridgette. Is that her name then? Bridgette?'

'Oh lor'. Don't you go telling her that I told you her name or anything else or you'll get me into trouble. Matron doesn't allow us to use our first names, says we're to keep ourselves distant from the patients. I think she's afraid we'll become too familiar with you men if we let you know our names.'

'And yours, pretty Nurse Weatherall, what do they call you?'

She flushed. 'See? I told you, we're not allowed to let you address us by our first names.' She softened at seeing his face. 'But when Matron's not around you can call me Martha.'

He relaxed. 'Martha it is. Martha and Bridgette, my very own angels. I promise I'll be a model patient.'

'Good, now let me put this tray over your covers, the food will be here shortly and until your arm gets better you'll need a hand to help you eat.'

--§--

It was later that evening when the ward door opened and Bridgette Mathers stood in the doorway. She looked tired, almost drained but when she saw Tom staring expectantly at her she summoned a smile and walked over to him.

'Hello there, you look a great deal better than you did earlier today. Did you manage to eat something?'

'I tried but after a diet of bully beef and biscuits for so long it was hard to swallow anything so decent as the fish we were given. Sorry.'

'I won't let the cooks know, don't worry.' She moved closer and his nostrils caught the scent of her perfume. 'Won't you get into trouble wearing perfume?' he asked and she laughed, a short, grim laugh.

'Miss Green and I often argue about that very thing. Her rules include no toiletries at all whilst on duty and while I don't wear any during theatre hours I do put a few drops on when I'm finished. I find it takes away the smell of chloroform and the stink of gangrenous wounds. It's also my way of dealing with the smell of so much death. I've a good stomach for the sight of the wounds themselves but it's the smell that upsets me most so I lose myself by the expedient method of a few drops of perfume. Why do you ask, do you like it?'

He was taken aback for a second time by her candour. 'It's rather nice but you must excuse me, I'm afraid the stench I've experienced these past few weeks would make an abattoir seem sweet by comparison. With the unsanitary conditions out there on the peninsula you'll need all the perfume you can muster when our wounded come onboard, we must stink to high heaven.'

She looked pensive. 'The wounded don't bother me at all, poor boys, their smell is the least of their troubles. But I digress. I'm here to give you some information about the other chap with the same name as you.'

'Did you speak with him? Is he really...?' Tom asked eagerly but she shook her head, making her curls bounce in an attractive manner. 'Hold on there, let me speak. I went to Medical Reception and made enquiries. This chap is definitely called Walter Thomas Harding and he's a corporal in the 7th Middlesex. As far as I know he was born in Canon Street, Bury, and he's 21 years old. There's no mention of any next of kin.'

'That's him! That's my brother, Walter. Walt. We were both born in Bury so it must be him!' Tom cried and made to throw his covers back but she stopped him.

'What do you think you're doing, get back in there, there's no way you're going anywhere.'

'But, he's my brother. I must go to him.'

'You can,' she told him soothingly, 'but please, not tonight. You've been pretty badly wounded yourself so stay in bed tonight and rest. In the morning, after surgical rounds, I'll get an orderly to fetch a wheelchair and take you to see him myself if I'm not required in theatre. And only if I think you're up to it. Walter's asleep just now, he's recovering from a nasty case of dysentry so he needs all the rest we can give him. Both of you can get a good night's sleep and I'll take you to him tomorrow, I promise.'

He started to argue but the look on her face made him realise what an effort it had been for her to come and visit him as she'd promised.

'I'm sorry,' he said contritely, 'in my eagerness I forgot how tired *you* must be feeling, I've been laid here doing nothing but rest whilst you've been working. Flat out by the look of it, too, was it bad?' She nodded, a shadow passing across her pretty features. 'There were some dreadful wounds. We never fail to be amazed by the different ways something as small as a bullet or a piece of shrapnel can cause so much damage to the human body. Two men died as we operated but it was maybe a blessing for them. It's not so much the wounds themselves but the time taken for the men to be properly seen. So many cases arrive with advanced gangrene and all we can do is amputate.

Colonel Horrocks is a great surgeon but even he despairs. We lose a lot post-operative, purely to shock, their weakened bodies can't take the trauma of surgery so long after having been wounded. The medical services onshore do their best under trying conditions but are, for the most part, non-existent. Not enough doctors or supplies. Healthy men die for lack of prompt first aid, so many more could be saved but by the time they reach us for many it's too late. Many burials at sea are carried out on the way to Alexandria of men who've died needlessly.'

She lifted her head. 'On our last journey we had so many wounded the vast majority spent the entire crossing simply lying on their stretchers, crammed onto the upper decks. Men were everywhere and we just couldn't cope, the death toll was horrific. It was an utter shambles and if those back home that planned this monstrous affair could see the results of their incompetence they would be ashamed. But let's not get too morbid, rest now and I'll see you tomorrow.'

184

'The badge you're wearing, what is it?' he asked and she looked down at the badge containing a white cross on her breast.

'Oh, this. I'm a sister in the QAIMNS,' she said simply, 'that's the *Queen Alexander Imperial Military Nursing Service*. Most of the nurses onboard belong to it, there's QAIMNS serving here in the Mediterranean and also in France. The badge was devised by Queen Alexander herself, the motto *Sub-Crucia Candida* simply means, *Under the White Cross*. Now, enough, you need to rest. Goodnight.'

'Goodnight, Bridgette.' he called as she left. She reached the door and looked back, a frown on her face at his use of her first name. 'Martha!' she breathed, her face twitched once in annoyance and she was gone.

He spent a restless night, tossing and turning, his thoughts going back to the days spent with Walter as boys, their tights and the bonds that had grown up between them travelling through childhood without parents. Aunt Elsie had been a good surrogate mother to them but it had been just the two of them that had lived and played cheek by jowl. Now, after a long time he was going to see Walter again, here of all places and he spent the night willing the clock's hands to spin faster.

Morning dawned and after a quick breakfast he looked eagerly to the ward door. More patients were awake and the room hummed with the quiet murmur of conversation as men laughed and joked with their neighbours. The portholes had been opened to admit some fresh air in and the atmosphere in the ward was pleasant and relaxing. Fred Wooller waved without speaking and Tom acknowledged the greeting with a diffident wave with his good hand, immersed in his expectations. At last the ward door opened and a male orderly entered pushing a wheelchair, followed closely behind by Bridgette Mathers.

He pushed back the covers and tried to swing his body out of the cot but the effort was too great and he fell back with a groan.

'What do you think you're doing, do you want to injure yourself, you fool!' she blazed, standing at the foot of his cot. 'Now listen to me, serjeant, if you don't do as you're told you can stay where you are. Understand?'

'Your eyes are so attractive when you're angry, Bridgette, has anyone told you that?'

The orderly sniggered and she rounded angrily on him. 'Don't you encourage him, Wheeler, I've enough to do without adding fools to my list!' She turned back to Tom. 'You! Stay there and let us do the work or you're going nowhere.'

She bent over him and took his good arm. 'Wheeler,' she commanded 'don't just stand there gawking, man, come and help me get Serjeant Harding into the wheelchair.'

Her cap was close to his face and he could smell the freshness of her hair. As her head moved closer he murmured into her ear, 'You've changed your perfume today, a pity, I was getting to like the other one.' and was rewarded by a pink flush spreading over her face. To hide her embarrassment she busied herself in assisting the orderly move Tom into the wheelchair, keeping her eyes averted from his face. When he was safely seated she stood upright, chest heaving as she caught her breath. Still she wouldn't look at him and he caught the amused look on Wheeler's face and returned the man's grin.

'Right, now that's done let's get you out of here and go see this man you think could be your brother. We can't stay long, Surgical Rounds have been delayed owing to the time taken operating last night but they'll be along later so you need to be back in time for those.'

She motioned to the orderly and Wheeler dutifully moved over and took the arms of the wheelchair. Pushing Tom towards the open door he began exchanging cheery greetings with other patients but a sharp word from Bridgette Mathers stopped his chatter in its tracks and he pushed Tom through the doors in a morose silence. The door led to a long passage, at the end of which was a doorway that Tom presumed led up onto the open deck.

'You're lucky,' she said walking alongside him, 'most of the wards are well below decks but yours is situated just below the Promenade Deck so we'll have you out in no time getting some fresh air and sunshine on the voyage over to Egypt.'

'Where's my brother...this other Harding, then?' Tom enquired.

'Not too far, actually, just along here and down one deck. We have electric lifts so there's no problem in taking you to him. There is a stairway nearby but this is much more convenient. I hope it is him, by the way, it sounds too good to be true so I don't want you getting your hopes up. Ah, here we are, careful now.'

The wheelchair was deftly positioned inside the lift door and she pressed a button as Wheeler squeezed in and the door closed behind him. No-one spoke and after a short hum of electric motors the lift juddered to an abrupt stop and she pressed another button to re-open the door. They exited the lift into a similar corridor to the upper deck and Wheeler grabbed the handles and resumed pushing.

At the end of the corridor an open door beckoned and Wheeler turned into another bright, open, airy ward, filled like Tom's with two rows of cots but with no portholes to admit the passage of fresh air. They were under the waterline now and he could appreciate the change in the ward temperature compared to the one he'd just left. It was warmer down here, a lot warmer, the heat reflected in the pallid, sweating faces of the men occupying the cots.

Ignoring the stifling heat and the rank smell, Bridgette Mathers walked slowly along before stopping near the middle and gesturing to Tom with a finger on her lips. Following her gaze he looked across the cot to the man lying asleep and concentrated hard. As his vision cleared he saw a gaunt, haggard face with eyes tightly closed, its head cushioned by clean pillows. He struggled to reconcile this wasted figure with the picture of Walter that he'd carried in his mind since they'd last seen each other and gestured impatiently for Wheeler to move him closer.

'Walter? Walt? Can you hear me, it's Tom.' he breathed quietly and the man's features twitched. Walt's eyes opened slowly and focussed on the figure sitting in the wheelchair looking at him. He frowned, a perplexed frown as if struggling to comprehend what was happening.

'What's up, Walt, cat got your tongue? Can't you greet your own bloody brother?'

'Tom?' he answered weakly. 'Tom? How? What...?' He rolled over on his side and looked more closely. 'Oh, God, Tom, it's really you.' Tears formed in his eyes, great wet tears that rolled down his face, becoming intermingled with those of his brother's as they hugged each other fiercely. Walt's hand stroked his older brother's head tenderly as he gazed into Tom's eyes.

'Watch it you clot, my bloody head hurts. And my arm, what a state to greet you in.' Tom said through his tears and they hugged each other closely again.

'I'll leave you for now but you can't have long, we need to get Tom back to his own ward shortly.' Bridgette informed them as she turned away, trying to hide her own emotions at the sight of the two brothers embracing but neither man heard her. Years of separation rolled away as they contemplated each other, robbing both men of the power of speech momentarily.

'What did you...?'

'How long have you…?'

'Sorry, you first.'

'No, go on.'

'When we…'

Words burst from their lips and they spoke in torrents, exclaiming volubly, filling in the details of their lives since last they'd met. In this way an hour flew by in animated conversation until Bridgette looked in consternation at the watch on her uniform blouse and spoke softly.

'I'm sorry, boys but we've got to go now. Tom, tell Walter we'll bring you back tomorrow but for now the both of you need some rest. You've three long days to chat once we get underway so say goodbye and we'll be on our way.'

Reluctantly the two parted and Wheeler pushed Tom back into the corridor. He waved a last time to Walt and sat back with an air of satisfaction.

'Thank you, Miss Mathers,' he said quietly, 'I don't think you'll ever know what you've just done but I can never repay you for this.'

She smiled, touched by his sincerity and moved closer. 'I'm glad we could reunite you and Walter. What a story to tell your families in later years of how you met after all this time, on a hospital ship of all places. There's no need to be so formal, either, Matron has a thing about Other Ranks and first names but so long as you don't use it when she's around I think you could carry on calling me Bridgette.'

There was no answer and when she looked down, Tom Harding had fallen asleep. 'Oh well, so much for my seductive ways.' she said, sighing. Wheeler laughed aloud but at a wintry glance from her the smile swiftly left his face.

--§--

Bridgette Mathers let go the slides holding her cap in place and shook her curls free, letting them bounce on her shoulders whilst critically examining her reflection in the mirror above the washbasin in her sparse cabin. The rank of Sister had given her the right to her own cabin. It wasn't spacious but meant she could retire here of an evening after a long day on the wards or assisting in the operating theatre and relax without the silliness of the younger girls annoying her. They meant well, she knew that but their youth overcame their sense of responsibility sometimes and she could easily lose her temper with them. God knew she had one, something she'd inherited from her Scottish father, lost to her only a year ago but he lived on in her heart and when she felt depressed or lonely she would think of him and days spent in his company and her spirits would soon lift.

He'd taught her well, given her the wisdom to see the world as it really was and to treat fools accordingly. Knowing that, it had always been a surprise that her career in the QAIMNS had progressed without hindrance until she'd reached the elevated position of Sister. It would be easy to stay on and wait to reach the dizzy heights of Matron of her own hospital or ship but in her heart she knew something was missing and that the road leading to further promotion was one she couldn't or wouldn't contemplate.

The war had changed hers and so many others lives in ways they couldn't begin to fathom; the fighting and casualties on a scale incomprehensible a few years ago and recently she'd begun to feel more and more melancholic with every new transport of wounded souls that arrived onboard. Joining the nursing service had been of great satisfaction to her, until now. Days blurred into all too readily into each other, the early excitement of foreign travel and warm climates long subsumed into tiring shifts tending the seemingly endless queues of shattered souls that cried piteously for her attention. Something was missing from her life and with every passing day she found herself mourning for what might have been.

She sat and quietly brushed her hair with an ivory-handled brush, long, deliberate strokes, pulling it through her auburn hair in a purposeful manner as she glanced at herself in the mirror. She'd divested herself of her blouse and pinafore, sitting on the chair amid the humid closeness of the cabin in her slip. A light dusting of freckles dusted her shoulders and she turned this way and that to examine them critically. They showed up against the paleness of her alabaster skin but she thought them not unattractive and her gaze followed her body's contours as she brushed.

Men found her attractive, she knew that. Her features would never be called beautiful but she had a quiet prettiness that a lot of men had admired, with white, even teeth and high cheekbones that accentuated her green eyes, a throwback to her Scottish ancestry. A good figure, full breasts together with a slim waist and long legs that all showed up well when set against the close fit of her uniform turned male heads whenever she walked out.

It might all have been so different if she'd stayed at home but she'd harboured no regrets until recently. The things other women sought, a husband, children, had seemed so unimportant but quietly within she knew that she'd swop this life in an instant to be part of someone who loved her and she loved in return. She shivered in spite of the heat in the room. That's what you get from wishing for the impossible she told herself angrily and shook her head in despair. Wishing for things that could never happen led nowhere. She'd resolved long ago to put the pain of her past behind her and face life without letting anyone see beyond the facade she maintained and gain access to her inner self. The days of love and happiness were buried in her past and had ended long ago.

Thinking about another life brought Tom Harding's face to mind and a wry smile touched the edge of her lips as she thought of his cheekiness when he'd first been slung aboard. She'd have to watch herself with him, although he was rather good-looking in a serious sort of way she'd need to keep him from getting too close, give him no encouragement. He was just another injured soldier and that was the way it would stay. Miss Green would be watching her like a hawk, as she did all of them in her attempts to keep them distant from their charges. Shipboard romances were for exotic foreign cruises, not the grim reality of tending badly wounded men in wartime.

Still, the strength of the emotions she'd experienced on seeing him meet his long-lost brother had both surprised and worried her. In amongst all the pain and suffering of the men she'd tended, bringing the Harding brothers together had been a special moment and the conflicting feelings it had aroused within her had lasted throughout the rest of the day. Coming upon Tom Harding in the ward and watching him as he slept had brought a strange sense of maternal longing in her, one she'd swiftly suppressed but even now the memory of that longing had the power to unsettle her.

She finished brushing her hair and bent to wash in the tepid water in the basin. The operating theatres would still be fully occupied at this late hour and she had an early call booked for the morning when she'd be needed again. Yawning, she turned down the coverlet but prior to getting into bed hesitated before opening the small drawer of her bedside cabinet. On top of some letters lay a gold chain and locket and she picked it up and held it to her bosom. She lowered the locket and slowly snapped it open. Contained within each side was a photograph of a smiling face and she looked closely before snapping the locket closed again and returning it to the drawer.

A quick half hour, she'd promised herself she'd read for half an hour and then try to sleep, that way any painful memories could be mercifully blotted out. She reached for the book sitting on top of the cabinet and brought it close to her face. Squinting hard, she tried to make out the typescript but her eyelids drooped wearily as the events of the day overtook her tired brain and the book slid unread onto the floor.

Chapter Ten.

Aegean Coast 23rd May.

'Can it be fixed, Heini?'

Oberleutnant Zur See Waldemar Schachter looked anxiously down into the depths of his U-boat from his perch on the bridge as his Maschinist looked upwards at him through the same gap.

'I'm not sure, Kapitan, something's not quite right with the trim but what, that's the question. Bauer's gone to have a look aft but for now we'd better stay on the surface.'

'*Verdamnte!*' the 26-year old banged the edge of the rail in frustration as he contemplated his next move. He looked back at the frothing wake his small Coastal Type submarine, *UB-3*, was spreading on an otherwise placid sea and thought quickly on his next move. He was due in Istanbul shortly with his vital cargo of spares and this setback would cost them precious time. His small craft travelled faster on the surface using its Daimler diesel engine but the thought of not being able to dive should they come across enemy ships worried him more than he wanted to admit.

Schachter ran a nervous hand through his thinning blonde hair as he considered his options. A graduate of His Imperial Majesty's Marine Academie 04/06 Klasse, he'd undergone a thorough grounding in the responsibilities of command and was acutely aware of those responsibilities to the wellbeing of his crew but this was wartime and different rules applied now. *UB-3* was his first independent command since graduating and he was keen to make a good impression on his superiors. His parents back in Wilhelmshaven had been so proud of his success and his posting to the U-boat base at Cattaro high up on the upper reaches of the Adriatic coast had made him determined to make his mark there.

They'd already had a brush with a French destroyer since leaving Cattaro and if the cargo he was carrying wasn't so urgently needed in Turkey he'd have about-turned and headed for the safety of home. Damn the French, the destroyer had caught *UB-3* off the Greek coast on the surface and fired a salvo from her ageing guns before they'd been able to make an emergency dive. A near miss aft had affected the ability of the vessel to manoeuvre, at first thought confined only to the rudder but it was soon obvious something else was wrong and until they found and repaired this latest problem they'd be sitting ducks.

She'd twisted this way and that at her top underwater speed of 5 knots in shaking off her pursuer but it had been at a cost of vital time and the running down of their electric motor's batteries. Now, their single diesel engine of 60hp was pushing them along as fast as it could at its maximum speed of 6 knots, burning precious fuel reserves as they attempted to make up for the time lost.

His boat was one of a class of smaller coastal attack submarines laid down in 1914, *UB-3* having been launched only two months previously. Built in sections in the Germaniawerft yard in Kiel, Germany, along with others of her class she'd been transported by rail down to the base at Pola on the Adriatic and assembled in the *Seearsenal* of the Austro-Hungarian Navy, the KuK. (*Kaiserliche und Königliche Kriegsmarine.*) After a short work-up in the Adriatic following her assembly they'd embarked food and fuel, together with their cargo and prepared for their first war patrol.

This was to be a voyage to Istanbul, delivering spares for two German battleships. SMS Goeben and SMS Breslau had escaped the attentions of the British Mediterranean fleet the previous August and had been handed over to the Turks, albeit still retaining her German crews. Now renamed *Yavuz Sultan Selim* and *Midilli* respectively, they relied on both overland and underwater resupply, their latest demands being for spare parts for the ship's wireless sets. After delivering her cargo *UB-3* would stay on in Istanbul and join the newly-formed flotilla to be based there.

At only 28 meters long with a beam of 3 yards, living conditions onboard *UB-3* were cramped enough for her 14 man crew, a situation made worse by the boxes and crates stowed in every nook and cranny along her puny length. After much discussion, Waldemar Schachter had loaded these spares, plus food and other items aboard the submarine, retaining against all advice the two older type CO6 AV torpedoes already loaded within the bow tubes. With a combined weight of over 1500kgs he'd been warned that these weapons would slow him greatly when set against the amount of cargo he was carrying but he'd retorted that the security they brought was worth the risk, words he now badly regretted as his vessel wallowed sluggishly in a rising sea. Besides which, it would have taken far too long to unload the torpedoes and he'd been eager to set off.

It was no use, he decided, he'd have to rid himself of the weight that the torpedoes added to his trimming problem but another part of his brain protested at the waste of just firing them uselessly into the sea.

Old as they were they could still be useful to the planned u-boat flotilla that was to be based in Istanbul and it was this fact that made him reluctant to divest himself of them and the added security they brought by their onboard presence.

The light was dimming fast and it would be dark soon so best to leave making the final decision for another hour or two and then decide. The currents in the Dardanelles were said to be exceedingly tricky to manoeuvre among so it might be prudent to have rid the boat of the *eels* by then. A pity, it would have been a feather in his cap to have expended them on an enemy steamer or warship but he was pragmatic enough to realise that that would bring another set of dangers into being.

Add to it this damned problem of the boat's stability and he couldn't risk submerging until they'd found the cause and rectified it. Better to leave things as they were and continue on the surface like this and pray they didn't meet an enemy ship. He closed his eyes and let his thoughts and his boat run on and on.

--§--

Walt Harding slowly opened his eyes. His right hand refused to move and he looked down to find it being held tightly by his brother Tom's uninjured hand, his brother who sat in a wheelchair alongside the cot Walt lay in. Tom's eyes were also closed but as he felt Walt move he opened them wide and both men smiled together.

'I thought I was dreaming yesterday, Tom,' Walt murmured, 'I just couldn't believe it was true when I opened my eyes to find you sat there.'

'Well, brother, it's not a dream and we really are here, of all places. Private Wheeler brought me to see you this morning but you were fast asleep so I toddled off back to my own ward and waited until this evening to try again. There's so much more to catch up on but first things first, how are you feeling today?'

Walt arched his back, trying to find a more comfortable position before twisting his face into a sour expression. 'Pretty weak, I must say. I'm running a temperature but I was only sleeping cos they woke me early this morning and gave me a bloody enema,' he said angrily. 'It felt terrible but they insisted, said it would do me the world of good...'

'So that accounts for the smell in here.'

Walt looked suspiciously up at his brother but Tom stared back with a look of complete innocence.

'Yes, well, so they gave me this enema to help me.'

'And did it?'

'I still feel lousy so I wouldn't know. The nurse over there says they'll be giving me a few more over during the voyage to try and cleanse my guts of all the rubbish that's accumulated there, me and most of the other blokes in this ward. It's made me feel more tired and a damn sight weaker, I can tell you although I have to say I was treated far better than on my way down to the beach at Cape Helles.'

'How do you mean?'

'The bastards tied the bottom legs of my trousers together with string to stop any shit leaking out onto their damn stretcher and I was swimming in it by the time we got there!' He looked at his brother with a guarded expression, in time to see Tom's face twitch as he tried in vain to suppress a smile.

'I thought so. You're finding this funny, aren't you? Don't laugh, you bastard! How would you like to feel your innards spilling out in liquid form, I thought I'd never stop. I still do.' His words made Tom smile even more and try as he might to be annoyed, Walt's lips twitched too and both men burst out laughing at the mental picture he'd painted so vividly.

'I pitied the poor nurse who had to cut my trousers off when we arrived onboard; she screamed and jumped sideways out of the way of the torrent that flowed from my clothing. Poor lass, she was only a young thing, probably thought of nursing as wiping fevered brows and taking temperatures, not cutting pants full of shit off tired, wounded men.'

They laughed even more uproariously at these comments, the noise waking several sleeping patients and attracting a scowling, harassed nurse who scurried over and harangued them into a cowed silence.

'So how are you?' Walt asked after she'd gone and by way of a reply Tom flexed his injured arm. 'This was only a flesh wound, stung a bit but it's feeling a bit better every day so I'll soon be able to ditch the sling. Although I might keep it on when we reach Alexandria, I could use it to gain some sympathy from all those lovely sheila's that I'm told go for an injured bloke. As for the head, it's still sore but I'll survive. My eyesight's a lot better today so I can see your ugly mug a lot clearer.'

'I'll give you *ugly mug* and what's this about *sheila's*?' Walt retorted, 'God, Tom, you're beginning to sound like an Aussie!'

They fell silent at his words. After a short contemplative pause Tom spoke again. 'It's where I reckon I'll be staying, Walt, the country's huge and there's so much a man can do if he sets his mind to it. Why don't you come out and join me? This war won't last forever and when it's over Australia will be needing a new influx of good blokes to replace those it's lost, men who'll knuckle down and make a go of things.

Come on, say you will, it'll be so good to have you with me. We can look for something to do together. There's lots of opportunities and what's waiting for you back in Blighty? Please, Walt, say yes, you'll love Queensland.'

Walt smiled at his older brother's enthusiasm. 'Oh, Tom, you were ever the adventurer. No. don't look like that, I was only kidding, although you've always had the wanderlust about you. As for me, well, I'm not sure. Tell me a bit more about Australia on the way over to Egypt and I swear I'll have a good think about it. You're right about not having anyone waiting for me back home but it's still a big decision to up sticks and move.'

'I know, I know, but don't forget you'd be with me.'

'That's what I'm frightened of.'

They both laughed heartily again, drawing another frosty look from the harassed nurse.

'What's this, laughter? We'll soon stop that, I won't have laughter on my wards!' Both men looked up guiltily at the sound to see the smiling figure of Bridgette Mathers at the end of the bed. They'd been too engrossed in each other's company to hear her approach.

'Don't do that. I thought you were Miss Green, Bridgette, it was a passable enough imitation of her to put the fear of God into us.'

'Bridgette? Well I never, Tom, on first name terms already, are we?'

'Shut up you clot. Bridgette, this is Walter, my brother, you couldn't get a word in edgeways yesterday but he's feeling a lot better today after his enema this morning and was wondering if you could sort him out with another, says he's really beginning to enjoy them.'

'Tom!'

'Alright, Walt, keep your hair on, I was only joking.'

Walt gazed at Bridgette Mathers appreciatively. 'He's lying, I do remember you from yesterday only I was a bit taken up with this lout.

Tom didn't tell me he had a lady friend onboard already, though, he always was a fast worker, was my brother.'

Now it was Tom's turn to feel aggrieved. 'Bridgette…Miss Mathers,' he protested, 'Don't believe a word he says, I never called you my *lady friend* as he's trying to make out.'

She looked exasperatedly from one to the other. 'Men! Why is it, given half the chance, you behave just like children?' she said scornfully, ignoring their banter, 'Where's Wheeler? I left him here with express instructions to keep an eye on you.'

'I think he went for a stroll on the upper decks, he said he wouldn't be long.' Tom shrugged phlegmatically.

'Don't lie to me, Serjeant Harding, if I know Private Wheeler, he'll have his nose in the linen room door canoodling with one of my nurses. Stay here and don't move, we'll be leaving shortly.' She flounced off, watched admiringly by the two brothers.

'Fine temper there, Tom, don't you think? Nice girl though, are you really friends?'

'Come off it, I only arrived the day before yesterday,' Tom complained, 'don't you read anything into my use of her first name either, young man. She's a Sister and you don't get to that rank taking up with the likes of you and me.'

'Now I know you're interested in her, you devil.'

'Please yourself!' Tom answered sharply, 'Best I'm off before you see what my real temper sounds like!' `

The brisk return of Bridgette Mathers followed closely by a sullen-looking Private Wheeler put paid to anymore conversation. After making his farewells, Tom was pushed to the door of the ward. A harsh thrumming noise sounded suddenly below his feet and he started in surprise.

'Aha!' Bridgette put a steadying hand on the wheelchair. 'That's it then, we'll be off fairly soon.'

'I don't follow you.' Tom said.

'That's the main engines starting so we must be sailing shortly.' A rattling of chains filled the air and she nodded her head. 'There, you see? They're lifting the anchors. We've taken as many wounded as we can manage, all the beds are filled.' She turned to Tom. 'There was a cease-fire the other day onshore to allow both sides to bury their dead. Apparently the smell from the unburied bodies was lingering over the whole of the peninsula, they say the Turks lost at least ten thousand men on the 19th so conditions in the trenches must have been horrific.'

She shuddered and crossed to one of the portholes, looking out into the harbour. 'Darkness isn't far off but Captain Treadwell will want to have enough light to aid our leaving harbour. Once we're at sea it doesn't matter, we'll put all our lights on to let other ships in the area know we're a hospital ship.'

'Do you really think that would bother the Huns if we ran into one of their submarines?' Tom said quietly, 'The men in the ward were discussing the sinking of the Lusitania only this morning. The swine that sank her didn't care a fig that she was carrying women and children onboard or the fact that a great number of the passengers were neutral. This ship would make a fine prize for any U-boat captain worth his salt.'

'Don't worry,' she reassured him, 'there's been no report of U-boats in the area and Captain Treadwell will have ensured that before making his plans for sailing. Besides,' she added confidently, 'we're a hospital ship, we're covered by the Geneva Convention so no-one would dare attack us.'

'Ask the survivors of the Lusitania if the submarine that sank them played by the rules. This is war, Bridgette and men become worse than animals in wartime. Believe me, I've seen it.'

She stared at him thoughtfully as she digested his words before shaking her head. 'No, Tom Harding, I'm not going to enter into an argument with you. Look, I've made the crossing three times now and never felt one iota of concern, let alone seen an enemy submarine. Don't worry, we'll be fine. We'll get back to the ward now before Miss Green plays merry hell with me, she always likes to have a head-count before we sail, to make sure none of you men have somehow sneaked off the ship to return to the fighting.'

'You are joking, aren't you?' Tom retorted, 'It's the other way round. Have a good look under the beds, you should be looking for men who've sneaked onboard to escape the fighting, not go back. No-one in their right mind would want to exchange their berth onboard here to go back to the hell they've left ashore!'

--§--

The sea continued to rise, a deep swell that made the slender laden-down craft roll heavily under the extra weight of her cargo. Waldemar

Schachter clung tightly on to the guardrail as he and the lookout both jostled for a firm footing in the cramped confines of *UB-3*'s miniscule bridge atop the U-boat's upper deck.

'We'll give it another five minutes and then you and I can go below and get some supper, Walther.'

'*Zu befehl, Herr Kapitan!*'

He punched the lookout lightly on the shoulder. 'Not so formal, Walther, we're at sea now, away from all those landlubbers who haven't a clue what we fighting men put up with when we're out here on the waves. I bet they...'

'A ship, sir, look over there! A large one, too!'

'Where?'

Schachter craned his neck to follow Walther's pointing fingers. A speck on the horizon astern, silhouetted against the slowly sinking sun caught his eye and he grunted in admiration of his lookout's keen eyesight. 'Good God, I see her now, you've done well picking her out in this light. Right, my lad, down below and let's see what we've got here.'

They tumbled into the bowels of the conning tower and Schachter spoke sharply over his shoulder as he deftly spun the control wheel above him, locking the hatch into place and sealing them in. 'Heini, quick, a large ship behind us, catching up fast. Get your recognition charts out and let's see what we've got.'

He crossed quickly to the periscope housing and spoke again as he unshipped it from its housing.

'Prepare to dive!'

'*Kapitan?* Should we be doing this, the boat isn't safe, we need to know more about the trim problem before we commit ourselves to diving. The batteries aren't fully charged either, which will also limit our submerged time.'

Schachter laughed gaily. 'Heini, Heini, stop worrying, we're not going to go deep, just enough to hide us from any lookouts the Britischer might have. Diving stations! Now! Bauer? Take us down carefully to periscope depth, ten metres to begin with. Helmsman, come round to '

'*Jawohl, Herr Kapitan.*'

UB-3 lurched ponderously as the trim valves operated by their separate levers opened and the inrushing seas forced her bows under the water as she smoothly slid into a shallow dive. The pressure hull creaked and groaned as she dove deeper; sounds that made those in the vicinity cast an anxious eye on the needle of the depth meter. When she'd levelled off and the bubbles stopped streaming past the optics of the periscope, Waldemar Schachter hunched over the eyepieces and concentrated hard on the image of the far-away ship. 'Hmn, she looks like a big steamer. Heini, come and see, give me your opinion. What do you think she looks like? See how many funnels you can make out.' He wriggled out of the way and let the other man take his place.

'Well?'

'A moment, sir, ah, I have him now. Oh.' He stepped back, aware of his commanding officer's impatience but mindful also of his duty to speak the correct words lest there be no misunderstandings.

'From her silhouette, she's a liner sir, possibly a Castle Line ship. She has four funnels which marks her out as a very large one but from the lights she's carrying she's almost certainly fitted out as a hospital ship.'

'Are you sure?' Schachter tried to disguise his disappointment but his demeanour left the other man in no doubt as to his true feelings. 'Look again, are you certain she's what you think she is?'

'Well, I can't say for certain at this distance but the lights, they tell…'

'So she could be a decoy, carrying war supplies or fresh troops to the British just like Lusitania was doing in the Atlantic weeks ago, only this time our Britischer's pretending to be a hospital ship. What's her present heading?'

'Let me see, I make it, um, NNE, around 038 degrees. About five degrees off our own course, sir.'

'There!' Schachter's voice was triumphant. 'I told you. If she *was* a hospital ship she'd be heading in a different direction to us, away from Mudros. There's something fishy going on here and if Egypt *is* her destination she should be on a far different heading, round about 080 or 085, I would say. No, what we have here is another ruse by the British to fool us into thinking she's one thing when in reality she's another. This Britischer's a troopship, I'm certain of that. Ready the torpedoes and swing round on a heading to intercept her.'

'*Kapitan*,' Heinrich Molders' voice was strained. 'are you certain about this? World opinion damned *Kapitanleutnant* Schwieger's action in sinking Lusitania, he and all the crew *of U-20* are being talked of as war criminals. We could surface and stop this ship, make her heave to while we examine her. If she proves to be a troopship in disguise we could use the torpedoes on the surface, that way it will also be much safer for us.'

'Heini, you're behaving like my old grandmother with all this worrying! Stop her with what? We have no deck gun and they'd just laugh at us if we surface and they spotted us whilst passing by at high speed, if they don't ram us as an afterthought. There's no way I'm letting these troops reach the shore to kill more of our Turkish allies, sinking this ship could make a dramatic difference to the campaign.

No, my friend, we carry on our preparations to attack. If we turn back onto her now there should be enough time to set up a perfect shot in this light as she approaches, we'll only have the one chance and by God we're going to take it. Besides, it'll make the perfect start to our operational career.'

'Of course, sir, but I still think.....'

'Don't be such a wet rag, man! Look here, Heini, what better present than a fat liner in the bag? Quickly now, get ready to launch our *eels*, this is a far better way to get rid of them then just firing them into an empty sea. Set the torpedoes' firing depth to three metres, that should be more than ample.'

In spite of the strain they were under his enthusiasm infected them all and the crew bent to their tasks with renewed vigour. Grinning broadly but aware, too, of the tension building up, Waldemar Schachter ignored his throbbing head and put his eye to the periscope again.

--§--

Captain Nathaniel Treadwell, commanding *HMHS Fyvie Castle*, paced the bridge with a satisfied air. Since leaving the comparative safety of Lemnos harbour earlier in the late afternoon he'd swung his ship round in a large arc towards the distant peninsula to avoid any incoming ships. Admiralty signals had advised of several troop transports arriving that evening at Lemnos from Alexandria so he'd prudently sailed away from the island in a north easterly direction to avoid being caught in amongst them going the other way in the hours of darkness.

The reason for the lateness of these arrivals was the recent sighting of German submarines in the area and although he thought there was no substance to the present concerns he fully appreciated the need to take precautions. Better to be safe than lying at the bottom of the sea, hence his decision to leave Lemnos later than he would have under normal circumstances.

They'd left without an escort, being a hospital ship meant they should fear no-one but he stroked his beard thoughtfully as he mused. The battleship *Queen Elizabeth* had left for Malta, he'd heard, possibly never to return, citing problems with her engines. If so, that boded ill for the military. She'd performed well using her main armaments but naval shellfire was not the answer. More troops were needed to break the stalemate but at the rate the fools in command of the campaign were using them up there'd be none left by August.

He roused himself, time to take a closer look at their track and intended course. On a darkened sea the last thing he wanted was to have to manoeuvre smartly at speed to avoid some idiot's blacked-out vessel blundering along happily in the dark, unaware of his presence. The bright lights shining down *Fyvie Castle's* entire length *should* alert other ships but with some of the captains commanding merchantmen these days you just never knew. He sighed, by taking the course he'd ordered they'd be well clear of the incoming transports and he ordered the helmsman to hold the wheel steady. In an hour's time, when it would be fully dark, they'd swing round and head for Alexandria at full speed in order to land their casualties as quickly as possible.

--§--

The hubbub in the ward increased as the evening meal was served. Many had groused in the manner of soldiers at the lateness of the food's arrival but calmed down when told it was due to the preparations for leaving harbour. Now they were finally at sea, those who were able to converse with their neighbours wore happy smiles as they anticipated the crossing to Egypt and the prospect of some weeks spent in recuperation before being sent back to rejoin their units.

Tom sat on Fred Wooller's cot playing cards with the awkwardness of being one-handed hindering his progress. Discounting his blurred vision he'd won the odd game but the triumphant smile on Fred's face had planted the seeds of suspicion that the deck they were using had been tampered with in some way. No matter, Fred was grateful for the company. His legs were healing well and Martha Weatherall had informed him about the increasing usefulness of prosthetic legs.

She'd also promised to visit once they reached Alexandria and already had written two or three letters home for him, ready to post as soon they were alongside.

Fyvie Castle ploughed her way onwards as they dealt the cards. A faint humming below his feet and the gentle swaying of the water inside the glass on the bedside locker were the only indications to Tom of the ship's progress through the water.

'She's a fine lass that Sister Mathers, Tom, got her eye on you too, I fancy. I've seen her looking at you from the corner of her eyes when she comes in, mate. You want to watch it, Matron Green'll get jealous, must be years since she 'ad a man.' He cackled at his own joke and Tom joined in.

'Put a sock in it, Fred,' he murmured, 'women like Bridgette Mathers are not for the likes of you and me. On no, a beautiful girl like her will catch the eye of an officer, a doctor, an *Iodine King* or one of those swankers that have a wad of war stories but never stepped onto a battlefield.

I've no doubt she'll nurse back to full health a handsome, red-tabbed staff officer with scratches on his swagger stick caused by fending off crazed battalion commanders who dared to demand to see a real battle plan that would work without it slaughtering all their men. And after marrying this *Hooray Henry* she'll retire to the country with Mr La-di-dah Blashford Bollocks to raise golden-headed children and Labrador dogs. Though in which order, I'm not quite sure yet.'

'You don't say!' Fred exclaimed gleefully'

'Oh yes. It'll be; "*Oh Dahling, do go and see what Alphonse is up to…. I think he's cutting up the gardener in the potting shed*" Or: "*Cyril, put Nurse Smethers down this minute and come and eat your greens otherwise you won't grow up to be as big or as important as Daddy!*" Something like that.' He strutted up and down making sweeping movements with his sling coincide with his verbal caricatures, causing the watchers to hoot with laughter. The laughter died down eventually and they returned to their cards. Tom hitched his pajama bottoms up and tied the belt of his dressing gown tighter round his waist as he reached for the deck of cards.

'Did I hear my name mentioned, Serjeant Harding? Just who is this doctor or staff officer I'm supposed to marry?' A dry voice broke in on their reverie and both started guiltily.

'Bridgette, Miss Mathers, I didn't see you come in. Fred and I were just having a quiet talk, speculating on the end of the war and the suchlike...'

'And?'

He jumped from the bed with an effort and looked at her enquiringly.

'Forgive me...and?...and what?'

'You mentioned staff officers and doctors, not to mention Labradors I believe. Why doctors, was it for any particular reason? I've just come from a stint in the Officers Ward where I happen to have talked with quite a few medical men, is that why you feel free to poke fun at me? Well?' There was steel in her reply and he flinched.

'Oh, no, I just...you see...it was Fred...'

'It most certainly was not me, miss. He said it all by himself!'

'Thanks, Fred! Well, alright Bridgette, I did just speculate on what would happen if you—'

'Who've you been talking to, Martha Weatherall? That girl! Always spreading unwarranted gossip. Is that why you did it, to taunt me about the past, did you both have a good laugh at my expense? Well? What do you know of me that gives you the right to make such fun?'

He stepped back, awkward in the presence of her anger.

'Martha? What has she to do with this? Bridgette, I never—'

'It's *Sister* Mathers, Serjeant Harding.'

'Look, she never said a word, all this silliness is of my doing, I was only trying to cheer the boys up with a bit of tomfoolery. You mustn't jump to conclusions.'

'I'll thank you to keep such opinions to yourself, Serjeant Harding! And get yourself back into bed, you've no right to be out just now!'

She strode out of the ward, head held high, cheeks a fiery red, leaving Tom dumbstruck. Fred Wooller sniggered loudly then subsided, chastened, as he saw the stricken expression on his friend's face.

'Go on then, Tom, go after her and speak to her, better let her know it was only a bit of fun. If she'll listen!'

'Bridgette, wait.'

She spun round and advanced down the corridor towards him, eyes blazing.

'No! Don't speak, how dare the two of you discuss me like that as if I'm some sort of heifer fit only to raise children and dogs! There's more to me than that, Tom Harding!'

'Bridgette, please, it was only a lark, we were only funning. Two soldiers having a laugh and keeping everyone around us amused.' He spoke earnestly and she recognised the contrition in his voice but the anger was still fresh. Wounds she thought long healed re-opened, raw memories that made her lash out indiscriminately and the roaring sound of blood rushing in her head gave her the impetus to hurt someone as she'd been hurt, to make the man opposite as miserable as his words had made her feel.

'Don't speak to me again, go back to the ward and get back into bed. I'll send Nurse Weatherall to see to you but from now on when we meet it'll be on a professional level. You're a patient and I'm a nurse and that's how I shall deal with you from now on. Do you understand?'

She advanced down the corridor towards him and he retreated in shocked surprise from the ferocity of her anger. He tried once more.

'Please, let me explain. It was just a silly remark.'

'*Goodnight*, serjeant.'

--§--

'Both torpedoes ready, *Kapitan*, set for three metres as ordered. Inclination 90 degrees, range 250 metres.'

'Good, Heini,' Waldemar Schachter breathed, grasping the periscope handles firmly as he stared fixedly through the optic. He experienced a momentary flash of panic but ignored it and stared at the target's silhouette steadfastly. There was no mistake, this was a Britischer employing a *ruse de guerre* in order to escape them. Time to go to work. 'She'll be in range any second now, a perfect shot. Stand by...wait...Now! *Torpedo ein, los!*' A pause, a heartbeat. '*Und zwei, los!*' A hand punched the torpedo release button once, paused, and punched it once more.

The 45cm-long sinister shapes leapt from the tubes and accelerated towards their unsuspecting prey, gathering speed as they quickly bridged the distance between their mother ship and its target.

--§--

'Bridgette, I...'

'Don't you listen? I said *Goodnight*. Just go.'

205

As she turned to walk away the ship staggered and lurched sideways and a massive thump from up forward threw them both off their feet.

'*Whatthe...?*'

A second massive thump rang out, this time from aft of where they lay and they were picked up and slammed bodily down again as the ship rolled violently to the right. Before they could rise shakily to their feet the lights flickered and extinguished, leaving them in a stygian blackness reeking of cordite and dust. From a distance behind Tom the sound of men screaming erupted as the wounded were dumped unceremoniously onto the ward floor.

'Bridgette?' he gasped, 'Are you alright?'

Her shaken voice echoed eerily from the dark, getting closer as she crawled along the floor towards him. 'I...I'm here. What–what's happened, have we struck something?'

He found her and held her tight whilst she clung to him. 'I think we've been torpedoed or struck a mine. Can't you smell it? The air stinks of explosives which means something has hit us.'

As he spoke the ship lurched again, settling into a decidedly nose-down attitude and listing heavily to their right. Hoarse shouts came from all directions, intermingled with the cries of wounded men and she struggled from his grasp.

'We've got to get back to the ward, those poor men. . .'

'Bridgette, listen to me, the ship's sinking, get yourself on deck and look to yourself before she goes under. Do you hear me?'

'I can't just leave them, they're my patients, Tom.'

His mind froze.

'Oh, God, Walt, he's below us, he won't stand a chance in his present state.'

'You see? Go to him quickly, now, Tom. I must go back to the ward, see lf l can help the men in there up onto the decks. Wheeler should still be there, he'll help me.'

'Bridgette!'

'Tom, go now, see if you can find Walt. Hurry.' Before he could answer she'd crawled away and he was alone in the darkness. Disorientated, he pulled himself to his feet, his wounded arm throbbing fiercely and made his way in what he thought was the right direction by feeling his way along the walls. The sling impeded him and he tore it off angrily before resuming his quest.

At the end of the corridor he felt the outline of the lift's door and pulled frantically. Nothing budged, the door stayed firmly closed and he realised with a start that the power to the lift had died along with the lighting. Fighting back a surge of panic he thought furiously. The stairs, when they first visited Walt, Bridgette had said the stairs were nearby. He moved further along the corridor and almost fell into the hole the stairway made in the floor. Feeling for the banister he gingerly moved downwards, blurred vision straining to pierce the blackness.

All around him the sound of shouts, screams and, ominously, something he'd never heard before, something altogether more sinister came to his straining ears. The ship creaked loudly in agonised protest as her hull flexed under the sheer weight of thousands of gallons of seawater rushing into the gaping holes in her side made by the torpedoes. The first torpedo had struck on her starboard side forward of the bridge whilst the second one, hitting her two seconds later, had exploded aft of the main engine-room, knocking out her generators and, more importantly, the electric pumps. With the main source of pumping out the water pouring unabated into her disabled hull, *Fyvie Castle* began to settle lower in the water, allowing even more water to flood in through unauthorised open portholes adorning both sides of the ship.

As the torpedoes hissed away from their tubes, Waldemar Schachter kept his eyes firmly on the target. 'How long now?' he called over his shoulder.

'Three seconds to impact, *Herr Kapitan.*' A voice spoke out of the gloom and Schachter exhaled deeply, excitement growing as he gazed across the water in anticipation. This would show his comrades in the Officer's Mess at Cattaro what he and his boat were capable of. A massive column of white water visible even at this distance in the fading light reared up alongside the ship's bridge as the first torpedo's 122kg warhead punched into the liner's side. He'd scarcely drawn breath before a second identical column appeared at the stern and seconds later, two dull thumps echoed across the water to the waiting men's ears.

'Both hits! Look at her, she's sinking, we've hit her with both our *eels*, Heini!' Schachter could hardly contain his emotion and from in front and behind of his cramped position he could hear shouts from the crew as they joined in his celebrations. Their elation was short-lived. The boat pitched upwards in a frightening manner and Schachter reeled back holding a bloodied face as his cheek smashed into the periscope. Cries of triumph changed rapidly to fear as the boat bucked wildly, throwing men to the floor as it corkscrewed violently upwards. All thoughts of victory forgotten, Waldemar Schachter fought to stay upright as he hung on to an overhanging valve wheel.

'Heini, what's happening?' he gasped, 'Bauer, level the boat out and keep us submerged.'

The Helmsman's frightened voice answered him. '*Kapitan*, she won't answer the helm fully and we're broaching fast. What should I do?'

Heinrich Molders' words brought a sense of calm to the situation. 'We've lost trim, *Kapitan*, that's why we're broaching. We'll shoot out onto the surface soon at this rate so if we can control the boat when we do surface we should be able to level off then. Bauer, stand by to—'

A harsh, grinding noise interrupted his speech and the boat staggered to the right. 'She won't answer the rudder at all now, it's jammed fully to starboard, sir!' Bauer cried, his voice rising. Before Schachter could open his mouth the boat crashed heavily from the depths onto the surface like a porpoise, bow hanging in the air like a shark's nose before slamming back down into the swell. Without levelling off as Molders had hoped she would, she continued to slide underwater in a steep dive to starboard.

'Open the valves and bring her back up!' Schachter shouted above the hubbub, 'Heini, help Schneider on the *Diving Piano* and bring her nose up or we're all dead men! Get those not needed to move aft and help trim her out of this. Hurry.' There was no mistaking the urgency in his voice and Molders sprang to the platform where the diving-valve levers known as the *Diving Piano* were housed. These valves, 24 on each side, were used to open and close the tanks to allow the U-boat to dive or ascend, a complicated affair made worse by the tendency of the U-boat to pitch up and broach as the weight of her torpedoes being fired lightened the weight of the boat.

Heinrich Molders grunted with the strain of moving the levers and imperceptibly the nose of the U-boat began to rise and level off. As Schachter allowed himself a small sigh of relief a glance at their compass indicator made him pause to observe their heading. His mind raced as he noted the spinning dial and tried to remember their sinking target's heading, furiously superimposing the two onto each other. If the Britischer had turned to starboard under the *eels* impact and their own rudder was fixed immovably for the moment in the same direction there was a distinct chance the two could meet unless *UB-3* could be taken deeper. It was all a matter of whose turning circle was the greater

A thrumming noise in the distance grew louder with each passing second and Schachter realised with mounting horror that his calculations were correct, the Britischer was bearing down on them as it sank and they were in grave danger of colliding with their own prey as their paths intersected.

'Heini, forget levelling off, for God's sake take us deeper!'

'But *Kapitan*...?'

'Do it. Now. Get them men forward, bring her nose down!'

The noise of approaching screws was deafening now, a roaring sound that transfixed their concentration as the *Fyvie Castle* bore down on them, all the while sinking lower in the water as the life left her. The U-boat's arrested dive was resumed in a panic-stricken haste, eyes looking fearfully up at the ceiling of the conning tower. A shouted command brought the men who'd run aft back into the forward end of the boat and she began to heel over sharply.

'Come on, come on.' Schachter prayed, willing her to dive quicker as the noise above grew to an ear-splitting shriek. The noise was too loud now for shouted commands so he waved his arms vigorously in an effort to spur his men on. The bow angle increased and a surge of hope coursed through him as he dared to think of survival.

--§--

Captain Treadwell stared anxiously as the running figures scurried across the decks below where he stood on *Fyvie Castle's* bridge. It was hopeless, the ship was foundering fast and his focus was now on ensuring as many of those onboard reached the safety of the lifeboats before she slipped beneath the waves. Boats were already being lowered and his officers had their orders but he fully appreciated the need for the ship to lose way before they could think of launching them. Although her screws were slowing down rapidly in response to the loss of steam pressure they still had some way before she could come to a complete stop and launch the boats.

So far there was no sign of panic amongst the crew but that could easily change. Although there was a bit of a swell the sea state was calm for the moment and once they'd come to a stop it would be the work of minutes to begin launching the lifeboats. How long did they have? It was a question he had no answer for and a feeling of dread passed through him as he contemplated what could happen in the next few minutes.

Her bows were dipping lower as she took on more water. He hoped the watertight compartments would hold up, God knows her longitudinal bulkheads had been strengthened like all ships since Titanic's tragic loss but he couldn't guarantee them holding back the sea for too long. A shudder ran through the ship followed by a grinding, tearing noise and his eyes opened wide in surprise. This was totally alien and a different sound to that he'd anticipated accompanying their sinking.

He turned swiftly to the waiting men alongside him. 'Alright, everyone, it's time for us to leave, we've done our duty and there's nothing left, she'll be gone soon. Make your way to the sides and see if you can find a boat. Bernard? Did the radio operator get the distress signals off? Good. Well done, now off you go and good luck.'

Waldemar Schachter's face turned pale as the noise above them grew to a crescendo, blotting out any coherent thought from the furious pounding noise assaulting their eardrums with a maddened cacophony of sound. He opened his mouth to scream but any words on his lips were drowned, literally, in a torrent of ice-cold water as the 17,000 ton razor-sharp, barnacled hull of the *Fyvie Castle* sliced through *UB-3's* pressure hull like a hot knife easing its way through butter. Victor and vanquished met in a screech of tortured metal which lasted only seconds as the broken halves of the submarine folded inwards and plunged uncontrollably to the sea-bed cocooned within a great cascade of air bubbles. Above her victim's broken carcass, *HMHS Fyvie Castle* shook herself momentarily and continued underway, slowing down and sinking lower, ever lower, in the water.

--§--

Breathing hard, Tom reached the bottom of the stairs and peered round in an attempt to get his bearings. No need to close his eyes to remember, the blackness was impenetrable so he shuffled along with his good arm held out as a shield, all the while attempting to find the ward door that would take him to Walt. The screaming rose audibly around him as badly-wounded men cried piteously for help and assistance and his blood ran cold contemplating his fate should he fail to find Walt and make it back to the upper decks.

Shouts and running steps filled his ears but he ignored them all and pressed on down the sloping deck. A sound of heavy, panicked breathing burst out of the darkness but before he could react the figure staggered past him moaning uncontrollably in its fear as it sought to escape. He willed himself along the corridor, heart hammering in his chest, fear threatening to unhinge him and the breathing escaping his tortured lungs in short painful gasps spurred him on as he stumbled sideways along the sloping deck. His head was aching badly now from a combination of his wound and fumes but he steeled himself and crept on.

A harsh, scraping, grinding noise from below made the ship shudder in her death throes and he held his breath until the noise stopped as suddenly as it had started. He found the door and fell through the doorway into Hell, where a blast of hot air greeted him. Over a short space of time, what had once been a bright, cheery and orderly existence was now a darkened, seething mass of humanity where fear ran unchecked amid the smell of evacuated bowels and putrefaction. Somewhere in the darkness lay his brother but as he stood mutely amid the confusion, the chaotic cries of alarm and sounds of terrified human beings, he began to lose all hope of finding Walt

'Help!'

'Nurse, someone, please, help! I can't move. For God's sake...!'

'Oh God!'

'Walt? Walt, are you there?' he screamed desperately, trying to make his voice heard amid the pandemonium. 'Walt, it's Tom, can you hear me?'

'Over here!' a weak voice answered him and he headed to the sound, his heart hammering. From the dark a hand snatched at his jacket and he pulled free from the man's terrified grasp in a reflex action.

'Don't leave me, for pity's sake, I can't move. Please, don't leave me!' The man's voice raised an octave but Tom moved away from him, recoiling at this fresh horror.

'Tom...' The voice sounded nearer and Tom moved at an increased pace. He stumbled against a soft form lying inert on the floor and withdrew from it hastily. As he stretched to pass over it the figure moved beneath him and spoke weakly.

'Tom, is that you? It's me, Walt, I'm stuck.'

'Thank God!' Tom dropped to his knees and fumbled in the dark to make contact with his brother. 'Where are you stuck?'

'My leg. I was thrown out of the bed when the ship stopped suddenly and I think my leg's jammed in something. I can't see and I'm too weak to free myself. What's happened, why have the lights failed?

'I think we've been torpedoed.' Tom told him, trying to sound calm as he felt in the darkness for whatever had Walt held fast in its grasp. Walt began to cry, softly. 'Go Tom, get away and save yourself, there's no point staying here with me and both of us drowning.'

'Stop that talk now, Walter Harding!' Tom hissed fiercely, 'We're in this together. Do you think I've come all this bloody way to lose you like this, we're brothers and we'll get out of this together so shut up and let me think. God, what's that smell, don't tell me you've...?'

Walt broke in quietly. 'I'm sorry, there's been no-one to help. I've done it in my...'

'My fault, I should've known better than to embarrass you like this, Walt. Forgive me, we're in enough trouble without me adding to it.' His questing fingers found Walt's thigh and he moved down along its length.

'*Ah*, got you.'

'What is it?'

'It feels like a meal trolley's fallen over and your leg's trapped underneath. Right, I've only the use of one hand so you'll have to help me, Walt. Twist this way and give us your hand. No, here, not over there. *Ah*, there, hold it there. Now, together!'

They both heaved simultaneously and the heavy object moved slightly.

'That's scared the bugger, let's do it again. *Heeaave!*' This time it moved imperceptibly but a little bit more than before and both relaxed, breathing heavily.

'Tom, Tom!' Walt implored him. 'Please, it'll take too long, we're not going to do it and there's not much time left. Go now, save yourself. Please!'

'Not? Since when does a Harding say *not* and since when did you become an expert on ship sinkings? One more time and make this a good 'un, you dozy shirker. *Heeaave!*'

'*Aaah!* My leg. Stop, my leg, it's taking my leg off!'

'Stop crying you baby, the bloody thing's off your damn leg now!'

They clung together in relief, bathed in each other's sweat before Tom roused himself. 'C'mon now, Walt!' Tom gasped, 'We've got those stairs to negotiate.' He reached over and pulled at Walt's arms. 'Here, take a hold of my dressing gown sleeve, wrap your other arm around me and don't let go, do you hear me?'

'I'll...try.'

'*Ow!* Not that bloody arm.'

'Yes, sir. Sorry, yes, serjeant!'

'Keep up the jokes and we'll be out of here in no time.'

The black humour of the situation kept them going on the desperate journey to the upper deck, one of chaos and confusion, of falling over bodies, grimly shutting their ears to the piteous cries of trapped men and desperately negotiating their way round numerous obstacles and fallen furnishings. The ship had settled lower in the water by now and her list to the right had increased dramatically. More than once as they struggled upwards Walt implored Tom to leave him and save himself but he refused to relinquish his hold and dragged his brother along by sheer willpower alone. Eventually, on the point of collapse, they circumvented the last stairs and pushed open the door to the Promenade Deck.

Both men stood utterly exhausted, blinking owlishly in the dim light. They emerged to a screeching sound of venting steam as it wailed forlornly from the funnels high above them. *Fyvie Castle* was dead in the water now and only empty, deserted decks greeted them, davits and falls flapping in the slight wind being a witness to the boats on this side of the ship having already been lowered. The ship's list was more apparent in what light remained and her bows were pointing dangerously low. Apart from the whistling sound of the steam it was eerily quiet but faintly from the other side of the ship they could hear renewed shouting.

They staggered to the side and looked down. No lifeboats were apparent on the surface of the water. 'It looks a long way down, Tom, what do you think?'

'I think if we stay here, we're dead anyway so we've no choice. She won't stay afloat for much longer so we'd better hop off now.'

He looked round. 'Wait here.' he said, running into the murk and returning with a discarded lifejacket, a bulky affair in canvas-covered cork, and offering it to Walt. 'Quickly, put this on.'

'Tom, we could share it, why sh—?'

A sudden roaring noise made them both spin round. The sea was advancing relentlessly, swiftly, at an accelerated pace along the deck towards them in the deadly manner of a tiger stalking its prey and they both gasped in shock. *Fyvie Castle* had given up the struggle to remain afloat and the hungry sea was in no mood to wait any longer to claim its bounty.

'Quick, no arguing, she's going, get over the side. Now!' Walt hesitated so Tom grabbed his arm, pushed the lifejacket into his brother's faltering arms and helped him over the handrail before awkwardly straddling the rail himself and leaping into the sea. The impact drove him deep, the shock of hitting the water driving the air from his lungs before he automatically kicked out, shooting to the surface on the crest of a wave, spluttering and gasping as his aching lungs ingested mouthfuls of seawater.

He looked round in panic, alone on an empty, black sea. 'Walt, Walt, where are you?' No answering cry greeted him and his heart froze as he trod water frantically before striking out in a doggy fashion paddle in an attempt to distance himself from the sinking ship. From fifty yards away she still towered above him, a dark, massive bulk blotting out the panoply of stars that had appeared overhead and as he watched, fascinated, her shape changed suddenly. The stern lifted smoothly and hung there almost vertically for several long seconds before sliding quickly beneath the surface.

A whirling vortex of water ensnared him in its tentacles, dragging him under and he struggled frantically to escape its clutches before it released him abruptly, spitting him from its grasp in a welter of foam. Far below he could hear the faint sounds of her sinking, a grinding and groaning noise as the heavy machinery within her bowels broke free and she accelerated into the depths but here in the darkness his ears became attuned to a new phenomenon.

A low moaning like cattle lowing in their byres reached out across the surface and he realised with horror that he was listening to the sound of people drowning. Out there in the growing blackness, men and women were struggling for their lives in the emptiness of the sea, clinging desperately to whatever they could find and losing strength and hope before sinking below the waves.

An overwhelming sense of tiredness enveloped him, the strength of his limbs ebbing away as he trod water but by turning onto his back he found he could use his one good arm to propel himself along. Saltwater forced its way through his clenched teeth causing a hacking cough as it seared his throat and lungs but he paddled grimly on. The other arm and his head stung viciously where the seawater had leached through the bandages and attacked the raw wounds but he ignored the pain and swam, paddling towards the harrowing sounds in an attempt to locate Walt.

Something bumped against his side and he recoiled in horror, his mind flashing back to Mudros harbour. Sharks? The object gave a wooden feel to his touch and he breathed a sigh of relief as he recognised it as a wicker chair. Other objects floated haplessly on the surface, chairs, planks of wood and other remnants of the ship intermingled with bodies, lots of bodies, mostly floating face down. He recoiled wildly from one he swam blindly into, that of a young man floating face up, eyes wide-open, staring into infinity. A puzzled frown creased Tom's features as he focussed on the body. The creased uniform jacket the man was wearing looked foreign, one Tom had never seen before and he appeared to be covered in some kind of evil-smelling fuel. Hastily he paddled away from the corpse only to bump into another and then another. The sea appeared to be carpeted with them and a low groan of despair escaped his lips.

A large buoyant object floated into his path and he grabbed eagerly at a rope hanging from its side, holding on tightly whilst he felt his strength returning. It was the upturned half of a ship's lifeboat and looking along its length he was aware of another pair of hands holding onto a similar strand of rope. The rest of the body was immersed in the sea, its head out of sight and as he watched, aghast, the hands opened and the unseen figure slipped silently below the surface.

He lost count of time as he clung there. Gradually the cries around him quieted and it grew dark as he pitched helplessly in the troughs of the waves. A white object drifted towards slowly towards him out of the gloom and he indifferently observed its approach through bleary eyes until it was close enough to make out the shape of a person, dead he assumed, tied within the straps of a bulky Board of Trade cork lifejacket. He or she made no movement but as they drifted closer the shape of its hair became more familiar and with a gasp Tom made out the inert figure of Bridgette Mathers.

He released his hold on the rope and paddled over to her, cupping her head under his arm as he frantically checked for signs of life. She was cold to the touch, her eyes tightly closed but as he moved her head she coughed weakly, a dribble of water passing from her lips. Spurred on by her movement, Tom grasped hold of one of the lifejacket's straps and towed her back to the comparative safety of the upturned lifeboat.

'Bridgette, it's me, Tom. Can you hear me?' He spoke softly into her ear but her eyes remained firmly closed in a pale face and a hard knot of anxiety formed in the pit of his stomach. Shaking her shoulders as best he could brought no response and his anxiety grew. At last he was rewarded by her eyes fluttering open momentarily and she looked round in panic without recognising him, hands beating at his chest ineffectively as she fought against him.

Rising and falling in the growing swell, he caught hold of her hand and thrust it through a loop of the rope, anchoring her by her elbow to the side of the shattered lifeboat. Satisfied she wouldn't drift off he concentrated on holding her head free of the water, ignoring the knife-thrusts of pain that lanced through his injured arm as he grimly supported her. Her eyes closed again and she lay inert as they bobbed around. He cast his gaze past the wreckage, straining his eyes to see if anyone else out there in the darkness could help. Faintly at first, growing stronger with every passing second, he heard a voice in the distance and his hopes rose.

'Over here, we're over here!' he shrieked. No-one answered and his spirits fell before he roused himself and called again.

'Help! Help! We're over here!' This time he heard an answering call and renewed shouting with increased vigour. A minute or two later, guided by his weakening voice, the dark shape of a lifeboat appeared out of the gloom on the peak of a wave, oars biting deeply as the rowers strained to propel the lifeboat in his direction. The oars were shipped raggedly as the lifeboat came alongside and willing hands helped him to push Bridgette Mathers' inert figure into its innards.

216

With the last of his rapidly diminishing energy he was quickly pulled aboard by friendly hands.

Lying gasping, shivering, fighting the urge to throw up on the wooden frames biting into his back, he became aware of a pair of eyes studying him keenly. 'Ah, our Antipodean friend!' a voice spoke, and as his weakened body gave up the struggle to remain conscious and the night claimed him he dimly recognised the voice as that of Matron Green.

--§--

Morning found them alone on a gently rolling sea. During the night the swell had dispersed what lifeboats had made it away from the ship and although they had heard faint shouts for hours afterwards, sunrise brought only an empty horizon. Tom woke stiffly to the smell of vomit, a sick feeling in his own stomach and sore, aching limbs from his sojourn on the floor of the lifeboat. The dry squeak of oars invaded the silence as the boat rose and fell listlessly in the swell. His sodden clothes had partially dried and the blinding headache he'd experienced on being pulled into the boat had receded so he shrugged the discomfort aside and contemplated the events of the preceding hours.

Walt was gone, he knew it, the dull ache in his head confirmation that his newly-found brother was dead. He tried to pull himself upright but his wounded arm failed him and he collapsed into the well of the lifeboat by the stern with a stifled cry of pain. Lying there in the warm sunlight uncaring and feeling the ravages of thirst, his body rolled to and fro as it responded to the motion of the boat cresting the peaks and troughs of the waves. A finger poked him sharply in the side and he glanced up in anger.

'You. Are you going to lie there forever, man? Get up, we could use you on the oars.'

Reluctantly he eased himself to a sitting position, focussing on the face of Matron Madeleine Green as she frowned down at him from a standing position in the middle of the lifeboat. Weakly he lifted his arm. 'I'm bloody well wounded, can't you see that? Aren't you supposed to be a nurse?'

'Don't take that tone of voice with me, young man,' she retorted, 'I've people far worse than you manning the oars so get yourself up here and give one of them a rest!'

217

Struggling to his feet he stood unsteadily and tried to maintain his balance. A fresh breeze wafted across his face, the brisk saltiness of the air restoring his strength and his humour. He pulled a wry face, glancing over at the matron. 'Please excuse my bad manners,' he smiled, 'I've only one good hand but it should be enough to pull on an oar for a while. Where would you like me to sit? Before I do, is there any chance of a mouthful of water, fresh water, only I'm feeling a bit parched you see.'

Blithely unaware of his feeble attempt at sarcasm, it was her turn to apologise. 'I'm sorry, you've been laid down there for so long I should've realised you'd be feeling dehydrated.' She sat down, reached behind her and pulled out a small grey tin. Carefully pouring a measure into a metal cup she handed it over to Tom. 'Be careful with it, soldier, we've not much water and God knows when we'll be picked up so we'll have to ration it for as long as we can.'

'Someone should take charge of it, then!' he gasped, half-choking as the tepid liquid ran down his throat.

'Easy there,' she murmured, taking the cup from him as he coughed and spluttered, '*I've* taken charge of it, you don't think I'd let you men decide when to drink do you, it would be gone in no time. Now, do you think you could relieve Alistair over there, poor dear, he's been rowing for hours without a break.' She pointed to his left and Tom turned in that direction.

One of two figures bent over an oar weakly lifted an arm in acknowledgement at hearing his name and Tom took a good look around the boat at the other survivors before making his way on shaky feet over to where Alistair awaited him. The lifeboat was crowded with a mixture of men and women, soldiers, nurses and ship's crewmen, fifty or sixty altogether, he reasoned. An overpowering stench wafted around the seats, the result of many of the occupant's seasickness and he gagged and fought to keep bile rising from the pit of his stomach and shaming him in front of all these strangers.

A man's face stared at him and for a brief moment hope flared as he thought it might be Walt but the man turned and his hopes fell. This man looked nothing like his brother and his despair returned unbidden. He looked, too, for a sight of Bridgette Mathers' uniform but was unable to find her in the lank, apathetic faces that peered blearily back at him. He turned back to Madeleine Green.

'The nurse. Sister Mathers, you picked her up. Is she alright?'

Madeleine Green pointed forwards in exasperation. 'She's recovering back there, she was unconscious when we picked you both up, poor girl, so I had her placed under the awning at the far end of the lifeboat. Now, please, do you mind doing as you're told?' Tom looked towards the bow but saw nothing except the awning flapping emptily. Five feet away he saw the ward orderly Private Wheeler staring blankly at the floor but the man gave no sign of recognising him and Tom forgot him as he squeezed through the press of people to the oar Madeleine Green had indicated.

Alistair eased himself gratefully from his seat and smiled apologetically at Tom. 'Thanks awfully.' he whispered before sliding past to where the matron gestured for him to sit. Taking his place, Tom glanced sideways at his rowing companion, an older man, a coloured member of *Fyvie Castle's* crew that he'd heard referred to as Lascars. A term used to describe one as coming from the Indian continent, the man gave no indication of Tom's presence and continued to sit head down, mumbling incoherently to himself.

'Right, chaps, you've had a good rest so let's do some more rowing. Altogether now, *puuuulll.*'

At the sound of her voice, those slumped over the oars roused themselves and glared at Matron Green but she ignored them and sang out again. 'Come on, show us what you're made of. Don't give up. Lt Smithfield, sit up straight there and pull with the others.'

Reluctantly, the rowlocks creaked as first one then the other began to strain at the leather-bound oars. Tom took hold of the slippery wood with his good hand and pulled feebly at it. The Lascar next to him snarled toothlessly at him and pulled with gusto, slobbering angrily as he gesticulated for Tom to use both hands. Tom pulled at his salt-encrusted shirt to reveal his wounded arm by way of explanation and the man gasped as he observed the filthy blood-stained bandages. He stopped rowing long enough to clap Tom on the back by way of a silent apology and together they began pulling at their oar in a lopsided frenzy.

--§--

In this way they moved across the water, sliding up and pitching down in a corkscrewing fashion. When Tom faltered, the Lascar would wait patiently until he was ready to pull again and then take over most of the rowing. Hours passed, with frequent rests and at

219

long last Matron Green signalled for them to rest and eat. Under the hungry eyes of the boat's occupants she broke open a metal tin of the emergency supplies and began handing out pieces of ships biscuits and cups of water. Tom tried his biscuit gingerly, placing a corner of it in his mouth and attempting to bite a part off. It felt as hard as a piece of teak and he made to throw it angrily over the side but his hand was stopped by his rowing companion.

Waiting until the water cup reached them, the Indian dunked his biscuit in the fresh water and gestured for Tom to do the same. Grudgingly he copied the man and to his surprise found it more edible as the action of immersing it in water softened it enough to allow him to swallow a morsel. A chuckle leaked from the man's lips and he dug his elbow into Tom's side in obvious amusement. Tom's lips twitched in response and together they leaned on the oar in satisfaction and watched their companions scrabble for the biscuits and a splash of water.

The sun was directly overhead now, a bright yellow orb that seared his eyes when he looked up and he thought deeply about their chances of survival. Thirst would become a problem in the hours ahead, the sparse water rations would help eke out what little remained but if help didn't reach them soon the water, or lack of it, could be a flashpoint amongst the hungry and thirsty sunburnt survivors.

Nightfall arrived as a blessed relief from the sun, bringing with it a marked drop in the temperature and no sign of rescue. The night was bitterly cold so Tom and his rowing companion moved closer together, bodies locked as in a lover's embrace, drawing strength from each other's heat. In this way they remained huddled until the dawn. During the hours of darkness Tom awoke to hear quiet splashes and when the sun's rays drove away night's shadows he could see empty places where the worst of the wounded had lain.

The next day passed in a torment of hunger and thirst with arguments springing up about the size of the rations, in particular the water. Just as Tom had feared, several officers in the boat tried to use their rank to obtain larger portions but were slapped smartly down by Matron Green, leaving a seething air of resentment apparent on all sides. An unremitting sun glared down on the boat, leaving no shade to retreat to and causing the raw agonies of sunburn to add to those of a mounting thirst. Little attempt was made at rowing, those sitting at the oars dabbled feebly at the water, content to allow the lifeboat to drift along with the prevailing current.

Nightfall at the end of the second day brought other problems. A faint splashing noise followed by slurping sounds brought Tom awake in an instant and he peered at the man sitting in front of him. The figure turned away, making gobbling noises as he did so and Tom realised with mounting concern that the man had been leaning well over the side and was drinking seawater in great gulps from his cupped hands.

'Stop it, you fool,' he hissed, 'you'll kill yourself drinking that stuff.'

The man wrenched round angrily. 'Keep your bloody mouth closed and salute when you speak to me. I'm an officer I'll have you know.'

'It's still far too dangerous to drink seawater,' Tom replied evenly, 'sir! And I'm not saluting anyone in this damn boat.'

'Oh yes, we'll see about that when we get to Alexandria, laddie.' the officer snarled. 'Now mind your own damn business, I'll do as I please.'

'It's your funeral.' Tom shrugged as the officer turned and began leaning over the side again. The man was risking his life with the stupidity of his actions and tired and exasperated, Tom fell into a fitful sleep, conscious only of the movement of the boat and the lapping of the waves against the woodwork. He still hadn't caught sight of Bridgette Mathers and that only increased his anxiety.

He woke an hour later to a great shout of alarm. 'Sit down, Major Burnside! Grab him, someone, before he hurts himself.'

Tom looked wearily up to see the officer with whom he'd argued during the night standing upright in his seat, brandishing an imaginary pistol as he wavered on the slick wood, thrashing his arms wild-eyed at the lifeboat's occupants.

'Take cover!' he yelled wildly, 'Watch out! They're coming….. No. Don't! I won't let you take me…'

Tom leant forward rapidly and grabbed his legs but the major kicked backwards viciously and he fell, winded, into the scuppers. Before he could regain his feet the major uttered a piercing cry and dived headfirst over the side into the sea. A shocked silence was broken as Tom grabbed the edge of the rail and looked back. A slight swirl was all he could see on the surface and he sat back and put his head into his hands.

By midmorning of the following day, more empty places told of the growing number of deaths among them. The major's death forgotten,

221

impatience and anger coupled with a raging desire for water led to vociferous arguments and one or two occasions survivors had to be physically restrained to stop them lunging for the supplies Madeleine Green now kept stockpiled under her seat. The situation was reaching danger levels and in order to avert the growing crisis she decided to try and raise their spirits.

'Alright, everyone, it's getting to hot to row just now so while we save our strength for later, how's about a singsong?' A collective groan rose up but Madeleine Green blithely ignored them and began to sing in a thin, reedy voice. *"Rule Britannia... Britannia rules the..."*

'Put a sock in it! What about an Aussie song?'

'Well, I never...'

'Come on you blokes, ignore the sheila. Don't let her dictate what we're gonna sing. How about: *"Once a jolly swagman camped..."*

"Rule Britannia..."

"...by a billabong..."

'A ship, oh my sainted aunt, look, a bloody ship!'

'Where?'

In an instant the singing contest was forgotten as they all craned their eyes anxiously to peer in the same direction a soldier stood up in the bows was pointing. 'I see it, over there on the horizon. There, there, look, can you see it?' More people took up the cry and the hardier of them stood up, frantically waving items of clothing.

'Over here! We're over here! Oh God, make them see us!'

'Please, calm down. Lt Smithfield, take charge of some men and see if you can rig up a sail or something to let them know we're here.' Madeleine Green was unflappable and the officer to her right sprang forward at her urging and delved into the small locker built into the middle of the lifeboat. A crewman squirmed over to help him and together they wrestled a large red piece of canvas from its depths. The mast it should have fitted to lay splintered and useless in the bottom of the lifeboat.

It was the work of seconds to unfold the canvas and with the help of others the two men held it triumphantly aloft. It caught the breeze and the craft heeled over dangerously, spilling several of them from their places on the thwarts as they lost their balance in their eagerness to be saved.

'Be careful!' she admonished them, 'We don't want to lose anyone now.'

222

The lifeboat picked up speed but the pace went unheeded as everyone kept longing eyes on the faint smudge on the horizon. 'She's turning our way, look everyone, she must have seen us. *Hooooraaah!*'

'Wait a moment, what if she's a Hun boat, or worse, Turkish?' The speaker, a thin red-faced man with a sparse moustache and the uniform of a lieutenant was viewed with contempt and he hastily tried to make amends. 'Look, all I said was she...'

'You. Shut up, you bludger, or you'll taste my fist, mate!'

'I say, just who do you think you're threatening? I'll have you...'

'She is, she's turning, coming this way. Quick, keep waving everyone.'

Enmity abandoned, men and women jumped up and down, waving whatever came to hand and embracing each other in an ecstasy of relief. The smudge coalesced into a dark shape and within minutes the sleek outline of a destroyer took shape under the thin trail of black smoke that billowed behind her as she raced towards them, White Ensign fluttering cockily from her masthead. The foam in her wake frothed to a frenzy as she slowed and placed her engines in reverse, allowing her to glide noiselessly towards the madly cheering throng that lined the sides of the lifeboat.

'WHAT...SHIP?' An officer leaned from the side of the destroyer and shouted through a megaphone. Madeleine Green stood up and replied in a high, emotionally-charged voice. '*His Majesty's Hospital Ship Fyvie Castle*, sunk three days ago.'

'Roger. Well done, ever since we picked up a Marconi message giving your last known position we've all been looking for you. Come over to the side and we'll take you onboard.' A scrambling net was lowered at the lowest point of the ship and the lifeboat manoeuvred below it. A rush developed as people surged towards the net but Tom hung back and watched as the fittest among the survivors climbed upwards before being dragged onto the destroyer's deck by friendly hands. A hand tapped his shoulder and he turned in surprise to see the Lascar looking gravely at him. Smiling, the man reached out a hand and Tom placed his in the man's leathery embrace.

Together they made their way to the side of the lifeboat and taking a firm grip on Tom's dressing gown belt, the man began to climb one-handed, his muscles standing out like cords as he took Tom's weight in his other hand. Tom used his good arm to help their progress as best he could and with both men planting their feet securely in the net, they inched towards safety and a minute later both lay panting on the warship's wooden deck. A sailor attempted to pull the Lascar away.

'Get away from him.' Tom stopped him. 'Leave him be, that's my mate.' he said sharply and the sailor walked off shaking his head. The two lay bonded together, feeling the strength of the sun on their backs, smiling into each other's face in silent acknowledgement of the debt that had grown between them as all around the lifeboat was speedily emptied. Eventually, Tom roused himself enough to watch keenly as the non-walking survivors were gently retrieved. There was no sign of Bridgette Mathers amongst them and he reasoned she may well have been disembarked in the minutes he'd lain there.

As he continued to stare his arm was roughly pulled by a sailor trying to force him to rise. 'Come on, me old, up on yer feet, d'you want to lie there all day?'

'Have you picked anyone else up, perhaps, survivors from another boat?' Tom croaked hopefully but the man shook has head sadly. 'Sorry, pal, you're the first we've sighted. There are other ships looking but the skipper wants to get back and land yous lot first. C'mon, down we go an' have a nice cup of kye.'

'Kye?' Tom asked bemused.

'Yeah. Best wet of navy cocoa this side of the Suez. Our chef does it a treat so get your legs moving, chum. If yer lucky he'll have plonked a goodly tot of rum in it.'

Tom tried to picture his brother floating, alone, out there on the sea with no hope but his mind baulked at the thought and he reluctantly allowed himself to be led away and helped through a gangway into the warship's interior.

Once all the survivors were onboard the destroyer's captain increased speed, reaching Alexandria the following day where they were swiftly guided alongside the quayside. A fleet of motor ambulances with canvas sides were soon in attendance and began the task of transporting everyone to hospital. Two orderlies helped Tom down the gangway into the cool interior of one of the vehicles and slammed the tailgate shut. He tried vainly to catch a glimpse of his friend and saviour the Lascar but the tailgate slamming left him lying in the shaded interior as the vehicle moved off.

224

A short journey later they pulled up in the courtyard of a large building. 'Here we are, chum,' one of the orderlies cried, helping Tom alight. 'No 15 General Hospital, gonna be your home for a while now, I reckon.'

'Hang on, mate,' Tom answered, 'I'm with the Australians, should I be here?' The two men looked at each other in perplexion. 'Dunno. This is where we were told to take you all. Not to worry, pal, we'll leave you here and let them decide where you're to go.'

Ignoring his protests they procured a wheelchair and pushed him through the doors at the front of the building. The entrance opened out onto a wide, imposing corridor smelling of floor wax. White fans hummed overhead bringing a sense of coolness and peace and in spite of his concerns Tom felt himself relax as the men pushed him towards a large desk marked **Reception**.

'Aha!'

They were stopped in their tracks by a large figure barring their way and Tom looked up with mounting dread to see Matron Madeleine Green staring down at him. 'Harding, isn't it? I've been looking for you. I'd like a word with you if you don't mind, please come with me. Leave him there, you two, I'll see to this man.'

Her crumpled uniform was stained white with salt from their ordeal but she still commanded a regal air and the orderlies jumped with alacrity to obey her. She turned about and Tom lifted himself from the wheelchair and followed meekly in her footsteps. As she crossed the corridor to an open office door she spoke over her shoulder.

'The first thing I did on arriving here was to ask them to check on your whereabouts. Please, do come in.' The office contained a small wooden desk and two chairs and she indicated which one he was to seat himself upon.

'I shall be leaving here shortly, to travel to Cairo and report on the disaster we were both lucky to survive, Serjeant Harding. I couldn't leave without first thanking you personally for your bravery in saving Sister Mathers and also for trying to save poor Major Burnside. He went quite mad, you know, I think through drinking seawater. Thirst can do terrible things to sufferers and I believe he wasn't the only one to try it.'

'I did try to tell him not to.' Tom murmured dryly. He looked across the table at her. 'There's someone who was on the ship with me, I must find out if he survived. Would it be possible to find out if anyone else was picked up?'

'Just you sit here and relax, young man. I've ordered a pot of tea and when you're quite ready the orderlies will come for you and they'll see you're settled in alright. We'll keep you here for the time being until we find out what happened to this person you mentioned, I'm sure an extra bod won't be noticed. Just don't get yourself noticed or someone will want to know what an Australian is doing here. '

'How very English.' Tom replied with a wry smile, 'Tea. Thank you matron. This person, he's actually…'

'My goodness, look at the time!' she cried, interrupting him and looking up at the clock on the wall behind him. 'We'll talk later about who you're looking for but right now I must fly. I shall be reporting your courage to the right authorities when I reach Cairo so take care of yourself, serjeant. I hope you recover fairly swiftly.'

'Not too swiftly.' Tom smiled, 'I'd like a fair rest before going back.'

The smile faded from her features. 'You're right. Take as long as you can in that case, and try to come out of this debacle in one piece. Good luck, serjeant.'

She left and shortly afterwards a discreet knock on the door heralded the arrival of the tea. After sipping a cup he ventured out into the corridor and made his way back to Reception.

'Ah, there you are,' a rather severe-looking nurse exclaimed, 'we were getting worried, thought you'd ran off on us.'

'Look,' Tom asked desperately, 'I know it's all a bit too soon but would you know whether or not any other ships have picked up survivors? My brother, Corporal Walter Harding of the 7th Middlesex was on the ship with me and I haven't seen or heard of him since the ship sank. Would you have heard of him or any other survivors from other boats, perhaps?'

Her face relaxed into a wide smile. 'Come with me, please. I think you'll be interested in who is …ah, here we are. Try in here.'

She pushed open the door and gestured for Tom to come closer. 'A destroyer found him. They were just about to abandon the search for survivors when a keen-eyed tar spotted him clinging to a spar of driftwood, apparently so tightly they had to physically prise it from his grasp to get him onto the ship.'

Hardly hearing her words, Tom stared past her to the recumbent figure lying huddled amongst the white sheets of a hospital bed. His heart gave a great leap and from a distance he heard the nurse turn and walk away, leaving him staring through suddenly moist eyes at the sleeping form of his brother for the second time in a week.

Chapter Eleven.

Turkish reserve trenches.

He was floating on a sea of pain, every slight movement of his limbs causing him to stifle a cry lest he be discovered. By lying inert, he let the sea-swell wash over him until the pain subsided and it became bearable enough for him to stiffly stretch his arms and legs and sit up. A loud buzzing noise filled his head but he ignored it whilst trying to make sense of his surroundings. The noises of battle, the last sounds in his consciousness before the blackness had enveloped him, were gone now and he sensed a change of circumstance, that of an alien space and time.

He was lying on dry, arid sand and all around was silence and a great overwhelming sense of darkness. Stifling a groan he twisted to his left and looked up, lying back and letting his elbows bear the full weight of his body whilst ignoring the pain lancing through his injured shoulder. A pale, watery moon, its beams a dim silver light on the ground before him, cast strange shadows on the desert floor. Far away in the distance a low, dark line appeared to signify a range of hills but in the nearness of the desert surrounding him he sensed nothing, only the vast emptiness of space.

When the tide of pain had ebbed still further he rose with an effort and took a faltering step forward. With no conscious sense of direction an unspecified, inner choice made him head towards the moon overhead and he followed what he perceived to be a faint trail on the desert floor below his feet. The air was perfectly still, an eerie portent of something about to or of that which had already happened and he shook his head in bemusement at the lack of stars overhead in what appeared otherwise to be a clear sky. Somewhere far away he heard the hoot of an owl and his heart froze at the sound. To an Armenian owls were evil, harbingers of death, and his breathing increased rapidly to a ragged whisper.

A presentiment of something evil lurking in the darkness from which he should turn away grew stronger with each step but his feet seemed to have decided on a different direction to that which he wished to follow and in his bemused state he let them lead him on. A silent shape flitted past on the far edge of his peripheral vision and his lips curled in both disgust and disdain as he recognised its form. A jackal, the eternal desert scavenger, what was it doing here in this alien landscape far from its prey's normal habitat? As it slid away into the shadows it was joined by another and a few steps later a fresh animal loped quietly by without heeding him and his disquiet grew.

One was strange enough but this many? What was there here for them to bring them so far from their usual haunts? A new sense, unbidden, welled up inside him, that of foreboding and he looked round for clues which could explain these feelings. Nothing stirred and in his trancelike state he continued to walk on. His feet hit an obstruction and the effort spent in keeping his feet sent fresh waves of pain through his aching shoulder and side as his arms flailed wildly for balance. Cursing, he glanced down for the cause of his stumbling and recoiled in fright at the sight of a human torso gleaming palely in the moonlight.

He stepped forward and looked again. There was no mistaking the arched ribs and breastbone that poked mutely from the drifting sand which had piled around it and as he followed the shape of the skeletal remains he was shocked to see an empty-eyed skull grinning up at him. Its half-covered jawbone clearly showed the ravages wrought by the jackals and as he stared closer, two lines of heaped sand denoted the skewed position of the skeleton's legs and his uneasiness grew as he peered further into the dim light.

Another mound outlined a fresh set of remains nearby and as his shocked eyes became accustomed to the gloom he became aware of many more such mounds stretching seemingly into infinity. He was on the outskirts of what appeared to be a graveyard, a huge ossuary, the last resting place of whom or what he was unsure. His confused mind failed to re-arrange these jumbled thoughts into something resembling coherent insight and he took several hesitant steps further into the scattered remains in order to understand clearly what had happened here.

This was no modern site of battle; the ground lacked any signs of the damage high-explosive shells wreaked and what lay before him in the sand failed to match the violence he'd seen on bodies that were flung in all directions when such shells exploded nearby. The skeletons were devoid of all clothing although some scraps still clung tenaciously to their owner's bones and he bent forward to see if he could recognise their origin. The cloth was not of any military uniform he'd seen and his uneasiness grew.

His foot touched something small and he glanced down. A small, white object gleamed faintly up at him and he reached for it unconsciously. It nestled snugly in the palm of his hand and as he turned it around realisation hit him like a blow to the stomach. He was holding a skull, a child's skull, the back of which had been shattered by a savage blow to the head.

Recoiling in horror he dropped the skull to the desert floor and looked round again. In the pale, dim light, the small mounds had gone unnoticed but now he could see them, clustered around the adult remains. This was no graveyard, this was a charnel-house, a place of execution, not burial, and the people whose remains littered the desert had been brought here and murdered.

But who were they and what were the supposed crimes that had brought them to this dismal spot? The bones held no clues he could see but he moved aimlessly amongst them, head down, looking closely for other clues that could unravel the mystery. An answer came while he wandered, a small object lying in the open near a skull and his fingers closed round it eagerly. It was an earring, a woman's earring and as he studied it he recognised the square shape dangling on a thin, silver filigree chain as being that of Armenian origin.

228

His breathing quickened, his heart began to pound and he sank to his knees, mouth open, eyes unseeing as the full portent of his discovery hit him. These were surely his people, Armenian Turks who had been taken from their village and brought here to be foully robbed and then done away with. He found his voice and the desert reverberated as Artoun Seferian lifted his head and howled, a high, feral ululation of grief. The prowling jackals nearby lifted their heads in startled fear at this sudden intrusion and loped swiftly into the security of the night as the sounds of his anguish carried far out into the wastelands.

The sound stopped abruptly as he pitched forward onto his knees and wept, the tears intermingling wetly with the dryness of the desert sand. Hegine, oh, my poor, dearest Hegine. His beautiful, gentle wife was dead, he realised that now. Private Kaplan's words had indeed confirmed the awful truth, evil had happened here and that truth was too much to contemplate. Their son must have died too. Never again would he hold his son, Khat, and exult in his closeness, the beauty of that which he and Hegine had created. Teetering on the edge of madness he tried to banish any thought of how his loved ones could have met their death but utter despair wracked his body, together with his sobs, and within the loneliness of eternity he grieved for his wife and son.

A series of flashes together with a low rumbling gathered in intensity from behind him but he ignored it as he knelt there, head in hands, contemplating the emptiness of the future. A torrent of noise swept suddenly over him, knocking him to the ground, reawakening the pain from his wounds and he cowered under the onslaught of the tearing, crashing sounds. Pressure waves lifted him bodily into the air and flung him down again, pushing his face into the sand as he struggled wildly for breath, the pressure of each grain invading his mouth and suffocating him with its cloying embrace.

Abruptly, the noises faded into the darkness that had enveloped him and he cautiously opened his eyes.

--§--

'Ah. Finally you're awake. We thought we'd lost you.' A calm voice registered amongst the manic seeds of his confusion and he looked up from where he now found himself lying, under a dirty blanket on a reed-packed floor, and into the inquisitive gaze of the German officer, Leutnant Brückner. His left arm was covered in a filthy bloodstained bandage, tied roughly across his wound. Distracted by the sudden change in time and place, his eyes tried to fathom out his new surroundings by the light of a flickering oil lamp and the German noticed his puzzlement.

'The noise? Don't worry, it's just our enemy letting us know they've taken in fresh deliveries of shells. They've expended a lot on the front line a kilometre away and now they're giving the reserve trenches a taste of it too. We're quite safe here, this dugout was constructed well and it's also quite deep. How are you feeling, a bit groggy, hmn?'

A cloud burst within and an overwhelming sense of relief coursed through his mind as he digested the German officer's words. The weird atmospheric sensations he'd experienced in the desert had somehow been manufactured by his own febrile imagination, none of it could therefore be true! In his gratitude at this revelation he began to rise, babbling incoherently but Brückner leant over him and made soft soothing noises as if speaking to a child. 'Don't struggle, lie there and recover. You've had a nasty time of it, I fear, but we didn't find you until this evening. Private Kaplan heard a sound and under the cover of the dark he went out and brought you in, you must have crawled back from the enemy lines where you were wounded.

Quite remarkable, your survival. We lost so many of our fellows. Casualties were dreadful, many dead and missing but you, my friend, with *Allah's* help, were one of the lucky ones. The enemy's bullets cause dreadful wounds but you must have been knocked down by one of their home-made grenades as we took a lot of rusty metal fragments from your shoulder. I think that and the shock of being wounded caused a reaction as you've been quite feverish for the last two or three days, calling out in your sleep and thrashing around on the floor. We were quite worried for a while but look at you now, apart from that bandage you look the perfect picture of health.

The doctor cleaned your wounds every day so you should make a good recovery. Oh, and another thing, the captain was so pleased with you and your late friend's bravery he lifted the sentence hanging over you. When you're back to full strength you're to rejoin the battalion as a free man. Good news, eh, but it gets better.'

He leant forward and continued. 'Until you're able to resume normal duties I've told the captain I'll take you as a servant. You interest me and there's still so much I want to learn about your ways and religion. When you're able to talk more I'll send for the *imam* and he can offer you spiritual comfort. Come, Yilmaz, rest. Sleep. We'll get some food down you later but for now only a sip of water is allowed.'

Artoun offered up his lips eagerly as a *nefer* dutifully poured a thin stream of cool water down his parched throat. When the private had finished helping him drink he lay back on the rough pillow beneath his head and slept. His last thought was a picture of Hegine holding Khat in her arms as he had left her, a warm smile on her face and his son's small hand waving furiously.

In the days that followed he tried not to concentrate on them but applied himself to resting and allowing the healing process to continue. The regiment had constructed some tents well behind the trenches, under the shelter of the pine trees, almost invisible from the air and it was to one of these he was assigned to recover. He was fed lentil broth, bread when it was available and drank plenty of cool, clean water that came from a local well. Leutnant Brückner visited him from time to time, checking up on his progress, making desultory small talk, the subjects ranging from various aspects of the war to the flora and fauna surrounding their positions.

Two weeks after his rescue he was deemed fit enough to carry out light duties and made his way to where the German had commandeered a small dugout. During the day the heat could be almost unendurable but by contrast the temperature dropped sharply at night and Brückner had been glad of the warmth his dugout provided. He heard Artoun's approaching footsteps and popped his head out of the entranceway.

'Come in, come in,' he greeted Artoun enthusiastically, 'I just had a delivery of some cheese, would you like some?'

Artoun shook his head in perplexion at the man's solicitous greeting, completely different to that of any Turkish officer he'd had dealings with. As an ordinary soldier he would've been lucky to be met with a snarl and a swift kick if he failed to move quickly enough yet here was an officer greeting him pleasantly and asking if he wanted to eat.

Brückner saw the perplexion and guessed the reason behind it. Motioning Artoun to come inside he gestured for him to sit on a rickety bench whilst he sat down on his bedding on the floor. The atmosphere inside the dugout was stifling but the German ignored the heat and spoke quietly. 'You'll excuse me if I take something myself,' he said, 'only I've had nothing this morning. The captain calls for us at the most inconvenient times and this morning was no exception.'

He looked inquisitively at Artoun before continuing. 'I asked for you to be my manservant because it will give you a chance to recover fully. If you were to go back to the regiment they'd make you work a lot harder than I would and you need more time for that arm to heal before going back to the firing line.'

'Thank you, *efendim*,' Artoun stammered, 'I cannot thank you enough for helping me in this manner. I hope to serve you well and...'

231

'How is the arm, no problems now?'

'No *efendim*, I was always strong and this helped, I feel, in my recovery. Apart from a twinge now and again I...

'A good thing it was your left arm, eh? As a Moslem, to have your right injured would have been more of a social disaster, don't you think?'

'I suppose so.' Artoun smiled weakly, all the time wondering where this strange conversation with the quiet, seemingly placid foreigner was headed.

'You're name isn't really Yilmaz, is it?' the Leutnant asked abruptly. 'Well?'

His question was a sharp blow to Artoun's stomach. '*Efendim*, I... My name...?'

'Please, don't take me for a fool. Out with it, man, who are you really?'

'But I...'

'I said, don't take me for a fool!' Brückner snorted. 'You're not a Moslem, whoever or whatever you pretend to be. I've watched ever since you and your friend were sent to this battalion for punishment, you don't act like a Moslem and unlike your late departed friend you've never spoken to the *Imam* that I'm aware of. When I spoke to you in the dugout just after you'd been brought in and mentioned the *Imam* coming to speak with you I thought you looked perturbed but put it down simply as the confusion of a badly-wounded man. Now I know you were scared he'd suspect the truth if he visited you. There's something definitely different about you and if you hadn't been part of the punishment squad your fellow soldiers would have sniffed you out long ago.'

'We were not allowed to speak with the *Imam*.' Artoun spoke desperately, trying to suppress his fear. 'Because we were under sentence of death the *Imam* stayed well clear of us. He made it quite clear that we would not be under *Allah's* protection as a result of our sins and could only atone for our misdemeanours by dying bravely. That's why he ignored our existence.'

'Prettily spoken but untrue, I fear. You play the part of a Moslem soldier very well but there's something about you that just doesn't quite fit in. What is it, I wonder? You look Turkish, a trifle paler than some but I've seen lighter-skinned Ottomans than you so just what is it about you that causes me such unease? I observed your friend speaking with the *Imam* on several occasions but you, never. Last chance, Yilmaz, if that *is* your real name, and then I call the guards and the captain can question you further.'

Artoun stared at him, his mind racing. The choice was simple enough, talk or not, it was the consequences of either action that were to be feared. His mind made up, he began to speak.

'I'm Artoun Seferian, late *onbasi* with the 66th battalion until it was removed from a train and murdered by men who a short time previously we looked on as comrades. I alone survived to run away and rejoin my family but I was unlucky enough to be captured and made up the name of Yilmaz, a Moslem name, to escape detection and almost certain death. They sent me to Konia for punishment as a deserter and it was there I met Arif Bilgili and we were sent here with a punishment squad.'

'Ah, I was right, I thought you had the look of an NCO about you, someone used to giving orders, not taking them. Seferian? That's an *ermeni* name, isn't it?' Brückner looked at Artoun keenly and he returned the stare defiantly.

'Yes, I'm *ermeni* and a loyal Turk too, although that was forgotten when they slaughtered my comrades. That infamous day we were *Gâvurs*, their name for those not of their faith, *unbelievers*, and that was probably why we were to be murdered. For the simple reason that we believed in a different god. You wouldn't understand...'

'No?' Brückner answered softly, 'I'm Jewish, Seferian, do you know what that means? I owe my rank and good fortune to a distant relative but make no mistake, there have been many times when my allegiance to his majesty, the *Kaiser*, has been questioned. We Jews are tolerated for now but one day...' He broke off and stared at Artoun.

'The question is, now what do we do with you?'

'If you inform the captain of what I've just told you, I'm a dead man.' Artoun said simply. 'He can't afford to be caught up in my troubles so it might be better if you told him and he can have me killed. That way, you won't attract any trouble yourself.'

'For a simple man you speak very eloquently, Artoun Seferian. I'm touched by your concern for my welfare but the thought of turning you in, shall we say, never crossed my mind for a second. I told you just now that I'm Jewish, do you realise what that information could do to me in the wrong hands? No-one in the group of German officers who came to Turkey to assist Enver Paşa knows that fact but now you do. So you see, we both have a secret to keep.'

'But you're an Islamic scholar, *efendim*, you told us that when we first met. Surely that means...'

'I said I was an Islamic scholar, that's true, you're right on that account. Strange, don't you think, that a Jew should find so much to admire in a religion that can be focussed on his own destruction? However, I did *not* say I was a Mohameddan. I didn't come here to stir up old hatreds, I'm Jewish by birth but my family and I are non-practising members of our race. I came here as a German officer in the service of my country to help Turkey through her confrontation with the Western allies, our enemy. By keeping my own religion quiet I can get on with my job, which is to help your country defeat its enemies.

Besides which, Islam is a gentle religion. The men who killed your comrades did not do so in the name of *Allah*, they did so because they are evil. War casts many strange shadows, my friend, and its darkness cloaks us all. I grieve for your loss but, please, do not let the circumstances interfere with the truth of what happened. Politicians and their hatred of others cause wars, not the simple people who get caught up in such affairs. Your friends died because of men's twisted ideals, not through the simple act of devotion to a supreme being.

Rest easy, Artoun Seferian, my lips are sealed, as I hope yours are too. You can continue with your duties as my manservant and I'll continue to afford you what protection I can. When we're around others our relationship will be as an officer to his servant, you understand. I'll continue to call you Yilmaz but in private we can at least act as human beings. Agreed?'

Artoun reached over and shook the hand Brückner held out. 'I shall be your shadow, *efendim*, ask and I shall be there.'

'Good. Now do your duty. Clear off and let me sleep, it's too hot outside and I think a nap is in order. That's all, you can go. Come back later when I'm awake and we'll talk further. And stop calling me, *efendim*. A simple, plain *Sir* will do, or *Herr Leutnant* at a push. Alright?' He hunkered down on his blankets without waiting for an answer and closed his eyes.

Taking his actions as a dismissal, Artoun turned and left the dugout. Further down the trench two soldiers sat in an upright position who glanced up curiously at his passing but he gave no indication of having seen them.

'You. Stop there!'

He turned to see the angry, contorted face of the *chaoush* who had so grievously troubled him and Arif bearing down on him. 'Yes, sir, what is it?' he enquired innocently.

For an answer the man lifted his hand and slapped Artoun hard across the face, a stinging blow. 'Where've you been, I've been looking for you, you dog!'

His face smarting, Artoun made as if to answer but the NCO lifted his hand to strike him again. Something in Artoun's demeanour stayed the blow and he stepped back. 'Don't stare at me like that you insolent cur or I'll have you flogged until the flesh hangs down your back! Answer me, I asked, where've you been?'

'Doing my duty, *chaoush*, seeing to the German officer as I was asked to.'

'Who said this?'

'The *efendim*, he visited me while I was recovering and told me I was to be his servant.'

'We'll see about that,' the fat NCO blustered, 'I wasn't told and as far as I'm concerned you'll be placed where I can keep my eye on you, Yilmaz. I don't like you, you're not like the rest of these good, honest soldiers and if I can use up scum like you before putting my men in danger then I will. Do you understand me?'

'Perfectly, *chaoush* but if I were you I'd speak to the captain first, he might have a different idea.'

'Dog! You'd threaten me? We'll see who laughs loudest, your friend Bilgili thought he was too smart for me and look what it brought him. Ha! I'll sort you out like I did for him, you'll see.'

'As you wish.' Artoun replied calmly enough though a fierce temper coursed through him at the mention of Arif Bilgili. The *chaoush* stared at him for several long seconds before abruptly turning on his heels and making his way past the two recumbent soldiers, kicking one of them savagely as he passed.

--§--

The following day, after breaking his fast, Artoun made his way back to Brückner's dugout, where he found the German holding up a dark pair of long socks.

'Ah, Yilmaz, take these and see if you can get them clean for me, could you? They can just about stand by themselves and are starting to make my feet sore. I've asked for fresh supplies but no doubt it'll take months to get them. Do you think you'll be able to wash them one-handed?'

'I'll see if I can beg some hot water from the cook and wash them with soap.' He turned to leave then swung back impetuously. 'We have a *nefer* in my company, Kaplan is his name. He told my friend Arif Bilgili that our leaders had begun moving whole villages of the *ermeni* people away to the hills for resettlement and that it was common knowledge that many of these villagers were being slaughtered. Have you heard of this, is there any truth in what this man says? He says you were speaking to the captain about it.'

Brückner noted the anxiety in the man's tone and moved quickly to suppress it. 'You must know how rumours like this start, Yilmaz, a man hears something and tells his friend who passes it on to his friend, who then passes it on to another and so on. Very soon the whole story has become distorted and instead of— look, take my asking for new socks for example. By the time it reaches HQ, if it was passed down the supply chain by mouth, I reckon they'd have been informed that I'd lost my legs. You see what I mean? There's probably some innocent explanation for all this, it could be that in order to protect certain villagers it was necessary to relocate them. Am I making sense? Is my Turkish good enough to make that explanation to you?'

'I see what you're getting at but there must have been some truth in the story for Kaplan to pass it on.' Artoun answered slowly. 'Forgive me but how does a story of moving villagers for their protection turn into a tale of slaughtering them and robbing them of all their possessions? That's what Kaplan said is happening. Your Turkish is very good now. I understood perfectly what you meant to say.'

'Thank you, I've been listening to a lot of conversations in order to improve my command of your language. In answer to your questions, the captain did mention something in passing to me about relocations in Anatolia but I wasn't paying much attention to him, his choice of words was quite hard for me to follow the conversation properly. However, now that you ask I'll make discreet enquiries and see if I can learn if there is any truth to this man Kaplan's babbling. Where is it you're from? Do you have a family in the area that this man Kaplan described?'

'I think it best if I don't tell you that, sir. Let's just say that I'm from Anatolia and that's where most of the actions are apparently taking place. As to a family, my wife Hegine and son Khat await me when this war is over. Now do you see why I worry so?'

'You're a lucky man to have such fine people waiting for you. Back in Germany I have no family other than my parents and they grow older with each passing day. Try not to worry, I'll do my best to find what news there is. And now, my manservant, do you think you could go and clean those socks for me? Although the heat makes me take to the shadows during the day, my feet freeze overnight. We go back into the front line the day after tomorrow and I'd like a soft pair of socks to keep my feet warm so off you go.'

As Artoun made his way down the trench, Bruckner shouted. 'Stop!' Puzzled, Artoun made his way back to the Leutnant. 'I forgot to tell you, the captain had a word with me last night. Apparently one of his *chaoush's* complained that you'd attached yourself to me without being assigned by him. The captain was furious at one of his NCO's speaking to him in that manner, struck the man with his fist and knocked the poor chap over.

When the man arose the captain told him *he'd* authorised your transfer as my servant and who did the *chaoush* think he was. After shouting at him for some time he knocked the poor man down again so be careful, Yilmaz, I fear you've made an implacable enemy there. He won't forget the beating and why he received it.'

Artoun nodded and hurried down the trench, Brückner's words racing round his mind. Preoccupied as he was he failed to see the rifle butt poking out from a dugout entrance and he sprawled full length as he tripped over it. Winded, his wounded arm sending white-hot needles of pain coursing through his body, he looked up into the bruised, scowling face of the *chaoush*.

'Think yourself clever, eh, you bastard!' the man hissed through gritted teeth. 'Got yourself a protector, have you? The *Aleman* won't be with us for ever and when he goes, or catches a bullet, you and me will have some fun then.'

Artoun said nothing. He rose painfully, gathered up the Leutnant's socks and backed down the trench keeping his eyes firmly on the *chaoush* until he was able to turn a corner and make his way to the field kitchen and a grumbling cook.

--§--

The following day preparations were made for a return to the trenches. Brückner seemed happy at their imminent departure, whistling snatches of a gay tune through his teeth as he packed his knapsack. 'Do you know who that is, Yilmaz?' he asked, 'Wagner, that's who! A brilliant composer, German of course. An anti-Semite, too, by all accounts but I can forgive him even that when he writes such wonderful music as this. *Tra-la-la...*'

'You seem happy this morning Herr Leutnant, is there any particular reason?'

'But of course, we're going back into the front line. What better reason could there be for making a chap happy than the prospect of another fight? It certainly wasn't because of your washing my socks, they feel harder than when I took them off. What did you wash them in, mud?'

'I'm sorry,' Artoun articulated apologetically, 'the cook had thrown the hot water out and I couldn't find any soap so I had to wash them in cold...'

'Oh, do stop whining, Yilmaz. I couldn't care less how or what you washed the damned things in! We're going back to the front, leaving these reserve trenches shortly so clean socks are now the least of my worries!'

'Is that a reason for rejoicing?' Artoun asked hesitantly, 'All we do is throw ourselves at the enemies defences and die in large numbers, what is there about dying like that that can make a man feel so happy?'

Brückner stopped his whistling and looked sternly at Artoun. 'You must have more faith in our leaders. Our General Liman Von Sanders and your own Colonel Kemal worked wonders in stopping the enemy making any advances, they've not moved forward a single centimetre since we stopped them above Ari Burnu. Those strange Australian fellows have found out what it's like to be on the end of German shells and Turkish bullets and for the time being they're dug in and unable to move. Now that Esat Pasha has taken full command of the Northern sector, with our strong positions and artillery all we need do is wait for them to attack and they'll founder like waves breaking on the Aegean shore.'

'They fought well,' Artoun answered, 'we were unable to throw them back into the sea when they landed, I have heard, and since that day they have fought stubbornly. The night I was wounded they fought us to a standstill, we failed to pierce their lines and ended up losing many men.'

'Those days are past, Yilmaz, I can assure you. The British and Australians lack the artillery they need to make an attack succeed so we hold the upper hand. Our tactics are correct for the situation we find ourselves in, strengthen our defences and wait for them to come to us. Besides which, their generals are such incompetents. If they'd only pressed harder in the first days of the landings we would have been in severe trouble. The movement of troops by General Von Sanders, however, was a masterstroke, we pushed them back and they just sat there without knowing what to do next. Our losses have been heavy, that's true but along with their losses we are also sapping their will to continue.

They are far from home, fighting a war they don't seem to really believe in. On the other hand, you, my friend, are fighting for your homeland against the invader. See? It makes a man fight that much harder and I'm sure they've had a sharp shock by coming here and thinking they only had to make a rude noise and Istanbul would fall into their hands without a single shot being fired. Well, they've learned the folly of that approach, haven't they?

Anyway, enough of this chatter. Come, help me with my packing and we'll see what transpires next, eh? I have to speak with the captain shortly so sit here and guard my pack from your scavenging brethren until I return.'

'Did you find out any more of what Kaplan spoke of, sir?'

'No, and now is not the time to go poking my nose into matters such as those. When we arrive at the front I'll have a quiet word, I promise but for now let's concentrate on making sure I don't leave anything behind.'

'Just where is it we're going?'

'I heard the captain say something about the battalion joining with the 2nd Division, there's a good chance the enemy will try a breakthrough and we're going to help our brothers stop them. Now, for the last time, stop this chattering and come over here and help me with my pack. You'll have to do your duty and join the others in the trenches, as will I but I'll make sure you don't have to do any manual work. Can we get on, there's not much time left?'

--§--

By marching overnight the battalion moved into its new positions. In passing the unit they were relieving, little was said, no words exchanged. These men looked worn out, torn filthy uniforms with glazed, dead expressions in their eyes. They were Arabs from the Asian side, known for their penchant of shooting recklessly and randomly at any sound and Artoun was one of many in his own battalion thankful they'd not have them as near neighbours.

The smell reached them when they were still several hundred yards from the trenches, a dry, foul smell of death and decaying bodies mixed with the reek of excrement. Some of the new men who'd joined recently as reinforcements gagged but were mercilessly flogged by NCO's moving amongst them, hissing fiercely as they kept order with the knout.

Each soldier was issued with 100 rounds in clips and three days supplies before filing into the trenches. 'Keep your ammunition clean,' a grizzled NCO growled, 'I don't give a damn if your uniform's fall off your back and your boots wither and drop off your feet but woe betide any man who I see neglecting his *tufek* and ammunition. It's all that stands between you and Paradise and while that might sound promising, *Allah* be praised, your country requires you to send many of the enemy opposite to their Hell before you shuffle off your own mortal coil. Got it?' No-one answered, each man shouldered his rifle and took his place in the line silently without any banter or small talk.

Daylight found them huddled in the bottom of the trenches, yawning as the day broke with a pink-tinged dawn. A muffled *crack*! from the bay next to them caused Artoun and his companions to look up in concern but a *nefer* furthest away peered round the corner and spoke in an excited tone.

'It's that idiot, Mohamed! The enemy shot him. They're taking his body away now. The *chaoush* is not pleased Listen to him shouting at the others.' The thought of the dead man and his passing sobered all those crouching down and Artoun noticed with a wry smile that since the unfortunate Mohamed's premature demise everyone crouched that much lower.

The sun climbed steadily overhead, an orb that burned their eye sockets if they were foolish enough to look up. A smattering of rifle fire erupted and carried on until mid-morning but no-one near him joined in, everyone content to conserve both their energy and ammunition. A sweating *nefer* crawled down the trench, muttering profusely. As he made to pass, Artoun held out a restraining hand.

'Where are you going in such a hurry, my friend?'

'The captain, that son of a whore, has decided that he wants to know what the enemy is doing. I've been told to go to the edge of our trenches and see if I can spot any movement on their part.'

'How far away are the enemy?'

'I don't know, if I survive I'll let you know.'

He passed on down the trench, still muttering and was lost from sight. A few minutes later a single shot rang out and the soldiers glanced at each other in consternation. Ten minutes passed before a shuffling sound put them on their guard as the *chaoush's* reddened face peered round the corner.

'Yilmaz, come here!' he ordered and Artoun started at the sound of his name. Obediently he made his way along the trench floor doubled over in a crouch until he was level with the NCO's florid face.

'Where's your *tufek*?'

240

'I can't fire it because of my injury, my arm's not strong enough to support the weapon so the leutnant said to leave it behind for now.'

'You cur!' the *chaoush* spat. 'Take yourself to the end of this trench where you'll find a deep hole and I want you stay there and observe the enemy. Smartly now, don't take all day!'

'What happened to the last man?' Artoun asked.

'Don't question my orders, do as you're told!' the chaoush roared angrily, 'Just get yourself along there and let us know what you can see.'

'But I was told I wasn't to be…' Artoun protested but the *chaoush* held up a restraining hand. 'I don't care what you were told, your protector has gone to HQ for our orders and while the captain is resting *I* give the orders. You're no good to me manning the line without being able to fire your *tufek* so what better use for you than as an observer. Now, for the last time, get your arse off to where I ordered you or face the consequences. Take your time when you get there and count their numbers. Let us know how many of them you see and how close their forward saps are. Go!'

Reluctantly, Artoun squeezed past the *chaoush* and prepared to crouch down.

'Crawl!' the *chaoush* ordered.

'My arm… I'd be better off crouching.'

'Crawl!'

Artoun crawled, biting his lip as his injured arm grazed the trench wall. He inched awkwardly in this fashion until he was able to round a corner when he slowed and leant against the side of the trench until his failing strength returned. Once rested, he resumed his journey towards the observation post, fear mounting as he neared his objective. Three *nefers* urged him on and he joined them, panting with both exhaustion and trepidation.

'Are you the new observer?' one demanded roughly and in spite of his fear Artoun smiled. 'You could call me that, although the *chaoush* has a different name for me.' he grinned and the three privates snickered.

'What happened to the last one?' Artoun asked, dreading the answer.

'We told him to keep his head down but he didn't listen, insisted on taking a long look to observe the enemy's strength and an *infidel* drilled him, right through the forehead.'

'Where is he now and how far away are the enemy?' Artoun looked down at a large, damp patch of what he took to be blood on the floor matting. 'This is the second time I've been made to act as an observer, the Johnny's are not going to miss me this time by the look of it.'

The *nefers* snickered again. 'We dragged him down here and heaved him over the parapet like we were told to. I nearly got shot too!' one answered indignantly, 'As far as we could ascertain, the *infidels* are only sixty to seventy yards away. Hey, maybe you could let us know when you come back. *If* you come back at all, friend.' At this, the three men broke into raucous laughter.

Nettled, Artoun left them and made his way to the far end of the trench where it bulged out into a larger, roomier space. He guessed this was where he was to make his observations from but he knew the enemy would have this spot under observation themselves and any movement could be fatal so he squatted on his haunches and ruminated on his next move. His mind clear he moved forward and cautiously raised his *kabalak* on the fingers of one hand. *Bang!* a shot sounded and the headgear flew from his fingers and crashed into the far side, a neat hole where his forehead would have been.

By his reckoning the enemy would now wait for the next unfortunate to be sent to this spot and so would relax their guard for the next half hour. He squatted awkwardly against the side of the trench yards away from the observation post and began to dig frantically yet carefully with the tip of his bayonet. In a few minutes he'd made a small slit beneath the parapet large enough for his eyes to see through which he shored up with a shell fragment.

Satisfied with his efforts, he slowly eased one eye over the hole and held his breath. No shots sounded and he slid sideways until both eyes filled the aperture and he could look down on the panorama before him. He drew breath sharply as he recognised the sprawled mounds of bodies littering the ground between the two lines.

No-mans-land was filled with the results of earlier failed attempts to break the deadlock that had existed since the landings and he now understood where the awful stench of putrefaction originated from. Bodies from both sides, blackened and burnt by the sun lay pointing in all directions, some swollen so grotesquely that their uniforms had ripped asunder, exposing yet more flesh to be broiled by a pitiless sun.

The corpses were covered in a heaving black mass of flies and a pungent odour filled the air, blown hither and thither by the breeze. Intermingled with the sweetness of the myrtle it formed a stench which defeated all attempts to overcome it and Artoun took a deep breath using the sleeve of his tunic as a mask before staring further into the void between the two antagonists.

The Australian trenches, he guessed, were seventy yards away and judging by the movement along them, were heavily manned. Cooking fires along their length only served to remind him of his gnawing hunger but he counted those he could see and committed them to memory. The information could prove useful if he made it back alive. Behind the front line trench were several more, communication and reserve trenches and again by the sheer amount of movements along them he concluded that they too were also heavily manned.

He stayed in that cramped position for another hour, hardly daring to move as he observed and mentally recorded all that he saw. Satisfied, he retrieved his headgear and retraced his steps back to where the three soldiers waited.

'What! You're back! Did you bother to take a look as we heard no shots bar one and thought you'd had it. The *chaoush* has already been informed.'

'Then he'll he delighted to see me return, back from the dead!' Artoun observed dryly, 'You never know, he might want to come down here and observe the miracle at first hand for himself.'

'Now I know you're not right in the head!' the soldier snorted. 'That fat pig might share the trenches with us but he's never to be found anywhere there might be danger.'

Leaving them to their grousing Artoun made his way to the dugout that comprised the company HQ. As he neared the entrance he recognised the figure of Captain Çelik in deep conversation with Leutnant Brückner.

'Look here, all I'm saying is my understanding of the matter is that your man volunteered to go forward and observe the enemy at close quarters himself. I'm sorry to hear of his death but you know we need that information, Brückner, even you...' He broke off and followed Brückner's quizzical gaze over his shoulder, his eyes alighting on Artoun as he approached them.

'Well, there you are, here is the soldier himself, come back to us. A miracle!' His face assumed a grim expression. 'If I find that damned *chaoush* has overstepped the mark I swear I'll...'

'Sir. *Nefer* Yilmaz begs to report his findings of the enemy forces. I observed them for a long time and can point out on the map, if you show me, where and how they've disposed of their troops.' Artoun spoke forcefully.

The captain stepped close and frowned. 'Good man, you've done well but tell me something, Yilmaz. The *chaoush* told me personally that you'd volunteered, even though you knew it meant almost certain death to go. Is that true, did you volunteer?'

Artoun looked squarely at the captain and spoke with as much emphasis as he could. 'Yes sir, that's quite true, I volunteered. Someone had to do it and I was honoured to make the journey down there and observe as best I could.'

The captain punched Artoun's arm lightly with a smile. 'We'll make a soldier out of you yet, Yilmaz. Good man, accompany me and the leutnant here into my dugout and you can show me what you saw. HQ will be delighted at your news, Esat Pasha is convinced the *infidels* are cooking up something big and if we can show him what we've gleaned today it could have a great influence on the outcome of our preparations.

Come, the two of you, let's partake of coffee and some fine sweetmeats my wife sent me, this has all the makings of a good day.'

Ignoring the look of surprise on Brückner's face, Artoun bowed his head and followed the captain into the dugout. That night he dreamed of his wife and son again, seeing the faces of them with clarity as he contemplated his situation. Poor Hegine, she and Khat would be lonely without him, wondering when they would see him next. A fierce determination welled up inside, it was over for poor Arif but *he*, Artoun Seferian, would see his family again even if it meant moving heaven and earth to get there. So be it, someday in the near future they would all be together. With those thoughts uppermost, he slept.

--§--

As a result of Artoun's observations, the trenches were heavily fortified. Each night, a company of Turkish engineers swarmed around the defences, laying heavy wooden logs across the parapets under the cover of darkness. These fitted snugly together and made it impossible for attackers to jump down into a trench, pushing them towards the heavily-fortified entrances. More loopholes were made in the parapets, allowing a clear field of fire across the broken spaces of no-mans-land and a stock of ammunition and peculiar black, egg-shaped Turkish hand grenades was positioned at all the key points of the defences.

Maxim machine-guns were strategically placed and boxes of canvas-belted ammunition laid ready nearby, the gunners fussing over their charges as one would over a small child, cleaning and oiling the mechanisms daily. Captain Çelik was everywhere, shouting and bawling his disapproval as he berated one man and praised another, pushing and pulling until finally the defences met with his complete satisfaction.

'Let the *infidels* dare to attack us now, men,' he declared, puffing on an aromatic cheroot, 'we'll hurl them back to their own positions and then roll them back into the sea!'

Chapter Twelve.

Alexandria, June.

He looked up as the door opened and a small group of white-coated medical officers exited the ward, talking noisily. A petite, dark-haired nurse detached herself from the group and walked over to where he sat, smiling warmly at his quizzical expression.

'Serjeant Harding? I thought it might be you. You can go in now, the doctors have finished their rounds and I can let you have a few moments with your brother.'

'Thank you. How is he, has there been any….?'

She stopped him with a wave of her hand and another smile. 'Don't worry, he's a lot better, The fever's left him after this latest setback and although he's still very weak the doctor's a lot happier now than this time last week.' Her smile faded and her eyes clouded. 'He's one of the lucky ones. Many of the poor lads we take in are too weak by the time they reach us.'

She shook herself. 'There I go, getting gloomy again. Please, do go in but don't stay too long.' Ignoring his stammered thanks she walked slowly along the corridor as Tom opened the door and entered the ward.

The acrid stench of diarrhoea hit him like a blow to the face and he recoiled from its assault to the back of his throat. Coughing, he brought a defensive hand up to his mouth and looked round to see if he could see where they'd moved Walt. A pale, wan face halfway down the ward drew his attention and he slowly moved along the double row of beds in that direction. Amongst the low murmuring he recognised the sounds of unconscious men muttering sibilantly in their fevered tossing and turnings and he thanked God with a guilty heart that his brother wasn't laying there amongst them.

Walt Harding opened his eyes as Tom reached him and gestured weakly with a limp hand. 'This is becoming too much of a habit, don't you think, me having a quiet kip and waking up to find you rifling through my gear!'

Tom snorted. 'You cheeky bugger! Is this the thanks I get for coming here for the past weeks looking down on your ugly mug and hoping for at least a half-decent conversation?' Tom continued, more gently, 'You've been in a right state but I'm glad to see that you're beginning to look a darn sight better now. Beats the time just after we arrived, you were out of it for a whole week chum. Lying there, pretending there was

246

something wrong with you!' He laughed but Walt noticed the concern in his brother's eyes and his gaze softened.

'Sorry Tom. I'm nowt but trouble to you, aren't I?'

'I could agree with you there, as a brother you do know how to get on my wrong side. Are they treating you well?'

'They're angels, I've never been so well looked after in my life. I…Oh, did I tell you Bridgette comes in to see me from time to time?'

Tom looked up in surprise. 'No, you didn't mention it. Do you mean Bridgette Mathers, the nurse from the ship?'

Walt snorted. 'Don't come the innocent with me, Tom Harding. Is there another Bridgette you know of

'Sorry, Walt,' Tom mused, 'I didn't mean it the way it came out, it's just that…Bridgette? I've not seen or heard of her since ending up here. I did ask but you know what they're like, these medical bods, no-one would tell me anything. I took it she'd been moved to another hospital. When did she start visiting you?'

'No, no. She's here. Really. I think she was ill but when she recovered they put her in a different part of the hospital, the amputees, she said, and she sneaks away now and again to look in.'

'Well, there you go, all this time I'd thought she was gone and she's been here all along. What do you two talk about?'

Walt started guiltily but recovered quickly. 'You're not jealous are you, Tom?'

'In your eye!'

Both laughed but the exertion caused Walt to double over in a paroxysm of coughing and Tom moved swiftly to his brother's side. Walt fended him off and the bout passed.

'You couldn't get me a drink of water could you, I'm parched.' he hissed through clenched teeth.

'Stay there, I'll be right back.'

Tom left the bedside and hurried to the door, colliding with a soft body as he passed through the doorway. 'Oof! Sorry, I was tryi—Bridgette?' Tom Harding stepped back at stared at Bridgette Mather's reddening face as the two contemplated each other. She was wearing the same perfume from their first encounter and he inhaled deeply at the fragrance of her proximity.

'Tom. Serjeant Harding.' She recovered her composure and looked steadily back at him, a grave expression on her face. Standing close he continued to stare, tongue-tied, half-enunciated words and sentences whirling round his head. Finally he stuttered.

'What—how did you..? Look, it's marvellous to see you. Walt told me you were here. I never knew, I did ask but no-one would or could tell me anything. How are you? What about the others, that young girl, what was her name…. Martha Weatherall, was she picked up too?'

Bridgette Mather's eyes filled with tears. 'Martha died, she went back into the ward to see if she could help her patients and was never seen again. And…and Fred Wooller too. We lost over four hundred people that night and among those lost were twelve of our nurses. It was only a miracle that I survived, apparently I was rescued by….' She tailed off, unable to frame the words.

'I'm sorry to hear about Martha and poor Fred.' Tom said contritely, 'He was a fine man and she was a lovely girl, it's a shame she lost her life trying to help others.'

Her mood changed instantly as she recalled the brief conversation she'd had with Matron Green before the Matron had left for Cairo. After asking how she was feeling, Matron Green had congratulated Bridgette on her lucky escape on the night of the *Fyvie Castle's* sinking. The disappointment she'd felt when the older woman had praised *young Harding* for being her saviour came to the fore as she regarded Tom. It would have meant so much if Tom had been her saviour instead of his younger brother and the deep disappointment she felt welled up and changed to a feeling of ire.

'Yes, you'd know all about that, Serjeant Harding!' she exclaimed scornfully, wiping her eyes.

'What do you mean by that?' Her change of mood took him by surprise and he unable to keep a sharp edge from his voice as the question escaped his lips.

She spoke harshly, an icy expression on her features. 'I've been here since we were landed from the navy destroyer. Some rest and I was able to continue my duties. Not that you'd be bothered. You'll excuse me.' She made to push past but he put a hand on her wrist and restrained her.

'Bridgette, stop! What is this silliness?' he growled, the euphoria of seeing her evaporating at her words, 'We've just met again and this is how you greet me? Have I offended you in some way or do you still harbour a grudge still over that stupid remark I made back on the ship? I apologised, had you forgotten that but at least we're alive, people we both thought a lot of lost their lives that night. Is that a reason to act so uncharitably?'

She looked pointedly down at his hand and he let it drop. '*Silliness*, after what happened that night, you have a nerve to accuse *me* of silliness,

248

Tom Harding? Now, if you'll let me pass I have work to do. In there.'
She gestured at the ward door and he stepped to the side to allow her to
pass.

'My brother's in there. Walt. You remember him, do you? *He* might
look on you as a friend but it's obvious I've sunk pretty low in your
estimation.' A fierce anger grew inside Tom and she winced at his words
before her own temper rose to match his.

'Walt, oh yes, Serjeant Harding. I've got good reason to remember him,
at least *one* Harding conducted himself like a man that night.'

He recoiled from her accusation, trying to fathom a reason for her
obvious displeasure whilst a flame flared white-hot within. He stepped
closer. 'A man?' he hissed, voice taut with suppressed anger. 'Just what
does that mean, *a man?* Who are we talking about here? Me? What was it
I didn't do, Miss Mathers, that makes you look at me as if I were some
kind of monster?'

She made as if to answer but he savagely cut her short with a chopping
gesture of his hand. 'Don't answer! For some reason your mind's made
up with whatever nonsense it is you're harbouring in that head of yours
and not even the truth is going to make any sort of difference. My
brother lies on the other side of the door, *Sister* Mathers, seriously ill
from the dysentery that brought him here. I'd be obliged if you could act
like the nurse you make yourself out to be and bring him some water.
Good day.'

He walked away, stiff-backed.

'Tom! Come back, please, I'm sorry.'

If he heard her he gave no sign and continued to walk down the
corridor, rounding the corner and passing out of sight. Feeling decidedly
miserable she pushed the door open and entered the ward. What was it
about him that made her so defensive; made a man like Tom Harding
the recipient of the savage temper she knew lurked within her inner self?
She hardly knew the man yet he evoked deep emotions, bringing to the
surface dark days that she'd rather lay hidden.

Yet what troubled her *had* happened, there was no excusing her feelings
or the way he looked at her that could change the facts. Matron Green
had told her the simple truth of what had happened the night of the
sinking and no matter how she felt she couldn't change it. The
disappointment she'd felt on hearing that it was Walt who'd saved her
and not Tom had clouded her judgement, making her think less of him
no matter how hard she'd tried to think otherwise. Summonsing a smile

on her troubled face she walked among the beds looking for Walt Harding.

A faint smile touched his lips as she stopped opposite him. 'Hello, Sister Mathers... Bridgette.'

His innocence brought the smile back to her face. 'Hello, Walter, how are you feeling now?'

'I'm a lot better, the medicine they're giving me is helping greatly. I don't seem to be as hot and bothered as I was when I first got here. Did you see Tom just now? He said I've been in a fever for over a week but I can't remember a darn thing.'

'Yes,' she said flatly, 'Tom and I met, briefly. He said you needed a drink so I'll just go and—what? What is it?'

He clutched his stomach and looked embarrassed. 'Oh God, quick, could you bring me a....'

She ran from his side, throwing open the locker halfway down the ward, extracted a metal bedpan and rushed back to where he lay helpless. A loud, flatulent noise sounded as she guided his fumbling hands and he was able to push it under the bedclothes. 'Please, sister, could you at least leave me until it's past?' he hissed, 'You shouldn't have to wait there and watch, well, you know.'

'Walter Harding!' she scolded him, 'I'm a nurse, and used to this sort of thing. Let me know when you're finished and I'll dispose of the contents.' Whilst he lay there, hunched over in pain as spasms racked him, she glanced with a professional eye at the clipboard fastened to the end of the bed. He'd been prescribed emitine hydrochloride injections in order to treat his dysentery and it seemed they'd been successful in alleviating some of his symptoms. But not all of them.

An explosion of sound interrupted her inspection of the board and she averted her eyes in order to spare him further embarrassment. Eventually the sounds ceased and she moved to take the bedpan from his trembling arms. The watery contents caused her to draw breath in an audible hiss and he turned from her, muttering quietly.

'Sorry.'

'Sorry? Don't you ever say that word to me again, do you hear?'

He turned to face her, features creased in puzzlement. 'Why, what did I ever do that makes you feel that way?'

'Don't you remember, Walt, can you remember anything of what happened that night?'

'I'm sorry, do I remember...?'

250

She smiled, a quiet smile that lit up her face and his heart leapt. 'Walt, you saved my life that night on the ship, had it not been for you I'd have died along with all the others who were lost.'

'Did I?' Walt spoke slowly, his face twisted as he tried to recall the events of the sinking, 'it's all a bit hazy–in my mind I seem to recall Tom pushing me over the side and feeling the coldness of the water and the next thing I knew I was in an ambulance on my way here. Bridgette, are you sure it was me who saved you, is it possible there's been some kind of mistake?'

She looked squarely at him, lips set in a stubborn manner. 'There's no mistake, Matron Green spoke to me soon after I arrived here and told me the whole, wonderful story. She said I'd been kept afloat all night by the Harding boy and that if it hadn't been for your heroism I'd have drowned on that awful night. So you see, Walter Harding, I have you to thank for my life and it's something I shall be grateful to you for the rest of my life. But for you, my ....' She stopped and he waited for her to continue but she switched her gaze to the end of the ward and continued in a different vein.

'We'll talk about this some other time but for now you need rest so lie back here whilst I take this away.' She draped a cloth over the bedpan and moved to leave him.

'Wait! Stop. Bridgette, when you see Tom next, could you ask him to bring me a razor, I'd like to shave and feel human again. Please.'

'I'll bring you a razor myself, there's no need to bother your brother.' With those curt words she marched down the ward and swept through the door, leaving him staring after her in amazement. What had he said to have made her respond in that way, had her and Tom come to some sort of disagreement? Too late he remembered he'd forgotten to ask for a drink and looked round desperately. 'Nurse!'

Alexandria, June.

'Well, serjeant, you appear to be recovering nicely, the arm injury has healed quite well. Stretch it this way for me, can you? Good. Now the other way. Better. How's your head, any more pain, any funny turns?' The elderly medical officer straightened up from his examination of Tom's arm and began to wrap a light bandage around the wound site.

'No sir, I get the odd twinge but it feels better each day. As for the head, I still get an odd bout but it's been a few days since the last.'

'Good, good. We'll leave it another week I fancy and then start some exercises, try to build up those wasted muscles on the arm. Don't be in a hurry to get back, you won't thank me for sending you. How long is it since you were repatriated from Helles?'

Tom thought hard. Time had passed so easily since landing in Alexandria that it was easy to forget just how long he had been there. 'I was taken on the ship at Anzac. It must be over four weeks, sir, a bit strange with nothing to do but lie around all day yet I didn't realise just how long I'd been here until you asked. How are things over there, we hear the odd bit of news but it doesn't sound as if things are going too well.'

The MO's face darkened. 'It's a bloody disaster. We're quite overwhelmed by the scale of the casualties as no-one envisaged the sheer numbers of you poor chaps appearing at the docks. We farmed a lot out, opened new hospitals all over the bally place, even sent some to Cairo and as far away as Malta but still the ships keep arriving with hundreds more poor souls, all crying out for decent treatment. Those blithering idiots back in Blighty need shooting for the balls-up they've created out here.'

He glanced at Tom, a guarded expression on his face. 'You were at ANZAC Cove?' When Tom nodded, he continued. 'It's being kept a secret but we lost one of our warships off ANZAC a few days after you were evacuated, the *Triumph*. Seems she was torpedoed by a German submarine, could even have been the one that sank your ship, serjeant. The one thing they said would never come to pass happened.

She was conducting firing exercises at the Turkish trenches when she was hit and rolled over in full view of the men ashore.' He snorted. 'His Lordships are grateful that only seventy-odd men were lost, a trifling sum given the number dying ashore. Hah! Tell that to their widows!'

He stared overhead at the ceiling before continuing. 'This bloody war! What an adventure it must have seemed at first but we're beginning to count the true cost now. And it isn't just the rankers who are bearing the brunt, there's many a senior officer turning in his grave after stepping ashore and paying the price. Majors, Colonels, even a bloody general.'

'A general?' Tom asked, disbelieving. You're kidding, sir.'

'Aye, laddie, a general I said, and one of yours too!'

'Ours? Who?'

'Bridges. Major-General Bridges, a sniper got him, shot him in the thigh I believe and he bled to death. It seems even the higher-ups are not impervious to a copper-jacketed Mauser bullet. Nothing they could do for him, apparently, poor devil.'

His voice had risen but realising this he dropped an octave and continued. 'Meanwhile we go on suffering, a lack of everything you know, medical supplies, drugs, bandages, nurses and doctors. Need I go on? The only thing we're not short of is bodies, the wounded, the dying and the dead. They're in abundance, the vast majority hopeless cases before they even arrive. Some just don't stand a chance, we operate round the clock and they still die like flies.' He passed a weary hand over his face. 'Anyway, got to go now, back on duty this afternoon. You look after yourself and I'll see you again soon.'

That afternoon Tom sat on a seat in a shaded hospital verandah and gazed out at the canvas tents adorning what had been the front gardens. The doctor had been quite correct in his assessment, the wounded lay everywhere, crammed into overcrowded wards and overflowing into every available free space. Harassed medical staff did their best but many of the shattered bodies arriving at Alexandria's docks were destined only to fill a space in the rapidly-growing military cemeteries.

His hand searched and found his pocket empty. Strangely enough, he'd not missed it for months but now he felt an overwhelming urge to fill a pipe and draw a deep breath of fragrant smoke into his lungs. Quelling the thought he leant back in his wicker chair as an image of Bridgette Mathers, unbidden, danced before him. He'd seen her several times since the fateful day in the ward alongside Walt but she'd made no sign of noticing him and in his temper he'd ignored her also.

Walt was improving daily, although the food was pretty basic, the daily injections and the rest had done him a power of good. He'd talked enthusiastically of rejoining his battalion back at the front but Tom had urged him to make the most of the rest and he'd listened to reason. In his heart Tom dreaded losing him back to the hell that awaited them all and as the time drew closer became more morose with each passing day.

That anger surfaced whenever he thought of Bridgette Mathers and her treatment of him, at a loss to understand what on earth had got into her that day. She'd greeted him as if he were a leper, some form of pariah, and judging by her cool manner had no inkling of knowing it was he who'd saved her life. He shook his head in exasperation, it was no good, one day he'd meet with her again, couch his questions in a better manner and see if he could make sense of her hostility.

High from across the bay the reedy voice of a muzzerein sounded from the tower of a mosque, calling the faithful to prayer in the age-old manner, and he listened intently as the incantations carried over the still air. There was something quite reassuring in this simple act of faith and he relaxed as he continued to sit and listen. In a land not too far away, the horrors of the war he'd left continued to claim fresh victims daily but here in the balmy, late afternoon he felt a sense of peace overtake him and he gratefully drank in the feeling.

'Penny for them, chum?'

He'd assumed the verandah was empty but he turned to see a huddled shape in a wheelchair pushed up against the far corner. 'Look at them!' the figure spoke bitterly, 'Making all that noise. If I'd got my rifle I'd shoot the bastard's off'n their perches, disturbing a man's peace with all that guff.'

'I think you'll find that's their priest calling them to prayer.' Tom replied mildly.

'Prayer? I'll give them bloody prayer!'

'Look, what it is you have against Mohammedans?'

'I'll tell you what I have against the bastards, mate. It's because of them I'm bloody well here and if I hadn't come all this way I wouldn't have lost me fucking leg, now would I?'

'Oh, come on,' Tom protested, 'these simple people are our allies in this war, you can't hate them for your troubles, surely? They didn't start the war, they're caught up in it just like you and me.'

'Well, bugger me! Pardon me for daring to give you my opinion! What are you, a *scab-picker* or just another loafer who's never seen a trench in his bloody life? Let me tell you, I....'

'No, let me tell you.' Tom rose and walked over to the huddled figure, his hand outstretched. 'Tom Harding, Serjeant, 9th Australians. Wounded at Anzac.'

There was a long, profound silence before a grudging hand was raised in response. 'Archie Robertson, corporal, and don't I feel an idiot!'

Tom laughed. 'We're all entitled to our opinion, Archie Robertson, even one a trifle extreme as yours. Hang on a mo'.' He retraced his steps and dragged the wicker chair over, placing it down next to his new companion. 'Now, where were we?'

'We were discussing what a blithering, big-mouthed idiot I am,' the man exclaimed wryly, 'sorry for calling you those names, I should have known. Now I can see you properly you've got the look of a fighting cove about you.'

Tom settled into his chair. 'I'm sure the medical orderlies are well used to being called scab-pickers, Archie but the loafing bit I *could* take offence to!'

'Alright, alright, don't rub it in, I said I was sorry, didn't I?'

'Apology accepted. What brings you here, then, did you say you've got a gammy leg?'

'Not gammy, missing.'

A silence stretched out between them.

'A bit careless, did you lose it here in Alexandria?'

'Naw, what do you think? Some bloody wog cut it off cos I left his brothel without paying? Fat chance there. Our platoon serjeant was a right bible-thumper, watched us like a hawk, one look of a hard-on about a fellow and you scrubbed the fucking latrines for a week!'

'So what did happen?' Tom asked softly.

'Which mob did you say you were with, Tom—is that your name?'

'Yes, Tom's fine. I'm with the 9th Australians, we went ashore in a place called Ari Burnu, on the first day. Bloody awful. You?'

'1st Lancashire Fusiliers. Same. We went in at a place some staff berk had called 'W' Beach. It was a massacre, we were shot down like dogs before we'd even landed. The navy took us in close and then made us row the rest of the way. The bloody Turks were waiting for us and started machine-gunning us while we were still packed like sardines in the fucking boats. I got hit in the leg, fell overboard and that was the end of my war.

Our company commander, Captain Willis, was a bloody hero. He was everywhere, shouting at the men and cheering them on. It was just a slaughter, bodies and blood everywhere. How he wasn't killed I'll never know. Anyway, I nearly drowned but I managed to paddle to the shore in a sea of blood and hang onto some barbed wire until our chaps finally cleared the beach and they started to collect the wounded. My hands were cut to shreds but there was no way I was letting go.'

At the mention of the name Willis, Tom's expression darkened as he thought back to a morning in the past and the sight of Billy Willis dropping to his knees, blood pouring from his side. If he'd noticed Tom's sudden discomfort, Archie Robertson ignored it and blithely carried on.

'Most of my mates copped it so I suppose I'm lucky, I just lost me leg. It took days to evacuate us so by the time I got here on the ship it smelled bloody awful and they cut it off. The stump's healing pretty good, they tell me, and I'll be able to be sent back to Blighty in a month or so at this rate.

Mind you, that's my career as a fucking trapeze artist gone to blazes!' he concluded gloomily.

'You were a trapeze artist?' Tom asked incredulously.

'No, course not! What do you take me for, I just said that to make you feel sorry for me, get you back for taking the piss outta me earlier!'

'You cheeky sod!'

They ruminated in silence.

'This place was a school you know, before us lot came and made a right royal mess of it.'

'You don't say. No wonder the bogs are so small, made for bloody kids not great big lunking soldiers, were they?'

'I mean it, Archie. It could've been worse, look at what we had on the beaches. Nothing!'

'Yeah, I know. Fancy a fag?'

'No thanks. I smoked a pipe once. I've given up.'

'Lucky you. So how did you get here then?'

Tom sighed. Patiently he explained the sinking of *Fyvie Castle* to an open-mouthed Archie. '…and then we were picked up and brought here. Me and my brother, his saving was more a miracle than mine, poor lad. He's got a dose of dysentery, which reminds me, I must get myself off and see if I can't grab a couple of minutes with him before they close the ward for the night. Which one are you in, Archie?'

'Ward Nine, mate, same floor as this. You?'

'Ward Five, next floor down. Right, time I was off. I'll see you around.'

'Oi, Tom, you said you was an Australian. Not sounding like that you isn't, what part of Australia are you from, then?'

'Wigan. 'night, Archie.'

--§--

The following morning, after breakfast and the morning rounds had been completed, Tom strolled down the corridor and up the stairs to the verandah he'd vacated the previous evening. The early morning coolness was dissipating fast and the day promised to turn into a warm, humid experience. He sat in the wicker chair and contemplated his fingernails. The verandah door banged noisily but he continued to stare into space.

256

'What! You again? Can't a man find some bloody peace anywhere? This is *my* verandah, I'll have you know! I'll tell the orderly to make you scarper next time he drags me here.'

He turned, grinning, to look into the smiling face of Archie Robertson. 'And a good morning to you, too, Archie. Did we sleep well? Hows the leg today?'

'No I bloody well didn't! Me leg's killing me but who listens, eh? I shouted at the orderly who pushed me here for banging the 'ell outta my leg but the bugger just ignored me.'

'Let's get you in here then.' Tom said, rising and moving over to the wheelchair.

'Oi, careful!'

He sighed. 'I'm trying, Archie. What brings you back to this spot so early?'

'I could ask you the same question but you don't have the sister from Hell looking after your ward, do you?'

'It's not Sister Mathers, is it?' asked Tom, his heart quickening.

'No, she's a cracker, I wouldn't mind a few rounds sparring with her. Naw, I'm talking about Sister McQueen. Now that is some bitch, she makes Hawkins, the platoon serjeant I was telling you about last night seem almost saintly.'

'Why, what's the matter with her?'

'Everything, the fucking cow!' Archie burst out heatedly, 'Reported me for smoking in bed, didn't she! One sodding fag and you'd think I was trying to start another Great Fire of London!' He looked out over the verandah. 'Not much of a view is there? All I can bloody see is tents, where's the gardens?'

'Archie,' Tom replied gently, 'I think they *are* the gardens that you're looking at, the tents were needed for more wounded coming in.'

'Bloody marvellous, cooped up in here and now there's nothing to look at.' Archie huffed gloomily.

'Hang on, I've an idea. Right, let's get you turned about!' Tom grabbed the handles on the wheelchair and deftly spun it and its agitated occupant round to face the opposite direction.

'Stop it, you berk! All I can see now is bloody walls, at least I had some view before you stuck your oar in!'

'Oh, shut your moaning, Archie we're not stopping here. Off we go.'

He pushed open the door, leaning forward with his free hand and proceeded at a fast pace down the gleaming, polished floor of the corridor. Ignoring the outraged protests of several white-starched nurses

he sped on until he came to a doorway in the centre of the corridor.
'Righto, here we are then, time for a spot of mountain climbing.'
'Eh?'

For an answer, Tom leant down and pulled at Archie's hospital
uniform jacket with his good hand. 'Give us a hand, Archie. Hold on
tight and up we come.'

'Whoa! What the hell are you doing?'

'Taking you for a ride! Put your arms around my neck but don't
strangle me or we will need a doctor' Hoisting Archie's limp body over
his shoulders one-handed he pushed open the door to be confronted by
a stairwell. 'Up we go.'

'Up? What the bloody hell's going on?'

'You said you wanted to have a better view so I thought I'd take you to
see one?'

'What?'

'The roof, you clot. We're going to have a seat on the roof, there's a flat
bit up there that makes a nice viewing platform.' He held tight to
Archie's trouser bottoms and hitched his injured arm higher up by
Archie's groin, trying to avoid the empty flapping leg which held his
stump.

'Oi, watch where you're putting your hand, mate, I've heard all about
you Australians!'

'Shut up and hold on!'

Archie remained silent as Tom climbed the stairs leading to the roof,
sweat pouring from him with the weight of his burden. His injured
shoulder began to nag him, sharp needles of pain reminding him why he
was a patient but he bore the pain stoically with clenched teeth and
struggled up the stairs.

At last he made it to a small door and swinging Archie round, fumbled
with the door catch. It defeated him for several seconds but finally gave
way and they stumbled out into bright sunshine. Breathing hard, he
squinted downwards as his eyes became accustomed to the glare.

'What do you think, Archie?'

'Humph! All I can see from here is your bloody arse, put me down you
berk! And it's too bloody hot!'

'Oh, right, sorry!' He leaned forward and gently laid Archie on the
floor. 'Give me a mo', I need to get my breath back. God, you don't half
weigh a ton. And stop moaning, will you?'

'I'm not moaning! It's all that wholesome army grub, packs weight on a man.' Archie answered with a look of false modesty, 'Although looking at my manly form you'd never know that.'

'Now just stay there and don't wander off, I'll be right back.'

'Comedian!' Archie growled.

Tom returned in two minutes, triumphantly clutching two wicker chairs. '*Ta-ra*! Your seat for the show sir, would you like to sit in any particular row?'

'Just help me up and cut the funnies!'

'Typical, no bloody gratitude!' He grabbed Archie's jacket and between them settled him into one of the chairs, placing them in the welcoming shade of the doorway. Tom swivelled his around and joined Archie. From where they sat, high above the hospital they could see over the city to the bustling harbour beyond. Feluccas under sail threaded their way in between larger, more modern craft, creating a multi-coloured canvas of the ancient and the new worlds. Grey battleships swung lazily on their anchors under a bright blue sky out in the shallow bay and over in the commercial harbour the wharves appeared tightly packed with drab transports and supply ships.

If he swung round he could make out the dark shape of greenery stretching away to his right. The Nile wasn't far away, the vast delta it had formed in splitting so near to the sea covered hundreds of square miles and reached nearly all the way to Cairo, a hundred and thirty miles upriver. An offshore breeze brought a tang of citrus to Tom's tongue and nostrils and he imagined it came from the orange and lemon groves that constituted the greenery he could see from his lofty perch.

'Go on, admit it, tell me you're impressed.'

'*Humph*! I said it's too hot!'

'See, I knew you would be. Did you know that over there was one of the Wonders of the World? The Egyptians built a lighthouse here, the Pharos of Alexandria in 280BC, I believe. It was three hundred feet high and…"

'You know what it reminds me of?'

'No, tell me.'

'Karachi.'

'Karachi?'

'Yes, Karachi, Sindh Province, India, one and the same. Are you bloody well deaf? That's where we were before we came here, I was having a lovely time in the sun 'til the Bosches started their tricks and before we knew it we was on a troopship beetling back to Blighty. Nuneaton to be

259

precise. What a dump, I wasn't half glad to be back on a ship headed for Egypt although they didn't tell us bugger all 'til we arrived in Alexandria docks. A waste of a journey, we could have just hopped off on the way to Blighty instead of sailing there to get bleeding cold and then coming back here. Typical army, haven't a clue how to manage a war.'

He pondered a moment. 'How's your brother doing?'

'He's fine, I popped in on him last night but he was sleeping. The nurse on duty said he's doing fine, still on liquids but they hope he'll be able to eat solid food shortly.'

'What, liquid bully?'

They both laughed at Archie's description of the state that the bully beef reached them on the peninsula, a foul-smelling, liquid full of rancid fatty deposits. To starving men it was all they received and so was forced down with many imprecations at the high command that had deemed it fit enough for the troop's consumption. A deadly side-effect from consuming it was an enormous thirst that rendered fatigued men prostrate with dry, dust-caked mouths, swollen tongues and agonised fantasies of cool running water.

'Just let Frey Bentos ask me to endorse their bloody meat, I'll give them hell, see if I don't! Anyway, you said the other night you was from Wigan Tom, is that the truth?'

'Nah, me and Walt, my brother, we're from Bury.'

'You lied to me! Doesn't matter, we're near neighbours I'll have you know. I'm from Radcliffe meself. What made you join the Australians, then?'

'No big mystery. Me and Walt were orphans, our mam and dad died in a house fire but we were saved and our aunt, Elsie, took us in and brought us up. Did a good job too but I didn't fancy staying down the mines all my life so when I could I took off to Australia to make my way in the world.'

'What's it like, this Australia, is it all it's cracked up to be?'

Tom thought for a while. 'I'd say—Look, if you're decent and honest and want to work, there's work there but if you want the easy life and to live off the efforts of others you'll have a hard time of it. It was just beginning to work out for me when the war came so I figured I might as well see the war with the country that gave me a fresh start rather than travel all the way back to Blighty and end up doing the exact same thing. It's funny, I think of myself as Australian now. I still speak like a Brit but my hearts with …'

'And your brother, what of him?'

'Will you stop interrupting me! Walt, he joined up because I couldn't send for him on the money I was earning at the time but now it's different. I'm hoping that after the war we can both make a living together, as brothers, and make a go of something between us.'

'How about me, do you think they'll take a cripple hopping along on one leg? I joined the regulars because I didn't want to end up down the pit like my dad but look where it got me, buggered hands and a leg that's buried not too far from here, I'll wager.'

'Course they would, Archie, you could always take up as a one-legged trapeze artist, very popular in Sydney, I'm told.'

'Oi, cut out the funnies. I told you, you're a lousy comedian.'

They sat in silence, each taking in the view and interpreting it in his own way, content in each other's company and the lack of the need for conversation. Eventually, Tom stirred. 'Much as I'd like to sit here for the rest of the day it's starting to get a tad too hot for my liking and it'll be time for grub soon, I wager so I'll take you back down, my old mate. Let's get you over to the door and we'll go down the same way we came up.'

'Why, what time is it?'

Tom reached into his tunic pocket and took out his father's watch.

'About ten to eleven, I reckon.'

'Huh! Not if you're using that cheap-looking bit of tat, it ain't.'

'That's my fathers watch I'll have you know. Real silver too.' Tom protested.

'Call that a watch? *This* is a watch!'

Archie Robertson fumbled in his jacket pocket, grunting with exertion. His hand re-emerged holding a large, gold hunter pocket watch and he held it up for Tom to see. 'Lemme see now, you're dead right, nearly eleven so definitely time for a cuppa and a wad. Alright, Sir Galahad, let me hop onto your shoulders and we'll be off in the Donkey Derby. Come here will you, I can't reach you from where I'm at now.'

Tom noticed the livid weals on his companion's hands but refrained from speaking out. They'd be a result of the wounds Archie had suffered from hanging onto the barbed wire on the fatal morning of his regiment's landing, an experience he would not be grateful to Tom for the remembering. He tried a different tack.

'That's some watch you have, Archie, a family heirloom?'

'I should cocoa! I picked it up in Karachi from a native jeweller off the Bunder Road. I had intended to take a tram down to the Empress Market to see if I could pick a nice bint up for a spot of mutual comfort but it was too hot so I decided to go elsewhere and I dunno, I saw this in the window and went in. Me and the old Indian bloke who owned the shop had a bit of a tussle and a haggle and I bought it. Cost me a packet, too, but we both came out of the transaction thinking we'd diddled the other and it's been my pride and joy ever since. Real gold, you know.' He proffered it up.

'Are they your initials on the case?'

'Observant beggar, aren't you? Well, I could say they are and they are but they're not my initials, if you see what I mean.'

'You've lost me.'

'Look, it's not that hard, even for an Australian. That's why I bought the bloody watch, it has the same initials as me inscribed on the outside. See? A.R... Archie Robertson. Only the date's different. Look.' He opened the case and Tom peered closely at the elegantly scribed copperplate inscription inside.

East India Company.
Cawnpore.
1856.

'How weird, it must be a relic from the Indian Mutiny. Now let me see, when was that? 1857 or thereabouts, I think. Your man here must have lived in Cawnpore before the mutiny started.'

'I'm blowed if I know, chum, it had the same initials as me and that was the reason I bought it. And it tells perfect time, too. Now when I go out in mufti I look a proper toff, a well- heeled gent.'

'I'm jealous, Archie, it's a fabulous watch but talking of time, if I don't get us both down from here sharp-ish, we're both gonna be in trouble and I for one don't fancy having a con-flab with that Sister McQueen you told me about.'

'Perish the thought. Just get a bloody move-on will you and stop gabbing.'

'Right, I'll leave the chairs here They'll come in handy for our next little tête-à-tête.'

--§--

He strolled into the ward, whistling sibilantly through his teeth, a smile on his face as he remembered the bellows of rage coming from Archie's ward after he'd left him outside. He had to hand it to him, he'd been spot on in his description of the infamous sister, he could hear her all the way down the stairs to his own floor.

'Harding? You've got mail. Two letters, I put them on yer bed.'

'Thanks.'

He frowned. Mail? Who'd be writing to him, he only had Walt and Elsie in the world and neither had written in years. He hurried over to his bed and took in the two envelopes with **Forwarded Mail** stamped across them, lying on top of the covers. One was in a faded blue, official-looking type so he opened it first, stepping back in shock and surprise as he read its contents. The first page of onion-skin paper merely read:

Whereupon it has pleased His Majesty
to bestow upon Sjt Thomas Harding E Coy
9th Battalion Australian Imperial Force
the **Distinguished Conduct Medal**
for Bravery in the Field.
Dated this Day.
3rd June 1915.
GVR.

The second page was the citation for his award.

On several occasions Sjt Harding has displayed outstanding bravery, leading to the route of enemy forces pressing home attacks on positions held by this NCO and his men. During the initial landings at ARI BURNU on 25th April Cpl Harding, as he was then, showed extreme gallantry under heavy fire when ensuring the safe landing of the men under his command. It was due to his fortitude and the disposition of his men that they were able to take up positions and frustrate any attempt by the Turkish forces to oust them from that position. Similarly, in the area known as PLUGGE'S PLATEAU, on 4th May this NCO and his platoon repulsed all attempts by the Turks to force the company position after the battalion was heavily shelled. It was during this attack that Sjt Harding gallantly rescued his platoon officer from certain death when he ventured out into no-mans-land and effected the rescue of his officer whilst under heavy fire. On another occasion on the 19th May, Sjt Harding received gunshot wounds to the head and arm whilst the battalion

263

withstood a further attack but continued to urge his men on until he was removed from the action to receive medical attention.

Signed.

R.A. Salisbury. Major.

C.O 9th Battn AIF 23rd May 1915.

'Oh my goodness!'

He sat cross-legged on his bed and read and re-read the recommendation. There was no doubt, it was his name on the documents. A quiet elation grew within, someone in higher authority had deemed him fit for recognition of the tasks he'd carried out since the chaos of the landing at Anzac Cove and the award of the medal was a result of that recognition.

He'd have to tell Walt, he'd be so pleased for him. He'd go now. No, best wait, Walt would be sleeping, he'd leave it until this evening. The excitement subsided, leaving a quiet satisfaction. Did he feel a different person? No, but the ribbon would mark him out, there'd be no immediate change to his circumstances but his comrades would know him by the ribbon he could now wear on his left breast. He scanned the citation again but it held no details of when the medal would be bestowed. Never mind, he was content to let the army catch up with him. Tomorrow, he'd see about it tomorrow.

His gaze drifted to the other letter lying on the bed covers and opened it automatically, his mind still on the news he'd just received. Another shock was in store as he read the opening lines. It was a letter from Australia, written to him by the hand of Loretta Treharne, Mark Treharne's wife.

'Busselton.'

Trenton Station.

Queensland.

6th June 1915.

Dear Tom,

May I call you by your first name? I do hope you forgive my forwardness in doing so but Mark wrote of you so often in his letters before the landings that I feel we know each other as friends. I write this with the gratitude of a wife in giving thanks to the man who has delivered her husband safe and sound back to the loving care of his family. Nothing I put down on paper can convey my feelings for the miracle you brought about in saving my husband. All I can do is thank you from the bottom of my heart and hope that God will spare you too in this dreadful war and bring you safely back to your loved ones.

Mark spent two weeks in hospital in Egypt before being repatriated and is now on his way back to us and will need further treatment in a Brisbane hospital. Whilst in hospital he had his letters written for him by a nurse and writes warmly of the times he spent with you and the men under him in Egypt before setting out for the peninsula. He is quite blind and the doctors have held out little hope for his sight to be restored but at least he has been spared, unlike so many poor souls whose families mourn in their passing. Since the landings at Gallipoli the newspapers have been filled with little else but the heartache of the lengthening casualty lists.

We have been blessed with a beautiful little girl, Abigail, who was born on the 1st May and I know her proud father will be besotted with his 'little darling' when he can finally hold her. We are hopeful that he will be allowed home in the weeks following his treatment where we can care for him in his own surroundings.

My husband asked me to write and tell you that when this war is over and we are victorious, as assured we will be, you must return to Queensland and join us here. Mark will need someone to assist him in the running of this place, I can do my part but it requires a man, a true friend, to help him overcome the handicaps God has placed before him and I can think of no-one else suited to that task but yourself. Please say you will, Australia will have need of strong decent men to build our fledgling nation into one that will astonish the world.

I leave you with my grateful thanks and a prayer for your continuing good fortune.

With Sincere Best Wishes,

Loretta Treharne.

Tom sat in quiet meditation as he digested the contents of Loretta Treharne's letter. The strength of the woman showed through in her measured words and he felt touched by her concern for him, a serjeant in the army in which her husband had held the King's commission. Compared to her husband's rank he was a mere mortal but she'd written to him as an equal with none of the class distinction he'd been accustomed to during his formative years in England. Perhaps this was why men like him felt so attached to and so fiercely proud of their adopted country. It had taken them in and given them the feeling of belonging, of equality and in all of them had been fostered the urge to repay those feelings of security.

'Grub's up, Tom, are you coming?'

'Uhh, what? Oh, right. Be with you in a mo.'

'Good news?'

He pushed the letters under his pillow. 'Something like that.'

--§--

Later that evening he looked down at the wan, smiling face of his brother and tried to decide where to start.

'Tom, you look like the cat who's stolen all the cream. What's up, have you had some good news?'

'You could say that, Walt, it's knowing how to explain it all to you.'

'That's not like you to be lost for words, why don't you start at the beginning?'

Tom stifled a grin and sat down at the foot of the bed, staring at Walt's expectant face. 'Well, it's like this...' He spoke slowly to begin with as he tried to collect his thoughts and turn them into sentences that made sense. Walt's eyes opened wide as he described the Turk's attacks on their position and his rescue of Mark Treharne. 'Do you mean to sa...?'

'Shh! Let me finish.' He ran quickly through the rest of his story, explaining the letter from Mark Treharne's wife and her entreaties for him to come and join them after the war's end. Eventually, he came to the end and sat in silence as Walt continued to stare at him with shining eyes.

'Tom!' he burst out, 'What a story, I can't believe it! What a woman to write to you like that, offering you a job but you deserve a bloody medal for what you did. They should give you the Victoria Cross for saving that man.'

'Not quite, Walt, that's what I was coming to. They've awarded me the Distinguished Conduct Medal, can you believe it? After all that happened on the first day too.'

'You did say something queer about that to me when we met on the ship, Tom, why did you hark back to it, what was so awful?'

Quietly Tom recounted in a dispassionate voice the story of the soldier he'd fired on in the blazing scrubland, omitting none of the details. Walt listened silently, his eyes moving from his brother's face to the window and back as Tom spoke on. When he'd finished, Walt leant forward with and effort and softly squeezed his brother's hand.

'Don't let that get you down Tom. I can see how badly its affected you but no-one could blame you, I'd have done the very same. You put a poor cove out of his misery, what were you to do, leave him to die a horrible death on his own? Nah, you did him a favour and I'm proud of you. Buck up, come on, try to forget it and when they pin the medal on you, wear it with pride, you deserve it.'

'I know what you're saying, Walt but I have to live with it, they're giving me a medal and I killed a fellow soldier, a mate.'

'Get away with you, can't you see? My brother's a blooming hero! Tom, I'm so proud of you I could burst. I—'

'Walt, please, keep your voice down.'

'Oh shut up, you nincompoop. You've just been awarded a bloody medal and you want me to keep quiet about it? Not on your nelly, chum, when I can get out of bed I'm gonna shout it from the top of the roof. *"My brother's a hero, Tom Harding is a hero!"* You see if I don't.' His voice faded away and he sank back, coughing, onto his pillow.

'Walt? See, I told you to calm down, you'll give yourself a right turn if you don't.' He saw the change in Walt's face in frantically trying to control his coughing and turned around to see the figure of Bridgette Mathers looking quizzically at the pair of them.

She ignored Tom and directed her comments to Walt. 'Are you alright, Walt, I heard the noise and came over to see if I could help.'

'No, I'm fine, Bridgette, just a coughing fit but, please, don't be concerned, I'm alright now. See? It was Tom and his news what set me off but I'm better now, I swear.'

'News?' She arched her eyebrows and Tom suddenly felt deflated. The anger he'd felt at hearing Walt's casual use of her first name evaporated as he looked at her, trying to conceal his confusion and embarrassment as she waited for him to speak.

'Go on Tom, tell her.' Walt urged him but he shook his head stubbornly and moved off the bed. 'I must be going now, Walt, I'll look in later if I get a chance. Take care of yourself, I'll be back. And Walt, don't breathe a word on that *other thing* we just discussed. Promise?'

Walt raised a weak hand in acknowledgement and Tom stepped back to leave. In passing he was aware of her proximity but any quickening of his pulse at her nearness was tempered with the remembrance of the last meeting between them both. She lifted her head as if to speak but it was he who ignored her now.

'See to the lad, please.' He spoke brusquely and was past before she could respond, heading for the ward door and leaving her looking at his departing back in dismay.

'Bridgette, is something wrong, have you and Tom quarrelled?'

She forced a smile to her face and busied herself smoothing his covers.

'No, Walt but I do think sometimes I get on the wrong side of your brother.'

'Oh, that's easy enough for me but why you?'

'I don't know but enough of this, lie back and let me sort this bed out for you. And while I do it you can tell me all about Tom's good news.'

--§--

Tom Harding strode down the corridor, seething at the events of the previous minutes. Damn the woman, she'd brought him right down to earth, destroying any lingering euphoria he'd felt at the arrival of the letters. What was it about her that made him want to mean something to her yet resulted in nothing but ill-feeling between them whenever they met? Best forget it, he'd go and visit Archie, see if his foul-mouthed yet amusing outlook on life could restore his good humour.

A familiar face swam in and out of his vision and he spoke aloud. 'Wheeler? It's Wheeler, isn't it?'

The man with the Red Cross brassard on his arm turned to face him, his puzzled expression at hearing his name changing as he recognised Tom.

'I know you, you're that Australian cove what was on the ship with us. How'd you get here, this is a British hospital, don't you lot have your own one up in Cairo?'

'They let me stay here, my brother Walt was on the ship with us. You took me to see him, remember?'

Private Wheeler's face took on a crafty twist. 'That's right, I remember now, you was mooning around that snooty bitch Mathers, I took you down with her to see that other cove. Your…'

'Keep a civil tongue in your head, man!' Tom snapped, '*Sister* Mathers outranks you by a long chalk and I'll not let you talk of her like that, you hear?'

'I was only funning, chum,' Wheeler whined, 'no need to get shirty over my little joke. Look.' He leant over and a large bag he'd been carrying on his left shoulder dropped with a loud *thud!* to the floor. 'How about some nice oranges, real tasty they are, I guarantee it.'

'Where'd you get them from?' Tom asked curiously, forgetting his anger.

Jack Wheeler's face changed again, becoming shifty. He looked furtively round and stepped close to Tom. 'I've got contacts, see, that can get me anything, in or out of the hospital. What do you fancy, some other fruit, beer, cheap cigarettes? I can get pretty much everything. A woman?' He stepped even closer and spoke again in a conspiratorial whisper. 'For a small price I can get you an Arab bint in here and the use of a storeroom for an hour if you want. You tell me and…'

'How much are the oranges?' Tom asked curtly.

Wheeler looked him up and down, mentally gauging how much he could get away with. 'Three *piastres* a dozen. That's a fair price for all the trouble I have to go through.' he added in haste seeing the frosty expression on Tom's face. 'Honest, I wouldn't try and diddle you serjeant. Look, I'll throw in some fresh grapes with them, how's about that?'

'Fine,' Tom answered grimly, 'but they're not for me. I'll pay you what you're asking but I want you to squeeze the oranges into a jug and take it to my brother, Walter Harding, in Ward Eleven. You got that?'

'Harding, Ward Eleven. No trouble, I'll take it there myself, chum.'

Tom dug in his trouser pocket and brought out a handful of change. He counted the coins into Wheeler's waiting hand and placed his hand firmly over that of Wheeler's until the man looked up into Tom's face.

'Mind you do that now, I'll make sure that you do.'

'Consider it done, serjeant.'

Tom nodded in acknowledgement and walked away, missing the look of hatred in Wheeler's eyes as he watched his figure recede down the corridor.

'Think you're special do you, me lad, we'll fucking well see who has the last laugh, won't we!' He looked down at his hand and spat on the coins resting there before pocketing them, hefting the burlap bag onto his shoulder and walking away in the opposite direction,

Chapter Thirteen.

Alexandria, June.

The following morning Tom Harding stepped out of the ward door and prepared to walk upstairs and see if Archie was game for another trip to the roof. He'd only taken four or five steps when his way was blocked by a woman in the starched white uniform of a nurse and his heart sank as he recognised Bridgette Mathers. He made to pass but she put out a restraining arm, an anxious look on her pretty features.

'Please, Tom, don't. I need to speak with you, is there anywhere we can talk in private?'

His heart lurched. 'Why? Is it Walt? What's happened?'

She laid a cool hand on his arm. 'No, Tom, Walt's fine. It's you I'd like to talk to. So, could you spare me a few minutes?'

Tom looked searchingly but saw nothing but concern in her expression. He gestured down the corridor. 'Come this way, there's a spot I take one of the lads to for a quiet chat, we can go there.'

Dutifully, she fell in behind him as he moved off and followed as he headed for the doorway leading to the stairs. He looked swiftly up and down the corridor before signalling her to pass through the open door and ascend the stairs leading to the roof. Following closely behind he let the door swing shut, oblivious to the silent figure watching their passage from the concealment of a ward door just feet away.

'Hello, hello, just what's going on here, then?' mused Jack Wheeler as he watched them both disappear. 'Well I never, *Miss Goody Two-shoes* and her fancy man. In broad daylight too, who'd've believed it!' Stowing the knowledge in the back of his mind for later he strode away, whistling, a smug smile on his face.

Tom led the way and opened the door at the top of the stairs, stepping back to allow her to pass and walk out onto the roof. 'My goodness!' she exclaimed peering in all directions, 'What a beautiful view, you can almost see Cairo from up here.'

'Not quite.' he mused quietly and was rewarded by a wide smile. The ice broken, she moved across the space and eased herself into one of the chairs, peering out over the harbour as she waited for him to join her.

'What is it you wanted to speak to me about?' he asked curiously, 'I thought I'd be one of the last people you'd want a conversation with?'

'That's just it, I'm so confused I don't know what to do or think. I'm not some blushing schoolgirl being asked out without a chaperone, neither do I believe in ship-borne romances but since we met I've been unable to think straight. Something about you makes me want to confide in you but there's a gulf between us, made wider by my wanting to keep you at arm's length. Why would that be? I'd like to think better of you but what happened that night when we...' Her voice tailed away. '...when the ship was lost. I can't put those events out of my mind. And yet, I'm flattered by your attentions. Do you see what I'm trying to say?'

'No.' he replied flatly, misunderstanding her distress. 'I seem to have a strange effect on you, Bridgette but there's nothing complicated about me, you're a beautiful woman and as a man I'm attracted to you. Is that so awful?'

'Yes, I mean, no. Oh look, this is so strange. The war has had its effect on us all and changed how we act. Please try and understand; time means so little nowadays, the time we used to spend in meeting and courting has been swept away by the war but I've become scared to trust anyone, scared of being hurt again and in giving way to those these feelings I push people away in order to avoid any complications.'

'But why? I wouldn't hurt you.'

'I know but that gulf exists between us all the same. It's why I feel so miserable. I'm exhilarated that you want to like me and confused because if I let you I might end up feeling low and lost again. It's so complicated. If only it had been you—'

'Had been—?'

'Damn you, Tom Harding!' she burst out, 'Let me finish, this is so unfair. I came to speak with you to lay the ghosts that have come between us and again I find myself unable to speak the words that can make you understand. Why do I find it so hard to unburden myself? I've seen so many young men in the last months, what is it about you that makes you so different? Why can't we be friends? Is that being forward, my thinking this way?'

'I can't answer that, Bridgette and what about if? If you can't trust someone with your feelings, Bridgette, you'll end up a lonely, bitter woman and for someone like you that would be a tragedy. I can't promise you that in coming to know more about me life would ever be a smooth path but one thing you should understand is that I would never, ever, deliberately cause you pain.'

'I think I realise that and I want to apologise for acting like a fool, Tom. You must think me a spoiled, stupid child for the way I've acted since we met. I can't explain it, we meet as adults and speak yet there's this—oh, I don't know, this strangeness between us. I've been so rotten to you, for all the wrong reasons. Someone told me things that may or

271

may not be true, things that concern you and like a fool I believed them without asking you first. Now can you understand what I'm trying to say?'

'I haven't a clue what it is you've heard about me but I can tell you this, Bridgette. People can be the most vicious animals on earth, telling the most hideous lies in order to get their own way. What I'm trying to say is that you mustn't believe everything you hear or accept facts at face value, there's always another explanation.

If you asked me to explain how I feel I'd be at a loss to spell it out. We could say it's the conditions we've met under but I don't know, I only know that in spite of everything when I see you a light flickers inside me and I want to go on seeing more of you. Have you ever felt like that about a person?'

'Once, and I suppose that its put me on my guard ever since, made me keep people who could mean something at arm's length.' She continued. 'In spite of trying to put you out of my mind for all the wrong reasons I find myself hoping I'll meet you again. But enough of the past, before I broach the subject that's been troubling me I believe congratulations are in order. Walter told me of your news, Tom, the Distinguished Conduct Medal no less, are you not proud of yourself? I think it's simply wonderful that your bravery has been honoured in this way.'

'Trust Walter,' he rasped, a pang of jealousy lancing through him as she spoke his brother's name, 'I hope that's all he gave away. I'll wager he greatly exaggerated my exploits in order to make me out a greater hero than he already thinks I am.'

'No, he just said you'd been awarded the medal for several acts of bravery since the landings, he didn't mention any particular event. I can't begin to imagine how the war is going on out there, it must be a very cruel affair.' She spoke softly, catching him off guard by changing the subject, 'I mean, I know it must be horrible living under the conditions you face, judging from what other men have told me but when I ask about the actual war side of it they just clam up on me.'

'What is it you're asking me to tell?' he said slowly. 'Beautiful scenery, flowers whose scent tears at your heart and clear blue skies but everywhere you look there are corpses. Birds sing above the constant sound of gunfire. We see each other from across the trench lines, sometimes yards apart but instead of greeting each other like neighbours would, we see who can kill the other first. Men I never knew and never will. Men who until we came to their country meant no harm to me but now all I want to do is kill him and him me.

Until you've actually been there, stood sweltering in the early morning in the trenches and heard the man next to you gasp his life out and you can't do a damn thing about it... Bridgette, I can't spoil your innocence and tell you the truth. Think of it as a gallant adventure played out by heroes who meet their death with a stiff upper lip and a smile for the enemy. The reality is far too dreadful to contemplate, I assure you.'

She stared at him wide-eyed, taken aback by his vehemence. 'I'm so sorry.'

'It's alright,' he answered her gently, 'really it is. I surprised myself; this is the longest I've spoken about it and not to a fellow soldier but to a beautiful woman who came here to tend to us. It's just that—we men, we like to make it sound far more dramatic that it actually is. We award ourselves medals in order to disguise the incompetent way we butcher our fellow human beings in unimaginable ways and in numbers to great to comprehend.

My apologies, I'm trying to convince you that war is somehow noble when you see for yourself the results of the savagery we endure each time a new batch of wounded arrive here. Having been under fire and seen the awful things human beings do to each other makes me think that this war will go on for a long time. Our generals will want nothing less than the total waste of all the fine young men who came here for an ideal and found a different kind of values prevailing. Does that make sense to you?'

'Yes, I think you've put it quite succinctly, Tom. You're right, although I can't imagine in my wildest dreams how bad it is but thank you for trying to spare me. I see the results in the shattered bodies we try so desperately to mend.' She stopped and looked down at the floor and he waited for her to continue. When it became clear that she'd finished speaking for the moment he broke in.

'Can't we talk about something different, totally different to this damned war?'

'I'd like that.' she smiled, shy yet comfortable in his presence. 'What though? I've been so horrid I'm taken aback that you'd want to talk to me at all.'

'So, what awful thing is it I'm supposed to have done?'

'Not now, Tom, can we speak about that matter later? For now I'd just like to sit here and relax and enjoy the view.'

'Alright but don't go too near the edge. Promise?'

They both laughed, the awkwardness between them vanishing.

After a while, she turned to him and spoke softly. 'What did you do before you enlisted, Tom?'

'After I arrived in Australia I turned my hand at a lot of different jobs. I was a miner back in England but I'd always wanted to escape the drudgery of a pit job and emigrating seemed to be the answer. That way I could always have the sun on my face, I hated the dark. Still do'

'Any regrets?'

'In a way. The dream was to find a good living and send for Walt but it never materialised. Poor Walt, he probably hates me for leaving him and gallivanting off but I never seemed to have enough money for his passage.'

'Were you never lonely?' she asked questioningly.

'All the time.'

'So how did you cope with missing home?'

'I read avidly,' he replied, laughing, 'everything and anything that came to hand, from newspapers to Euclid. I'll have you know I'm a walking encyclopaedia. In the depths of the night I'd wake up and reach for a book, I found reading a cheap novel or a more serious subject by candlelight helped ease the feeling of being far from home. I suppose I was craving the education I never got back in England. I took to reading more and the more I read the hungrier for knowledge I became.

I made some good friends during my wanderings and so it seemed the natural thing to do to enlist when the war broke out, pay back a bit of what I thought I owed Australia for taking me in. But enough about me, what about you Bridgette Mathers? What made you throw yourself into this war, isn't there a sweetheart waiting for you back home?'

'No.' she replied shortly, 'No-one.' She changed the subject abruptly. 'What about your parents?'

'They're both dead,' he explained, 'there was a fire in the house and my parents were overcome by the smoke. My father liked to smoke a pipe after work, while he read. The word was that my mother went up to bed and he fell asleep and the pipe dropped to the floor and started the fire. We were saved when our mother dropped us from the upstairs window into the arms of rescuers below but she couldn't be saved. Our aunt Elsie who lived nearby took us in. Elsie was a spinster but she brought us up as if we were her own and for that Walt and I will always be grateful.'

'I'm sorry to hear that. So, Tom Harding, do you have someone back home holding a torch for you?'

'What a quaint way to put it,' he grinned. 'I should be so lucky.' He smiled, anxious to lift her spirits, 'I was too busy looking for work and ending up in some weird far-flung parts of the Outback to think about meeting women. But you, Bridgette, you're a fine woman, the sort any respectable beau would count himself lucky to stroll down the promenade arm in arm with. Why've you not been snapped up already?'

She laughed delightedly. 'I wish you'd met my father, Tom Harding, he'd have given you short shrift if he'd heard you talking like that. My mother died when I was quite young and I have no recollection of her but he was a wonderful man with no time for fools. He died suddenly at home, over a year ago. A blessing, perhaps, for whatever comfort that knowledge has brought as this conflict would have broken his heart.' Her voice softened. 'You remind me of him so much, perhaps that's why I'm drawn to you.'

'Now look who's talking.'

In spite of her sad thoughts she laughed again, a rich, throaty sound. 'We have a saying in Scotland for people like you, you'd be called a *sook*!'

'A what?'

'A *sook*. It means someone who's trying to worm his way into your affections, you see what I'm hinting at?'

'Perish the thought, ma'am!' he replied with an innocent expression and his heart leapt in his breast as she responded to his advances, throwing her head back in laughter but then she straightened and gazed at him intently.

'I had a locket in my cabin onboard, it contained a photograph of my father. I lost it when the ship sank. I didn't think anyone could replace him but—'

'There you see!'

'Let me finish. When I see you I have this feeling of—something different coming into my life, yet—there's so much to say and if I do speak what's on my mind I'm scared that you'll walk away and want nothing to do with me again. My head's in a spin, Tom, and God only knows when it'll stop.'

He frowned and stared back, a studied, blank look on his face. 'Bridgette, what is it you're trying to say, is it the rank difference between us that bothers you? I'm Australian now, don't forget, and we don't give a stuff about rank or station, it's what's inside a person that counts not the bloody clothes on their back.'

275

'No, Tom,' she hastened to reassure him, 'I don't care a fig who sees us, my rank and yours have nothing to do with what's troubling me. It's...'

'Bridgette, tell me for Christ's sake, don't lead me on here and then clam up. If you've something to say, just come right out and say it. Oh God, don't tell me you've brought me all the way up here to inform me where babies come from? You're too late, Bridgette, the padre on the boat over tried to tell us, stupid bastard, but we just laughed him off the mess deck. He thought he'd sit us down and ...Bridgette?'

A tear trickled slowly down her cheek and she buried her head in her hands, sobbing quietly.

'I'm so sorry, I didn't mean to upset you with my joking.' He knelt down in contrition and pulled her head into his shoulders. She rested there for a minute or so until her composure returned and sat upright again, fiercely wiping her eyes.

'I'm alright.' She looked at him tenderly. 'You're a fine man, Tom Harding and I could dream of letting myself fall in love with you but it wouldn't be fair.'

'I don't understand.' Tom stammered, 'Are you trying to tell me you're already married? Tell me, Bridgette, for God's sake, kill this suspense before it kills me!'

She met his gaze and gathered her thoughts before answering. 'Tom, you and I could never have a life together, not after what happened to me. I'm so embarrassed by the mistake I made and it's not fair to burden you with that knowledge.'

'Let me be the judge of that.' Tom replied softly.

She hesitated before answering in a quiet voice. 'I was still suffering form the trauma of losing my father when we were sent here. He was my world and I went to pieces. I foolishly allowed myself to be seduced by a doctor on the ship thinking it would help heal the pain but he abandoned me soon afterwards. I thought I'd found love but he obviously considered it as something else.

We were found out and he was removed to another post ashore without giving me another thought and I was lucky to keep my job only through Matron Green's pleading for me to remain with her. Before he left, all the nursing staff were informed of my conduct. He boasted to many people of how he'd made love to me and, as you might believe, I've been dubbed a *scarlet woman* ever since.'

She finished speaking and looked to see what effect her words had had on the man sitting opposite her.

He continued to look at her calmly, without a trace of the distaste she expected to see.

'Is that your dark secret, is that what you were scared I'd find out? Tell me, is that why you became so angry with me on the ship the night of the sinking, I was only funning, you know.'

'Yes,' she admitted, 'I overheard you speaking with the other men and thought Martha Weatherall had told you all about me. She always was a bit of a gossip and I was mortified to think you were having a laugh at my expense. I'm afraid I let my temper get the better of me and I tore into you without thinking. Can you forgive me?'

'How did the others onboard find out?'

'I'm not sure.' Her eyes darkened as she relived the pain of those days. 'I think, I'm almost certain that he informed one of the male orderlies and that man was the one who spread the word around the ship. Now do you see?'

'Forget them all, Bridgette, forget all the hypocrites who've never known love or life.' He took a deep breath. 'There's something I want to say so could you hear me out? Come to Australia with me when this is all over, where no-one will care a hoot except what you are deep inside. We can settle there in the sort of world you're dreaming about. It's a huge country and we can go anywhere we please, be anyone we want to be. I even have the promise of a good job, too.'

In a few short sentences he outlined the letter he'd received from Loretta Treharne, playing down the part he'd played in her husband's survival. 'Mark Treharne's blind and needs someone to help him run the place so you see our prayers could be answered by taking up his offer. Say you'll come with me, I know it's a scary thought right now but come with me, make a new start and a new life.'

She arched an eyebrow. 'Tom Harding, are you proposing?'

He stopped short before laughing sheepishly. 'I think I am. Sort of.'

She leant across the space between them, eyes shining. 'You're a good man and I'm grateful for your offer but I'm also scared, Tom. Are we not rushing into things neither of us has properly thought out? Think about what you're saying, think about the commitment you'd be making. Are you sure of all this?'

His lips hovered near hers. 'Bridgette, you're wearing that damn perfume again! It's the one thing that's cemented my offer. I couldn't face life without smelling it over and over again. Say yes.'

She laughed nervously, unable to tell if he was serious or not.

'Tom, you seem to have thought of everything in such a short time but there's also Walt to consider. You'd never leave your brother now that you've found each other, what about Walt?'

'I've told Walt he can come out to Australia when this is all over and we'll make a go of it together. Mark Treharne's promise of a job would extend to taking Walt with me, I'm sure of it.'

She settled back and laughed infectiously, a mellow sound that warmed his heart. 'Be serious, you fool! I could—what was that?'

'What was what?'

'I heard a noise, there, from the other side of the door!'

Tom rose and swiftly pulled the door open. From below came the sounds of someone hurrying down the stairs and they stared guiltily into each others face.

'Right, Bridgette, I think we'd better scarper, now, before whoever that was comes back with reinforcements. I don't want to get you into trouble...what?'

Her shoulders shook with suppressed laughter. 'It's too late for that, Tom but I see what you mean. What shall we do?'

'You can stop cracking the funnies for a start,' he growled, 'I'm the comedian about here, or so Archie says.'

'Archie?'

'Never mind, I'll explain about him later. Right, you go down first and if the coast's clear take off to the left. I'll give you a minute or two then come down and make my way off to the right. Got that?'

'Yes, and Tom, thank you.'

'For what?'

'You don't have to, you know?'

'Bridgette, my head's starting to spin, what don't *I have to*?'

'You're a decent man, Tom did I tell you that earlier? I meant you don't have to honour the offer you made upstairs, I'm sure once you think about it you'll come to realise it could ne—'

He pulled her close and placed his lips over hers, forcing her backwards into the wall of the doorway. They stayed that way, aware of the proximity of each others bodies, joined together by the pressure of their lips for several, long seconds before he released her and said, shakily, 'No more nonsense, Bridgette, get going before I try to seduce you here and now. We'll talk again later.'

She nodded weakly and disappeared from sight, her heels making a clattering noise as she descended the stairs to the corridor. He leant against the upper doorway, his heart hammering. This new twist in his feelings for her surprised and elated him and he began to feel the faint stirrings of hope that maybe, possibly, something good after all could come out of this grotesque war. As he opened the ward door and surreptitiously slipped inside, a memory surfaced and he pulled up short, nettled. In all the excitement he'd forgotten to discuss the one matter uppermost in his mind, that of the night of the sinking and his part in it. He relaxed and let a faint smile drift across his face. Never mind, there was time enough to talk to her about it, a lifetime if his newfound hopes were to be believed.

--§--

He was still smiling the following day when he opened the door to Ward Nine and walked down the rows of beds.

'You there!'

He turned to see a large, white-starched matriarch bearing down on him, wearing a sisters uniform and a look of extreme displeasure.

'Yes, ma'am, can I help you?' he asked innocently.

'I asked where did you think you were going! Well?'

'Not very far, obviously, with these wounds,' he replied tongue in cheek, 'I thought I'd take a stroll and see if my mate, Archie Robertson was ready for a promenade with me.'

'Well, you thought wrong! Corporal Robertson has been absenting himself far too often for my liking, without permission, and I've decided to put a stop to it. Now, turn around and make yourself scarce out of MY ward before I report you for your insolence. I'm...'

'You must be Sister McQueen, am I right? I must be,' he said, noting the look of surprise on her face, 'your reputation precedes you ma'am. Could you tell A-r-c-h-i-e...' he enunciated his friend's name slowly and carefully in order to cause the maximum annoyance and was rewarded by her face turning a deeper shade of purple, '...could you tell him Tom Harding sends his regards and I'll look in later.'

Ignoring the strangled noises emanating from her throat he opened the ward door and strode back down the corridor.

--§--

'You'll get me bloody killed, pulling a stunt like that, you berk!' Archie groused as they sat in the late afternoon warmth, staring over the harbour from their perch. 'Sister McQueen went to town on me after

279

your little visit. Ranted on about her *reputation* and what the hell had I been saying? *And* what was I doing inviting Australians to *her* ward to visit? Gawd help me, she regards you lot as worse than dirt on her slippers. With that woman, cleanliness is next to godliness and I'm only here because she took an attack of the vapours and disappeared to recover. God help me if she comes back and finds you've spirited me away.' he concluded gloomily.

'Look Archie, where would you rather be, back in the ward or sitting here with me, enjoying the view? Say so now and I'll whip you back there before the dragon reappears. I don't give a monkey's, you tell me!'

'Alright, alright, keep your hair on, I was only telling you.'

'Telling me what?'

'That cow. McQueen. She's got it in for me and now she's got it in for you. I wouldn't be surprised if she rats on you to the Hospital Director.'

'But what could they do to me, I'm an Australian?'

'Move you to another hospital you berk, is that what you want, to leave your brother? You've got a cushy number here, mate, don't spoil it by letting some fat cow like her have you thrown out on yer ear cos you upset her. Savvy?'

'Hmn, you're right, Archie, I see what you mean. Alright, next time I want to take you anywhere I'll turn up with a bunch of flowers and charm her down off her broomstick.'

In spite of himself, Archie saw the funny side and joined in Tom's laughter. When they'd calmed down he looked sideways at his companion and asked, 'What was it like for you on the first day, Tom, was it the same slaughter we rowed into?'

'Depends on what you mean Archie. Listening to how your lot copped a packet I suppose we landed without too much of a fuss, even if we *did* land on the wrong bloody beach. We all lost mates and our casualties amongst the officers were pretty high but it was just a bloody great mix-up once we got ashore. No-one landed where they were supposed to and no-one had a clue, initially, where the hell we were meant to be in the first place!'

He stopped, a mental picture of Billy Willis and another, darker episode, pushing to the forefront of his memory and Archie waited for him to continue.

'Those first days were awful and they just kept getting worse. None of us knew what we'd let ourselves in for and it broke my heart to see so many good men go west in some stupid stunt before they'd even begun to make a contribution.

All because of some pom officer's cock-up, those bastard's couldn't organise an orgy in a whorehouse, believe you me. They turned us from being the finest bunch of men I'd ever known into an army of ghosts, that's what we are now, the ghosts of the Dardanelles. In later years our grandchildren and our widows will visit Gallipoli and say, *"What the hell did they come here for?"* and who will there be to give them the right answer? *"Your menfolk died because we didn't have a fucking clue how to fight a war!"*

I tell you, Archie, if General Sir Ian Hamilton ever came to ANZAC Cove to speak to the ordinary man he'd be riddled with bullets, *our* bullets, before he stepped ashore on the beach.'

'I'm sorry, chum, I didn't mean to upset you,' Archie said gently, 'I thought it might do you good to talk about it, like'

'I did go on, didn't I?' Tom replied wryly but Archie protested, 'No, Tom, I didn't mean to sound as if I was annoyed with you. What you just said sent a shiver down my spine. You made it sound so real, it sounds like we were all pitched into the same hell.'

'We were.' Tom answered in a quiet voice. 'I think of it every night, especially...' he broke off.

'Especially what, chum?'

'What would you, say, Archie, if I told you I killed a man?'

'Tom, me lad, don't get annoyed at my answer but that's what we came here to do, isn't it, to kill folk?'

'What if it was one of your own men?' Tom replied slowly, picking his words with care.

Sensing his distress, Archie Robertson though deeply before replying just as carefully.

'Tom, this is war and in war, strange things happen to us all, things we'd rather forget. This man, was he a pal of yours?'

'I never saw him before, couldn't even tell you what he looked like either. When I came across him, he was lying helpless in the middle of burning scrub, badly wounded, I think, and on fire. Anyway, he couldn't get out and I couldn't get in to help him so he screamed at me to kill him. Screamed, Archie, like a stuck pig... The hair stood up on the back of my neck. I'd just seen my best pal bayoneted by a Turk and shot his killer but this was different, this was a fellow Australian, in pain, begging me to shoot him!'

'And did you?'

'God help me, yes! I stuck my rifle into the flames and pulled the trigger. He never screamed again after that and I ran back and rejoined my own battalion as if nothing had ever happened.'

'And you've blamed yourself ever since? What for? You did a badly-wounded man a favour, did the decent thing. What could you do, sit on your backside and let him burn to death?'

'No, but...'

'No buts to it, Tom. If I was stuck in a situation like that, slowly burning to death and a man, a man, Tom, not some half-witted coward, came along and put me out of my misery, I'd fly up to heaven singing his praises. Give me your hand so I can shake it. Brave men are hard to find and you, my chum, have just told me a story that makes you one of the finest.'

'It gets worse, Archie, I received a letter the other day, they're giving me the DCM. Can you believe it? After an episode like that, they're going to reward me with a bloody medal.'

'Hallelujah! That's all I'll say on it, Tom Harding, besides my congratulations and praise for our generals. Some dimwit has come to his senses and dished a medal out to the right person for a change, not one of his own staff wallahs. We'll have to see about getting hold of some, ahem, *squash*, so we can make a toast to your good fortune and... eh? 'oo the bleeding hell are you?'

A face had appeared at the door, unheard until he filled the doorway with his presence.

'Are you Corporal Robertson, mate, Ward Nine? Sister McQueen told me to look for you, says she wants a word, sharpish, and I was to bring you back if I found yous.'

'Shit! Trust her to want me, I must be in for a verbal from her. Right, mate, now that you're here, you can help me down.' He turned to Tom. 'Sorry, Tom, got to go, this cove'll give me a hand, you stay here and enjoy the view.'

The man sauntered out onto the verandah and with a start Tom recognised the surly features of the hospital orderly, Jack Wheeler. At the same time, Wheeler recognised him and a twisted grin settled over his face.

'Well, if it isn't my old mate, Serjeant Harding. What are you doing up here, sarje, chewing the fat and enjoying the view like the corporal says? You can see lots of pretty Arab bints from up here, if you had some binoculars, that is. How's about it, shall I get you a pair for your next visit?'

282

'Don't talk rot, Wheeler, and whilst you're here, did you deliver those oranges I paid you for the other day to my brother?'

'There's no need to get all nasty now, sarje, is there? Your brother got his squash that night, delivered it meself in person so's I could get a glimpse of that tasty dish, Sister Mathers. Likes her men big, I'm told.'

The last part was spoken in an insolent, suggestive manner and Tom's temper flared hotly. He lunged forward.

'You make any more cracks about Bridgette Mathers and I'll...'

Wheeler stepped deftly back, evading Tom's challenge. 'Oh, it's Bridgette is it now, you being a serjeant and her a nursing sister. Tut-tut, serjeant, wouldn't the matron like to know about that?'

'You foul bastard!' Tom blazed, 'I'll see you in Hell!' He lunged forward again but only succeeded in knocking Archie Robertson out of his chair and onto the verandah floor. His temper disappeared in an instant and he bent down in contrition.

'Sorry, Archie, I shouldn't have lost my temper. Are you alright?'

'Don't worry, Tom, I lost a leg, not me senses, I'm fine' He looked angrily up at Wheeler. 'You, take that fucking smirk off you face and help me up then we'll go and see to your Sister McQueen, see if we don't.'

As Wheeler bent to pick him up, careful to stay out of Tom's reach, Archie spoke again. 'I'll sort that baggage McQueen out and see you later, Tom. Tomorrow morning be alright?'

'Yes, Archie, I'll come round for you and see how the land lies after I've visited Walt. Could you do me a favour, do you have the time on you? I think I might have overstayed my leave from my own ward but at least we've got decent staff on ours, unlike yours.'

Archie fumbled in his jacket and brought out the gold hunter watch Tom had seen previously. 'It's ten past four, chum, and you could be right. Best you bugger off smartly, leave me with Mr Smartarse here, he'll get me back to the ward with no bother. Won't you?' he added threateningly, addressing Jack Wheeler.

Wheeler's attention was fixed on the watch in Archie's hand.

'Oi, did you hear me?'

'Er, no, sorry, corporal, what was it you wanted?'

'I said, you berk, you'll take care of me, won't you?'

'Ah, yes, we'll have you downstairs and in the ward quick as you like, you'll see.'

'Good, so what're you bloody gawping at?'

Wheeler's face took on the crafty expression Tom had seen when they'd discussed the price of the oranges destined for Walt.

'The watch, corp, that's a mighty smart piece. Is it real gold?'

'Course it is, what did you think it was made of, tin? Now get me up from here, will you?'

'Would you be willing to sell it to me, I'd give you a real good price for it. You'd be surpr...'

'Shut the cackling and get me up, I said! The watch isn't for sale, now or any time, you hear? Get that into your thick skull. There's a wheelchair at the foot of the stairs so help me to the fucking ward before I kick your arse with the one good leg I've got left!'

Chapter Fourteen.

Alexandria, June.

The next few days saw a massive influx of wounded brought in using the same canvas-covered motor vehicles that had taken Tom and so many others to the hospital wards. Men lay groaning everywhere in huddled heaps in the corridors as the wards overflowed, the nursing staff unable to cope with the steady streams of unkempt, often delirious figures that landed at their doors. Many of the wounded carried the strong, dank smell of gangrene with wounds festering under the cover of filthy bandages.

Tom and the rest of the walking wounded already on the road to recovery were confined to their wards as the hospital struggled to sort out the injured into some semblance of priority and it was days before Tom could make his way to Walt's ward. His brother sat upright in bed, reading a week old newspaper, frowning at its contents as Tom entered and placed himself on the end of the bed.

'Hi, Tom, nice to see you again. Have you seen this?' He thrust the paper indignantly at Tom. 'The stupid clods, they've got General Hamilton reporting fresh gains and driving the Turks back on all fronts. For God's sake, it says here they expect Krithia to fall at any moment! Who writes this rot?' Leaning over, he threw the paper to the floor in disgust.

Tom laughed. 'Never mind, little brother, it probably says inside that the Kaiser has offered peace terms if we'd only put our arms away and retreat back to Egypt. Course it's all rot, what did you think, that the government would allow the real truth to be reported? If people back home knew what was going on out here, Hamilton and all his generals would be on the next boat home, tied up in chains! And that would never do so they go on filling the papers with nonsense and hope that the general public don't read it, study the casualty lists and put two and two together.'

'We've lost another battleship, Tom, did you know that? The paper says that *HMS Majestic* was torpedoed two days after the *Triumph*. That makes three so far and the ward gossip is that they'll withdraw the rest of the fleet and then where will that leave us?'

'Forget that for the moment, how are you feeling today, you're looking a whole lot better than last time I was in?'

'I'm feeling quite chipper, Tom, I really am. They also say that Italy has joined us at long last and that should make a big difference. Maybe they'll even send some troops right away to help us out. Or some food, spaghetti would make a fine difference to eating bully don't you think?'

'Aren't you being fed well enough here, the food's not that bad is it?'

'Of course, but you know, a lot of how I'm feeling is also to do with the care I'm getting here. The nurses treat you like heroes and they say if I continue to improve I'll be discharged in another two or three weeks and that means a return to the peninsula. I won't be looking forward to that.

Bridgette comes in most days and fusses over me so. Sometimes I get real embarrassed by her attention, especially when she calls me her *Special Hero*. I keep telling her I only did what anyone else would've under the same circumstances but she still insists on saying that if it wasn't for me she would never have survived that night the ship went down.'

'She calls you *what?*' Tom asked incredulously, his voice rising in spite of himself. He tried to control his feelings as he stared grimly at his brother, fighting a rising sense of disbelief and panic as he listened to Walt. Her *Special Hero?*

'Why, what did you do for her that was so special?'

'She says I saved her life, kept her afloat until she was rescued. I told her I can't remember a blessed thing about that night after I hit the water but she still keeps telling me that it was me?'

'Where did she get that information from?' Tom growled, his voice causing Walt to look at him sharply.

'I say, Tom, steady on, why are you getting so upset? I know you have a sweet spot for Bridgette but there's no need to start shouting at me just because it was me that saved her and not you!' Walt snapped, his own temper rising. 'Anyone would think you were jealous.'

'Walt!' Tom snapped back, 'Before you go on, take a moment to think. Go back to the night the ship foundered. How could you have been in any state to save anyone when you couldn't even save yourself? I came down to your mess and found you and helped you up to the side of the ship. Do you remember that happening? Can you then honestly say you were in a fit state that night to rescue anyone, let alone Bridgette Mathers?'

'I've tried to remember Tom. Every time she mentions it I try to envisage myself catching hold of her and keeping her afloat but it's no good. I just can't remember! All I feel is the coldness of the water and hearing you call for me and then—then it all goes black and I wake up clinging to a piece of wood and some sailor is shouting at me to hang on. There, are you satisfied now?'

'Walt,' Tom replied in a softer tone, 'I think Bridgette has the wrong idea about how she was rescued and from the information she was given by somebody, whoever it was, you seemed to fit the bill. Do you see what I'm getting at? Someone else saved her. She's just mixed the information up.'

Walt pondered for a moment. 'There was something she said that didn't make sense. Hang on, what was it—oh this bloody memory of mine. I know, she said Matron Green told her, said *she'd* said it was the Harding boy who'd brought her to the lifeboat. There, you see, it must have been me after all!'

Tom said nothing but looked at his brother searchingly. Walt reddened under his gaze and became uncomfortable, licking his lips and flexing his hands vigorously. A thought struck him and he stared at Tom angrily.

'Oh my God, I know what it is, you want me to think it was *you* who saved her, that's the truth of it Tom, isn't it? You're besotted with her. I know that much and now you want to worm your way into her good books by passing yourself off as her saviour! Tell me, Tom, am I wrong in thinking that?'

'No,' Tom replied steadily, 'you're not wrong in your assumption. It *was* me who pulled her over to the lifeboat, only Matron Green got us mixed up, not Bridgette. How is it you weren't rescued with us if it was you that saved her? I don't think the matron knew there were two Hardings on the ship so it was an easy mistake to make but you're wrong on the other count Walt, I don't need to make a story up about saving anyone to be in favour with Bridgette Mathers. We've spoken about after the war and she...'

'I knew it!' Walt shouted hotly, 'You worked your bloody charm on her and she fell for it! You think that because I owe you my life by coming back to the ward for me that night you can steal the one woman who cares for me and not you! Well, it won't work Tom, I've seen right through your little game and I tell you, it won't wash. Not with her, and certainly not with me, you rotter! It was like that time you stole dad's watch, you knew I wanted it but you kept it, you selfish bastard!'

Tom stepped back in astonishment. 'Dad's watch? Walt, you're feverish and talking rot. Aunt Elsie gave me the watch, you know she did. I didn't steal it, I was the eldest son. The watch was always going to come to me. If it means that much to you, I'll give you it. Just don't tell me I stole it. And where did you get the thought that Bridgette Mathers and you could—don't you see...?'

'You cold-hearted bastard!' Walt hissed. 'Keep the bloody watch! Now I know it was all about you, Tom, you don't give a fig for me as long as you get what you want. You'll throw your medal at me next, tell me what a pity it is I don't have one to dazzle her with. Go on get out, out of this fucking ward now and stay out, you hear?'

'Walt, I...'

'Out! Nurse? Nurse?'

Tom rose heavily from the bed. He turned and looked at the distraught face of his brother and said gently, 'Think on what I said Walt. You'll realise its all true. Nothing I said was for my benefit but at this moment you'd believe I was the Devil if someone put that idea before you. When you've calmed down, send me a message and we'll speak again. I'll not be back until you want me to come.'

Walt ignored him, his lips compressed into a thin line of hate, eyes looking straight ahead. Sighing, Tom walked from the ward as an anxious nurse bustled up the aisle towards them.

--§--

Bridgette Mathers hummed as she deftly folded the sheets into a pile and placed them on the shelves of the voluminous cupboard she stood in. She turned to leave and pulled up as the doorway was filled with the sneering face of Jack Wheeler.

'Well, if it ain't Miss Goody Two-shoes,' he smiled, 'Where's your boyfriend, he's not hiding in there with you is he? Oh no, don't tell me you and he have just had a...'

'You swine!' she cried, stepping back from him, 'What on earth are you talking about?'

Wheeler advanced on her, forcing her back into the depths of the cupboard. 'You know who and what I'm talking about, you cheap tart. That bloody Australian, that's who?'

She caught her breath, scared at his easy manner with her. 'Private Wheeler, if you don't stop this nonsense immediately, I'll scream for help and have you arrested. Do you hear me? Get out of my sight, now!'

His answer was to advance closer still and grab her lapel, pulling her close. His rank, unwashed smell drenched her nostrils and she struggled frantically to no avail. He pinned her to his torso like a moth on a lepidopterist's mount, mouth brushing her ear and she gagged at the foul smell of his breath.

'I know,' he whispered, 'oh I know what your fancy man's been up to. Some hero he is, shot a man, one of his own soldiers he did. Killed the blighter, boasted about it too and the poor helpless sod wounded and unable to stop the bastard from doing him in!'

'You lie!' she blazed, wrenching free and turning on him. 'Tom Harding would never do a thing like that!'

'I 'eard him with my own ears miss, told me and his mate the spiv with one leg that's what he done. Fancy that, shooting one of your own men. What sort of a bloke could do that, eh? I'm telling you, straight up, that's what he said he did and you'd better believe me. The thing is,' he whispered menacingly, 'what are we gonna do about it?'

'What do you mean, what are *we* going to do about it?' she asked in surprise.

'Yeah, *we*. You see,' he continued slyly, 'if you was to give me certain *favours* like I'm sure your Australian friend is enjoying then this doesn't have to go any further, does it?'

'What!'

He wrapped an arm round her, pawing at her bosom, breathing heavily. 'Look, how about I shut the door of this here cupboard and then I'll explain better. No-one will miss you. I certainly won't, if you get my meaning.'

Pulling a hand free she delivered a stinging blow to his face. 'You guttersnipe, do you really think I'd give myself to someone like you? Let me tell you, Wheeler, you've just ...'

'Don't you fucking dare!' he snarled, face twisted in a malevolent scowl. 'Don't go all hoighty-toighty on me, you snooty bitch! I'm a patient man, I'll give you until tomorrow afternoon and if you don't come over with the goods by then I'll have a quiet word with the Hospital Director and your chum will be on a capital charge before he can fucking sneeze! We still shoot people out here only we do it legal like, after a nice court-martial, unlike your Aussie's idea of justice. Think about it, you've got until tomorrow, I swear!'

She lent against the warm sheets, eyes closed in horror at his words and when she opened them again he was gone. She stayed leaning against the linen for some time as she pondered what Wheeler had told her. Pulling her blouse together she straightened her dress and cautiously opened the door before looking up and down the corridor. It was surprisingly empty and she slipped surreptitiously out of the cupboard and walked away, thinking furiously.

Tom's entry into Ward Nine the next morning was blocked by his old adversary, Sister McQueen. In his dark mood he moved to push brusquely past her but she laid a surprisingly gentle hand on his arm. 'Serjeant Harding, could I have a quiet word with you, here, through there.' She gestured at a small ante-chamber just inside the door and Tom followed her with a furrowed brow. What was the old cow up to now, what new evil was she about to visit on him. The sister pointed to a chair and said quietly, 'I think you'd better sit down, I have some bad news for you.'

'For me?' Tom asked in surprise.

'It concerns, Corporal Robertson, Archie. I have to say, that... Oh, look, there's no other way to say this so, please, bear with me. Archie's dying. I'm sorry, he's not got very much longer.'

Her quiet words stunned Tom, quelling any retort on his lips. He took a seat in stunned silence, shaking his head in disbelief at her words.

'I don't understand–I mean–he looked alright when I last saw him.'

'Look Tom...may I call you Tom?' He nodded, unable or unwilling to fully comprehend the import of her words and she continued. 'I know you and he had grown really close during your stay here, he only has a widowed mother as family back in England and it was good that he found someone like you to make him forget his wounds and talk with.'

'But I don't see, how did...?'

'Gangrene, Tom.' she enunciated with care, 'It's the biggest killer of all those poor men who arrive here and continues to take its toll long after we think we've conquered it. Archie's wound started to bleed again and when we examined it, it was obvious that the gangrene had re-appeared. We're so short of everything, drugs, bandages, well, you know, you've been here long enough to know what I mean. His body system is so low that it can't fight the infection and he's sinking lower with every hour. He hasn't got long. He's become delirious and I feel he won't survive the night.'

'Oh, God,' Tom croaked, 'we had such laughs and I really thought he was getting better.' He buried his head in his hands as her words struck home and she moved to lay a cool hand on his shoulder.

'Would you like to sit with him?' she asked. 'Only we're so busy with the other men that I can't spare anyone and it would be such a shame if he was to leave this earth alone, don't you think?'

He raised his head, moved by her simple kindness. 'Thank you, sister, I'd be glad to. Poor chap, I was so looking forward to him going home. Look, I'm sorry I was so rude when we first met."

She smiled faintly at him. 'It's quite all right, I know the men think I'm some sort of harridan... Don't!' she interjected, holding up an arm, 'I know that's what they call me, on a good day. We have a hard job to do here, Tom, and discipline is sometimes called for. I can be quite hard when I need to be but believe me, I do know the sorrow loss brings.' She pulled herself together. 'Never mind that, you go and sit with your friend and if you need anything, please let me know,'

'Thank you.' Tom replied simply.

He hurried from the room and made his way to Archie's bed. A pair of sheets had been draped respectfully around the bed and he pushed them aside and looked down at his friend. Archie Robertson lay asleep, his pale face almost matching the pillow in its whiteness and Tom's spirits sank to see his friend brought so low. He shuffled to the top of the bed and sat down carefully opposite Archie's shoulders.

The only sound was Archie's stentorian breathing, a loud snoring that filled his bedspace. Tom peered closely at his face but Archie gave no sign of recognising his presence so he continued to sit, staring out from the open window beyond the bed. Archie had commandeered this bed when a former occupant had left for England, declaring it had the best view of all the ward beds. Well, Archie, Tom thought, it won't be doing you much good for any longer. The thought saddened and depressed him and he bent low, rubbing his forehead with his free hand.

'Tom? Is that you, Tom?' A low voice broke into his reverie and he looked down into Archie's pain-filled face.

'You're awake. How do you feel?'

'Bloody daft question to ask a dying man, ain't it?' Archie responded weakly.

'Sorry.'

'Don't be. I do know what's going on in here.' He gestured feebly at his body. 'I'm sort of running out of steam. Pity, I'd have liked to take that job you promised me in Sydney.'

'Job? In Sydney? What job was that, Archie?'

'Don't tell me you're gonna welsh on me, you Aussie bastard. You know, the one-legged trapeze artist!'

Tom groaned in his despair. 'Archie, if I could I'd take you there myself, you'd make a cracking trapeze artist, one leg and all.'

'I know. Tom?'

'Yes?'

'Could I ask you a big favour, chum?'

'Archie, just ask.'

'Could you sit here for a while longer and hold my hand? Only remember, it's not like we're engaged or summat.'

Tom felt for his friend's hand under the covers and was shocked to feel how feeble Archie's pulse was. He clasped the hand firmly and brought it up onto the top of the covers, laying it down gently underneath his own, trapping Archie's fingers with his own.

'That's nice,' Archie whispered, 'Tom, did I ever tell you of the girl I once asked to marry me?'

'No, you never did.' Tom replied softly through his tears.

'She was a fine lass, from Bury like yourself, only her dad didn't approve, you know.'

'Why?' Tom asked, 'you'd have made a fine catch, Archie. What did he say was wrong with you?' There was no reply, just a sibilant hiss and when he lifted his hand, Archie's fell limply back onto the bed. He wept then, tears for Archie and all the other poor unfortunates who'd set out with such high hopes only to see them founder on the rocky shores of the peninsula.

--§--

He sat for a while, staring into space as he tried to come to terms with Archie's passing and before leaving, gently folded Archie's arms across his chest. The door to Archie's bedside locker yawned idly open and he frowned and pulled at the doors further. A quick glance inside confirmed his suspicions and his lips compressed into a hard, thin line before he straightened up, touched Archie's cheek and walked swiftly away.

A nurse walked towards him, a questioning expression on her pretty face but he dared not trust himself to speak and she passed him by with saddened, knowing eyes. He walked blindly upstairs to the verandah he and Archie had shared and it was there that Bridgette Mathers found him, looking disconsolately over the harbour below.

He turned sharply, relaxing as he recognised her. 'Bridgette, I'm glad you came,' he began, 'I've just left my friend Archie. He...'

'Tom,' she responded in a low voice, 'I've been everywhere looking for you, what's going on? After all we said to each other I can't believe you'd

292

act like this. I've just left Walt, he's in an awful state. Tom, how could you deceive your own brother like that?'

Her accusing stance rudely interrupted his train of thought and he glanced questioningly at her, thrown off balance by her manner. 'I'm sorry. You said, *deceive*, why on earth would I do that? I don't understand, what's this all about?'

'You know damn well!' she raged. 'Walt told me you said it was you who had rescued me the night of the sinking, not him. Tom, that's an outright lie, you couldn't have done anything that night, not with your injuries. Matron Green told me herself it was Walt so why would you do this?'

The swift change in her attitude towards him left him reeling and he hastened to quell her anger. 'Bridgette, I swear I told Walt the truth. If Matron Green had explained herself better you too might not have misunderstood the truth of the matter. She never knew about Walter being onboard and his being my brother unless you mentioned it to her. Did you tell her?' he demanded. She shook her head, unable to meet his eyes. 'No, I thought not. You couldn't remember anything that night after the ship sank and neither can Walt. Everything I told Walt was true, I went back down into the ship after I left you, found Walt trapped and released him. I helped him to the ship's side and we both went over the side as the ship foundered. He had dysentery, for God's sake; do you think that gave him superhuman strength enough to help you? *I* found you floating in the sea and *I* supported you for hours until help came in the shape of the lifeboat and Matron Green.

You and I were in that lifeboat. If Walt had helped you to it why wasn't he picked up with us as well? I didn't tell Walt this to make him feel less of a man, I told him everything to put a stop to any misunderstanding. If Matron Green informed you that the Harding boy rescued you, it was you who made the wrong assumption that it was Walt, do you see…?'

She broke in hotly, the floodgates of her anger a raging torrent at his questioning. 'Are you really asking me to believe you when a woman who was actually there swore it was Walt who came to my aid? And if that wasn't enough, what about this soldier you shot, one of your own men? Would someone who killed one of his own in cold blood become a would-be rescuer of women on a sinking ship? Not likely, a foul coward like that, he'd want to save his own neck not that of others.' Her temper was well and truly roused as she berated him in the white heat of an emotional loss of control, all rationale gone. 'Do you realise after what you've done that you could be shot if the authorities find out!'

Tom Harding's face turned deathly pale as he listened.

'Stop now. Who told you of that incident?' he said quietly, with an intensity that pulled her up short.

'You don't deny it, then?'

'I asked you a question, Bridgette Mathers. Who? Not Archie Robertson, I do know *he'd* never betray a friend's confidence, so who?' She shrank from the steel in his voice and suddenly felt quite alone. An inkling of impending disaster loomed before her but in her rage she blindly carried on, all the while unaware that her angry words were opening a yawning chasm between them. In her desire to wash away the humiliation she'd suffered at the hands of Jack Wheeler she dismissed her uncertainties and they remained unspoken, stillborn, as she continued to flay Tom with her accusations.

'You know fine well who it was that told me and it wasn't this Archie Robertson. Tom, you boasted about it to this person, he said you took great pride in speaking about killing a helpless, wounded man.'

'He said *that*, and you believed him? Without coming to me and asking for an explanation you'd take his word against that of mine?'

'What was I to believe, that it was all a lie? You've already lied to your brother, don't deny it, so who's to say you wouldn't lie to me about this or deny all knowledge of it?'

He stood up slowly and brushed imaginary sand from his clothes whilst trying to quell his raging inner feelings, choosing his words before turning to look at her. His voice carried with it an air of sad finality.

'Bridgette, I could be accused of lots of things but not a liar, a coward *and* a killer. Not at the same time, surely? There are so many questions here and so few answers. What do you really know, or think you know? I told of certain matters that had happened in confidence to someone I believed would keep them safe. It's obvious he had as little regard for me as you do now, he used that information to try and drive a wedge between us for his own ends and it's succeeded. You two deserve each other so go to him, be with him, he wants you and I'm done here. All the things I'd hoped and cared about will not be found between us now.

What I did that first day will haunt me forever. I see that poor beggar's face every night. Every night! But if a crime *was* committed as you allege, I'll answer for it to a higher authority than those incompetents on the other side of the water. A poor man's death, someone I'd never met before or knew, lies on my conscience and I'll bear that responsibility for the rest of my life but I defy anyone to regard that death as a crime. No-one, not a real soldier and comrade, would censure me for my actions so what gives you the right to call my compassion an act of murder? You ask, *"What if the authorities find out?"* You stupid, misinformed woman, *all* the deaths staining my hands have been done on their behalf. What the bloody hell do you think we're doing here?'

He pushed past her and she heard his footsteps echoing down the stairs and swayed dizzily, holding faintly onto the door as she frantically digested his words. How could she believe that a brave, decent man like Tom Harding would bare his soul to one such as Jack Wheeler but there was no mistaking the fact that Wheeler *had* given her that information and Tom hadn't denied a single word. Something was gravely wrong here. How did he think she could be involved with anyone as foul as Wheeler and where had he found out that the orderly had made his loathsome advances to her?

Just what was his relationship with that blackguard? It didn't add up; in her heart she knew she'd made a huge mistake in her easy acceptance of his guilt and that thought stayed with her as she made her way shakily across the verandah and sat down on the wicker chair. A premonition that her life had changed irrevocably in the instant she'd accused Tom Harding washed over her and she slumped against the rail.

'Oh, God, what have I done?'

--§--

Two floors below, Tom made his way along the corridor, seething, his mind a sea of emotions. It was obvious to him that Walt had spun some story to Bridgette Mathers enough for her to fly at him as she'd done. How else had she found out about the death of the wounded soldier that first day of the landings and what other lies had his brother poured into her ears? A small fire ignited in his belly and blazed higher as the harsh words she'd flung at him were poured onto the flames. When next he spoke to Walt there were some harsh truths to be told.

In his anger he barged into another figure without looking and opened his mouth to apologise. 'Sorry, mate... *You!*' The other man turned to escape but Tom restrained him. 'Come here Wheeler, I want a word' Tom looked the sullen figure opposite up and down. 'I was right, I thought you'd stolen it, you bastard.' Jack Wheeler squirmed from Tom's hand and began to hurry in the opposite direction but to no avail. A hand of steel clamped itself round his shoulder and he was forced round to confront his aggressor.

'That chain you're wearing, take it out of your top pocket. Now, God dammit!'

'Eh?'

'I won't ask again, the chain, pull it out of your pocket. Show me what's on the other end.'

Reluctantly, Wheeler did as he was ordered and the two men looked down at the gold hunter watch nestling in his palm.

'I'm only going to ask you once, you fucking weasel, where did you get that watch?'

'*Ouch*, lemme go!' Wheeler whined, 'You got no right to...*oof!*' A fist sank deep into his midriff as all Tom Harding's pent-up emotions were put into the blow and he doubled over in pain and surprise. He would have fallen but Tom grabbed him as he fell and jerked him upright.

'Now, answer the question. Where did you get that watch?'

'You know damn fine.' A wheeze spilled from Wheeler lips as he tried to suck in breath, '*Uuh*. Your mate sold it to me, only this morning. I gave him a good price for it, too, he said he needed the cash for...*Uurggh!*'

Tom struck him once with his good hand; a terrible crushing blow on the cheek and Wheeler fell as if pole-axed. Bending over his recumbent figure, Tom rasped, 'Archie Robertson died today. He's not been gone but a few hours and you robbed his corpse, you ghoul! A good man died and scum like you live and rob them of all their precious belongings.'

Wheeler tried to speak but Tom hoisted him up one-handed, struck him again and Wheeler slumped to the floor unconscious. Tom bent and plucked the watch from his fingers. Another thought struck him as he looked down on Wheeler's sprawled figure. 'You!' he breathed. 'It was you who spread the word about Bridgette Mathers round the ship, wasn't it? You wanted her and there was no way she'd look at a bastard like you so you made sure everyone heard about her troubles, didn't you?'

He kicked Wheeler viciously in the stomach and hefted the watch. 'There are better folk in this world more deserving of this than you. If I see you again, I'll kill you and that's the truth!' He left him lying on the floor and walked away oblivious to the stares of the passers by.

--§--

They came for him as he sat sipping a ruminative cup of tea in the canteen, two heavily-armed Provost Corps men and a weedy, thin-faced civilian. 'That's him!' the civilian cried, 'That's the creature who assaulted my medical orderly. Arrest him at once, serjeant!'

'Yessir. Alright, chum, you're to come with us and no messing, do you understand?'

'Perfectly,' Tom said calmly, 'can I have a few moments to put my kit together for safe keeping? I need to do that as there's so many thieves hanging around here.'

He was escorted to a large office belonging to the thin-faced man who turned out to be the Hospital Director. Settling himself importantly behind the desk the Director looked round as Tom was led in. 'We'll not take long here, do you know the penalty for assaulting a medical orderly in the pursuit of his duties. Let me tell you...'

'He's a thief, he robs the dead.' Tom interrupted quietly but his words carried to all in the room.

'You have no proof of that.' the man blustered.

'Archie Robertson, a corporal in the 1st Lancashire Fusiliers, died today and that creature of yours robbed him of a gold pocket watch while Archie's body was still warm. I saw Archie with the watch, Wheeler offered to buy it and was refused and the next I saw of it your orderly was wearing it.' Tom stated bluntly. 'Wheeler told me he'd bought it but that was all lies. Archie Robertson was dying, there was no way he'd part with that watch on his deathbed, no way at all.'

'Where's the watch now?' the Director asked sharply, 'Don't tell me, you kept it, for, ah, good luck I assume.' he smiled smugly.

'Wrong.' Tom replied steadily, 'I have my own, look, here it is. What would I want another one for? You see, mine came with me when I was wounded. Aussie medical orderlies don't rob their mates.' He added blithely, 'What's the term the men have for you RAMC chaps? *Rob All My Comrades*, isn't it?'

He continued. 'I took Corporal Robertson's watch to the hospital Post Office after gaining Archie's home address from the ward sister. It's on its way home to his mother, the rightful owner, right now. It's true,' seeing the look of surprise and disbelief on the Director's face, 'go and ask the sister and then take yourself off to the Post Office. I made sure I was recognised when I was there, they'll confirm that a package containing a watch was sent to Mrs Robertson of Bury, England. I packed it in front of them so they could all see the package's contents.'

'*Harrumph*! Most irregular. But there's also the matter of the assault on Private Wheeler, you'll still be facing charges over that matter, my good man. That should wipe the smile off your face!'

297

'I'm sorry, sir, but I don't think so.'

'What? Damn your impertinence, do you think you're going to get off scot-free? Think again.'

'I think *you* should, sir. You see, I'm not here with the British army and I don't think you have jurisdiction over us Australians, something to do with you British shooting a few of us in the Boer War without asking.'

Perplexed by this sudden turn of events the Director turned to the Provost Corps men. 'Is this true?' he demanded, 'Is he telling the truth?'

The Provost Serjeant thought for a moment then slowly nodded. 'I 'aven't a clue about the Boer War but if he's an Aussie then I reckon he's telling the truth, sir. We'll have to turn him over to them and let his own people deal with him.'

'Get him out of here now!' the Director demanded, 'I want him on a train to Cairo today, do you hear? And when I find out who let an Australian stay in my hospital there'll be hell to pay.'

'Yes sir. Alright, you, come along now.'

They marched along the corridor but when they were clear of the office the Provost Serjeant pulled up short and turned to Tom.

'Right, chum. Before we go and collect your kit and stuff you on a train, as Mr Davidson's wanting, you and me are going for a little walk to my office, have a quiet word, like.'

'You think so?' Tom said heatedly, 'I've only one good arm at the moment but let me tell you, serjeant, I'm not going to take your *quiet words* without a fight.'

'Don't be so bloody stupid, man, you 'an me are going to have a quiet celebratory drink while you tell me all about our Private Wheeler. That little shit's been getting his way far too easily around here, thinks he's *Cock of the North* but now with your help we're going to take him down a peg or two.

Making a few bob flogging dodgy fruit is one thing, robbing your own comrades is another and I'm not having it here. You'll be on a train to Cairo tonight alright, but that bastard's going in the other direction. They've had a bad run on Medical Orderly's over at Cape Helles, for some reason they're quite unable to stop a bullet so we're going to send them Private Wheeler and see if he's any different. I wouldn't give him five minutes, especially as I'm gonna write a note to my pal over there, he'll make sure Wheeler gets placed in the thick of it.'

Nah, don't thank me, you've done us a favour giving that sod a good hiding. He whined something about you being involved in a shooting but he's a liar and I told him that to his face straight. Getting rid of

298

him'll send a message to anyone else contemplating something similar. We take care of you proper soldiers over here. Savvy?' Now let's go and 'ave that *chota peg* I was babbling about.'

--§--

Replete, he settled back into the cushioned seat of the carriage as the evening train pulled out of Alexandria on its way up the line to Cairo and for him the delights of No.1 Australian General Hospital in Heliopolis. The journey normally took five hours and if he was lucky, on arrival in the capital he'd be able to catch an electric tram out to the hospital, formerly an upmarket hotel, in the suburbs. The Grand Hotel and its two thousand rooms had been requisitioned as a military hospital soon after the arrival of the ANZAC Corps. A gloomy rumour going round was that the authorities only requisitioned it when they saw the British plans and realised how many casualties the coming campaign would bring.

He'd not had time to confront Walt but no matter, the serjeant and his men had found him a second-hand uniform to replace his hospital garb and a pack for his kit, all the while ensuring his glass was filled until it was time for him to leave for the station. They'd pushed past the crowds of hawkers and stalls filling the concourse to bundle him safely into the carriage where he now sat.

The soothing effects of the alcohol had gone some way in dimming his anger and despair and although the air was enticingly balmy, a sweet scented evocation of the East, he was oblivious to its charms as he slumped deeper into the seat and mulled over the day's events in his mind. He'd miss Archie's funeral and at the present time that hurt far more than his altercation with Bridgette.

A beggar pressed his face against the window, his pleading cries of *"Baksheesh, sahib!!"* going unheeded as Tom stared blindly past him through the glass. A sharp pressure on his left buttock forced him back to the present and he delved into the trouser pocket on that side and looked down. Nestling in his hand was a gold locket, one a medical orderly had haggled for on his behalf in the bazaar. It was to have been a present for Bridgette, to replace the one she'd lost but he thrust it angrily back into his pocket and tried to remember.

In his fatigued state he failed to pick out the events that had overtaken him so quickly but his strength deserted him and before succumbing to sleep's embrace he thought once more of Bridgette Mathers and her hate-filled accusations. All his hopes had been dashed, leaving him with the bitter, sour taste of ashes in his throat. She was wrong, so very wrong but it was too late to address the matter now, best to let it lie. Forget her and get back to the Peninsula and the friends he'd left there.

As for Walt, he felt a deep sense of betrayal at his brother's actions in relaying their private conversation in order to alienate Bridgette Mathers. That his disloyalty had succeeded he could only sadly concur and he tried to picture his brother's face and imagine the triumph he must now be feeling. Sleep would not be forsaken and before he could bring Walt to the fore he slid into a deep, dreamless cocoon.

--§--

'Oh my back.' Madeleine Green straightened up and ruefully arched her back after climbing out of the motor ambulance that had brought her back to the hospital. Cairo had been a welcome rest but she had needed to get back to her charges and now here she was at last. The journey back to Alexandria had been long and she'd arrived stiff and sore but that was small beer to what lay ahead.

As she dropped her suitcase in the cool interior of the portico she saw a familiar face and smiled. 'Sister Mathers, over here!' she called gaily. Her smile faded as she saw the anguished look on the nurse's face.

'My goodness, what is it my dear?'

'Matron, thank God you're here, please, I must talk to you.'

'Yes, yes, of course, let me call an orderly and we can go to my—'

'No, it can't wait. Tell me, please the night we, I was saved. Who was it that saved me, can you remember? Please Matron, it's most urgent. You once told me it was "*the Harding boy.*" Can you remember which one?'

'Which one? Why, there only was one, Miss Mathers, you know, the one who saved you. Now what was his first name? Oh dear, this memory of mine. Wait a minute, he was Australian, a real gentleman and a hero, if you ask me. Tom! That was his name, Thomas Harding!' she concluded triumphantly.

Bridgette Mathers slid to the floor in a dead faint, leaving Madeleine Green gaping foolishly at her.

'Oh my goodness, whatever's come over the poor girl? Orderly? Orderly!'

Chapter Fifteen.

Anzac Cove. July

The sun's rays beat down on the upturned faces crowding the lighter as they neared the beach. The sun was a bright shining orb in the clear sky and Tom was grateful for the shade his slouch hat granted him from the effects of the searing heat. Looking round, he was amazed to see how the cove's appearance had changed in the months since he was last there. The scene was almost unrecognisable from the early days of the landings; makeshift lean-to's and holes dug into the hillsides had given way to more substantial constructions and a sense of permanence. Jetties stretched their way several yards out into the water and everywhere he looked he could see piles of sandbags strengthening the dugouts and great dumps of ammunition and foodstuffs set back far from the water's edge.

The greatest change he observed was in the attitude of the men themselves. Gone was the boundless, carefree enthusiasm of the early days, replaced it seemed by a surly, sullen air of forbearance. Scowls evident on the faces of those inhabiting the beach told of every movement begrudged, carried out in a stoical fashion without smile or banter. A shell sent up a white wall of water far over to their right but no-one on the beach moved save the new men who shuffled closer together. This outward feeling of discontent was evident in the old hand's clothing, many wearing ragged shorts and torn shirtsleeves with khaki strips poking out from under the rear of their caps, making each soldier sporting them look like a foreign legionnaire in silhouette.

'Strewth, mate.' the man to his left muttered, 'Looks like a bloody goldfield settlement. All we need now is a bar at the end of the pier and we're set for a good time.'

'I wouldn't count on it.' Tom replied, squinting into the sun as he tried to get his bearings.

The soldier glanced curiously at him. 'You bin here before then, cobber?' he enquired.

'You could say that.'

His companion looked round at the hills gleaming above them in the heat of the midday sun. The sound of rifle fire reverberated faintly from their tops and he listened curiously. 'Is that where the Abduls are dug in?' he enquired, 'Seems a long way to go for a fight, if you ask me.'

'Don't worry, they're not that far away and believe me, you don't have to go to them for a fight, they come to you.'

'So you've seen some action, then? I can't wait to stick one of those dirty bastards.'

'Don't be so eager.'

'So you *have* been in a scrap with them?'

'Some.'

'What was it like?'

'You'll find out soon enough.' The soldier shrugged his shoulders and turned away to resume his looksee. Tom opened his mouth to speak but held his tongue. He hadn't meant to be rude but it was no use, nothing he could have explained would have prepared the young man for what was in store. Better he find out himself the hard way rather than rely on someone else's memories, his enthusiasm for killing Turks would soon wane after a week in the lines. He shifted his pack nearer his feet and frowned.

Lying by his left foot was a bundle of firewood, thin sticks of wood tied together with string. Each of them had been given a bundle as they'd left the transport but no-one had explained where or how they were to dispose of the sticks. Firewood was obviously at a premium here and for a moment he toyed with the idea of leaving the bundle on the floor of the lighter but his thoughts were interrupted by a sharp, grinding noise as they edged alongside the main landing place of Watson's Pier.

'Right, you lot, everyone out and report to that bloke over there with the red armband.'

Grumbling, they hefted their packs and rifles and did as they were told, angling off the pier to where an important-looking 2/Lt stood impatiently waiting, a red armband prominent on his left arm.

'Come on, come, you men, get a move on, we haven't got all day!' he shouted.

'Hold yer horses, mate, we're doing our best.' a young private protested but a fierce glare from the officer quelled any further protest.

'Line up over here in order of rank and we'll get you sorted out as quickly as possible.' As they moved to obey he suddenly dropped his clipboard and dived full length on the sand. Without thinking, Tom grabbed his companion from the cutter and dragged him to the floor as the others looked on in amazement.

'What...?'

'Get your head down and keep it that way.' Tom snarled but his voice was drowned by the approaching scream of a shell. It landed seventy yards away, exploding in a massive cloud of sand and shingle and dimly through his ringing ears Tom caught the sound of a man screaming and knew someone had been caught by the deadly fragments. He turned anxiously to the soldier alongside him but the youngster shook his head. 'No, sarje, it's not me.' He pointed down the beach. 'Oh God, there.' His throat worked violently and he threw up on to the sand as Tom looked past him. Taking in a scene of sprawled bodies and mangled, bloodied flesh strewn a few yards from where they lay he shook the youngster's shoulder.

'Come on, son, up you get. There's nothing we can do, the stretcher bearers'll sort those poor buggers out. Thank God you've not been knocked, brush yourself down and let's find that officer and get off the damn beach before the Turks sling another shell our way.'

'Is it like this every day?' the youngster enquired as he picked himself up wiping his mouth. 'Only I'm sure I ticked a different box on my Attestation Form when they asked me what I wanted to do.' He looked back, his tanned face a deathly shade of white. 'Christ, I've never seen a dead bloke before, that's some way to complete my education!'

In spite of himself Tom laughed grimly. 'You'll get over it, mate. There's a lot worse sights to see here. Tom Harding, serjeant, ex-9th Battalion.' He said this by way of greeting, extending a hand. It was grabbed firmly by the fresh-faced private who smiled in response, although his face still held traces of shock.

'Cornelius Ryan, Coney to me mates, private, no bloody unit at all yet. They put me in some reinforcement mob but God knows I forgot the number, sarje. You don't think they'll send me back to Egypt for that, do you?'

Tom laughed. 'You'll have to think of a better excuse, I'm afraid.'

He was interrupted by the voice of the 2/lt calling them to him and without further ado walked over to where the officer stood.

'Welcome to Gallipoli, men, now where were we?'

When it came to his turn the officer scrutinised his clipboard before glaring at Tom. 'Serjeant Harding, right? You're out of uniform, serjeant, I have you down here as a DCM holder, is that true?'

As Tom nodded grimly in assent he continued. 'Well, it's no bloody good you turning up here without wearing the ribbon. You'll be going to 'B' Company of the 14th Battalion so as soon as you get there, indent for some ribbon and get it sown on your tunic. Got it?'

'Is there no way I can go back to my own mob, sir? I was with the 9th and…'

'Look, serjeant,' the officer snapped, 'I haven't got time to stand here and argue the bloody toss about where you *want* to go, I'm telling you where you *are* going so why don't you just do as you're told?' Tom nodded again, anger rising deep within him as he continued to stare steadily at the young 2/lt. His gaze discomfited, the man reddened before turning to the private stood alongside Tom. 'And don't stare at an officer like that or I'll do you for insolence, DCM or no DCM. Bugger off over there,' he pointed to a dugout on the far side of the hill, 'and don't let me see you again.'

Throwing him an immaculate salute, Tom marched away erect, contempt obvious in his posture. He was joined by a breathless Cornelius Ryan who slid opposite him. 'Did I hear that bludger right, sarje, you've got the DCM?' Tom glanced askance at him and continued to walk on but Ryan wouldn't be put off. 'Wow, fancy, I'm walking next to a hero.' Tom grunted sourly but the youngster ignored his response and chattered on. 'Did you kill a lot of the Jacko's to win your medal? What was it like?'

Tom wheeled round on him. 'Like I said on the beach, son, you'll soon find out.'

Unfazed, Ryan grinned. 'Keep yer shirt on sarje, we're going to be mates.'

'Oh yeah. How?'

'That bastard's sent me to the 14th with you. Same company too, so we'll be mates then, eh?'

'I just knew this was going to be my lucky day!' Tom breathed.

It wasn't just Anzac Cove. So much in his life had changed since he was last here. On arrival in Cairo he'd made his way to the Australian hospital in the former resort town of Heliopolis where he'd been perfunctorily examined and assigned to a ward for the next two weeks. At his persistent nagging a medical board had examined him and reluctantly granted his request to return to the front. The weeks spent in quiet contemplation on a hospital ward had failed to assuage the anger and sorrow he felt at his betrayal by Walt and Bridgette. A letter arriving just before his departure, marked *Urgent!* was savagely torn to shreds before an astonished mail clerk upon his recognising the scent of her perfume on the envelope.

It had been with no small measure of relief that he'd boarded the train back to Alexandria and the docks where a sleepy transport waited impatiently for the next band of lambs to be embarked for the slaughter. He'd recognised the frontage of the hospital buildings as they were conveyed from the station but had deliberately turned his glance away, a gesture of finality in a decision not to reconcile the past with the future awaiting him.

--§--

Back at Anzac Cove a helpful clerk in the Battalion HQ sent them on their way with directions, his helpfulness fortified by their present to him of the bundles of firewood. Fifty men of the 14th had been sent to man the firestep and so the clerk sent them to join the group who'd already departed. Together Tom and his young companion made for Monash Gully before the climb up a spur to the ridge above.

After negotiating Shrapnel Valley safely they turned into the entrance to Monash Gully. Ryan pulled at Tom's shoulder. 'What's that lot over there?' he enquired.

Tom followed his pointing finger. In a makeshift barbed-wire compound ringed by sandbags sat four or five dishevelled-looking men in drab khaki uniforms. Listlessly they swayed on their haunches as they looked around them from under towelling wrapped round their heads to ward off the heat of the sun.

'Those poor blokes? They're Turk prisoners, real Jacko's.'

'You don't say. Half a mo', I wanna have a quick dekko at them.'

Before Tom could speak the young Australian hurried over and stood gazing down on the prisoners. None returned his gaze and he looked round with a wide grin as Tom approached.

'Is this what we're facin', mate, they don't look that dangerous to me.'

'You'll find out soon enough, Ryan,' Tom rasped, 'they may not look like anything to you but they fight like hell and almost always never surrender. They suffer the same conditions we do and still come up game as anything. We're all the same in this shithole so take a good look, this is probably the nearest you'll get to a living one!'

He turned on his heel and after a moment's hesitation, Cornelius Ryan trotted after him. Together they resumed their trek in silence

'Hang on, cobber,' Ryan puffed as they climbed steeply upwards, 'this is killing me. No-one said we had to be bloody mountain goats to get there!' Recognising the wisdom of his young companion's words, Tom relaxed his pace and slowed to allow Ryan to catch him up.

They trudged on up through the maze of trenches and saps in silence, stopping from time to time to ease their packs off and take in huge gulps of warm, fetid air. A Turkish machine-gun opened up without warning and they hurriedly ducked down as the bullets sped overhead. Gunfire eerily reverberated from all sides but both men were too exhausted to notice from which direction the fire came and were perspiring freely when they finally reached their destination, a deep set of trenches at the far end of the plateau.

A sentry pointed out their company's positions. 'Keep yer heads down, mate,' a helpful voice cried and they ducked involuntarily, 'Abdul's been cracking on at knocking one of us all bloody morning.'

As if in confirmation a bullet *whirred* wickedly overhead and they redoubled their steps along the crowded trench to where a casual figure wearing the badges of a captain on his frayed shirt watched them approach with some amusement.

'You two must be the new blokes?' he said, rising to a half-crouch. 'Come on in and let's see if we can't whistle up a cuppa for yous. The name's Redford, no need to salute.' He turned and disappeared inside a dugout entrance and Tom pushed Cornelius Ryan's shoulder, impatiently gesturing for the youngster to follow. They dropped their packs outside and squeezed in, a fresh trickle of sweat leeching from them instantly in the sweltering atmosphere within the sparsely-furnished dugout.

'Holland!'

A dark unshaven figure poked his head through the entrance.

'What is it, Doug?'

'Get some char for these two. And get a bloody shave, we're on active service!'

'Yeah? That'll be right, mate.' the figure spat sardonically before disappearing from view.

Doug Redford laughed aloud. 'Don't mind that tosser,' he said easily, speaking to the two amazed men sat on the floor before him, 'we don't stand on ceremony here but Private Holland does take the mickey a bit too well sometimes. However, he does make bloody good tea so I tend to overlook his familiarity a lot of the time. Right,' he continued, 'who've we got here? You first.' he said, pointing at Tom.

'Serjeant Thomas Harding, ex-9th Battalion, sir'

'The 9th, you say. Were you with them on the first day?'

Tom nodded.

'I heard you blokes took a hammering that day. Would that be right?'

'Sort of.' Tom replied dryly, causing Redford to snort in derision.

'A modest man, by God! Well, serjeant, if you got through that alright we could use your experience here. And you?' he said, turning to where Ryan sat, 'What about you, son?'

'Private Cornelius Ryan, sir, new in from Egypt. Coney to me mates. I'm here to kill Jacko's for you.'

'Bugger me, I don't believe it,' Redford grinned, '*another* modest man!' Ryan squirmed in embarrassment but Doug Redford hastened to placate him. 'I'm only funning, son, take that look off'n your dial. Don't worry, you'll get lots of opportunities to kill as many Jacko's as you want. Dying is something they don't seem to mind, the way they carry on when they attack. Would you agree, Harding?'

Tom nodded grimly.

'He should know, sir, Serjeant Harding's got the DCM.' Coney Ryan found his tongue and at his words Doug Redford sat upright and appraised Tom with fresh eyes. 'The DCM? You don't say? There's not many of those been awarded round here,' he mused. 'sometimes I think we Aussies are deliberately overlooked but I heard some great news this morning. One of our own blokes has just been awarded the Victoria Cross, the first Aussie to do so. Name of Jacka, Bert Jacka. Do any of you know him?'

They both shook their heads as Redford continued. 'I joined this mob after his exploits in May at Courtney's Post. Apparently he went bush and started killing as many Turks as stood in front of him. Those he didn't shoot he used the bloody bayonet on. A one-man army so if you see him when it's time for some tucker, better let him have his first, eh.'

They both joined in the laughter which was interrupted by the appearance of some lukewarm tea in misshapen metal mugs swarming with flies and borne by a grumbling, sweating Holland. Swatting several large flies from his mug, Redford motioned for the other two men to join him and they gratefully accepted his offer, brushing clouds of flies from their lips as they hungrily sucked in the sweet tea. When all three mugs were empty, Doug Redford looked over to them.

'Right, now that's over and done with, I want you two to continue down the trench about fifty yards and ask for a Serjeant Lindsay. Got that? Good. Tell him I sent you and he's to fix you up with some tucker and that he's to use you tonight.'

'To use us, sir, what for?' Ryan's eyes opened wide in surprise

'We're going back to the beach area tomorrow to join the rest of the mob but before we do we've been told we're going over to surprise Johnny Turk in his trenches. Some bloody rubbish about taking new intelligence down with us. My eye! Now that you're here you might as well get stuck in with the rest of us.'

'Cripes! Orlright, I'm game for that. Thanks—' Ryan's words were lost as Tom leant forward and spoke rapidly.

'Come on, sir, he's just a boy, new to this. I'll go, no worry, but do you have to use him? He's only just arrived today and doesn't half a clue what's going on. Let him acclimatise first and then see what he's like.'

Doug Redford's genial features twisted into a grimace. 'Look, Harding, I know what you mean but I've got fourteen blokes already crook in my company and those left hardly have the strength to lift a rifle. Look around you, what you can't stuff in your mouth as soon as the tucker arrives, the bloody flies steal. You can't open your mouth and you'll get thousands of the little buggers crawling in. The men go crook in their hundreds every day, from dysentery, enteric fever, the trots, you bloody well name it and a bloke goes down with it.

We're all dehydrated because we don't get enough water but do HQ give a stuff? Do they hell! Those bastards on the beach get their allowance and more but up here the blokes are permanently dehydrated for lack of a couple of pints of water a day.

I'm told to stick it out until the next stunt and we'll push Johnny Turk back to the Bosphorus. Yeah? Not in my lifetime!' He passed a weary hand over his brow. 'Although we're going down the ridge tomorrow, we'll be back as quick as Christ lets us, you'll see. You two are a Godsend. I've been told to leap over to the Turk's trenches tonight and have a dekko and to do that I need good, strong, men. You two fit the bill.'

He glanced at Ryan's expectant face. 'Don't worry, son, I'm not leaving you out and we'll see you get through it alright.'

'No worries, sir, I won't let you down.' Coney Ryan could hardly contain himself and Tom's heart sank. He nodded at Redford and shuffled to the entrance with Ryan following him.

'Try and get an hour or two's kip before we go.' Captain Redford's last words hurried them down the trench and Tom swore savagely as his foot caught a sleeping man who cursed them roundly before subsiding back to sleep.

'Aw, come on, sarje, it won't be that bad.' Ryan protested and Tom rounded on him.

'Stop your chattering, you fool and listen. Can you hear that?'

'Hear what?'

'I said listen.'

After several seconds, Ryan shook his head in puzzlement. 'I don't get what you're on about, I don't hear a thing.'

Tom sighed. 'Can't you hear anything at all?' he demanded.

'Er, I… Sort of. There's a faint tinkling noise, now that you mention it. Like…cowbells. What is it?'

'It's rats, thousands of the little bastards. Little did I say, some are as big as horses but that's the least of our problems.'

'Hang on, sarje, how can rats make that kind of noise, it sounds like something metal's out there?'

'It is. Where do you think the bully tins go when the blokes have emptied the food out of them? Well?'

'I'm not sure where this is leading, what've bully tins got to do with it?'

'If a fairly small thing like a rat can make that sort of noise scavenging among the hundreds of tins our blokes have heaved over the parapet what sort of noise do you think we'll make later on tonight, in the dark, when we start tramping on those very same tins with our size nines and above? Not to mention the rotting corpses that are strewn everywhere. Step on one of them and you'll yell out, sure as Christ, when your foot goes straight through his guts. Now do you see what I'm getting at?'

'I think so.' Ryan replied slowly as he contemplated the import of Tom's words.

'You don't have to be able to see in the dark, all you need to do is listen,' Tom spoke quietly as they squirmed round a tight traverse, 'if the Turk's ears are as good as yours and mine they'll hear us coming through the gaps in our wire from a mile away. Redford knows it, I know it and now you know it. Captain Redford was right, try and get some kip when we arrive where we're supposed to be. It might be your last for some time.'

'Garn. You're just trying to scare me.' Coney scoffed but his open features twisted into a concerned frown as he continued to follow Tom down the trench. He stopped suddenly, causing Tom to turn. 'What's wrong now?'

'Strewth, the smell, what the flaming hell is that?'

'Oh, that,' Tom replied, 'it's the dead. Death and shit, all mixed together. You'll soon get used to it or join them. Have a good look, you'll see some of the corpses are strung out along the parapet. Better a dead body copping a bullet than another of us being knocked.' '

A paler Ryan followed him as they reached the scrape in the wall occupied by Serjeant Joe Lindsay.

--§--

'Psst!'

A silence ensued, followed by a renewed attempt to make contact. *'Psst!'*

'What, what is it?' Tom whispered hoarsely.

'Did the serjeant say I was to follow you when we go over, or him? I've forgotten.'

Tom looked sideways. In the paleness of the moon Ryan's face looked deathly white and a faint tic pulsed in the left-hand corner of his features. 'Look, just you keep your eyes on me and do what I do. Alright?'

The youngster gripped the pick handle he was carrying even tighter and tried to force a faint smile on his face. 'Thanks, mate, I'll be looking out fo—'

'*Shh.* Here's Lindsay, we must be going now. Keep your mouth shut and do as I do.'

'Rightho.'

Joe Lindsay passed them and as he did so, reached over and squeezed both men's arms. They nodded in return and he took a few more steps before lifting himself easily out over the parapet, gesturing for them to follow. The four other waiting solders hung back so Tom moved forward and followed Lindsay out of the trench.

It was pitch-black, with only a shadow of the moon providing scant light. His own breathing sounded like an approaching locomotive to Tom and he willed himself to calm down and regulate his breath. Dimly ahead of him he could see the upturned soles of Joe Lindsay's boots and he began to crawl in the same direction, taking care to plant his hands and feet carefully in front and behind. He carried a stout cudgel in one hand and made sure it, too, made no sound as he grounded it. Noises from his rear announced the arrival of the others and he breathed a trifle easier. The Turks were only forty yards away so it was imperative everyone kept as quiet as they could.

Tom and Coney Ryan had met with a wearied Joe Lindsay and after dumping their packs, tried to escape from the heat of the sun and grab a few hours troubled sleep. The evening had brought a tepid dish of, cheese and hard biscuits with some indifferent tea tasting faintly of muddied clay before a makeshift plan of attack had been explained.

They were to crawl over to the Turkish trenches and see how well-manned they were, hurl bombs into the nearest bay and try to drag a prisoner back with them. Living or dead, it didn't matter, it was explained, anything the prisoner's body gave up would provide useful information. Tom thought the plan ludicrous and a sure-fire way to lose men in the process but wisely, as the new man, kept his counsel.

The enemy trenches were a distant blur and he wiped the sweat from his eyes with his free hand and crawled onwards. He moved smoothly through the gap that opened up before him in the wire, careful not to snag his clothing on it but a sudden rattling to his left caused him to pull up sharply and he hissed urgently into the dark. 'Keep the bloody noise down!' The rattling continued and his anxiety rose. The Turks would hear the same noise any second now and all hell would break loose.

'*Whatthe*...!' A body bumped into him and he looked over in surprise as Ryan surged past, a fixed look of terror on his face. Tom reached out to restrain him but Ryan shook off his hand and before Tom's amazed gaze stood up and began to stride forward in great steps.

Forgetting his own fear, Tom stood, caught up with him and grabbed at Coney's hand. 'Get down you fool, you'll give us away!' he spoke in a low voice.

'Lemme go, sarje, I ain't crawling anymore like a bloody dog! Come on, let's run over there and give it to them.' Ryan spoke loudly and Tom winced.

'*Shh*, for God's sake!'

Whoosh!

A flare arced skywards from the trenches opposite and Tom froze as the landscape around him was bathe in an eerie, intense light. The sudden burst of light only served to unsettle Ryan more and he wheeled round, eyes like a hunted deer as he frantically sought to escape from the grasp of the blinding glare.

'Stand still, don't move!' Throwing caution to the wind Tom grasped hold of Cornelius Ryan's sleeve firmly and tried to quell his desire to run. 'If you move, we're dead meat.'

'Lemme go!' the youngster screamed as another flare burst directly overhead.

Ryan wrenched wildly from Tom's grasp and turned to run back but a sharp-eyed Turkish gunner had seen the movement and quickly swivelled his machine-gun in their direction. *Brrtt! Brrtt! Thwack!* A hammer blow struck the side of Tom's chest and he gasped in agony with its impact. He tried to remain upright but his knees buckled and he slowly fell to the ground, grunting with shock. Lying, full-length he felt earth trickle into his open mouth, brutally stifling any sounds of pain he might have made and he willed his hand to move in that direction to try and clear his throat. His fingers stubbornly refused to obey this

311

command as a feeling of light-headedness overtook him and a warm, wet sensation spread through his lower body.

From a long way distant he heard shouting and the scream of an animal in mortal pain. A body thudded down alongside him. Twisting round with an effort he gazed into the open face of Cornelius Ryan, a perplexed look on eyes that were rapidly glazing with the opaque filminess of death.

'Oh God, no.'

Painfully, he raised himself up to crawl in the youngster's direction only to fall as the shock of another round striking his left hip knocked him backwards. This time he felt bones break. *Brrt! Brrt! Brrt!* The firing seemed to go on forever, interspersed with hoarse cries and shouts from both sides but he lay where he fell, a warm lassitude filling his body as he floated languidly in a wet, storm-tossed sea. He drifted off, to be roughly jerked awake as the voice of Joe Lindsay whispered into his ear. 'I've got you, Harding, just hang on and we'll get you out of this.'

He tried to raise a hand in acknowledgement but his limbs refused to comply and he sank back into a dark, welcoming void. Dimly, from afar, a shot sounded and a body thumped limply down across his midriff. Blood burst from his lips as his mouth opened to protest this intrusion but the effort of speech was too great and he relaxed slowly as the life-force pulsed from his wounds. His last thought was of a hint of perfume, an icy fragrance that accompanied him all the way down the quickening slide to oblivion.

--§--

Captain Doug Redford watched in silence as his men filed down the trench towards him. 'I heard the firing Jackson,' he said in a low voice, 'any casualties.'

The corporal used a thumb to point behind him. 'The Jacko's were alerted by that new bloke, Ryan.' he said. 'He made a bloody racket and they opened up on us. Knocked Ryan and the other new bloke too, sir.'

'What! Ryan and Harding are both dead?'

'That's not all the bad news sir. Joe Lindsay went forward to try and rescue Harding and a Jacko got 'im too. The boys are bringing their bodies in now. We had to leave Ryan where he fell, I wasn't risking any more blokes to try and recover him.'

'Oh God! Alright Jackson,' Redford spoke wearily, 'take the bodies and get a few of the blokes to see that they're buried decently behind the parados. Come and see me when that's done and make a full report.'

'Rightho Boss.'

Long after Jackson had disappeared, Doug Redford stooped in a half-crouch, scanning the darkness for any signs of Turkish activity. In the distance a white flare rose slowly, bathing the gullies and escarpments in its brilliant light and throwing them into sharp relief. He waited until it had flickered to a spluttering end before turning back down the trench. There were reports to write and with luck he'd be able to grab a few hours disturbed sleep before dawn heralded the beginning of another bloody day.

Chapter Sixteen.

Above ANZAC Cove, July.

'Are you awake, Yilmaz?'

Artoun Seferian rolled over, instantly alert, and looked up.

'Yes, sir, what is it, has something happened, are we to move from here?'

The other laughed. 'No, no fear of that. I couldn't sleep and thought you might keep me company for an hour or so before a new day arrives. One more in our quest for survival, don't you agree?'

'Yes, sir.' Artoun replied, all the while cursing Brückner for the intrusion. He'd been dreaming about his wife and son and now he'd been robbed of all those pleasant thoughts to sit with an insomniac. Pushing his thin blanket aside he stood and glanced at the man regarding him from the far side of the dugout.

'Look. If you want to go back to sleep, please do so. It's just that I thought you and I could...'

'No, sir, I'm awake now and sleep will be hard to get back to. What ails you that you need to talk?'

Lt Brückner leant forward. 'It would appear that the fate which befell you and your comrades is not an isolated action, I've made further enquiries and Captain Çelik has had news of other, ah, *irregularities* in army units in the hinterland. And also, more disturbing is the news that whole areas of Anatolia are being purged of their Armenians. I tried to ask Çelik what he meant by this but he only laughed and said it was about time *those infidels* got what was coming to them. I started putting some thoughts together on receipt of this latest information and what you asked me about earlier, this business of Kaplan's talk of the Armenians being massacred and have come to a disturbing conclusion.

As an Islamic scholar I've always known that the Council of Union and Progress had been uneasy about the presence of so many different races and religions in the country so it's not hard to see where any thoughts of ridding themselves of the problem would come from. Already, I'm told, arrests of prominent Armenians have taken place with public executions occurring in order to set an example'

In spite of his exhaustion, Artoun thought quickly. 'We're not interlopers, sir,' he said hotly, 'we were encouraged by the government themselves to think of ourselves as Turks, after all.'

'Ah, my friend, but not Mohameddan. Turks in the lightest sense of the word, yes, but not Moslem you see? And there's the difference. Of course that's *if* the government are behind these actions but for years you non-Moslems have been treated differently, better than the Moslem peasants in the rural areas. You don't pay the same taxes, you have a different legal system, you...'

'At the end of the day, sir, we still owe allegiance to the land of our birth.'

'Which is? I think that's where the greater problem lies. Some, most, of the Armenian people crave annexation to Russia and if any actions are being taken against your people it would be because the rulers in Istanbul fear this desire for autonomy could lead to a break up of the Ottoman Empire. The Great Powers, France, Britain, even Germany, all have interfered with the politics of your country and it would seem that *Enver Paşa* and his cohorts have finally decided that now is the time to put an end to the interference.

Already, the *Ittihad* government has rid itself of thousands of Greek subjects by enforced repatriation and it was inevitable that, having carried out these pogroms, they would turn their attention to the plight of the Armenians. It would appear you stand in the way of preserving the empire, any thoughts of defeat bring with it a notion that the Armenians in Anatolia would then press the allies for an autonomous homeland and that Turkey will *never* accede to. Hence what appears to have already begun, forced relocations and the other many terrible acts that are now taking place. You, unfortunately, and your people are just pawns in a greater game, can you understand that?'

Artoun's heart raced at the German's chilling words. What could all this talk of *relocations* and murder mean for his family? Who would be left to defend them in his absence?

'What has that to do with simple people like my family who wish only to live their lives in peace, bring up their families in that same peace. We heard of atrocities against our people in Adana and other towns in 1909 and had hoped that by now the government realised what special qualities we brought to the well-being and finances of the country as a whole. So many Armenian tradesmen support the local—'

His words were interrupted by the sound of a flare soaring above them. It burst into life with a sharp *pop!* and both men looked up in surprise. The sudden transformation of night into day was followed by the sounds of a machine-gun stuttering into life and Brückner was galvanised into action.

'The enemy must be attacking, grab your rifle and follow me.' He smiled. 'We'll finish this philosophical discussion later but for now let's see what's going on. Hurry.'

Artoun needed no urging. Awkwardly he reached over for his rifle and followed the Leutnant down the trench. From somewhere up ahead loud shouts and hoarse cries sounded, spurring both men on. Within seconds they'd reached the front-line trench and Artoun peered cautiously over its lip as he tried to make out what was happening.

'Over there!' A private he knew only as Yusuf pointed excitedly. 'The *infidels*, a small party of them, they're trying to infiltrate us and murder us in our sleep.'

'Calm down, man!' Brückner snapped. 'Where are the enemy and from which direction did they come from?'

His words had a calming effect and Yusuf slowed his speech. 'We heard a noise in that direction, sir,' he pointed, 'and the next we knew a small party of *infidels* appeared, heading in this direction. Namik sent a flare up and when we saw them Hüseyin opened up with the machine-gun and two fell to earth. Others followed these men and so far we haven't seen them again but they're still out there. I think.'

'Good.' Brückner smiled. 'Well done to Hüseyin, that'll have given them food for thought. I dare say now they've been spotted they'll try and make their way back to their own lines. Tell Namik to fire another flare and let's see if we can't speed them up on their way.'

'At once, *efendim*.'

As they waited for the flare's revealing light to burst overhead, Brückner spoke sharply to Artoun. 'As soon as you see them, Yilmaz, try and take them. If we let them get away with this they'll become bolder and attack us every night.'

'I'm ready.' Artoun replied and awkwardly chambered a round into the breech of his rifle. The flare blossomed directly over his head and he shut his eyes to lessen its effects on his night sight. Opening them, he cast a glance across the broken ground, trying to pierce the flickering shadows.

'Look out!' A hand wavered and he looked to see a phantom slithering across the earth twenty yards away, pulling a limp form behind it. 'There!' A harsh voice bellowed into Artoun's ear and he swivelled to see the overblown shape of the *chaoush* alongside him, pointing furiously into the dark. 'Quickly, you dog, shoot the *infidel!*' He thumped Artoun hard on his injured shoulder and the rifle fell uselessly from his hands to the

316

floor of the trench. Stricken, his numbed limb on fire, Artoun could only gaze at the maddened NCO and this inflamed the man even more. 'You'll pay for disobeying an order, Yilmaz, I'll have you shot when this lot's finished.' the *chaoush* panted, stooping to pick Artoun's weapon up. He straightened and leant forward, sighting down the barrel. 'Watch and see how a real soldier kills his enemies.' He fired once and the phantom dropped out of sight. 'Now, throw grenades at them. Quickly!'

The man next to Artoun threw a series of grenades and these burst with a blinding light, robbing them of their sight for several precious seconds. In the silence that followed, a single shot rang out and the *chaoush* stiffened then sighed quietly as a large, dark hole blossomed in his forehead. He stood upright, swaying, before sliding soundlessly into the dirt.

'Get down!' Lt Brückner exclaimed, grabbing hold of Artoun. 'They're over there so keep an eye out for others.' The German pushed Artoun sideways as he strained to pierce the dark at the extremity's of the flare's brilliance and as he did so a red eye winked from across the ground to their front and a bullet snickered wickedly overhead.

'Be careful, sir, they're firing at us.' Artoun gave voice to his concern but the German gestured impatiently as he lifted himself higher in the trench, all the better to see further. Another shot sounded and Artoun sensed, rather than felt, the man next to him tense under the impact of a bullet.

'Are you alright, sir?' he asked anxiously but no answer came. Worried, he placed his rifle by his side and turned to speak again but stopped short at the sight of Brückner staggering back, both hands clutching his chest. Before Artoun's horrified gaze, Brückner tried to speak but a fountain of blood erupted from his mouth and he slumped tiredly to the trench floor and lay inert. Artoun dropped to his knees in a frantic attempt to aid the stricken officer but Brückner had already stopped breathing by the time he lifted the officer's limp, bloodied form up.

A crowd soon surrounded him in the confines of the trench as privates and NCO's gathered to see the end of the foreign officer in their midst. When Artoun finally roused himself and looked across the parapet there was no movement to be seen and he knew the enemy had taken their chance to escape and regained the safety of their own lines. Wearily, he asked Namik to help him carry the officer's body down the trench to their HQ and the fury of Captain Çelik.

--§--

317

The following morning Artoun was sent for by a still irate Çelik. 'Do you know the trouble you've landed me in, *nefer*?' he demanded theatrically from his seat in a small stone farmhouse at the rear of the lines.

'Sir, I must protest. The Leutnant did...'

'Silence! Don't answer back when I'm shouting. I've already lost my *chaoush* and now I've got HQ on my back demanding to know what happened to their precious *Aleman* ally. I'm trying to defend the sector here with the minimum of troops and with meagre food supplies and do they give a damn? No! They care more for that dead bastard than they do for the rest of the fucking army, of that I'm sure. They want me to send his body back for onward shipment to his family; it seems an honourable burial here amongst the rest of us is too dreadful a thought to contemplate.'

He rapped the table hard in his temper. 'I received a message five minutes ago asking, no, demanding I send the body back under escort. As if I have the men to spare. It's no use, you'll have to accompany the man back, do you hear?'

'Me? Why me, sir?' Artoun asked, puzzled.

'Don't question my orders, you dog! I'm not asking you, I'm ordering you! See that his body's delivered to wherever they want it to go before it's sent back to his homeland. He had a soft spot for you, it seems, so you can see him out of my sight. We should never have allowed him here but was I asked for my opinion? No, and now he's dead the shit is being heaped on my shoulders. Well, you, Yilmaz, can lessen that load. Go back with him and tell our masters that he died a hero's death fighting off the *infidels*.

Who knows, they might even award him the Medal of Merit. *Allah* himself knows I could do with the *Liyakat Madalyasi* pinned on my own tunic but not now, not after losing one of our esteemed allies who couldn't even keep his damn head down. What are you staring at? Go, you cur, before I have you soundly thrashed for bringing this trouble down on me.'

Stumbling outside the building, Artoun was met by another *nefer* leading a donkey which in turn was harnessed to a rough, open cart. Nestling on the back of the cart was a crude crate and Artoun guessed that it held the mortal remains of the recently deceased leutnant. Wood was in short supply everywhere with no coffins anywhere to be found but the Quartermaster had managed to get hold of a rough packing crate. It was not long enough to take Brückner's remains lengthwise so they'd simply bound his corpse like a crouching child's and crammed it into the cramped confines of the crate.

'Here, take them.' the *nefer* proffered the reins, 'I've got other work to do. Besides, the *infidel* should have been buried here within a day of his passing, like a good Moslem. These foreigners have no honour.'

'Where am I to take him?' Artoun asked, 'I've had no orders as to that.'

'The captain said to tell you that you must go to Gelibolu, there are still some *Alemans* based there and a ship will be waiting to take the body onto Stamboul. Leave your rifle here, you won't be needing it until you return. Here,' he held up a small woven bag. 'I scrounged some supplies for you so you won't go hungry on the journey.' He moved to depart but turned back. 'Don't even think of ditching him as soon as you're out of sight. Being a two-time deserter would mean a slow strangulation on the rope and in his present mood the captain will be more than happy to carry out such a task.'

--§--

The sun rose blood-red over the horizon and with its arrival Artoun roused himself and reluctantly walked over to where the donkey waited patiently, its large ears flicking absentmindedly at the annoying clouds of flies that crawled over its eyes and other facial extremities. He felt a sharp pang of pity for the animal but that was soon forgotten as he quickly harnessed it's loudly protesting head to the cart and they set off in the quickening dawn.

It was the start of their third day on the dusty track leading to the port of Gelibolu and he was feeling hungry. The food the *nefer* had given him, some dried lentils and stale bread, had not lasted beyond the second day and his stomach was making strange sounds as it forcefully reminded him of its starving plight. The donkey was also in a morose mood, it had not found any grazing since the previous day and was reminding him of this fact by making hoarse grumbling noises from time to time as they made their way along the track.

Luckily he'd had sufficient water in a large goatskin which he'd carefully eked out between him and the beast but it was no use, he'd have to find a depot somewhere in this wilderness and beg some food if he was to carry on and fulfil his mission.

He glanced at the crate and Brückner's words before the last attack which had killed the leutnant filled his mind. If what he had said was true then he, Artoun Seferian, should be on his way homewards as

319

quickly as possible to defend his family, not idling time away by carrying the ripe-smelling body of his officer to some Turkish town for onward shipment. What would happen when he reached Gelibolu? Would he be welcomed as a brother or imprisoned for being the bearer of bad news? He resolved to find a way out of this predicament before he reached the town and he let his mind wander as he and the donkey plodded on.

The tang of salt had filled his nostrils for some time now and he guessed that he wasn't far from the sea. With any luck he'd top the rise in front of him and find an army camp in the vicinity that could help him on his way. He pulled at the donkey's reins, cursing it for its stubbornness and his being there. It wasn't the animal's fault, he knew that but it was only human to look for someone else to blame for one's plight and the donkey fitted that position perfectly. It had a healthy set of sharp teeth and strong hind legs and he'd been mindful of both qualities when approaching it.

Arif Bilgili would have seen the humour in it. *"Yilmaz,"* he'd have said, *"only an ass could pull a donkey along the way that you do."* And laughed as he did so. At the thought of his friend, Artoun's thoughts turned a shade darker. He missed Arif and his frank and open manner. They'd shared a lot together and in a different place, in a different age they'd have remained as brothers and friends for life. Now it was he, Artoun Seferian, refugee in his own country who looked over his shoulder every day whilst his friend mouldered in a shallow grave far behind him.

To his intense disappointment, when he crested the rise in the track he saw only a small fishing village tucked in a tiny cove and not the army camp he was hoping for. A few small boats were drawn up on the thin slip of a beach and despondently he headed towards them. At the sounds of his approach, two children dressed in ragged garments appeared from a doorway of one of the cottages and solemnly watched as he headed for the streamlet he could see emptying into the cove.

As the scent of fresh water reached its dusty nostrils the donkey lifted its head, braying loudly and scared the children back indoors. It strained hard against his hands and pulled mightily to get to the source of the smell. Artoun let it have its head and the donkeys lips curled in gratitude as both of them buried their mouths in the shallow water and began to drink noisily. The crate containing Leutnant Brückner's body teetered precariously on the edge of the cart and he rose and lunged forward to catch hold of it before it fell to the floor.

He straightened up from his efforts, pulled at the donkey's lead and retraced his steps. A shadow fell across his feet and, looking up, he caught sight of a surly-looking male dressed in filthy clothes as ragged as the children's watching him silently with a dark scowl on his face.

'What is it you want here, and what's that on the cart?'

'Good day, sir, I'm on my way to Gelibolu, to deliver the body of my officer, an *infidel* serving in our glorious army and needed to stop for sustenance. Do you have anything I could buy, I have some *piastres*, not much but suffice to pay for some bread if you have enough to spare?' Artoun smiled reassuringly but his good manners were ignored.

'How do I know you're what you say you are and not one of those deserters we see passing here most days? All looking for the same as you only they don't want to pay for it. And how do I know that's a dead body you have in there?' he pointed to the cart, 'It could be something valuable that you're stealing and what you tell me is a pack of lies to disguise your true intentions.'

'Why would I lie to you?' Artoun replied evenly, 'Would a deserter really wander this forsaken part of the land dragging a cart containing a dead man's body?'

The man's scowl deepened. 'Now you make fun of me. If you are who you say you are, where's your *tufek*? Only deserters run round these days without their arms.' He turned on his heels and went back inside the cottage, slamming the door shut. From inside came the sound of raised voices followed by a sharp slap like the noise like a pistol shot. A woman's loud sobbing ensued and Artoun's eyes narrowed. So he was a woman-beater as well as an ungracious host. He turned to retrace his steps but a loud *snick!* broke the silence and he swivelled round to be confronted by the wavering barrel of a rusted rifle.

The rifle was an old muzzle-loading flintlock type, probably an ancient Miquelet and Artoun could see from where he stood that it was fully cocked. From this range the lead ball would cause him a grievous wound even if it failed to kill him outright so he took a step back and the man advanced towards him, the barrel never leaving Artoun's chest.

'Leave the cart where it is and go quickly or I'll shoot you down like a dog. Go I say, now!'

Artoun looked at the man's white face. Behind the would-be thief, a face hovered in the window of the cottage, screened by a lace covering and as Artoun continued to stare it slipped from view. 'Are you listening? I said go!'

Artoun raised his hands, palms held outwards. 'Alright, alright, I'm going but you're making a big mistake. My captain will send men after me and—'

'Turn and walk now or I fire.'

Artoun dropped his hands, turned and walked quickly back down the track. Once out of sight he doubled back and laid atop a dune, head covered by a large thatch of rough, coarse-growing sea-grass as he stared at the houses below. As he watched, the thief walked from the open door to his cottage, speaking angrily to someone out of sight of Artoun's questioning gaze. With a final bad-tempered flourish of his arms the man slung his ancient firearm over his shoulder and walked over to where the donkey stood patiently, grabbed the reins and began tugging the cart down the track without a backward glance.

As he lay there, thoughts ran swiftly through his mind. To leave now would see him captured again at some point and death would surely claim him this time. He'd been too lucky, the army would shoot him without mercy as a deserter. No, that way lay behind him, all he could do now was try and find a way back to Hegine and his son.

Artoun waited several minutes before standing up and walking slowly down the dune to the village. He walked towards the house the thief had left from but before reaching it the door swung open on creaking hinges and a woman dressed in a *chadour* stood in the doorway, watching him silently. He took a step forward and spoke hesitantly, mindful of the fact that he was alone with a married woman. 'My apologies mistress, but I must ask you some questions. Is that man your husband? He's stolen my animal and the cart, do you know where's he taking it? It contains nothing of value but I shall be in deep trouble if I don't get it back and deliver it to those waiting for its arrival.'

She contemplated him for several seconds before answering. 'That lazy pig Yusuf! He thinks there's something valuable in there so he's gone to the local camp where the men of the *Teshkilâti Mahsusa* live, in the hope that he'll get a good price for it. He's always there, hanging round them like a camp dog, begging for the scraps from their table.'

'It contains the body of my late officer, an *infidel* and the only value it has is to his family in another land far from here,' Artoun informed her sorrowfully.

'Then go,' she cried sharply, 'if he finds you here on his return he'll kill you!'

'You said Special Organisation, Artoun asked curiously, 'who are these men?'

She hesitated. 'I heard tell that they are men sent by the government to rid us of our internal enemies, those they call *ermeni*. Huh! Enemies? I've never heard of these people, we're all good Turkish people round here.'

322

Artoun shuddered and stepped back in shock, his heart pounding in his chest. What was the reason for the presence of this group of men here on the peninsula? Did they mean to carry out an examination of soldiers serving in the army here, with the sole purpose of ridding the army of any serving Armenians? Were there really special groups tasked with robbery and murder, all in the government's name? The words of the deceased leutnant flashed across his mind and he knew, with a deep sense of shock and foreboding, that this simple woman was speaking the truth and that what Brückner had told him was happening all over Turkey.

He realised, too, that if these men came and questioned him he might not withstand any detailed questions they might throw at him. Seeing his turmoil her attitude softened. 'Do you know how to sail a boat?' she said, pointing to where the fishing boats were drawn up on the beach. 'If you take to the track again he'll see you and the *Teshkilâti Mahsusa* camp is not ten minutes from here. They might want to accompany him back here and he'll have told them lies about how he came into possession of the cart and that will be sure to land you in trouble.'

He thought quickly. The boat? He'd never had any experience of boats but if it kept him from being questioned, or worse, by the thugs of the Special Organisation it looked as if that's all he had to keep out of their grasp. What had been a simple matter of the theft of Brückner's body now had the chance to turn into something altogether more serious. He looked at the woman. 'Which boat is his?'

She pointed again. 'You can't miss it, it's the one that needs the most attention, he only goes out in it when there's nothing left in the house. The children and I could starve and he wouldn't get off his fat stomach to help us. Go, take it, it'll be worth the beating when he comes back to find it gone.'

'Will you be alright?' Artoun asked worriedly, "I don't want to get you into trouble.'

She shrugged. 'I'll be alright, I'll tell him that you threatened me with a knife. He won't do a thing if the other men come back with him, as I'm sure they will. Go now before he does return.'

Stammering his thanks Artoun raced across the sand to where the boats lay. She was right, of all the boats drawn up on the beach only one was prominent in its peeling paintwork, warped wood and patched sail. Splintered oars and a faded sail lay carelessly draped over its transom and he took hold of its bow and pushed desperately. It slid easily over the sand to the water's edge and once afloat, he waded out still clutching the

323

bow and grabbed hold of the side to swing aboard. A distant shout made him swing round and he saw a small group of men, the thief Yusuf prominent among them, running over the dunes towards him. They were several hundred yards away but he knew he had no time to spare.

Fear lent wings to his efforts and he grasped a splintered oar and began poling frantically to put deeper water between himself and the running men. A rifle barked and a bullet hummed viciously over his head as he frantically redoubled his efforts, ignoring the pain from his wounded shoulder. The boat was shaking, anxious to be off in its true element and he settled back in the stern, set an oar on the bare side and pulled hard in an awkward, sideways manner as if manipulating a kayak.

Even without rowlocks the boat cut easily through the water and he began to draw away from the waiting men but as he grinned in relief he saw Yusuf run over to another boat nearby. Fear rose in his throat but the man's slumped shoulders told him that the other boats held neither oars nor sail and he relaxed as he glided further out to sea. A rifle barked again and he ducked but the bullet slashed harmlessly into the water several yards to his right.

A stiff offshore wind was blowing now and he moved gingerly forward to try and erect the sail laying in a tangled mass in the bottom of the boat. After a few false starts he saw how it was fixed to the worn mast and tried to guide it into position. His heart leapt with relief when it pulled free and a portion unfurled, cracking open and pulling the small boat along in a crab-like fashion. The group on the beach now looked like ants scurrying around an anthill and he allowed himself the luxury of a smile as he drew further and further away.

He was soon in deeper water, the light blue of the sea changing to the colour of indigo and the boat heeled over dangerously before the wind, taking in large amounts of water as it scudded along in a curious lop-sided manner. He tried bailing with his hands but saw that course of action was useless and looked round desperately for something to use. Nothing came to hand and as he searched, dark clouds covered the sun, a violent squall erupted and he was quickly drenched in an icy downpour.

The wind strength increased dramatically and the boat began tossing like a cork, bobbing and dipping as the white-capped waves grew in size and intensity. The boat's sideways motion increased, imparting a feeling of queasiness as she slewed and yawed peculiarly. All thoughts of controlling her were literally swept from his mind as more and more seawater poured over her gunwhales and she began settling ominously ever lower in the heavy seas. Quickly he stripped off his uniform jacket and bunched it up, thrusting it into a large crack that had appeared in the side of the boat but it was to no avail.

A heavy *crack!* told of the mast and sail parting company and he fought to stand before the boat lurched in a sudden, shuddering movement, pitching him over the side and he found himself struggling desperately in the water. Surfacing, he floundered and gasped as seawater forced its way down his throat, an action which automatically caused a paroxysm of coughing and choking as the acrid, acid taste of bile filled his mouth. Pain lanced through his injured shoulder and he gave way to panic, feeling muscles tear as he threw his arms out and attempted to swim in a sideways doggy-paddle. His efforts brought no relief and he could feel the remaining strength in his good arm ebbing fast.

Swept into the trough of a mountainous wave he saw the wreckage of the boat disappear out of sight as it was overwhelmed and his heart sank with it. More water entered his mouth and he choked violently as the wave drove him under. Kicking hard, he reached the surface spluttering and gasping for air. His shoulder felt numb and he knew that his ability to stay afloat was severely limited. A calm feeling of inevitability settled over him with this knowledge and he was going under for a second time when a strong hand took hold of his arm and he was hauled upwards at speed.

He landed in a tangle of limbs in the sodden, water-logged well of a small boat and lay there gasping like a stranded goldfish as his aching stomach purged itself of the huge amount of water he'd ingested. Too weak to move, he let his mouth open and retched great gobbets of green bile ands seawater while his arms and legs jerked spasmodically. Head pounding, he tried to rise but a gentle hand pushed him back down and he threw up again.

'Stay down there 'til you're finished,' a voice commanded, 'I don't want you throwing up over me!'

The boat's violent corkscrewing motion brought him no relief and he retched until it seemed his stomach itself lay washing up and down with all the other contents he'd brought up. '*Uurrghhhh!*' he groaned, curling into a ball and wrapping his arms around his lower torso in a feeble attempt to stop the convulsions racking his raw innards.

'Look, Berat, look at what your father has caught. This must be my biggest catch ever!'

Artoun stirred and groaned softly as he lifted salt-encrusted eyes upwards and caught his first glimpse of his rescuer. An old man sat in the stern of the boat two feet away, worn slippers touching Artoun's shoulder as he peered down in amusement at the wretch at his feet. The wind had knocked his turban askew and his silver hair blew in a wild straggle across his brown, wizened face but the glance he gave Artoun was friendly enough. He moved the boat's tiller as he spoke and the wind died as the craft steadied itself in coming about. Briefly, Artoun felt the stirrings of life flood back into his body before he suddenly bent as a spasm overtook him and he retched again.

When next he looked up, a small boy of nine or ten, he guessed, was also looking down at him with a curious, detached air. 'Forgive the boy,' the old man spoke, 'he doesn't get to see too many strangers. You were lucky,' he continued, 'we were making for home after this storm blew up from nowhere when Berat here spotted your boat in difficulties. You're not a fisherman, no-one would handle the boat the way you were doing and try to call himself so. We made in your direction and I was lucky enough to take hold of you as you were going down, for the last time I think.'

'You have my thanks.' Artoun muttered. 'I was going...'

'You were going nowhere, except to the bottom.' The old man spoke calmly, deftly turning the boat into a better position and twisting round in his seat to seek a path through the waves. 'Your hands have the look of a craftsman but...'

'I'm a carpenter.' Artoun interjected, 'from Gelibolu.'

'My friend, do not lie to me. You may have the hands of a carpenter but I don't know you and you're not from round here. We don't get travelling carpenters so I can only surmise from your clothing that you're a deserter from our glorious army.' The last few words were tinged with bitterness and Artoun looked up in puzzlement.

'I don't know what you mean, I tell you I'm only a poor carpenter.'

'You're not. What you *are* is a poor liar my friend but don't worry, me and Berat won't give you away. The army took my other three sons these past months and not a word of them since. I protested that I needed them to help me in my work but they laughed and dragged my sons away to fight their accursed war. May *Allah* the merciful forgive them for I cannot, however grievously the country needs soldiers they did not need to take all my sons except one.' He jerked a finger at the small boy sitting quietly in the bow.

'Look at him, still a child! Berat is the son of my youngest wife, how can he help take in the nets or bait hooks and haul a line up at his age?'

Feeling less nauseous, Artoun struggled upright to a sitting position. 'My condolences...?'

'Ahmet. They call me Ahmet Şimşek.'

'I too have a son, Ahmet Şimşek and it would grieve me to see him taken for some senseless war that is not of our making. You have my sympathy—'

'So you *are* a deserter? You wear the uniform of a soldier, that I do know.' Ahmet Şimşek spoke quietly but there was no mistaking the emotion in his voice.

'Yes.' Artoun answered him, lifting his head proudly. 'I had other reasons to leave but cowardice was not one of them. This war has made enemies of us all, even amongst those who should be fighting together. Let us say that if circumstances had been a lot different I would have stayed at my post to drive off our country's enemies.'

'I can only guess at the truth of what you're saying, I'm just an old fisherman but I've seen gangs of thugs swaggering round upsetting some people and terrorising others. What I've also seen are lots of young men, boys really, begging and stealing as they try to make their way home. Simpletons, some of them but the army took them without question, as it did my sons, to fight a war that was not of our making. You don't look like a coward. This son of yours, is he far from here?'

The wind had dropped as suddenly as it had risen and the boat was now nosing purposely ahead under the guiding hand of Ahmet Şimşek as Artoun took in his bearings and pointed. 'Over there, my village lies twelve, maybe fifteen days hard march from the other side. If I can I shall try to make my way home.'

Ahmet swung the tiller and the boat turned smoothly onto a new heading. 'Then that's where we're going. If I can do one good deed in this madness that has descended upon us all it must surely be to reunite a son with his father. I know of a small cove not far from here, safe from prying eyes where we can land you safely. And don't tell me your name, that way me and the boy can't give anything away.'

'I can't thank you enough.'

'Then don't!' Ahmet replied brusquely. 'My helping you is my answer to a country that strips an old man of his sons. What difference will three country boys, brought up only as fishermen, make in helping to win this war? Bah! A curse on them all. My wives weep at night for their sons and what can I tell them, how can I comfort them? No, my friend, I shall do this for my family and laugh inside whenever I see a fat Ottoman officer ride by. Berat, come and help your father with the sail.

You, carpenter, sit there and do nothing. Get your strength back, you'll need it for the road ahead. When we put you ashore, head left and take the road to Bandirma. Keep the morning sun on your right and from there you should be able to go on to find the railroad. From there on, you're in *Allah's* hands.'

Artoun nodded weakly in acknowledgement and rose to take a place in the bows as the boy moved forward to assist his father. The dark clouds were a forgotten memory as the sun beamed its warm rays down on them and he could feel his clothing slowly beginning to dry out as he sat back and took in the scene. The boat cut through the water with assurance and he felt his spirits rise. He was going home.

Later, he turned as he reached the top of the shallow cliff and waved as the boat slid back into the water to begin its return trip. Ahmet Şimşek had made him rest for an hour to regain his strength and then had Artoun don a stained and crumpled smock he'd wrestled from the confines of the boat's locker. An old fez from the same location was jammed on his head and at Ahmet's insistence they swopped footwear to complete a rough and ready disguise after Artoun had stripped off his puttees. The old man had also handed over a small package of food containing some evil-smelling dried fish, a portion of goat's cheese and a small pannikin of fresh water. He'd waved away Artoun's stammered thanks and roughly wished him well before setting back to the boat and shouting at his son to help him launch her.

Artoun took a deep breath and turned his back to the sea. He looked upwards at the sun and mentally gauged his position for the second time that day. Merghem, Hegine and Khat lay off to his left and a fierce determination welled up as he contemplated the days ahead. Nothing would keep him from them, nothing, he vowed and squaring his shoulders, began to walk. Slowly at first, then faster as the desire to see his loved ones mounted inside him.

ANZAC Cove, July.

The transport rocked gently in the swell as the waiting boats embarked their living cargo for onward travel to the beach. Leaning over the side, Walt Harding took in the scene at a glance. So this was Anzac Cove, he mused. Somewhere among these men his brother was living, maybe even now gazing on the ship as Walt looked shorewards. They would languish here long enough to land the latest group of ANZAC reinforcements before heading east to Cape Helles where he would rejoin his battalion.

Unconsciously his hand reached up to his tunic pocket and found the reassurance he was seeking. He'd had so much to think about since Tom's departure and the three day journey from Alexandria to this crowded cove had only fuelled his determination to make amends. The letter he'd taken delivery of was still there, safe from the day he'd lifted it out of Bridgette Mathers's open hand and promised faithfully to make sure his brother received it. They'd been such fools and if by ensuring Tom received the letter he could expiate his part in the misguided affair it would be worth any anger Tom might show to him.

He'd spoken long into the night with Bridgette before his departure, reassuring her of Tom's love and his own stupid part in their separation. Now, with her feelings plainly written on a few sheets of paper he was hoping desperately to find a way to deliver Bridgette's words and right the wrong they'd done to a fine, decent man. He'd put it in the post as soon as they reached Cape Helles and could only imagine Tom's reaction but hoped it would be one of reconciliation. There was so much to do, to look forward to and the past weeks had shown him how less of a man he was when deprived of his brother's love and guidance.

Wheeler's part in the misunderstanding had come to light when the Provost Serjeant had visited Walt to tell him of the business with the pocket watch and to explain Tom's removal from Alexandria to a hospital in Cairo. It hadn't taken long to put two and two together and for him to realise what a fool he'd been to turn Tom away in the manner he'd done so. Now he was on his way to make things right if only he could find a way to ensure Tom received the letter.

'Hurry up you lot, we haven't got all day, for God's sake!'

Walt looked down to where a frustrated coxswain was showing his annoyance at the laggardly manner the Australians and New Zealanders were boarding his craft. 'I'll be late for my tot if you lot don't hurry up so move yer arses and get in, will you.'

An idea took hold as he watched and germinated whilst he ran down the deck and hurriedly descended the ladder to the lower deck. 'Hang on there, wait for me!' he called breathlessly.

'Oo' are you, mate, you're not going ashore here, are you?' the coxswain's suspicious voice broke into Walt's fevered thoughts and he pulled up short, thinking frantically. 'Sorry, jack, my boss asked me to go ashore with you and deliver this letter in person.' He pulled the envelope from his pocket and proffered it at the sailor who stared at it with narrowed eyes.

'Are you sure, I wasn't told about no letter.'

329

'Honest, I just learnt of it myself. You know these bloody officers, leave everything to the last minute. The letter's for someone called Monash, a general, very important I was told. '

'Huh! Just my luck. If I'm late because of your officer's gallivanting there'll be hell to pay. What do I tell my petty officer?' He took a step closer but Walt snatched the envelope away from the man's eyes.

'Look, tell him what you like, I only know that this letter is pretty important and if it's not delivered you and me will be in the kack real deep.' Walt stared beseechingly at the man and the sailor lowered his eyes grudgingly in acceptance.

'Alright, but I warn you, I'm not hanging about when we get there. If you don't deliver it pretty damn quick I'll leave you there and you can explain yourself to whoever or whatever later. Clear?'

'Clear.'

'Right, that's us then. Push off forr'd and let's get bloody well going.'

He sat impatiently as they neared the shore, marvelling at his boldness and wondering just how he was to pull the stunt off. The easy bit was getting the coxswain to admit him into the boat, the hard bit was delivering the letter for onward transmittal and getting back to the boat before the disgruntled sailor left him, literally, high and dry. No matter, first thing's first. Find someone, impress on them the importance of the letter then back on the boat and aboard before anyone missed him. Simple.

They landed and grumbling loudly, the reinforcement party took their leave and assembled on the beach. Without waiting, Walt vaulted over the side and sprinted along the beach, looking round urgently as he did so. A large flag fluttered outside a large wall of sandbags and he angled towards it.

'*Oof!*' He collided with a figure exiting the dugout and both men sprawled headlong on the shingle. 'What the bloody hell do you think you're doing?' The other man, an officer wearing major's rank badges glared at him whilst beating his tunic free of sand as Walt sat upright.

'Sorry sir!' he gasped, 'Only I've just got a minute or two to deliver this letter before I have to go back to the ship.' He pointed out to sea and the major followed his finger. Mollified the man stood and put his hand down.

'What's this all about, you're a pom, aren't you? What the hell are you doing here, son?'

Walt accepted the offer of a hand and was pulled upright as the major continued to stare at him in a hostile manner. Throwing a hasty salute,

Walter explained, his voice garbled as words tumbled from his lips. 'This letter. Got to get it, my brother. Big mistake you see. Must...'

'Whoa there. Alright, mate, slow down and start again.'

Taking a deep breath, Walt did as he was bade and slowly recounted his story. The major smiled ironically. 'A sorry tale of love and war, eh? Rightho, give me a chance to think and let's see if we can get it to your brother as quickly as possible. Have you put his name and rank on the envelope? Yes? Good, that'll cut down the chances of it going astray or to the wrong bloke. See that dugout in the corner with the flag hanging from the entrance? Take it and explain yourself, they should be able to deliver it to him from there. That's the best I can do before you have to get back to the beach or that matelot's going to leave you behind. Safe journey.'

Walt swivelled round to see the coxswain waving frantically in his direction. He gulped, 'Thanks sir, you've done me a great favour.' and threw another salute the major's way. Without further ado he sprinted down the beach towards the dugout the major had pointed out. Running hard amongst the throng filling the beach he was aware of men around him throwing themselves to the ground but he kept running, arms and legs pumping hard as he neared the edge of the cove.

A loud, shrieking noise similar to an express train filled his ears and he was flung upwards in a maelstrom of sound, dirt, intermixed with shingle and a roaring, crashing assault that blotted out the sun and the beach in the aftermath of the shell's impact. Helpless in its grip he found himself flying sideways in a foetal position as a giant fist smashed him senseless to the ground, where he lay still. After a short time he attempted to rise but fell groggily to the ground, a loud ringing sound blotting out any sense of normality.

A fleeting image of someone standing over him was a snapshot in his peripheral vision but the man's words were lost to the darkness which rose up swiftly and claimed him. He was conscious of hands gently lifting him onto a stretcher and, later, a sharp smell of chloroform that lingered in his nostrils long after he was winched up into the cool, welcoming bowels of a hospital ship.

Chapter Seventeen.

Anatolia, July

Artoun Seferian walked and rode for four days, sleeping rough and gratefully accepting the offers of a ride from simple farmers who passed with their ox carts. On reaching Bandirma he'd carefully skirted the town and struck out for his next objective, that of Bursa. Another four days in this manner saw him pass through Bursa and he continued on his quest, belly growling with hunger but drawing closer with every passing moment to the railroad that he hoped would carry him south to his family.

No-one along the way asked where he'd come from or where he was going and in turn he volunteered nothing, content to sit and conserve his energy and indulge in small talk during the ten days that he travelled, sharing their simple, frugal fare as the latest cart carrying him drew closer to yet another a large town.

It was named Bilejik, the farmer solemnly informed him before departing and it was here he would find the railway. Walking carefully down a dusty street through its outskirts, a group of Turks laden down with all manner of goods approached him. The nearest, an old peasant carrying a large bundle of clothing on his back, waved him over.

'If you hurry you can still find some goods but you'll have to be quick.' the old man panted, pointing a free hand back in the direction he'd come from.

'Goods?' Artoun stood, puzzled.

'The street of the *Gâvurs* back there,' the man pointed testily, 'only hurry, everything will be gone soon if you tarry here.'

Bemused, Artoun waved a hand and began walking in the direction the old man had indicated. The peasant's use of the word for *unbelievers* troubled him but as he drew near he began to realise what the old man had meant. The location wasn't hard to find, a crowd gathered outside the dwellings egged each other on with loud cries and imprecations. People disappeared inside houses and re-appeared seconds later, carrying or pulling at large pieces of furniture and household goods. Shocked, Artoun caught the arm of a young boy as he raced by. The youngster tried to shrug off his restraining hand but Artoun clung on stubbornly.

'What's happening here?' he demanded.

'Let me go!' the boy whined, 'The *Gâvurs* have been sent away, the troops came early this morning and took them and we've been told to help ourselves before the *gendarmas* arrive and steal everything for themselves.'

Thunderstruck, Artoun watched as the houses were greedily ransacked by the mob. These were Armenian houses but where their inhabitants were he could only guess. Hesitantly he walked closer to the nearest house, peering inside the shattered downstairs windows. What he did see filled him with dread. A pool of blood was starkly evident on the floor of the room into which he was looking and a closer glance showed bloodied handprints covering a wall. Whatever had happened here, those living in this house had not been allowed to depart peacefully and a mental picture of his family flashed through his mind. Was this scene of destruction already being played out in Merghem?

He turned to go but this time it was his arm that was grabbed roughly and he found himself pulled speedily over the entranceway into the house. 'Come, come!' a voice sounded in his ear as his assailant dragged him unwillingly through the bloodstained room and into the rear of the house. Once there, his arm was released and he spun round to confront his erstwhile saviour.

A young Turk, unshaven and wearing shabby clothes held a finger over his mouth. '*Shh!* Sorry for the violence but I thought I'd better get you in here out of the street, the *gendarmas* are on their way and you and I will stick out like sore thumbs.' Before Artoun could frame an indignant response, the young man spoke again. 'You're a deserter, aren't you?'

'What? Me? How dare you, I'm a ...'

The Turk grinned slyly. 'Look at you, don't play the innocent with me and try to tell me you're a farmer on his way to market, not with those clothes? You're dressed like a fisherman but where's the sea? And if I'm not mistaken, they're army issue trousers you're wearing. Well?'

'Leave me alone or else.' Artoun snarled hotly at him and the Turk's face changed in an instant. 'You fool, how do you think I *know* you're a deserter, are we both not in the same predicament?' He thrust out a hand. '*Salaam*, brother, from one who's on his *holidays* to another. Mehmet Shukri, *nefer*, late of the Ottoman Third Army Corps.'

Artoun relaxed. 'Alright,' he allowed grudgingly, shaking the others hand reluctantly. 'Know me only as Yilmaz. What was it you were saying about the *gendarmas*?'

'That we'd better get out of here now before they arrive or we'll face some awkward questions.' The other replied, tugging at his newfound companion's sleeve. 'Come, follow me, it's time we were far away from here.'

Artoun pushed through the throng filling the doorway and followed the young man in silence, his head pounding with unasked and unanswered questions but he kept silent as they hurried along quiet back streets until the row of ransacked houses was far behind them. Eventually he came to a stop, rocking back on his heels as his companion strode on. Looking over his shoulder, the Turk halted before walking back, a questioning look on his face. Artoun held up a hand.

'Stop right there, Mehmet Shukri, not one more step until you tell me just exactly where it is you're taking me.'

An exasperated look crossed Shukri's face. 'Look, I told you, we need to get away from here, there's a railway station not far from here and we can take a train to the south. I take it you don't want to go back in a northerly direction?'

Artoun caught the other's sleeve. 'A train, are you mad? We'll be caught and then what?'

Mehmet Shukri laughed aloud. 'I know we've just met but trust me, Yilmaz, that's all I ask. I warned you about the *gendarmas* didn't I? If it wasn't for me you'd have been caught already so, please, just listen and do as I say and we'll get out of this damned town.' He trotted on and Artoun hurried to catch him up.

'But I've no money, how can I afford to travel by train?'

Another sly look passed over the Turk's face. 'Extend that trust a little more and all will be revealed, brother. Ah, here we are.' He stopped and gestured. 'The station. Stay here and try not to attract attention to yourself and I'll go and see how the land lies. Don't worry, I won't be long.'

Before Artoun could answer he strode off and turned into the dilapidated station entrance. Artoun huddled down, trying to make himself inconspicuous whilst he waited for Shukri to return. A few passers-by looked curiously at him but no-one spoke and his spirits rose. Perhaps miracles could happen and this stranger be his salvation. It was in God's hands, all he could do was wait so he cast his gaze downwards and did precisely that.

Within minutes he was joined by another figure who squatted alongside him. He looked up and Shukri grinned back at him 'That's that, brother, a train arrives within the hour and we have a place in the guards van at the rear. A trifle uncomfortable but it will save us from answering any uncomfortable questions. I've paid for us to go as far as—'

'Wait! I've no *Teskeré*, do you?'

Shukri looked sideways. 'That's where nearly all my money went, the ticket collector took a lot of bribing before he'd allow us to travel without passports. Don't worry, we'll be in the rear of the train and no-one will come along asking to see our *Teskerés*.'

'Just how much did you have to pay him, it can't have been cheap?' Artoun asked curiously. The Turk's answer sent a shudder through him. 'I gave the dog two gold coins, some silver *piastres* and a large women's necklace before he was won over. It's alright, it wasn't my money, so to speak. All I handed over was what I took from the house I found you in.'

'The *ermeni* house?'

'The *Gâvurs* house.' Shukri gently corrected him. 'Where they're going they won't be needing riches, not unless their God asks a payment for the entering of whatever passes for a *Gâvur* Paradise. It's about time they got their come-uppance if the stories of their infidelities are true.'

Artoun's stomach lurched at his companion's words. Said innocently enough, Mehmet Shukri had no idea who stood alongside him nor did he seem to have any idea of the full horror behind what he was saying. Here out of the mouth of an ordinary Turk, a deserter from the Ottoman army it could be rightly said but an ordinary Moslem too, was the confirmation Artoun had dreaded for weeks. A deliberate policy seemed to be in force that dragged Armenian's from their homes to God knows where and the Turkish populace accepted this as a fact. By doing so they actually applauded the bestial acts of terror visited upon a people whose only crime was to worship an different God and harbour thoughts of liberties withheld in the country of their birth.

He turned away lest Shukri saw the pain in his face but his companion chattered blithely on, unaware of his new-found friend's true identity.

'It was partly that which led me to desert, I was based in Ankara and all around were stories of riches to be had from sacking the *Gâvur's* houses and their persons. The problem was that our regiment's officers were taking all the good stuff for themselves and their relatives but then I heard that we'd begun to transport the *ermeni* by rail to Adana and beyond, to camps in the desert. The Special Organisation are organising bands of *Chetes* down there, robber bands especially set up to pillage these scum as they pass.' He leant over conspiratorially.

'Between you and me, some of their women are right lookers, eh, so I thought to hell with flogging my soul with the army and maybe ending up in a shallow grave in the Çannakale. No, I said, I'll get out of here and follow these people down to Adana and see what I could do down

335

there. My regiment will be sent to Çannakale soon but as I have an uncle in Adana, I'm sure he'll have connections with these *Chetes* and I thought now was my chance to escape, make my way to Adana and so make my fortune. Heh, how about you, Yilmaz, why don't you come with me and I'll have my uncle set you up too?'

Artoun's head swam and he clasped it in shaking hands, looking at the ground as he tried to refrain from retching. Mistaking his emotions, Shukri punched him lightly on the shoulder. 'It's alright, you don't have to thank me now. Maybe later, when we've both become rich. Now, we'd better get ourselves inside and wait on the platform, we don't want to miss our only chance of a getaway. Follow me and sit far away from the others waiting so we don't raise any suspicions as to what two young men of army age might be doing here.'

Blank-faced, Artoun followed Mehmet Shukri into the station and they made their way to the southbound platform, sitting alone at the far end and saying nothing. Wild thoughts buzzed in and out of Artoun's mind but he knew if he was to leave now he would be lost. Hegine and Khat would never know the truth of his attempts to find them so he stared wordlessly down at the ground and willed the train to arrive.

Eventually, a loud mournful cry told of the Adana train's impending approach and at a sharp dig in his ribs from Shukri's elbow he rose and joined the Turk as he waited impatiently for the carriages to come to a squealing, squeaking halt in a flourish of black smoke. They made their way swiftly to the rear of the train where more haggling took place before a surly guard stepped back reluctantly to allow them to enter his domain. Ignoring Shukri and the guard's anguished protests, Artoun settled on some official-looking mailbags and closed his eyes as the train set off once more.

He slept fitfully with Hegine and Khat's face drifting in and out of his sleep until a squealing of brakes told him they were slowing down. As he struggled to rise, Mehmet Shukri squatted alongside and addressed him. 'Slept well my friend?' he enquired.

'Where are we?' Artoun answered groggily.

'We're just coming into Eskishehir so keep your head down and don't let anyone see you.' Shukri shuffled over to a grimy window in the side of the guard's van and peered outside. 'I can't see anyone...Oh...Come quick. Brother, come and see this'

'See what?'

Shukri gestured impatiently.

'Just do as I say. Come, You mustn't miss this.'

Artoun stood up and stretched before joining his travelling companion at the window. The dirty streaks on the glass prevented a good view but as his eyes became accustomed to looking through the grime he could see what appeared to be a stationary train in a siding not a few feet from where their own train sat waiting. At first he thought the freight cars opposite were empty but a movement caught his attention and peering closer he realised the cars were full of people.

With mounting horror he tried to make sense of what he was seeing but his thoughts were interrupted by Shukri's amused snigger.

'By *Allah*, those are *ermeni* in there, they're transporting them by train now.' He guffawed coarsely. 'So this is how our esteemed government rids us of these accursed peoples.'

Artoun moved into the frame of the window, rubbing its greasy surface with his sleeve as he tried to see more. Alarmed at his actions, Shukri grabbed his wrist but Artoun shrugged off the man's restraining hand as he stooped and peered through the area he'd cleaned, gasping in shock at the scene unravelling before his disbelieving eyes.

Packed tightly into the confines of the freight car opposite was a seething mass of humanity, pushing in all directions for space and the very air to breathe as a wave of motion surged up and down the interior of their prison. Those imprisoned consisted mainly of women but here and there he saw a long-bearded elderly man sandwiched inbetween the supine figures of what he took to be children. A low moan escaped his lips as he looked on and witnessed their struggle for life and although he tried to tear his gaze away he could only stare, fascinated and appalled at the plight of his people.

'Look at them,' Shukri jeered, 'like rats in a cage. There won't be many of them left when they arrive, shoved in like that, wherever it is they're being sent.'

'Golgotha.'

'What did you say, brother?'

'Golgotha,' Artoun intoned brokenly, 'those people are on their way to their deaths. Can't you see that? Have you no humanity left in you?'

Mehmet Shukri shrank back from the look in Artoun's eyes. 'Alright, don't work yourself into a frenzy, my friend, they're only *ermeni*, after all.' he protested.

Artoun turned from the Turk and looked back across the gap between the two trains. Directly opposite from where he looked out, a small child in ragged clothing, arms thrust listlessly through a wide gap in the slats of the freight car in fruitless supplication was hunched down looking out through a hole in the side of the freight car. Periodically her face was flattened against the wood of the car as the seething tide of humanity behind her ebbed and flowed but she remained passive, guileless eyes staring out onto the tracks. As Artoun watched, she became aware of his presence and looked up, regarding him gravely and as their eyes locked he felt himself drowning.

Within those wide, brown eyes he caught a glimpse of the soul of the world. In that moment, with a gut-wrenching feeling of helplessness, he comprehended all the evil forces encompassing this persecution of the innocents. He shuddered but was unable to break the spell as both contemplated each other across eternity. Her face, with no trace of reproach, continued to gaze steadfastly at him and the connection was only broken as a jolting motion signalled the departure of Artoun's train. Her face blurred suddenly and he wiped his tears away as the train clanked its way from those travelling to a far different destination.

As the train picked up speed Artoun continued to stare after her small form until it was lost from sight. Sick at heart, he turned to see Shukri gazing at him, hostile suspicion in his narrowed eyes as he contemplated Artoun's wet cheeks. Eventually, Shukri spoke.

'What regiment did you say you were with, brother—?'

'I didn't.' Artoun cut him off in mid-sentence. The atmosphere in the guard's van changed suddenly, to one of distrust and hostility and Artoun's next words only served to confirm the Turk's suspicions.

'The world as we know it is changing, Mehmet Shukri, and the murder of these poor people will only hasten that change. Well may you scorn them now but mark my words, *brother*, the crimes the Ottoman empire commit today will come back to haunt you and all who participated in them.' The words escaped his lips before he could prevent his mouth from opening and the Turk's face hardened further.

Artoun moved towards the mail sacks and Shukri scrambled to stay clear of him. Fixing the man with a contemptuous stare, Artoun settled himself back on the sacks keeping both Shukri and the guard in view and tried to wipe from his mind all that he'd witnessed. The nightmare scenes continued to fill his vision and although the train's rocking motion imparted a gentle invitation to sleep he found it hard to relax as they clattered their way southwards.

The two Turks huddled together in a corner, speaking in low voices and looking his way from time to time. He knew neither felt brave enough to try to overpower him but nevertheless realised it would only be a matter of time until they summoned up the courage to try it together. It was after they'd left the small town of Kutahia that he sensed the time for action was imminent.

He pretended to sleep, moving his head from side to side in a convincing show of tiredness whilst all the while observing them through half-closed eyes. Judging the moment to have arrived, they began to crawl stealthily towards him and he waited until Shukri was a foot or so away before rising up and striking with the speed of a snake. Before Shukri could react to Artoun's assault, a terrible blow to the side of his head felled the Turk and he collapsed in a crumpled heap, sending fresh waves of pain through Artoun's shoulder. The guard stopped his advance in mid-stride, uncertain of what to do next.

'Don't.' Artoun threatened softly. 'Whatever it is you're thinking of doing—don't.'

The old man blinked nervously, retreating towards the rear of the carriage until Artoun's next words halted him in mid-stride. Thrusting a hand into his empty pocket, Artoun spoke quietly. 'Come here, unless you want my knife buried in your stomach.' The man's eyes blinked nervously and his lips moved soundlessly but he held his ground, tensing as if for a charge.

Artoun spoke again. 'Last chance. If I have to come to you, you die!'

The man's shoulders collapsed, muscles relaxing in surrender and he shuffled meekly over to where Artoun waited. Taking hold of the guard's limp arm, Artoun pointed at the unconscious Shukri. 'Quick!' he demanded, 'Unravel his turban and tie him up before he wakens.'

Soundlessly, the guard did as he was bade, pulling the turban from an unresponsive Shukri's head and winding it around the Turk's legs before pulling it tight around his hands. After checking the man's handiwork, Artoun gestured for the guard to sit on the floor alongside Shukri and when he'd done so, pulled his own turban off and used that to pinion the guard. Only when both men were laid alongside each other did he exhale in relief and slide to the floor as he contemplated his next move.

--§--

The train dipped and swayed as it wended its way south through the hinterland. Between Afion-Karahisar and Konia, Mehmet Shukri regained consciousness and regarded Artoun with baleful eyes, saying nothing, staring angrily at his erstwhile companion and maintaining his malevolent silence until they pulled into Konia. As they shunted alongside the platform Artoun stole a quick glance out of the window; all

339

looked peaceful enough but a sixth sense spoke of danger and he turned to see Shukri's lips open wide to shout a warning.

Bounding over, Artoun clamped a fierce hand over the man's mouth. 'One word and you die, *brother*!' he hissed and Shukri's eyes opened wide with fear. The guard's eyes rolled upwards and he remained silent. Artoun and Shukri stayed joined in this manner until the train clanked its way onwards, leaving Konia and Artoun's memories of his meeting with Arif Bilgili far behind. He released his hold and spoke.

'I met a man there in Konia, Mehmet Shukri, a fellow moslem like yourself but also a human being. His corpse lies mouldering on the battlefields of Çannakale but unlike you he acquitted himself with honour. He minded not what colour a man's skin was, nor to which god he prayed. During our brief time together he taught me what it is to know true friendship, one that bridges the hatred between our people and if you live I hope one day you too will come to gain such knowledge.'

'Hah!' Shukri spat, 'Who cares about such talk? You'll get what's coming to you, *ermeni* scum! I should suffer torments for eternity for helping you, I should have recognised you for what you were when we first met. When we reach Adana, what then, who is going to save you there? Heh?'

Artoun leant over his captive. 'We both wear the same uniform but like my friend Arif, I too fought with honour. You, on the other hand, betray both your country and your race in wishing only to kill innocent people and profit by their deaths. Who says you'll be alive when we reach Adana, Mehmet Shukri? Think on that for a while whilst I find something to eat.'

Shukri's face turned pale as he digested Artoun's words and their meaning. 'Come now,' he whined, 'don't let's quarrel, forgive my harsh words, brother. My uncle, he could still help—'

Artoun wheeled away, ignoring the man's babbling as he rummaged through the guard's rucksack. It contained some dried figs which he devoured greedily and a container of water which went a long way to easing his parched throat. Replete, he sat back and let thoughts of home and his family wash over him as they drew ever closer. His two captives remained silent as Eregli and Bozanti were left behind, daylight began fading to the dusk of evening and he guessed they must soon be nearing Adana.

The guard's fez had fallen to the floor when Artoun had tied him up so he reached over and jammed it on his own head. It was a trifle small but he reasoned that it would help deflect any suspicions passer-bys might harbour if they spotted him bare-headed. He waited until the train began to slow down and as he'd done weeks before, slowly slid the door open and vaulted from the carriage into the scrub alongside the track. Picking himself up, as the train clattered into the distance he took a wary look round before striding off.

Anatolia, July.

'Mama, mama, soldiers are coming.'

Hegine Seferian stopped what she was doing and held onto the edge of the rough wooden table, reeling in shock at the sound of the high, piping voice outside. Khat? Khat!! The idea left her brain no sooner than it had taken root and she winced before sadly walking to the open doorway. The memory of her dead son was uppermost in her mind as she watched the slight form of Jan Abalian running down the hillside shouting the very same words Khat had scant weeks before.

He ran straight to the back door, pointing and jabbering with the impetuousness and exuberance of the young and she had to hold and restrain him until he calmed and spoke more slowly. 'Hegine, Hegine, I saw soldiers, over there.' He pointed excitedly and the words tumbled from his lips in a rush. 'Lots of them, I think, they're making a big dust cloud and they're headed this way.'

His words spelt danger for them all and she felt sick at their import. Gathering her thoughts she rubbed her hands over her face, trying not to frighten the boy. 'Jan, go and get your mother and sister but be quiet, don't make a sound. Hurry now but whatever you do, don't let the soldiers see you. Understand?'

He nodded, wide-eyed and disappeared at a run as she whirled round and looked frantically at the state of the room. There was fresh food on the table, vegetables and some dry corn and if the soldiers entered they'd realise someone was living here. Running over she swept the table's contents into her hands and stopped, stricken. The chickens, they'd find the chickens in the coop and know for certain someone or somebody was in the vicinity. Before she knew what she was doing she'd opened the coop's wire door and flung the food inside.

The scrawny birds swooped on the new-found delicacies and began feeding avidly and with luck that would keep them quiet until the soldiers passed. As she waited for Jan and his mother and sister to arrive Hegine took stock of their existence in the weeks following their meeting. The morning after she'd wearily arrived, fresh from her horrors with the bandits and the death of her son she and Marem Abalian had thoroughly searched the empty houses accompanied by the two children, Jan and Elise.

All the non-perishable foodstuffs that they could find had been removed back to her and Artoun's house and stored. The perishables that were edible they'd quickly consumed over the next few days, eating hearty meals until everything had gone before it had a chance to rot. Jan had displayed a talent for rounding up the stray chickens that had evaded the clutches of scavengers in the surrounding countryside and he'd also walked into the hills with Oğlan, returning tired but proudly leading three goats he'd found wandering around, tethers still attached.

The goats gave them welcome milk and Marem had become adept at cheese-making, showing off the skills she'd learned in her own household. By staying together in the same house they'd given comfort to each other and a degree of protection, something she'd been grateful for when a group of three Arab traders had passed curiously through the deserted village a week later leading their heavily-laden camels. They would have tarried longer but the sight of Oğlan soundlessly baring his ferocious canines had added fresh impetus to their strides and after hurriedly bartering some fresh meat and bread for some of Hegine's precious jewellery, they'd hastily departed.

Perhaps they'd alerted the soldiers, she mused as she waited impatiently. No matter, it was all spilt milk now and the thing to do was to hide and let the soldiers pass through quickly without knowing of the women and children hiding in one of the many seemingly deserted houses. Her thoughts were interrupted by the arrival of Marem and her children and soundlessly she gestured towards the half-open door of the adjoining room. Marem nodded and pulled the two children with her as she passed.

Taking one last look round, Hegine joined her and together they all crouched low besides the rough-hewn bed and its covers. From outside she could hear the jingling of harnesses and her heart leapt as the sounds grew in intensity as the soldiers made their way slowly down the street in relative silence.

It was *Oğlan* who betrayed them. As the soldiers passed the hound rose from his prone position by the back door, a low intense growling noise rising from deep within his throat as he caught the scent of his enemies. Hegine listened in terror as the jingling stopped and a dry, laconic voice broke the silence.

'Halt! You, Ismail. Go and see what's causing that noise.'

'At once, sir.'

A pause followed. 'Sir, it's a dog, a big dog. It looks dangerous, what shall I do?'

'Shoot it now. I don't want the damn thing eating any of you, it would make my report more complicated than it is already.'

'No!'

Hegine rose and ran to the front door without thinking, her only thoughts for *Oğlan's* wellbeing. Opposite her doorway, mounted on a small grey pony a man in an officer's uniform stared at her in astonishment. By his side a wizened uniformed figure raised his rifle but the officer spoke sharply and he lowered it again. Both woman and officer contemplated each other and it was he who broke the silence. Raising his right hand in a mock salute he said,

'You have the better of me, we thought this village was uninhabited. And you are...?'

She stared back proudly at him, noticing his even features and small, thin moustache. 'My name is Hegine Seferian and Merghem is my village.'

'Is it indeed? And is there just you and the dog, or are there anymore of you hiding in there?' He pointed to the door at her back.

'A friend and her children,' she informed him, 'victims like myself of the brutality of those who were once our protectors.'

'Bravely said Hegine Seferian, but who are these *protectors* you accuse?'

'Those Turkish soldiers who came here and robbed us, took our young women and girls into slavery and killed everyone else.'

'Ah...' he coughed delicately and spat over the side of his saddle, 'Those neither were honourable Turkish soldiers nor were they your protectors, they were just bandit scum pretending to be the agents of the Turkish people.'

'I notice you did not say *ermeni*.'

His dark features flushed angrily and he chose his next words carefully as he leant forward. 'Let me introduce myself. I am Captain Salih Bayur, an officer in the *Gendarmara* sent here by our government to oversee certain events. These men accompanying me are my *Zaptiehs*, members of the same force. In answer to your impudent question, are we not all Turks, Hegine Seferian? Arab, Ottoman, *Ermeni?*'

'That was before you came and murdered us, and—,' she stopped overcome as Khat's face swam before her, 'my son.'

For an answer he dismounted awkwardly and walked towards her. She caught an antiseptic smell, a clean fragrance as he neared her but stood

343

her ground and gazed resolutely at him as he left the pony's reins dangling and crossed to her side. Standing in front of her she could see his left sleeve was empty and pinned neatly to the side of his tunic. A livid scar crossed his left eye, the socket of which was also empty.

'Look down the street, what do you see?' he demanded. She squinted in the sunlight and did as he bade, seeing a dim mass of figures halted some way from where she stood.

'Who are those people, more soldiers to do your bidding?' she questioned but he smiled grimly.

'Look again, these are your own people, my people. *Ermeni*, yes, but to me they are also fellow Turks.'

By now her eyes had become accustomed to the sun's glare and she recognised the truth in what he said. The mass of people she took to be soldiers were clad in a garb similar to her own, that of simple country folk. Armenians.

'We found them in the desert some miles from here, being guarded by some renegades who spun a web of lies when asked what they were doing with these people. We brought the people back with us and I'm on my way to headquarters for more orders.'

'Halit!' she burst out and he looked at her in amazement.

'How did you come to know that dog, Halit?' he demanded.

'He was here, some weeks ago when they took me and my son away and murdered most of us. I escaped and made my way back here. They said they had orders from the government, they said we were...'

'They lied!' Bayur said harshly, 'Evil men have taken the opportunity afforded by the war against the invading *infidels* to line their own pockets by committing crimes against a certain portion of the population. The *ermeni* people have borne the brunt of their hatred but the crimes carried out by those scum eventually will be avenged, you have my word on it.'

'It was soldiers who carried out those crimes.' she replied simply and he glanced sharply at her. 'Halit. It was he who informed us we were criminals to be relocated by the government. False words! We were marched from this place and most of us foully murdered in the desert, my beautiful son Khat lies there among the dead.' Tears welled in her eyes and his gaze softened.

'And your husband, what of him, was he too killed in this manner?'

She looked scornfully at him. 'Captain, not all *ermeni* are the traitors you think us to be. My husband, too, wears a uniform, that of a Ottoman soldier. He at least serves his country honourably, unlike those in similar clothing.'

344

'In which case I salute him as a fellow patriot.'

'Don't mock me, Captain, our son lies dead at the hands of those who in earlier times we would have looked to for protection. Now, I can only feel hatred towards you all.'

'Mistress Seferian, I mourn with you for the untimely death of your son and all the other innocents but believe me, the retribution for these crimes has already begun.'

'How?'

'Halit again. It was he who commanded the rabble escorting these people to their doom. I questioned him but he tried to bluster his way out, informed me that he had friends in high places and that if I failed to release him and his men he would see to it I was severely dealt with.

You may not believe me but I too have served my country faithfully for many years and was not inclined to listen for much longer to the lies of a cur who disgraced the uniform he was wearing when we arrested him. Yes, Hegine Seferian, arrested him and his renegades. My understanding is that these *ermeni* were to be transported to the Syrian desert, not led by Halit somewhere else to be murdered most foully. These people were being robbed before being slaughtered and so I followed my orders to the letter. All confiscated property becomes that of the state, anyone contravening those orders will pay the ultimate price.

As for Halit, I took him at his word and he is now communing with those friends in high places he alluded to. I had him hanged from the highest tree we could find on our way back here but before I did that I had his men shot with their own weapons, I couldn't have my men soil their good *tufeks* on those scum.

And now, my men are tired and hungry so we'll rest here awhile.' As he spoke, Marem and the children had fearfully joined Hegine by the doorway and he smiled to allay their fears. 'Come, all of you, join us for a simple meal. We have some provisions, not much but you're welcome to share what we have.' He turned to the private at his side.

'Take the pony and water her and when you're done, bring the other villagers up here.'

When the man had smartly led the pony away Bayur turned back to Hegine. 'You've given me an idea. Please speak with these people for when we've eaten we shall stay for the night and in the morning I'm going to leave them with you and return to my superior for further orders. We'll need shelter so if you could show us where we could rest I'd be most grateful.' He stopped at the look in Hegine's eyes. 'Don't worry; I'll leave two or three of my men with you. They're decent men and no-one will dare interfere so long as they're watching over you. Now, come, speak with these people and see what's to be done.' He turned back and smiled thinly.

'But please, first, tie the dog up, can you?'

--§--

In the morning he was up and about early, haranguing his men in order to be off without delay. Before leaving he spoke with Hegine. 'Stay here under my men's protection and I'll be back in a week or so once I have new orders concerning your wellbeing. The army has commandeered many of our horses for their own use so it is only we officers who ride. This makes travel a time-consuming necessity but my poor men are now used to me bawling at them from on high while they walk alongside.'

She looked up at him astride the pony. 'And where would we go?'

He had the grace to look embarrassed.

'My apologies. My men will keep you safe, Mistress Seferian. Don't worry, I hand-picked them and they will carry out my orders to the letter whilst I'm away. No-one will be allowed to disturb you, you'll see. Now, I must be off and report back, my superior will be most interested to learn of my findings.'

After a pause he turned back and gestured at his empty sleeve. 'Do you see this, Mistress Seferian? I was wounded in the Balkan War whilst serving with the army. A shell burst nearby and tore off my arm and damaged my eye as we were retreating. We passed through an *ermeni* village and the village doctor, a good fellow, saw my plight and urged my men to take me into his house.

He stripped off the filthy dressings, amputated what was left of my arm and cleaned my eye socket. He then dressed all my wounds and sent me on my way with clean bandages. If it wasn't for his succour I would have died on the road back to our barracks. So you see, I have a debt to pay, one that has weighed heavy on my mind since but now I have the chance to repay a stranger's kindness. I will not fail you.'

He turned in the saddle and gestured with his free hand. Instantly, his remaining *Zaptiehs* formed a column and at his command they marched away, rifles over their shoulders. Hegine watched until they were out of sight before slowly walking down the dusty street to where several bemused figures watched her approach. She'd spoken to several of the bewildered new arrivals the previous evening, showing them empty houses where they could rest. Now she stood, hands on hips as she looked at them and contemplated how to make contact.

'Listen to me!' she cried, 'I am Hegine Seferian, a woman from this village who has suffered just like you and know what you're feeling...'

An old man stepped forward, eyes full of hatred. 'Why should we listen to you when you've shown yourself to be in league with those bandits? It was people like them who dragged us from our village with the idea of killing us all so why should we trust you, what loss have you known in all of this?'

She looked keenly at him until he lowered his gaze. 'Loss?' she spoke softly. 'The bones of my son Khat lie out there in the desert, along with those of the people of this village. I alone survived, look around you, do you see any others apart from myself and another woman with her two children? We have all lost a part of our lives, some more grievously than others. The captain who has just departed has shown himself to be an honourable man, unlike those who came to your village and mine and committed such foul deeds. He could have left you to die, as my people did but he saved you instead and brought you here

Can you see those men the captain left behind? They are our guardians and our protection until his return. They will look over us and ensure no-one else can take or harm you.'

The crowd had swelled by this time and she began to feel nervous at them all staring at her but her fears were allayed when the old man who'd harangued her stepped forward to her side. 'You make me ashamed to have doubted you, mistress,' he said meekly, 'come, meet with my people and let us know what you want of us. I am Farhad Beklian, a one-time elder of our village before the bandits arrived and wrecked our lives. What words can I say to comfort you in the loss of your son?'

She felt hot tears prick her eyelids but stifled them as she advanced over to him and linked her arm through his, relieved to hear his words. 'None but I thank you for your kindness. Introduce me, Farhad Beklian,' she said, 'and let's see if we can help each other in this time of troubles. There's much to do here until the captain returns so let us make a start.'

Within seconds she was surrounded by a host of babbling people, women, children and old folk, all vying for her attention at once. Waving for Marem to join her she began separating the numbers into more manageable groups, walking them round and allocating new residences better suited to their needs than those they'd inhabited the previous night. Once everyone was billeted she walked over to where a fierce-looking moustachioed *Zaptieh* sat by the well under the hazel tree, awaiting her.

She bent down and pressed her hands together. 'Greetings, sir, and welcome to our village. The captain has informed us that you are to look over us until his return and for that you have our eternal gratitude. We shall eat soon, a goat is to be slaughtered and a fine stew made. Could you perhaps join us in our meal?'

The *Zaptieh's* face creased appreciatively in a wide smile, revealing heavily-stained yellow teeth as he responded. 'Goat stew? We've had nothing but lentils and stale bread these past days, a stew shall be a feast indeed.' He drew a long, sharp bayonet from its scabbard. 'Ismail here used to be a butcher before the army conscripted him. I'll get him off his lazy arse and he can do the slaughtering for you in return for a good plate of the stew.'

Uttering a mental thank you at his words she nodded hurriedly and waited until one of the other *Zaptiehs* rose slowly to his feet and waited for her to show him what he must do. The sacrifice of a precious goat would be more than compensated for by the goodwill her deed would engender between them. Summoning a smile to her face she beckoned and Ismail loped tamely over to her.

'So much to do.' she mused, leading the way to where the goats were tethered. The fields on the outskirts of the village were full of ripening wheat and the vineyards groaned under the weight of bunches of grapes, all planted before Halit and his men had wreaked their vengeance on them. Nearer the houses, many plots had vegetables running to seed and she knew that come the morning she'd have to chivvy what able-bodied people she could muster to help her. The choice was stark enough, gather in what they could and sort it for the winter or starve. Cutting the wheat, winnowing the sheaves and bringing the full bags to the storehouses in the village would be a back-breaking task but one that had to be faced. The alternative didn't bear thinking about.

--§--

Ten days had passed since the captain's departure. Hegine sat atop the hillside overlooking the village, the hound Oğlan at her side, and ruminated deeply. The *Zaptiehs* had won everyone over with their gentle ways and willingness to work with them to gather in the harvest. It had been hard work but most of the precious corn was now safely stored and she could begin to hope. An image of her dead son had invaded her sleep over the past two nights and as she grieved in silence, whilst sat in the long grass, her heart had reached out into the unknown. Her failure to seek Artoun out over the miles separating them and commune with him had left her depressed and unsettled and she longed for his strong arms around her to help assuage the pain of their loss.

While she watched, Oğlan interrupted her thoughts by leaping to his feet, whining. She glanced down in concern. 'What is it, boy?' Panting heavily, he lifted his muzzle and began sniffing the air, a low growl emanating from his throat. Staring into the distance in an endeavour to discover what he'd sensed, a dustcloud on the horizon caught her eye and she frowned, squinting into the sun as she tried to make it out.

With mounting dread she made out a body of men travelling in their direction. From the slowness of their approach it would be an hour or so until they reached the village but the knowledge brought no comfort. Scrambling to her feet she raced down the hillside with Oğlan, looking for the older *Zaptieh*, Ali, and his men.

Ali was sat in his customary seat by the well, dandling a small child on his knee but his smile faded when he saw her look of consternation. Setting the giggling child down he strode over. The dog growled deeply in displeasure at the man's proximity to his adopted mistress but she *shushed!* him angrily and he subsided at her feet. 'What ails, you, Mistress Seferian?' the grizzled *Zaptieh* asked and in answer she looked over her shoulder, anxious not to startle those people staring at her in bewilderment at her dishevelled state .

'Men, coming this way, they'll be here in under an hour.' she said quietly, trying to catch her breath and he strained to hear her words. Grasping their import Ali's farce hardened and he shouted. 'Ismail, Hasan! Get yourselves out here. Now!' Two bodies tumbled from doorways dragging their rifles with them and the *Zaptieh* berated them for loafing before turning back to Hegine.

'Never fear, this is why the captain left us here. You're safe with us, I'll go outside the village and warn them off. Keep everyone inside until I return, I can threaten all I like but if they see something worth robbing there's no telling what they'll attempt. Quickly, mistress, do it now. You two, come with me and make sure those *tufeks* are loaded. I'll skin your unworthy hides if I find myself threatening strangers with only empty guns to back me up.'

The three *Zaptiehs* raced off and Hegine chided those watching. 'You heard the man, quickly, go and hide in the houses. Stay there until told to come out.' Looks of alarm passed over their faces but the people did as

349

she asked and within seconds the streets were emptied. She was one of the last to do so, joining Marem and her children in the house before pulling the door firmly behind her. Oğlan grumbled his dissatisfaction at this turn of events but she pulled the hound close and buried her head in his thick mane whilst straining to hear any sounds from outside.

The next twenty minutes passed like an eternity but faintly she heard her name being called and she rose. Marem held out a restraining arm but she shrugged it off, pushed Oğlan into a corner of the room and cautiously opened the door a crack. Standing in the street outside her door was Ali, a wide smile lighting up his face.

'It's the captain, my officer, Captain Bayur, returns. They'll be here in a few minutes so forgive me if I take some time to smarten up. Good man he may be but seeing us like this without tunics buttoned up will send him into a rage.'

She laughed aloud in her relief as the *Zaptiehs* pushed and pulled at their uniforms. 'Come on out, everyone! Our saviour Captain Bayur will arrive soon so come, let us honour him with our thanks.' In ones and twos they came, reluctantly leaving the sanctuary of the houses to gather by the well and wait in a subdued silence for the soldier's arrival.

The jingle of a horses harness preceded the appearance of the captain astride his small pony, accompanied by a dozen men and for a moment her heart thudded wildly in her breast. Memories flooded back as she recalled Halit's scowling face and the grief that had followed. Her breathing eased and subsided to what passed for normal as round a corner trotted the pony bearing Captain Salih Bayur.

He saw her at once and lifted a diffident arm in greeting although he wore a troubled expression on his face. 'Mistress Seferian, look, did I not say I'd return?' He glanced at the three men standing to attention by the well. 'Ah, I see you've been taking good care of my fellows. I hope they've not imposed themselves too much on you. Hasan! You look positively fat, man, what've they been feeding you?'

Hasan giggled nervously and thrust his shoulders out. 'At ease, all of you.' Bayur slid from his saddle, letting the reins droop into the earth. 'Is that water cool? I've been a long time in the saddle and my throat's parched.'

'At once, *efendim*.'

Ali rushed over to the well and returned bearing a dripping waterbottle. Lifting it to his lips, the captain drank deeply before stoppering it and letting it slide through his fingers to the ground. He looked around with a keen eye, missing nothing.

'I noticed the fields look empty, was it a good harvest?' Hegine nodded in agreement and he continued to speak as the remainder of his men filed round the corner to join him. 'The vineyards, too, look as if they've given up a good crop. You've done well.'

'Everything we grew has gone well, captain,' she replied, 'God willing we should have enough supplies now to see out the winter.'

If he heard her reference to God he ignored it and turned to the group of soldiers milling round in confusion. 'Bring that dog out here and give him a drink. I want him in good shape when we leave here.'

A *Zaptieh* roughly pushed a dust-rimed figure towards them, a fez pulled low on its face and hands bound tightly in front. Hegine glanced at the captain in puzzlement and Bayur answered her unspoken question. 'We found this…this creature on the track a day's march away. He saw us and tried to flee but my men ran him down. A deserter, fleeing from the war in Çannakale over the water, no doubt. I say that as he refuses to talk but that's of no import, when we get him back to my superior's prison he'll face a severe beating and savage questioning before we shoot him!'

She felt a pang of compassion as she watched the lone figure sway on the balls of his feet. Judging by his response she judged the prisoner to be on the point of collapse and moved forward to pick up the captain's discarded water-bottle. 'This man is utterly exhausted, captain, do you want him dead before you question him?'

'Go on, give him a drink then, he's in no shape to cause any trouble.'

Hearing the captain's words she approached the prisoner, aware of a rank, unwashed smell emanating from his body and clothing. Gently lifting his lowered face she took in his gaunt, unwashed and unshaven appearance as she prepared to pour water down his parched lips. The fez tumbled from his head, giving her a clear view of his face and she staggered back in shock and incredulity.

'Artoun!'

The haggard face of her husband stared mutely into her eyes and Hegine Seferian dropped the water-bottle, falling limply to the floor. Thunderstruck, those around her stared in amazement as the prisoner dropped to his knees and vainly tried to take her in his bound arms before being bundled away by his escort.

--§--

351

She awoke to find herself lying on the bed in which she'd shared so many nights with Artoun and struggled upright. 'Ah, how do you feel?' She turned at the question to see Marem's concerned face and tried to rise off the coarse covers but her friend restrained her. 'Let me go!' she cried hotly, 'They have Artoun, my husband.'

'Hegine, calm yourself, no good will come of upsetting yourself this way.' Marem's words had a calming effect and Hegine relaxed, bursting into tears. 'Oh, Hegine, don't distress yourself, the captain's a good man. It'll be alright, you see.' Marem tried to soothe her but Hegine's sobs only increased in intensity.

'I don't understand, they called him a dog, a deserter. My Artoun would never desert.' Hegine wailed bitterly, 'You heard Captain Bayur, Marem, he said they're going to shoot Artoun! Why? What is this, what has he done for this to happen?'

'There, there. Calm yourself, I'm sure no-one's going to shoot anyone. It's all a mistake, you'll see. If your Artoun is the man you've told me about these past weeks then I'm sure he'll be able to explain himself to the captain and all will become clear.' Although she spoke with assurance, Marem's face knotted into a concerned frown as she remembered the captain's reaction to the identity of his prisoner.

--§--

'So. You are Artoun Seferian, a man from this village and husband to Mistress Hegine. Is that right?' Salih Bayur's face slowly reddened as the figure bound to a chair stared insolently back at him with compressed lips and said nothing. The silence grew between them, broken by the captain striking a boot with his whip in a show of temper. 'Listen to me you fool, do you realise just by finding you this far from the coast in your country's uniform I can have you taken out, flogged within an inch of your miserable life and then executed without so much as a trial? By *Allah*, you *will* answer my questions or that shall happen. And soon! Answer me, or...'

'Or else what? You're going to kill me anyway. I'm *ermeni*, dressed in the uniform trousers of an Ottoman soldier, that alone affords you the perfect excuse. Do you think that being *ermeni* I expect any protection, no matter what I wear?'

Bayur stepped back and stroked his thin moustache thoughtfully as Artoun carefully enunciated his words. 'Ahhh, it has found a tongue at last. What do you mean by those words...*no matter what I wear?* Speak!'

Artoun gazed distrustfully at the man before him before next doing as bidden. 'You wear the uniform of our country too, captain, as do your men outside also but unlike myself you remain safe from other than the enemy's bullets whilst you wear it.' He indicated Bayur's empty sleeve. 'And I see you, too, have paid a high price for that service'

'Stop speaking in riddles, man, what is this nonsense? How can this uniform spell danger other than from our enemies? Do you mean to try and persuade me that you know otherwise? You, a deserter and a coward who fled the battlefield to let others die in your unworthy place. Bah! I...'

'Listen and I *shall* speak.' Artoun spoke forcefully. 'Listen to what I have to say and then decide who is the liar, who is the coward and deserter.'

Captain Bayur leant against the table. 'Continue.'

In a low voice Artoun recounted the story of his journey from Syria and the massacre of his regiment when they were removed from the train. Bayur's face was impassive as Artoun spoke but his eyes betrayed him, moving searchingly over Artoun's calm visage for any trace of embellishment. He broke in once to question Artoun fiercely at one point then settled back as Artoun went on to enlighten him as to his being captured and the journey to Konia. He described his incarceration there and his meeting up with Arif Bilgili before being marched to the peninsula as punishment for his alleged desertion, ending the story with his tale of Arif's death in action.

Bayur grew still as Artoun told of the meeting with Leutnant Brückner and Brückner's subsequent death also. It was only when Artoun finished telling of his escape from the beach that the captain became visibly agitated.

'These men you called the *Teshkilâti Mahsusa*, where did they come from?'

'I don't know,' Artoun replied evenly, 'this was a name the woman on the beach gave to the men staying nearby. Up until then it was a name I'd never heard before.'

He fell silent and the captain gazed into space over his head, a vacant expression on his face. Bayur raised a finger, lowered it then began speaking quietly. 'I've heard of these bandits of the Special Organisation. And believe me, Artoun Seferian, these...I shall not deem to call them men...these dogs are not patriots in any sense of the word. Let me explain. Although technically still a soldier and under the command of the Army Council, I am *employed*, shall we say, by my superior, His

353

Excellency Hakim Paşa, the governor of this province of Halep who rules from Maraş. I command a police detachment in the province used for security purposes, although with the way the war is going I fear our tenure here will not continue for long. That, however, is another matter. Recently, His Excellency has had me investigate certain *happenings* occurring throughout Anatolia and what we've learned so far, and it's not that much, has shaken His Excellency to the core. Secret telegrams, sent in the dead of night to governors and government officials with verbal orders for actions against this people and those people. All without recourse to open debate or proper orders. Some have been removed for not carrying out the orders contained in these telegrams. Purges I would call them but His Excellency declines to speak of them as such.

Being a full cousin of the Sultan, His Most Excellent Mehmet V Reşad, Hakim Paşa has been able to distance himself from the criminal activities of those who would call themselves patriots and to refuse to carry out such orders that he finds distasteful and unjust. *They* would like to see him quietly disposed of but family ties are too strong. His spies in Maraş tell him everything, giving him plenty of warning of the fools in Ankara's meddling.'

'So you believe my story?' Artoun asked.

'What you tell has a ring of truth about it. If all of it is true, and I don't doubt you for an instant, this evil has spread further into the hearts and minds of men than we thought. Make no mistake, Artoun Seferian, there *will* be a reckoning. This is no *jihad*, no holy war taken up against your people. It is murder, pure and simple and retribution will not be long in coming when peace prevails.

The madness will drop from the eyes of men and the war will end but whether we finish as victors is not for me to predict at this moment. What I do say is that decent Ottomans, true Turks, cannot and will not condone this evil. The guilty will face a judgement, that I promise you.

We have heard other rumours, whispers that like the telegrams arrive in the night under cover of darkness. It is said that in certain places for a Turk to aid an *ermeni*, a fellow Turk by *Allah!* is to face death by hanging in front of ones own house before that is burnt to the ground as a warning to others. Have we really come to this? We would kill our own people for aiding their fellow citizens?'

He fell silent, closing his eyes and running his hands down his face in a gesture of helplessness. Opening them abruptly he sighed. 'Go, for tonight go find your wife and be with her. You are so lucky, Artoun

Seferian to have found one like her. That woman has kept this village and the people together through the strength of her will. And also through her love for you. I will spend some time this evening thinking of how to reconcile this situation and give you my decision in the morning. For now, seek out your wife and comfort her.'

Artoun hesitated. The captain's words had aroused a deep foreboding. 'My son, Khat, is he with my wife also? I ask this only because you have not mentioned my son in all the words that have passed between us and the absence of those words frighten me. Has something happened?'

Salih Bayur raised his head and spoke softly, sadly. 'I have a son and daughter whom I have not seen in months. It is not for me to explain. Do as I say, go find your wife.' At that, he rose and quickly untied Artoun's bonds.

--§--

She heard the sound of his footsteps and ran to the door, wrenching it open and throwing herself into his arms before he could lay a hand on the catch. 'Hegine.' he murmured, burying his head into her lustrous hair whilst crushing her to him. He held her in that manner for several moments before gently releasing her to gaze into her eyes and softly kiss her cheek.

'Where is our son? Hegine, tell me about Khat.' he whispered into her ear, drawing her into his embrace once more. At his words, she stiffened and drew back, leaning away from him so she could see his face as her eyes filled. 'You know?' she asked, wonderingly.

'I saw the sorrow in the Captain's eyes and guessed the truth, although I could hardly believe it. Tell me how our son died.' he answered brokenly and she felt her heart break at the pain in his voice. 'Oh, Artoun...' she collapsed in the strength of his arms and he held her tightly to him as the dam holding back her tears gave way.

'I ...I cannot—' she sobbed, 'he was so small and I couldn't fight back and they took him from me...and...oh, Artoun, our beautiful boy—' his tears mingled with hers as in a low, faltering voice Hegine told her husband how their son had died.

Whilst she spoke, often breaking down inbetween sentences, Artoun stroked her hair and wept with her for the loss of their son's innocence. The weeks of yearning had promised much for his hopes to be so cruelly dashed with her words and he wept as he recalled Khat's face, his eyes and the special bond that had passed between father and son. He could not envisage a future without the presence of their firstborn beside them but he knew instinctively that if he was to falter now it could break the fragile spirit of the woman he loved.

Marem Abalian entered the room silently and her eyes opened wide as she took in the two people holding each other. Behind her, a bewildered Jan opened his mouth to speak but she swept her son into her arms and left, quietly closing the door behind her. That night she slept in an unoccupied house with her children as Artoun and Hegine began the long journey of love and reconciliation.

As dawn broke, Hegine rose and boiled some hot water. Artoun joined her and she made him sit whilst she washed his face before carefully shaving around his mouth, leaving him with a fine, drooping moustache. Fresh clothes stored in the long chest under the window transformed his haggard appearance and she stepped back in nervous apprehension.

'There! You look so much better than you did when I first saw you yesterday.' He walked over and wrapped his arms round her, breathing in her fragrance.

'Dearest Hegine, when you told me of our son last night I thought my world had come to an end. Seeing you here, I realise that…'

'Shh.' She said. 'Khat isn't gone from us, Artoun, he lives here.' she placed a hand on her breast, 'When first I wake, until the moment my eyes close at night, our son is safe with me. With us. If God blesses us with more children, and I know that he will, we shall tell them of their brother who lives among the stars. I understand also that your grief seems as if there will be no end but the sun will shine on us again and laughter will come back to live in our house. Grieve for him, Artoun, for what Khat might have become but live also, for what we can make together in the years to come.'

She leant forward and placed a small object into his open palm. 'Look, Artoun, your son sends his father the silver chain you bought him.'

He said nothing but she felt his shoulders heave silently as he clenched the chain tightly before pocketing it. After a while, he cleared his throat. 'Before we can dare to believe in these things, there is the matter of the captain and his charges against me.'

She tore free from his hold and turned on him. 'Artoun, don't! Captain Bayur is a just man. He hanged Halit for his crimes and that brings hope to my heart. You see, he'll set you free as soon as he recognises the injustice you've faced.'

'I hear your voice and words Hegine but the matter is not ours to resolve, only Bayur can say what will happen and he *is* a Turk.'

As he spoke, there came a muffled knock and both stared at each other with strained glances before Artoun walked over and opened the door. Standing in the dirt, an embarrassed look on his features, was the grizzled *Zaptieh,* Ali. 'If it please you, sir, 'he began humbly, 'the captain would speak with you.'

'I'm coming.' Artoun replied and took Hegine in his arms. 'Stay here,' he whispered fiercely, 'let me talk to the captain alone.'

'Artoun!'

'No! Let it be this way.' He hugged her to him, disengaged and strode out into the sunshine where Ali waited patiently. 'Come,' Artoun said, 'Let us go and see what your master wants.'

She ran out and watched as he disappeared up the dusty street, disappearing into one of the houses taken over by the soldiers. When they'd disappeared from sight, she began to sob quietly, the tears running down her face whilst she wiped futilely at them with the back of her hand. Marem Albanian appeared as if from nowhere and together the two women stood in the doorway in a close embrace.

--§--

Captain Bayur looked up from his seat as the figure of Artoun Seferian filled the doorway. 'Ah, you came—' he began but Artoun held up a hand. 'Captain, whatever I have done is done but please, assure me that whatever happens no harm will come to my wife or these poor unfortunates you and your men rescued. They had no part in what has transpired and...'

'A pretty speech, Artoun Seferian, but totally unnecessary,' the captain growled, 'although the crimes you've committed are grave ones, it could be argued that those committed against you and your people are even graver. This no time to talk of punishment, I would look to a better ending.'

'I don't understand,' Artoun muttered, 'what are you saying?'

'Is it not written in your holy book that an eye shall be taken for an eye? In Islam we, too, follow that tenet. Make the punishment fit the crime, eh? An eye for an eye is a pretty philosophy indeed to consider, it can be said but does it apply in this case? Hardly.'

'My son—' Artoun began but the captain forestalled him. Bayur looked downcast, uncomfortable, and his eyes refused to meet Artoun's. His next words sent a shiver through Artoun.

357

'My apologies for not informing you when we met, I deemed it better you heard of your son from your wife rather from my lips. It would appear that some children are being wrenched from their parent's arms during the deportations, in order to bring them up as Moslems. I can assure you that my men and I have had no part in this business.' His words tailed off as Artoun stared at him.

'What is this evil?' Artoun demanded.

'It's true, the parents are forced from their homes and the children are left behind, to be cared for by the state and brought up in the faith of Islam.'

'Not all children are taken.' Artoun intoned softly.

'No,' the captain whispered, his face turning a haggard shade of grey, 'to my country's everlasting shame, some are not.'

'And shall we meet this same fate?'

'No, Artoun Seferian!' the captain spoke sharply. 'Whatever crimes could be lodged against you pale into insignificance when we weigh up the crimes of the greater populace. Villages have been stripped of their inhabitants but here *Allah* has given us the chance to show mercy and help rebuild lives.' His next words threw Artoun's mind into confusion. 'You commanded men in your regiment didn't you?'

'Yes but what—?' A commotion outside interrupted him and he looked inquisitively towards the door. It burst open a few seconds later as Ali strode in, his eyes wide in fear.

'Captain, sir, master, my apologies but there are men coming. Many men, soldiers.'

'Alright, Ali.' Bayur rapped, 'Stay here and watch this man whilst I go and see who our new guests are.'

'Sir.'

Captain Bayur walked slowly to the door before turning to confront Artoun. 'Stay here with my man and don't come out. It may be nothing but on the other hand—' he let his words trail away before leaving and closing the door quietly behind him.

He was back within minutes, rubbing his jaw thoughtfully as he entered the room, sorrow and fear mingling in his expression. 'These men are regular troops who've been ordered to round up the people here and march them to the nearest rail point, for onward travel to relocation in Syria. I've been given an hour to gather everyone together and then the soldiers will take the people away.'

'But how—?'

'I don't know,' he replied testily, 'I can only assume word spread after I made my report to His Excellency and someone reported those facts to the army authorities. I would have had you all stay here together under your leadership, Seferian, but these men are commanded by a particularly nasty specimen of an officer so remain in this house whilst I make an attempt to —'

'Captain,' Artoun spoke softly, 'I will not go with them and neither shall my wife, I know what awaits us in this so-called *relocation*. It would be better if you kill us both, here and now.' He gazed steadily at the captain and it was Bayur who looked away first. From outside a shrill piercing scream made them whirl round and Captain Bayur broke the silence, enunciating each word slowly in order that Artoun understood their import.

'As I feared, it has begun. Listen to me, Artoun Seferian. Before you arrived I promised your wife that nothing would harm her whilst she was under my protection and my word stands. Do nothing to draw attention to this house, stay calm whilst I go and find your wife and bring her to you with *Allah's* help.'

'And what of the others?' Artoun said softly. 'Can you not help them, also?'

'*Olmaz*. Impossible. I can do no more.' Bayur replied simply. 'Unfortunately their fate lies in others hands now, not mine. The soldiers will search every house but by keeping Ali outside he will ensure no-one gains entry and finds you here. My men are faithful to no-one but me so be sure you're in good hands. There is danger for us all should any of the other *ermeni* give you away but I will not go back on a promise made.

'The others, where are they going? What will happen to them?'

Again, Bayur's eyes refused to meet those of Artoun's.

'I'm told space must be found for those Moslems displaced from the war and the earlier conflicts.' He shrugged. 'Your people, and others, must go to be relocated so that these people, deemed to be more suitable, can take their place.'

'This is monstrous! Captain Bayur, take me to this officer, let me speak with him.'

'Enough, Seferian. Stop!' the captain cried harshly. 'It will do no good except to condemn you and your wife. Orders have been given from high-up and they will be obeyed. You and I have no say in the matter.'

He spoke in a more soothing tone. 'Listen to me. You have a chance to live. Think of what I have said and take it, I beg you, for the alternative is too terrible to contemplate. Do you understand?'

Artoun nodded mutely. Bayur nodded curtly in return and after a hurried conversation with Ali, slipped through the doorway and disappeared.

In the minutes following, as the cries, hoarse shouts and screams from outside intensified, Artoun suffered an agony of waiting. Dark thoughts surfaced with each passing second as the banging of doors and cries of frightened women reached his ears. When he could stand the suspense no longer, he sprang to his feet and opened the door before an alarmed Ali's gaze. Someone outside pressed back on the door and Artoun fell backwards into the room, followed by a sanguine Captain Bayur together with Hegine, Marem and her two children. The dog, Oğlan, was the last to enter, gazing curiously round before flopping down at Artoun's feet with a contented sigh.

'Your wife is as stubborn as you Seferian,' Bayur remarked dryly, 'she wouldn't come with me unless I brought these other people also.'

As Artoun rose and embraced Hegine, Bayur spoke. 'Listen to me, all of you, we are not out of danger, the soldiers have nearly gathered everyone together and will be leaving soon. Their buffoon of an officer has demanded that my men and I accompany them to the railhead to ensure no-one escapes on the way so we will have to leave you.

Do not make a sound. It was only through the will of *Allah*, may his prophet be praised, that I managed to save you but you are not safe yet. Stay in the back room while I round up my men and, please, keep the dog silent or he will be the death of us all.'

'What if one of the villagers tells the soldiers that we are missing?'

'Then pray for a miracle, Artoun Seferian, for that is all that can save you should that happen.'

'And what will become of you, should we be found?'

Bayur smiled. A sad smile. 'We have a saying, *Kadir ne ise o olur.* Whatever fate has in store, will be.'

His expression changed as he thought rapidly. 'There is a possible way out for you, though. When we are gone, you must strike for the coast. Make for Mersin and find a boat skipper to take you away from here. You speak excellent Turkish, Seferian, and your skin is dark enough for you to pass as an Ottoman Turk. If anyone meets you on the way tell them you are a trader bound for Haleb together with your two wives and your children where your mother is gravely ill. Take passage by boat across the gulf to Alexandretta and when you reach there strike out to the south for a place called *Musa Dagh*. I have a map in my pouch, I shall no doubt carelessly lose it when I go. You will find it, I'm sure, and put the directions I shall scribe on it to good use.' He smiled thinly.

'*Musa Dagh*? What is this place, I've never heard of it?'

'It means *Moses Mountain*, a holy mountain not far from Alexandretta. His Excellency's spies have heard whispers, they say *ermeni* people are travelling there in order to remain out of the reach of the troops and the police. They could even be planning to set up a camp and resist attempts to take them by force. I don't know. All I do know is that this might be your only chance, a slim one mind, of surviving this nightmare.'

He looked from one to the other.

'Take passage by boat? *Musa Dagh*? What is this you tell us, captain? Look at us, where do you think we can get the money to do as you say?' Artoun spoke angrily.

Before Bayur could answer, Hegine spoke up. 'Artoun, beloved,' she said hurriedly, 'the captain has given us a chance. I buried some money and the rest of my jewellery in the back garden underneath the chicken coop. It's there still so with God's grace we should be able to sell it for enough money to pay for the boat. If we can sail to Syria we might be able to make our way to Egypt from there. My uncle in Alexandria would take us in and we can make a new start. Please Artoun, we must try otherwise it will all end here.'

She held him tightly and he relented, his anger fading.

'My apologies to you, captain, for dismissing your bravery so lightly. What can I do?'

'Nothing for now. Wait until long after we're gone before you venture outside. Take my advice, all of you alter your dress, both you women look like *ermeni* at this moment so see if you can find some other form of clothing to change your appearance. I know it's not what you want but you must look like Moslem women and act like them too otherwise you'll arouse suspicion.

Keep the children quiet, one loose word from them and it could spell disaster for you all. The dog will help prevent curious people from approaching too closely but you'll need all your wits about you if you're to stay alive. You must excuse me now but I fear the time has come for me to leave you. May you find peace wherever it is you end up, *Allah versin*. God grant it.'

Artoun freed himself from Hegine's embrace and grabbed the captain's shoulder, shaking it vigorously. 'Words fail me, captain, I cannot thank you enough for what you've done. You are an honourable man and if we survive it will be because of you. I wish you a long life and if this

361

madness ends, who knows, perhaps we shall meet under happier circumstances.'

'And as fellow Turks.' Bayur said gently. 'When this is all over, Turkey will recover from the sickness that now covers her eyes and we shall be as a nation again. Do not hate all Turks, Seferian, keep that for those whose crimes against your people indict us all. Amongst all this pain and suffering there are some Turks who still retain their honour and who will do their utmost to bring about peace between us again in the future.

I shall write out a *Teskeré* for you and that, too, will be carelessly discarded, wrapped in the map I intend to lose before leaving here. Look on the ground by the well. It will be a complete forgery and you may never need it but if you do, proffer it with the assurance of a man handing over the real thing and you'll get away with it. Don't act cowed, that'll be a giveaway. And now, I've done all I can, the rest I leave to a merciful *Allah*. I must go or they'll send someone looking for me and that will never do. '

He raised his good arm and saluted them before gesturing to Ali. The *Zaptieh* sprang to the door and opened it a crack. Looking quickly out, Ali nodded and both men disappeared into the daylight. Seconds later, a loud bellowing told them that the emptying of the village had begun. Above a subdued wailing came the harsh commands of the soldiers as the human caravan slowly wended its way to the east and the fate awaiting them.

Artoun took Hegine in his arms and held her tight. He felt her heart beating rapidly and he moved to quell her doubts. 'This will end and we shall find freedom!' he hissed fiercely. He looked across to where Marem and her children stood, trembling fearfully. 'Come, come, you are all our family now.' The children ran over and clutched at his waist whilst Marem approached more slowly and buried her face in Hegine's shoulders, sobbing quietly.

'Those poor people...'she began but Artoun silenced her. 'Grieve for them later, as I shall too, but for now we have been given a chance to live and must make ready our preparations.'

'Hegine! Hegine! Are we going on an adventure?' babbled Jan excitedly. 'Will there be lots...?'

'*Shh*, child,' Artoun admonished him sternly, 'your silence is one of the many certainties we must count on if we are to find salvation. Do you understand?'

The boy nodded, crestfallen, and Artoun bent down and placed a protective arm around his thin shoulders. 'You and I,' he began more

362

gently, 'are the men of the house and it is to us the women, your mother and sister included, will look on as their protectors. Will you assist me in keeping them safe in the coming days?'

Jan's face brightened and he nodded animatedly. 'Good.' Artoun smiled. 'Then let you and I ensure that nothing we need is left behind.'

They stayed in the house for hours before venturing out. No-one inhabited the village but themselves, the windows looked down blankly on them and dusty trails blowing down the empty streets told of a village full only of memories and ghosts. The map and *Teskeré* was where Bayur had said he'd leave it and their last task was spent in rummaging through the houses for food and clothing to sustain them on the journey.

Each carried what he could, even the children were pressed into carrying a small bedroll of spare clothes. Hegine and Marem obeyed the captain's words by finding clothing more suitable to that of a Moslem woman. When they were ready, Artoun led the way to the southern end of the village, Oğlan ambling eagerly alongside. The afternoon sun was beginning to sink into the west as he stopped for a final look round. Seeing the raw emotion in his expression, Hegine moved to Artoun's side and smiled, a look of hope and encouragement.

'A better world beckons, Artoun. I dreamt of Khat last night and in my dream he was smiling down on us, wishing us Godspeed in our travels. We shall live, for him and all the others who will never return. Let us find this *Musa Dagh* the brave captain spoke of and join our people gathering there.' She looked up into his face, a question on her lips. 'But what of your tools, Artoun, do we leave them here or try to carry them with us? We may have need of them when we reach safety, how else will we make our living?'

Artoun squeezed her arm in return and pointed to the south. 'There is where our story in this world ends and a new life awaits in another. There will be no need then of tools. Trust in God, Hegine, and he will provide for us in the new beginning. Come, we need to be on our way. There are many dangers in our path but we will succeed, I'm sure of that. Let us face the future together.' Without waiting for an answer he began walking without a backward glance and after a moment's hesitation, the others followed him.

ANZAC Cove 1960.

'*Efendim*, we're here.'

Walter Harding started as the quiet voice broke into his reverie and he turned over to see the weather-beaten face of his guide staring down at him. The cove they'd grounded in was deserted with only the faint hiss of surf breaking the silence but a horn blast carried across the deep blue of the sea and he espied a large tanker across the water, carving her way imperiously through the waves. On her way to Istanbul no doubt, he reasoned, and switched his gaze back to the landscape of ANZAC Cove.

Although the years had been kinder to the countryside than the men who had once lived and fought here it had still changed immeasurably. He stared hard at the crumbling hillsides, willing his fading memory to spring into life and point out him relevant landmarks stored for so long in the recesses of his mind. Where were the dugouts, the jetties and tracks leading up from the sea into the scrub-covered hills above? It was difficult to think that this was where it had began and ended. So many good men sacrificed and for what? Lives had been changed forever as a consequence of their experiences, his own included, and he could only wonder at the incongruity of it all.

Foreigners were seldom seen in this corner of the world but he had no doubt that in the years to come the trickle would turn into a flood. This quiet setting would become a place of homage and pilgrimage for the many. His family of four adults and one impatient teenage granddaughter had taken passage from Brisbane to Alexandria, transferring there to a smaller steamer for the journey to Istanbul. On arrival they'd hired a large battered, estate car, bumping and wheezing down the dusty tracks to Maidos, now renamed Eceabat, with the aid of a Michelin map in a state of suppressed excitement and trepidation.

Arriving in the late afternoon they'd taken a ferry over The Narrows to Çannakale and to the modest *pension* recommended to them. From there it had been an easy task to hire a fishing-boat and its owner to take Walt over to the Peninsula and around the Hellespont. Walt had made it plain that the initial visit would consist solely of himself and the family had readily acquiesced to his request. Bridgette had her own reasons for coming and he wanted to include her in his pilgrimage but they'd both realised that the first time was for Walt alone.

Selim Erez had been introduced to them by the owner of the *pension* as someone proficient in English and familiar with the area they wished to visit and he'd readily agreed to accompany Walt as a guide. A sleepless night followed before he'd met Selim and the guide's son in the early morning at the harbour's edge and boarded. The fishing boat looked as weather-beaten as its owner but she was spotless and her engine fired at the first attempt, nosing them out of the narrow harbour into the current.

The fast waters flowing through The Narrows had swept them along and he'd engaged Selim in quiet conversation, gazing with interest at the outline of Kilitbahir fort on the far side. Selim pointed out the wide expanse of Eren Keui Bay and Walt realised as they drifted along that they were passing over the wrecks of the ships that had fired the opening shots and whose failure to succeed that day had led to the birth of the land campaign. Below them in the depths slept the souls of the sailors who'd perished here and the thought had brought a sombre tone to the occasion.

The wide mouth of Morto Bay had yawned before them but he'd quickly dismissed it. 'S' Beach had been a distraction, a minor landing that should have been better supported and he ignored its presence. Selim Erez and his son had erected a tarpaulin between the deckhouse and the stern to shelter Walt from the heat of the sun's rays and he'd gratefully made his way aft to lay down.

On rounding the Hellespont he'd slept in the early morning sun whilst the small boat's diesel engine pushed them laboriously north along the heavily-wooded cliffs, passing the wrecks of grounded lighters and rusting jetties that identified the landing-places of the British in 1915. The bulbous silhouette of Sedulbahir Fort and the killing ground of 'V' Beach loomed into view before slowly disappearing behind them. Here, men of the Dubliners, Munsters and Leinsters had been mown down by the defenders machine-guns as they emerged from the sally ports cut in the side of the steamer, the *SS River Clyde*, but there were no traces left of the ship now. The deaths of the men contained within her bowels were marked by the simple white gravestones of the cemetery contained within the confines of the bay.

'W' Beach, now renamed *Lancashire Landing*, 'X' and 'Y' Beaches all passed unseen as he dozed with his panama hat over his face, rocking easily with the swell of the boat as she headed northwards and to the destination he'd impressed on the skipper before lying down on a bed of fishing nets. Selim had looked worried at first but reassured by his calm demeanour had taken to involving himself with the boat, a task which took up his time during the hours taken in reaching their destination.

It had been Bridgette's idea to return here, a way of joining the past to the present and looking for the peace which had eluded him for so long. Gallipoli wasn't the normal tourist's idea of a visit but she'd nagged him for months to do something about it and her insistence had paid off when at last he'd relented and agreed to find out the ways and means of coming here.

--§--

While he dozed, faces from the past encroached on his semi-conscious state, welding themselves to his memories as the faint sound of gunfire reverberated in his ears and the sharp, acrid tang of cordite drifted across his nostrils. He slept in this manner, dreaming as they rounded Hell Spit and sat in silence as the boat hissed its way onto the beach before grounding silently in the shallows of ANZAC Cove. Whilst Selim, aided by his son Murat, dropped a length of rope tied to a large stone to use as a kedge anchor, Walt eased himself stiffly over the gunwhale and splashed ashore. His aching bones had been a lot younger on his last visit here, he reasoned wryly, and he flexed his shoulders brusquely before making his way up the slight slope.

The years sloughed away as he walked across the shingle and stared at the southern end of the cove. It was there that what he needed to find resided, there that the reason for making this long, arduous journey awaited him and he shivered involuntarily as his stomach contracted sharply. Fear? Possibly, but a sense of completeness also, of finally laying to rest the ghosts that had haunted him for so long. Selim having finished attending to the boat waited with him but his reverent silence imparted that he, too, realised the significance of the stranger's appearance in his country and what this area meant to the man in front of him.

He began walking along the beach but stopped suddenly. If he closed his eyes, as he was wont to do, he knew that when he opened them again a different scene would enfold. There would be the hum of men's conversations as they lugged stores up the beach from Watson's Pier, piled more ammunition crates into high dumps and splashed in laughing, playful groups along the edge of the burning sea. White woolly puffs of shrapnel would burst overhead, a sight once seen never forgotten and that had stayed fresh in his memory down the intervening years.

He closed his eyes, waited a while and then opened them, keenly seeking that which he sought. Disappointment washed over him. Instead of his imaginings the air was still, filled only with the muted sounds of the surf and the faint cries of gulls mingled with the whispers of ghosts. A large bird of prey wheeled slowly overhead, circling on the thermals as it keenly sought out its prey and on seeing it, his mind raced back to another day long ago, not far from this very spot, when he'd watched a similar bird. It could be that it was that distant bird's offspring, many generations removed but he knew in his heart it was a forlorn hope and watched wistfully as it glided away.

Strange how he could now recall with clarity that particular day on the peninsula so many years ago. Time had passed slowly but he could still recall coming round on a stretcher for the second time and seeing the hospital ship looming across the entrance to the cove had aroused a deep sense of tragedy. The physical pain was less by far than the mental burden he'd carried then and now and it was with some relief he'd gratefully accepted the warm descent into blackness that the morphia given by a solicitous doctor had brought. The journey to Egypt had passed uneventfully this time, giving him plenty of hours to lie there and think and he'd lingered impatiently on the quayside on arrival until a tender deposited him back at the same hospital he'd left just days previously.

--§--

It was there that Bridgette had found him; searching the casualty lists each day she'd seen his name and had hurried frantically to his ward for a tear-stained reunion. They'd talked long into the night until fatigue and the effects of his wounds made her realise the burden she was imposing on him and she'd left him to sleep. From then on she'd visited every day and gradually, an understanding had arisen between them, an acknowledgement of the mistakes of the past and an affirmation in the promise of the future.

The lowest point came during his recovery when Tom's effects were sent to him by the Australian authorities. The sight of the small fob watch and a gold locket in amongst Tom's pitifully few personal items and the realisation that this brought closure with no hope of redeeming himself almost broke Walt Harding. Bridgette was the one light in his darkest hours and although his brother's death hung like a cloud over them both, a desire to make amends for their combined loss was the catalyst that brought them closer together.

Walt recovered slowly and returned to the shores of the peninsula in time to see out the final, tragic days of the campaign. Lone Pine, the slaughter of the Australian Light Horse at The Nek and the disasters of further attacks at Cape Helles, Chunuk Bair and Suvla Bay had convinced those back home that the increasing losses were not to be easily borne. A groundswell of opinion had begun with the aim of halting more draining of men and resources and when Hamilton had written to Whitehall in August, asking for another 100,000 men before he could confidently predict a victory, he'd been peremptorily dismissed in disgrace.

Hamilton's successor, General Sir Charles Munro had been appalled at the prevailing conditions facing his new command from the very first day of his arrival. Shocked by what he saw, he made a stark recommendation to London that the whole campaign be abandoned and the peninsula evacuated. His report had Kitchener hurrying out there to see for himself but even he had to concede the wisdom of Munro's words. Whilst Kitchener vacillated in giving the orders, more men died, fell ill or were wounded unnecessarily and it wasn't until early December, with the winter fast approaching, that a decision was finally arrived at..

The evacuation itself was nothing but a miracle. The Turks were unaware of anything untoward as first the ANZAC's in December and then the British and their French counterparts in early January quietly left their positions and sailed away from the beaches in the dead of night over a three-night period. Leaving behind only smashed-up equipment, booby-traps and the graves of their dead.

Three mines going up at The Nek in the early hours of the morning of the 20th December signalled the end of a long, bloody campaign for the ANZACS that had achieved nothing but the beginning of a heroic chapter in Australia's folklore history that would last down the generations. The British and French suffered agonies at Cape Helles before they, too, slipped successfully away, the last British troops leaving on the night of 8-9th January 1916..

British dead at Gallipoli totalled 21,255. Australia mourned the loss of 8,709 of her finest sons, New Zealand 2,701.France lost heavily too, with over 10,000 Frenchmen dying on both sides of the Dardanelles and the Dominions losses continued with Newfoundland's loss of 49 and India's 1,558. Turkish casualties included almost 86,700 killed, twice those of the Allies. The wounded on both sides ran into hundreds of thousands, some of whom recovered but many would remain crippled for what was left of their lives.

Opprobrium and the apportioning of blame had already begun and carried on long after the last man slunk away in the night. In its aftermath the instigator of the doomed campaign, Winston Churchill, was ousted from office, swopping his top hat and stiff collar for the uniform of a fighting man to command a battalion in France.

--§--

Walt had left Helles without a backward glance on one of the last transports and spent a brief leave in Alexandria before re-embarking again in May 1916 for Marseilles and the Western front. Before leaving, he'd sought Bridgette out and together they'd wandered the streets and parks, talking animatedly of what lay ahead.

One afternoon, while walking with Bridgette near a busy bazaar, he'd rounded a corner and almost knocked down a heavily-pregnant light-skinned woman, accompanied by a dark, good-looking man and a large, black dog, who were in the act of exiting an Armenian jeweller's shop. The dog had growled menacingly at him and the woman had called to it sharply.

'*Oglan! Dur!* Stop!'

'I'm sorry, are you alright?' Walt had stammered but she'd smiled, shaking her head and opening her hands wide in an expressive gesture that told him she spoke no English. The man alongside her, her husband Walt had reasoned, had also smiled and inclined his head towards the woman.

After making their way safely to Musa Dagh, Artoun and Hegine, together with Marem, had fought alongside the other Armenians who had taken refuge there. After a siege lasting fifty days they were rescued by French and British warships and transported to Port Said, in Egypt. There they had parted. Artoun and Hegine slowly made their way to Alexandria while Marem and her children took ship for the New World with an Armenian widower, Rupen Kelegian, that she'd become attached to during the siege. Artoun and Hegine had watched them leave after shedding tears and hugging each other before resuming their own journey.

Now, unknowingly, two men whose very lives had been intertwined and shaped by the events happening hundreds of miles away met by chance. 'She...good' Artoun had stammered to Walt in broken English and the couples had regarded each other with faint amusement before going their separate ways. Holding his pregnant wife's hand protectively,

Artoun and Hegine Seferian had passed Walt and Bridgette by, the significance of their meeting being lost forever.

With Western Front beckoning urgently for fresh fodder Walt left a tearful and apprehensive Bridgette and embarked with his battalion, a body of men all strangers to him with few of the original soldiers he'd arrived with in Egypt left to swop experiences with. The three day train journey up to the Somme had thrown them together and drawn them into a close fighting unit, qualities in great demand when the vaunted offensive opened in July.

He'd been lucky to survive the latest example of the willingness of the generals to throw away men's lives in useless, wasteful attacks. Another wound meant more time recuperating, in a London hospital this time, followed by a commission as a 2/lt and a posting to Belgium where he'd endured the bloody horrors of Passchendaele in August 1917. It was only the correspondence he'd received from Bridgette during those bloody days that had kept him sane in a world on the brink of madness.

Later that year, Aunt Elsie passed away and he'd visited Bury one last time on a short leave to pay his respects where she lay at rest in the local cemetery. Her passing cut any ties that had held him to the mother country and he'd returned to the front with a determination to see it out, survive and make for himself a new life in the far-off country that beckoned. By now, Bridgette was serving in a hospital at Etaples on the Channel coast and he'd visited her to tell her of his plans and broach a question that had grown in him since meeting her again in Alexandria.

News of the Armistice signed in November 1918 had reached him as he wakened from a drunken sleep in Paris whilst on a three-day leave and he'd angrily rebuked the newsbringer until it became obvious from the loud cries and singing outside his hotel bedroom window that the man was telling the truth. Prior to being demobbed in early 1919 he'd taken stock of his life and wrote the letter that would change his life forever. Two months later, on demobilisation leave in London, he'd received a reply from Mark and Loretta Treharne and had lost no time in taking passage to Queensland.

He'd been received with great joy and the offer of a job made so many months previously to his brother had been honourably extended to himself and one which he'd gratefully accepted. Four months later, he'd stood on the quay at Woolloomooloo Dock in Sydney and watched, heart in mouth, as a smiling Bridgette had walked down the gangway of the ship bringing her out to join him and a new beginning.

On the train journey to Brisbane they'd stopped briefly to change trains at the small border town of Wallangarra as the two state's rail gauges were of different size. Standing under the ornate platform awning on the Queensland side of the station he'd quietly and formally proposed. To his relief, he had been accepted and the remaining hours clattering up the coast had been spent in both eager planning and quiet remembrance

Their marriage at Busselton was an informal affair but from those beginnings a deep love developed between them, helped in no small way by the memories of his brother's part in their lives. Loretta Treharne and her husband had made them both welcome and a life-long friendship had blossomed as the cattle station benefited from their administrations.

It had been Loretta who'd planted the seed of a return to Gallipoli in Bridgette's head, one he knew he had reason to feel ever more grateful for. Had it not been for her insistence it was doubtful he'd had dredged up the courage to return on his own.

The trip had been planned to include the whole family and now that he was here, standing in the place where so memories had their birthplace, doubts began to seep into his mind. The faces of his family swam into view and he blinked hard. Dear Jack. He'd watched his son's mental struggle over the years with a sense of pity, the boy had had his burdens to bear and it was a testament to his strength of character and courage that he'd borne that burden throughout the years of their collective grief. When this trip had been in the early planning stages Walt had asked Bridgette if they'd extend it and visit Egypt but she'd shook her head forcefully and there had been no further talk of it.

Their firstborn, 22 yr-old Corporal Adam Harding, lay at rest in a small peaceful cemetery near Tobruk where he'd been killed in 1942, fighting for a new kind of freedom against a resurgent Germany and her allies. They'd watched their son go to war with a sense of pride but when the awful news of his death arrived Bridgette had crumbled and never recovered fully from the loss. It was a punishment for the past she'd said, and no amount of comfort had caused her to deviate from that assertion. Time had partly healed the pain but he heard her sometimes in the night, sobbing quietly into her pillow, and knew that even now, eighteen years on, she missed her son with a longing the passing years could never assuage.

Bridgette the strong one, the woman whose strength he had needed so much in the dark days and who had helped him come to terms with his loss could find no peace in the depths of her own despair. Even Tom's death had not caused her the pain he knew she'd felt at losing Adam and

371

although they'd grown closer through the years that had followed, there were still times when she deliberately turned away from him so that he could not see the grief she still bore.

She'd become hysterical in late 1942 when Jack had arrived home one evening and announced that he'd volunteered to join the army and fight the Japanese, convinced she'd lose him also. Nothing would calm her fears but Jack survived to come back, marry and settle down to raising a family and working alongside his father at Busselton.

--§--

Walt straightened from his thoughts and strode quietly over to where Selim waited, smiling to show he understood, walking past the guide and through the open gate of the Commonwealth War Graves cemetery.

'Thank you, Selim, I'm fine. Is this where he...'

'*Efendim*, yes. We must go this way.'

The guide pointed to his left and Walt swung in that direction, picking his steps carefully.

Beach Cemetery opened out before him, the sparse headstones set low down on the ground in order to escape the deprivations of the fierce winter rains, all of them in view of the blue Aegean. He swallowed noisily as the fear returned; would the redemption he sought be here after all? A mounting sense of dread was quelled by the guide's calm voice. He'd told Selim which row he was looking for but in his troubled state found he could not comprehend where to start.

'Here *efendim*, over here.'

He faltered then, stumbling, but a strong hand caught him and guided him forward. He took in the headstones, each bearing a name and date. Some carried an added inscription but his eyes had suddenly moistened and he found it hard to concentrate on the messages they bore. *Believed to be buried in this cemetery...* caught his eye and he frowned, uncertain now. Another inscription caught his eye and he stooped to read it better. *Their glory shall not be blotted out....* The knowledge that what he'd hoped to find could be lost made him stop abruptly but Selim Erez understood his fears and gently led him down a flower-filled row to the end before hesitating, looking downwards.

As he stood, unable to follow Selim's gaze, he brought two objects from his pocket and glanced down. Nestling in his palm was a small, silver pocket-watch, their father's, and an old, faded, blood-stained letter. After snapping open the watch's face he held it tightly in his hand, forcing himself to look over to where two whitened headstones lay together, their bases a profusion of brightly-coloured flowers amid spiky grass and dry, arid soil. A mental picture of two small boys running, laughing, through the sprawled dirt of a colliery spoil-heap flashed through his mind and he let the memories overwhelm him in a wave of sorrow and longing.

'Come on, our Tom, try and catch me if you can.'

'Don't be daft, Walt, Aunt Elsie will skelp our lugs if we come home wi' coal dust sticking from us.'

'Scaredy-cat!'

His mind fast-forwarded to their meeting in the hospital ship. *'What's up, Walt, cat got your tongue? Can't you greet your own bloody brother?'*

'Oh, God, Tom, it's really you.'

And to the cool of an Alexandria hospital ward. *'Sorry, Tom, I'm nowt but trouble to you, aren't I?'*

'I could agree with you there, as a brother you do know how to get on my wrong side.'

He gasped at the intensity of the images and closed his eyes briefly. Keeping the watch in one hand he swept his hat from his head with the other, fanning his sweating brow vigorously. When he opened his eyes again the boys had disappeared and he was alone once more. A silence followed, broken by his guide's puzzled voice. *'Efendim*, look. This man, he nearly has the same name as yours.' Walt focussed on the stones and read the right-hand inscription first, slowly, his vision blurring as he tremulously intoned each word aloud.

1543 Sgt Joseph Lindsay.	*973 Sgt Thomas Walter Harding DCM.*
14th Battalion AIF.	*14th Battalion AIF.*
Died 13th July 1915.	*Died 13th July 1915.*
Aged 29.	*Aged 25.*
A loving son, sadly missed.	*A Brother in Arms and a true friend.*

He knelt and dug a small hole in the soil to the side of his brother's resting place with his free hand. Gently closing the watch and wrapping the letter around it, he placed them at the bottom of the depression he'd made and covered them in a thin layer of dirt before reaching out and running his hand over the headstone's inscription.

'Here you are, our Tom,' he intoned quietly, breaking unconsciously into the soft, glottal twang of their native Lancashire. 'It's been such a long time, I should've come to see you long before now. I've brought dad's watch back. It always was yours. And Bridgette has the locket you bought her; she wears it all the time.' He stopped, distraught by the gulf between them and the events that had finally brought him to this quiet cemetery overlooking the Aegean. 'As to the letter...well... Oh, Tom.' His voice faltered and died to a whisper. He stood up shakily and looked over to the scrub-covered hills beyond, vainly trying to hold his breath as years of torment, yearning and guilt broke free in a torrent from within the depths of his soul. Standing bare-headed in the sun, overcome by grief and holding tightly onto his hat, Walter Thomas Harding lowered his brow and wept.

Ghosts of the Dardanelles.

Speak softly,
stranger to this shore
lest your passing words might sully
The graves
of these young men who came before
to lie in peace
beyond each hill and gully
Look kindly
as you seek to comprehend
what brought them here, from foreign lands,
to die
In comradeship and faith
no finer end
Besides the blue Aegean. Where eagles fly
In leaving
save your tears for those who stayed
Far from their homeland's lonely
crags and fells
Who made a glorious death here, unafraid
Then praise these wraiths, their lost and earthly spirits
Ghosts of the Dardanelles.

Alan 2012.

Lightning Source UK Ltd.
Milton Keynes UK
UKOW052027051112

201712UK00019B/20/P